INFERNO

INFERNO

SHERRILYN KENYON

www.atombooks.net

ATOM

First published in the United States in 2013 by St Martin's Press
First published in Great Britain in 2013 by Atom
This paperback edition first published in Great Britain in 2014 by Atom

ISBN 978-0-7499-5767-4

Printed and bound in Great Britain by
Clays Ltd, St Ives plc

Papers used by Atom are from well-managed forests
and other responsible sources.

MIX
Paper from
responsible sources
FSC
www.fsc.org FSC® C104740

Atom
An imprint of
Little, Brown Book Group
100 Victoria Embankment
London EC4Y 0DY

An Hachette UK Company
www.hachette.co.uk

www.atombooks.net

To my boys and husband, who are always my greatest inspiration and endless source of pride.

And my friends for keeping me sane through every writing project: the mighty Kim brigade, Loretta, Jacs, Judy, Pam, Mama Lisa, Tish, and Trish. You ladies are the best!

And to the guys who help out on the site and behind the scenes: Parker, Paco, Michael, Howard, Ed, Derek, and Carl.

And of course, my wonderful SMP team: Monique, Matthew, Laura, John, Holly, et al—y'all rock!

And to you, the reader, for taking these fun journeys with me. Thank you so much for everything.

ACKNOWLEDGMENTS

While I am and have always been a huge zombie fan, I want to acknowledge two special people whose brains I picked while writing the book.

To my zombie savant and horror movie cohort, Evyl Ed, who also agreed to play Bubba in several Bubbisodes. Thanks for the invaluable insight and keen comments.

And to my favorite exorcist, Mama Lisa, who fights the good fight every day and who understands demonology in a way few people do.

Thank you both.

PROLOGUE

New Orleans
In the far distant future . . .

ilhouetted by the setting sun, and completely rusted out on the inside from his hatred of every living thing, Nick stood on the top of what remained of the old Jax Brewery building, watching his once beloved city burn to the ground. His demon's eyes flickered with hunger and self-pride, mirroring the fires that burned all around him. No longer possessing even a shred of humanity, he glanced at his hand, where he gripped a bloodied sword. From beneath his golden armor, his true demon skin showed its swirling black and red pattern. Lifting his chin, he stood tall and defiant, with his black wings spread wide. Fierce and terrifying to anything that neared him, he had finally come into his own.

And the massacre below was what fed him deep in his blackened soul.

Utter destruction and absolute human misery. There was no headier concoction. No better sight.

He couldn't be happier as he surveyed the aftermath of his war against the humans and gods.

Shattered helicopter pieces lay scattered on the asphalt and across the whole of Jackson Square. But those weren't the only remains lining the streets. . . . The grotesque sight would turn his stomach had he possessed any feeling whatsoever. However, his tender emotions, like the once great city and the humans who'd called it home, were gone.

Nothing except hatred and rage ruled him now.

As he watched, detached from it all, his demonic army feasted on the remains of the poor creatures who'd attempted to fight or those dumb enough to try and flee. Soon, there would be no one left to cry.

He laughed in triumph. He had won this war, and he reigned supreme. There was no one left to fight him now.

Suddenly, the wind carried something odd to his ears. He heard . . .

Human voices. Not shrieking in fear or begging for mercy like the others. These were . . .

Inside the cathedral. They were the voices of warriors preparing to battle.

But how? No one should be left.

Nick closed his eyes so that he could investigate the scene with his powers. Inside the once famed cathedral, screams from children rang out as his army pounded against the fortified door. Someone had piled the confessionals and pews against it to block his demons.

No, not someone . . .

Three women stood in the center of the nave ready to defend a handful of children and a small group of mothers who cowered behind the altar. Unlike the terrified ones who cried and whimpered in helplessness, the three women took stock of their weapons.

In his mind, he could see them clearly. Twin sisters he'd once called friends, Tabitha and Amanda, stood with another woman whose name he didn't know. She was familiar to him, but for some reason, he couldn't recall her. Not that it mattered.

Armed with swords, knives, and a crossbow, the women appeared battle-worn and exhausted. Still, they stood as fierce warriors, ready to fight to the bitter end. Tabitha's hair was dyed black while Amanda's remained their true dark auburn shade. As per her usual fashion, Tabitha was decked out in leather. Amanda's clothes were tight, yoga-styled, to allow her freedom of movement. The third woman wore guerrilla gear, complete with a Kevlar vest and combat boots. Her chemically straightened, long black hair was pulled back from her face and a deep bruise marred the dark skin of her left cheek.

"We can't hold them," Tabitha whispered to the other two women so that the children wouldn't overhear her.

Amanda lifted her chin in determination. "Then we die defending . . . just like our families did."

The third woman nodded. *"Acta est fabula."*

Tabitha and Amanda scowled at her.

She checked the edge of her sword before she spoke again. "The play is over? Caesar's dying words?"

Tabitha rolled her eyes. "I know what it means, woman. I was married to a Roman general. But dang, if you're going to quote Caesar, at least use *veni, vedi, vici.*"

"I came, I saw, I conquered?" Amanda asked incredulously. "Really? Nice try, Tabby, but unfortunately the only butts getting kicked today are ours."

A loud strike echoed as the doors heaved under the latest blow.

Tabitha growled. "They're coming through."

Amanda and Tabitha stood side by side while the third woman held her arms out. Fire engulfed her hands, letting him know that this woman wasn't human.

She was a goddess. . . .

Not Ma'at, who he'd grown up with, but she reminded him of the Egyptian goddesses he'd met and killed over the centuries. If only he knew which one.

Using her telekinesis, Amanda tried to hold the door. But all it did was give her a nosebleed as the demons broke through the wood and scattered the pews and confessionals in all directions. His army spilled into the building and headed straight for the children.

Like ancient soldiers, the women charged them and fought with an unparalleled skill. Tabitha took out three demons with one swing of her sword, while Amanda and the other woman killed even more.

For a few minutes, they appeared to be winning.

But they were no match for the sheer number of his forces as his demons overran them. Amanda went down first and then Tabitha as she ran to help her sister. With them out of the way, his army turned to the last woman and swarmed her. She held them back with firebolts for two minutes longer. But in the end, she, too, fell to the greater number.

The children and women ran for the back. Not that it did them any good. In unison, his army tore after them.

"Bon appétit," Nick whispered.

He started to turn away, until one demon caught his attention and held it there. Unlike the others, this one didn't battle or pursue the humans.

Dressed in black armor that appeared to ooze blood even though he wasn't wounded, this demon was more fierce than all of the others. Malphas surveyed the women's bodies with a look of utter disgust and sorrow.

Until he realized Tabitha was still alive.

He knelt by her side and cradled her head tenderly. "Tabby . . . I'm so sorry."

Grimacing, she opened her eyes as she labored to breathe. She laughed bitterly, exposing a set of bleeding teeth. "There are some things that sorry doesn't fix, Caleb."

"Shhh, don't speak. I can—"

"You failed us," she breathed, cutting Malphas off before he could continue. She licked her bruised lips, then went limp in his arms. Her eyes turned dull.

Tabitha Lane Devereaux Magnus was dead.

Wincing, Caleb held her close to his heart and stroked her bloody hair. "No, Tabby. I failed myself." He glanced to the other two women as tears filled his demonic eyes. "Most of all, I failed Nick."

Those words tore through Nick like a shredder. How dare his servant pity him. He was not some paltry human to be patronized as if he were nothing.

He was the Malachai. Lord and ruler of all the known universes!

His vision darkening with the weight of his fury, he manifested himself inside the cathedral, right beside Malphas. His gold armor gleaming in the dim light, Nick lifted his black wings as he towered over his servant. "You never did learn the proper tone or stance."

He grabbed Malphas by his throat and lifted him away from Tabitha's body.

"Go ahead," Caleb dared him. "Kill me. My only wish is that you'd done it centuries ago before I was forced to serve what you've become."

Fine then . . .

"I'm finished with you anyway," Nick growled in his face. He snapped Malphas's neck, then threw him against the wall so hard that his body went through the stone and landed in the alley outside.

Snarling in fury, Nick turned to go after those who'd fled, but as he took a step, his gaze went to Tabitha's arm. Blood stained her skin, yet that wasn't what had grabbed his attention. Rather it was the Latin words tattooed on her forearm. *Fabra est sui quaeque fati. She creates her own destiny.*

For the first time in years, Nick felt something other than fury and hatred. It'd been so long since he last had this emotion that it took him a full minute to name it.

Remorse. It ripped through him over what he'd done

to the people he'd once called family. To the very people he'd loved and protected.

Kyrian Hunter had saved him and his mother, and how had he repaid him?

He'd taken everything Kyrian had loved and destroyed it, and then he'd taken his life.

How did I become this monster? There was no one left to blame for his transformation. After all his promises that he wouldn't, that nothing could make him, he had given in. Nick looked down at his blood-soaked armor and clawed hands that had long ago ceased being human. He moved his gaze around the sacred room where he had marked all the major milestones of his human life, and saw what remained of it.

Only twisted, burning wreckage surrounded him.

Inside and out.

When had he lost himself so fully?

Throwing his head back, Nick roared in agony. . . .

Ambrose sat upright in bed, shaking from the premonition that had crept into his sleep.

Again.

Tears filled his eyes as he saw in his mind the image of Tabitha and Amanda dead on the same floor where he had attended countless Masses with his mother.

Where he'd once walked as an altar boy, and had sworn repeatedly that he would never become the monster his father was.

Instead, he'd morphed into something much worse. *How could I ever do such a thing?* How could he ever allow himself to deteriorate into such a beast?

Grinding his teeth, he wanted to purge the images out of his head. But they were there. Aching. Taunting. *Real.*

It was the future he saw, and he couldn't let it happen. No matter what it took, he had to save them all.

He had to.

"Nicholas?"

He flinched as Artemis sat up beside him and touched his bare shoulder. Worry furrowed her beautiful brow as her red hair fell around her slender shoulders in perfect curls. "You're trembling."

Ambrose shook his head in denial. "I never tremble. Nothing scares me."

She didn't believe it. He saw the truth in her green eyes as she brushed his damp hair back from his face. "Is it your dream again?"

"It's not a dream, Artie. It's a vision. Acheron was right. We can't change our fate. Only how we bring it about."

"Is that really what you believe?"

Ambrose raked his hand through his sweat-soaked hair. "No. I can't . . ."

He locked gazes with her, then spoke more forcefully. "I won't." In that moment, he felt his powers rising, trying to drown out his humanity and turn him into the creature he was born to be.

But he wasn't lost. Not yet.

"No one controls me," he growled in his demon's voice, pushing that darkness into submission. "Ever. I will *not* become the Malachai!"

He got out of bed and quickly dressed.

"Where are you going?"

He hesitated, then answered with more conviction than he'd ever had before. "To alter my past so that I can change my future."

CHAPTER 1

When most guys said that their girlfriend was going to kill them, it was a gross exaggeration or extreme paranoia. In the case of Nicholas Gautier it was a harsh, brutal fact. One so solid, he could chisel a check on it. Especially since the warning that his girl was an assassin sent to murder him had come from Death himself.

The one creature who would know a killer best . . .

As the old saying went, you couldn't argue with Death.

Stunned and numb from that unexpected land mine, Nick turned his attention to Nekoda Kennedy as she sat down in their chemistry class beside Nick's best friend, Caleb Malphas. For once her tight cream sweater didn't turn his mind to mush. Nor did the bright smile on her lips. Lips that held his attention and momentarily distracted his thoughts . . .

Yeah, okay, she really was seriously hot, from the top of her soft, shiny brown hair to the tips of her pink leather boots. And don't get him started on her green, green eyes that held an indelible fire so bright, it was scorching. But a man had to have some standards, and not being murdered by his girl was definitely one of them.

Teenage hormones be defied.

So then why did it feel like someone had kicked his tenders when her smile faded and sadness replaced the joy on her face? Why did it hurt him to see the uncertainty he caused *her*?

I am so messed up. . . .

That was the only reasonable explanation. No normal, sane person would care whether or not he hurt the feelings of a woman sent to kill him.

Except for Nick-Moron-Non-Normal-Gautier.

Nick dropped his gaze to the pink heart necklace she wore that he'd given her to celebrate their anniversary—and their escape from another near-death adventure. It had been a token of how much he loved her, and to let her know that her life meant a lot more to him than his own—that he would gladly die to protect her.

And yet she'd known the whole time that her mission here at St. Richard's was to end his life.

*Ain't this the crap heap? I swear my undying loyalty and
she swears to take my head.*

Why was he even surprised?

Because, in spite of the fact that he was half demon,
he wanted to believe in the goodness of others. That
deep down people were decent. Even nonpeople people.

And as her gaze held his, he no longer saw his chemistry classroom or any of his classmates. Everything
faded from his sight, except Nekoda. She looked so
sweet and innocent. Just like any beautiful teenage
girl. No one would ever guess she was anything except
normal.

Same with Caleb. With his dark hair and eyes, and
perfect build and features, Caleb was the quintessential
Mr. All-American Rich Kid. He bore no resemblance
to the winged demon Nick knew him to be.

For that matter, Nick looked normal on the outside,
too. Well, except for the hideously foul Hawaiian shirt
his mother had guilted him into donning. The only
bright side to wearing it was that it'd been known to
blind a few enemies sent to end his existence. Or crack
them up so badly that he was able to get in a cheap shot
before they killed him.

And it served as a great female demon repellant.
Human, too, for that matter.

But Nick was anything but normal.

I know what I am. That wasn't the question. He, like Caleb, was demonkyn, born and bred.

Nekoda's species was the one up for grabs.

Who are you?

No. What *are you?*

He'd asked her that question repeatedly. And every time, she'd refused to answer, and now he knew why.

Which meant she could be human, god, demon, soul-sucker, shapeshifter, Fringe Guard . . . there were so many creatures he'd learned about over the last year that he couldn't even begin to guess her origins.

For all he knew, she was some heart-eating ice cannibal. That at least explained the cold, bitter ache in the center of his chest.

"Are you planning to take your seat any time in the near future, Mr. Gautier? Or should I start class while you gape blankly in the center of the room?"

His classmates laughed.

Nick turned to glare at Grim over his shoulder. The famed reaper stood before the whiteboard, where he'd written the name "Mr. Graves."

Yeah, you are whacked, Grim. Totally.

But only Nick saw Grim's true form—that of a handsome blond man in his mid-twenties. Heck, he even saw Grim's scythe that was secured with a strap across the creature's back. To the rest of the room's occupants, including Nekoda and Caleb, Grim appeared as an average, chubby, middle-aged man in a cheap brown suit.

Yeah . . .

Nick would laugh, but Grim might take that as a personal challenge and decide to help Kody kill him. Yet what Nick couldn't get over was Grim's presence in this room.

It was a sad day when Death had nothing better to do than pretend to be a substitute chemistry teacher. . . .

No, it wasn't that simple. Someone in this room was going to die soon and Grim was here to toy with his victim. Nick could feel it with every inhuman part of himself.

But who?

Knowing he wouldn't have an answer today, he smirked at Grim, which probably wasn't the brightest idea. But far be it from him to ever let his common sense stop his stupidity. "By all means, commence . . . Mr. *Graves*. The last thing I'd ever want to do is keep you from your business."

Death gave him a lopsided grin. "Wise, boy. I knew you could be taught."

Nick didn't miss the sinister undertone and reference to the fact that Grim had been his tutor over this last year. The specter had taught him a lot of interesting things, but those powers had a bad habit, through no fault of Nick's, of backfiring. Because of that, Grim thought him to be dense and stupid. But he was neither. He caught on quick and saw things other people missed.

Including the fact that Grim had his own agenda where Nick was concerned. He definitely wasn't tutoring Nick out of the goodness of his black heart.

Nick had yet to uncover the truth of Grim's motivation, but in time, he would.

Still, this latest information about Nekoda rattled him. Did he dare believe it? Especially since he knew what a troublemaker Grim was. For that matter, Grim could easily be lying just to stir it up.

Trust her over Death. Kody had fought by his side countless times and saved his life. And yet . . . he heard Ambrose's voice in his head, warning him that he had yet to experience the betrayals that would one day kill him.

And his mother.

Sick to his stomach with that thought, Nick sat down between Nekoda and Caleb.

Nekoda reached out to touch his hand. "Are you all right?"

Nick slid his hand out from under hers. "Yeah, sure. Why wouldn't I be?" He pulled his backpack open so that he could grab the books he needed for class, but paused as he saw her frowning from the corner of his eye.

Are you really going to launch at my throat one day, Kody? After we've been through so much? That was the question he wanted to ask her. But there was no need to get into this while they were in class. His school rep was already so low he'd have to use a tractor full of dynamite just to blast it up to gutter level. The last thing he needed was to publicly accuse his girlfriend of being some evil demon sent to end his life.

Bad enough they think I'm a criminal and trash. No need to make them think I'm crazy, too.

He opened his book and tried to focus on words that had lost all meaning. *You should just drop out and forget this crap.* Not like school taught him anything he needed in real life. It definitely didn't teach him how to survive the predators who kept coming after him. How to avoid all the preternatural traps waiting . . .

Nick clenched his fist as an overwhelming urge to go tell his principal where to shove this useless curriculum went through him.

I can't do that.

It would break his mother's heart. And he'd be labeled a real loser by everyone else . . . even himself.

If Caleb could suffer through all the indignities, hassles, and boredom of high school with only an hourly complaint or two, he could, too. And unlike Caleb, he hadn't lived through the history and lessons that were being taught. To Nick, most of this was new.

What's going on, Nick? Why are you suddenly mad at me?

He glanced over to Nekoda, who'd pushed her thoughts into his mind. He started not to respond, but she was the only one who could hear his telepathy.

Who are you, Kody. This time it wasn't a question, he demanded an answer.

She glanced away. *You know I can't tell you.*

Yes, you can. You won't *and that's the problem.*

She sighed wearily. *Why are you on this again?*

Because I learned the truth a few minutes ago. You're here to kill me.

Her features blanched, confirming Grim's dire prediction where she was concerned.

Anger tore through him so fast and furiously that he could taste it. *Are you not going to deny it?*

She hesitated before she answered. *What do you want me to say?*

I want the truth, Kody.

Tears filled her eyes as she looked away from him. For a moment he felt like a heel for upsetting her, then he felt stupid for that emotion. What kind of chump worried about upsetting someone who'd been sent to end his life?

Nick Gautier.

Moron. Fool.

Bad dresser.

Major loser dork.

Kody touched his hand again. *The only truth that should concern you is that I care for you. Deeply.*

Deeply. Yeah, right. What kind of hackneyed crap was that? It ranked right up there with "He has a great personality" or better yet, "Why don't we just be friends."

Nick narrowed his gaze on her, trying to see the truth of her emotions. Did she really care about him or was she just that good an actress?

You are here to kill me. . . . Yes or no?

She pulled her hand back. *It's not that simple.*

He gaped at her. Was she serious? "What could be simpler than that?"

Every head in class turned to look at him. Nick felt his entire face heat up. Oh yeah, like puberty wasn't embarrassing enough. Now he had to shout out in the middle of class for no apparent reason.

"Channeling spirits again, Gautier?" Stone Blakemore—head jock moron—asked.

"Nah," Stone's best friend, Mason, said. "It's probably some mental disorder, like Backwoods Tourette's."

The entire room erupted into laughter.

Embarrassed and ticked off, Nick glared at the aptly named Stone, who was about as intelligent as the average rock . . . not to insult rocks.

Grim arched a brow. "Are you in the midst of some personal problem? Should I write you a pass for the counselor?"

Nick had to bite back the urge to insult his mentor, but only a fool taunted Death. And the one thing Nick had learned over the last year was that Death didn't have a sense of humor, and especially not when he was the brunt of the joke.

"No. It was a momentary jaw spasm."

"Then I suggest you try to control your bodily functions in the future." Death turned back to the board.

Nick ground his teeth. This wasn't the time and place for this and he knew it. He'd never been big into drama anyway. *Let's talk about this later.*

Kody stiffened. *Fine. I don't want to talk about it at all.*

Of course she didn't. Leave it to him to find the only woman in the universe who didn't want to talk about her feelings or their relationship. The only one who wanted to keep things status quo and undiscussed.

You all right?

Sighing, Nick nodded at Caleb. If they didn't stop silently talking to him, he was going to look seriously mental soon.

Worse, Caleb leaned forward and glanced meaningfully to Kody.

Great. Now the two of *them* were talking to each other and he couldn't hear it.

Nick raked his hand through his hair as his anger mounted. It was so fierce, it made his ears hum. Over the last few weeks, he'd noticed that his quick-draw temper getting worse. But then he'd always had anger management issues. Way too quick to ignite and even harder to calm. It was why he tried to be easygoing and to let things slide. Why he tried not to care about much of anything.

Yet lately, every little thing annoyed him.

Was this the demon in him gaining power? His future self, Ambrose, had warned him repeatedly about allowing his temper to rule him. Normally, it was Kody who calmed him down when he got into these moods.

Yeah . . . not today. Today, the mere mention of her name ignited his fury. He felt on edge and closer to losing it than he ever had before—except for those times when he *had* actually lost it.

C'mon, class. End already. I definitely need a time-out.

Why couldn't he have the power of time manipulation? According to Ambrose that was the only power he'd never possess. Not unless he stole it from others.

Of course, he did have the power of suggestive

persuasion. That one actually worked most of the time . . . but not with Death. *Dang you for teaching this class.*

It felt like torture, and not the usual my-class-is-too-long torture he was used to.

"Am I boring you, Gautier?"

Nick blinked as he realized Grim was talking to him. He chose to ignore the snickers and snide comments from the peanut gallery who were so easily amused, as most mindless creatures were, by his lack of attention. "Excuse me?"

"We're going over the periodic table. I've asked you, four times now, what is R-U, and what's its element category and atomic weight."

Like he knew that? Who in their right . . .

His thought trailed off as the answer popped into his head. "Ruthenium. It's a rare transition metal. The atomic number is forty-four and its weight is 101.07. It has a melting point of 2334 degrees Celsius and 4233 degrees Fahrenheit and a boiling point of 7502 degrees Fahrenheit. Anything else you want to know about it?"

Wait . . . Did he understand any of that?

Yeah, weirdly he did.

But how? Was this another power that would come and go, and that would never work properly?

Grim nodded with a grudging light of respect in his eyes. "So you *can* learn by osmosis."

That was one theory. 'Cause he had no other way to explain how he knew something he couldn't remember ever seeing. It had to have seeped into his skin while he slept on top of his chem book. That made sense to him. "Apparently."

"I always knew you were a freak, Gautier," Stone muttered.

Nick's temper exploded.

And so did Stone. One second he was mocking Nick and the next, his shirt caught fire. Nick jumped up with Caleb and half the class. Some of the girls screamed and ran for the door while Grim stood back with an evil gleam of hope in his dead eyes.

Brynna Addams grabbed the fire extinguisher from the wall and tried to work it.

Nick ran to her and held his hand out for her to surrender the red canister. Given the propensity of their old stove to spontaneously burst into flames whenever they used it, Nick had a ton of experience using these.

Brynna surrendered it without question.

Nick quickly moved to Stone and doused him with a giant burst. White smoke filled the room, and it wasn't until after the fire went out that it dawned on Nick how wrong he'd been in the past.

Guess I would put you out if you were on fire, Stone.

Who knew?

He was a bigger humanitarian than he'd ever thought. Then again, given Stone's typical behavior, he wasn't really doing anyone a favor by saving the jerk. He should have let Grim have him.

Nick held the fire extinguisher in his arms as several students cheered. Stone was soaking wet and covered with goo. For once, he looked at Nick with something other than disdain. If Nick didn't know better, he might even think that it was gratitude.

"Are you okay, baby?" Casey shrugged Stone's letterman's jacket off and wrapped it around Stone's shoulders. She wiped at the residue on Stone's face. "Speak to me . . ."

"Yeah, I'm all right."

Sobbing, Casey threw herself against Stone.

Grim took it all in stride. "Guess you'll be needing a pass to the nurse's office."

Could he sound any more disappointed? But then, Death didn't really blend with normal people, and most likely he'd been hoping for another body to claim.

Mason clapped Nick hard on his shoulder. "Quick

thinking, Gautier. Didn't know you had an actual brain in you."

The urge to turn the fire extinguisher on Mason was so strong that he wasn't sure how he kept from doing it.

Brynna stepped forward and touched Nick's hand. "You better let me have it before you give in."

Nick scowled. "Huh?"

She smiled up at him. "I know that look, Nick. I figure you're only seconds away from dousing Mason or using it to bash him in the head."

Nick let her take the canister from him. "Some people would consider that a public service."

"But not our principal."

Unfortunately, she was right. Mr. Head would have a conniption, and then Nick would have detention. And that was something he wanted to stay out of for a while.

Stone and Casey left the room and headed toward the office.

Grim cleared his throat to get everyone's attention. "Now that the drama is over and, sadly, no one died, we should get back to work."

As Nick returned to his seat, he caught the apprehensive glance that Nekoda traded with Caleb.

"What?" he asked her as he sat down.

"Did you do that?" she whispered.

"Do what?"

Set Stone on fire?

Scoffing, Nick started to deny it, but the minute he opened his mouth to speak, he realized something.

Two seconds before Stone had burst into flames, Nick *had* wished it on him.

Crap.

CHAPTER 2

I *set someone on fire.*

Nick couldn't let that one thought go. It was horrifying to think that he could cause something so deadly with nothing more than a single random thought.

My powers are *growing.*

But not his ability to control them . . .

If anything, that was getting worse, and they were exploding all over the place without any warning or reason whatsoever.

Power without control is worthless—Acheron's favorite saying. At least it was Ash's pet phrase any time Nick got behind the wheel and laid into the accelerator.

Damn it, Nick! You've got to learn to go slow and not rush off into traffic at warp ten, especially not when it's heading straight for you! Acheron's other fave rant where he was concerned.

In the past, Nick had ignored those warnings. Now . . .

The image of Stone bursting into flames was seared in his mind. Of course the burnt smell of Stone's werewolf hair hadn't really dissipated from the room. It clung to the air with a brutal reminder of what Nick had unconsciously done. One nanosecond of lapsed judgment and he'd almost killed someone. Granted, Stone was a jerk, but he didn't deserve to die for it.

At least not today.

Nick would have to ride herd on himself after this, lest he do some real damage to someone.

Suddenly, the bell rang, startling him from his thoughts. Nick jumped around a foot in his seat at the unexpected sound. *Talk about looking stupid.* Just what he wanted. Another reason to look awkward in front of his peers.

Caleb arched a brow at him. "You all right?"

"You didn't see another shadow, did you?" Nekoda asked in a hushed tone. A question he well understood, since the last shadow he'd seen had been a demon that one of his classmates had unleashed to wreak havoc with all their lives. Havoc he was still neck-deep in. While he'd been cleared of all the false charges Dina had made against him, rumors about the whole godawful situation that had led to his being handcuffed and hauled off school property abounded, and they clung to him with the tenacity of Velcro.

That thought didn't help his mood at all.

Nick narrowed his gaze on the necklace he'd given her. "The only demon I see right now is you, Kody."

She stiffened. "That's not fair."

"Neither is pretending to be my girlfriend while you're sizing me up for a body bag." He jammed his book into his backpack, then turned to glare at Caleb. "Did you know about that?"

"I still don't know what you're talking about."

"I'm talking about the fact that Kody's an assassin sent in to kill me."

Caleb went full-on into protection mode, letting Nick know that Caleb had been as clueless about her true intentions as him. *At least Caleb isn't in on it.* That made him feel a *little* better.

He put himself between Nick and Kody. "Is that true?" he growled.

Kody glanced around to make sure no one was listening to them before she answered. "It's not that simple, Malphas. I was sent to stop him from becoming what he's supposed to be."

Caleb scoffed. "Yeah, Nick, that sounds like killing orders to me."

Kody tried to step around him, but Caleb refused to let her pass.

"We're enemies, Nekoda. My job is to protect him from all threats. And now that clearly means *you*."

"You can't be serious." She looked past Caleb's massive shoulder. "Nick? Is this really what you want?"

"No. What I wanted was a normal girlfriend who only talks about shopping and fashion, and crap I don't care about. I have enough enemies moving in at my back. Last thing I need to do is put someone there I know intends to take a shot at me sooner or later." He jerked his backpack up and slung it over his shoulder. "We're done."

Nick turned and started for the door.

"You can't do this!" The sound of tears in her voice made his gut twist into a knot. "Nick . . ."

Don't turn around. He'd forgive her if he did. One look at the tears in her eyes and he'd be an idiot for her. He knew it. He couldn't stand to see any woman in pain, and he'd do anything to make one smile.

But not giving in to that urge was the hardest thing he'd ever done. Because the truth was, he loved her. He really did.

Love will make you stupid, kid. Trust me. You won't listen to anyone, not even your own common sense. That was the pet tirade of his boss, Kyrian. One he'd drilled into Nick's head. *Be careful who you give your heart to, Nick. Make sure that you hold hers before you hand over yours. Do* not *make my mistake.*

Kyrian Hunter was now an immortal protector because his wife had betrayed him in ancient Greece and surrendered him to his enemies to be brutally tortured and killed. The horror of her actions had scarred Kyrian so badly that he'd sold his soul to the Greek goddess Artemis so that he could take revenge on those enemies. In exchange for his Act of Vengeance, Kyrian had become a Dark-Hunter. Legendary soldiers, the Dark-Hunters fought to keep mankind safe from all the supernatural predators who wanted to put humans on their menus. It was an eternal life with a lot of perks.

Even so, Kyrian would have much rather stayed human and died poor than have the wife he'd treasured beyond all things betray him.

Love and loyalty above all. That was the one pledge that Nick subscribed to. Treachery was for cowards who didn't have the courage to fight face on. And while Nick Gautier might be a lot of things, he had never been, nor would he ever be, a coward.

No sir. If he was gunning for you, he let you know it in no-way-to-be-misconstrued words and actions.

And still his heart ached at the loss of Kody's friendship. At the loss of what could have been between them.

I am an idiot. Why else would he hurt this badly for a woman who'd planned to kill him?

When he stopped at his locker, Caleb clapped a hand on his shoulder. "Cheer up, bud. I know it feels like you just had your stones handed to you, but you will survive it."

Nick opened the door, not sure if he wanted to survive. "Have you ever had a woman betray you?"

"In ways you're too young to know about, Nick. Believe me, on the grand scheme of pain, this isn't so bad."

Funny, it didn't feel that way. Nick clenched his teeth as agony spread through him. He just wanted to go home, curl up in bed, and pretend this day hadn't happened. "Is that how you ended up enslaved to my father?"

"No."

Nick swapped out his books. "You're never going to tell me how he got ahold of your leash, are you?"

"Nope."

"Why?"

"Because one day, you *will* grow up and become a full-fledged Malachai. Your father will die, hopefully soon, and then I'll be free. But if I trust you with that information, then you'll know how to collar me. No offense, but I don't trust the demon in you not to turn on me and find me after I'm gone, and I've spent enough time as a slave. I don't want to live one day longer as one than I have to."

Nick was even more offended. "I'd die before I did that to you. You have to know me better."

"That's your human heart speaking and I respect that. But I also know that sooner or later that heart will be devoured by the darkness inside you. Then we won't be friends. I'll be a tool and you won't hesitate to throw me in a box and use me."

Caleb sounded like Kody now, and truthfully, Nick was sick of it. "If you really believe I'm beyond hope, why are you here?"

"Because my master ordered it."

"And if my father was dead?"

Caleb looked away. Emotions Nick couldn't name flitted across his features. It looked like Caleb was debating with himself.

"Well?" Nick prompted him for an answer.

Caleb sighed. "The only thing I know for certain is that if your dad was dead, I definitely wouldn't be in high school with you right now. I'd still be in bed asleep."

Nick laughed. He couldn't blame Caleb for that. He wouldn't be here either if he could find another way out. But that wasn't what concerned him. "Would you still be on my speed dial?"

Caleb narrowed those dark eyes on him. "I really want to hate you, Gautier."

Nick grinned. "Yeah, I'm like kudzu. I look all nice and harmless and the next thing you know I've taken root and it's too late . . . you like me." His smile faded as he saw Kody in the hallway, coming toward them. It slammed into him like a fist. "So how long does it usually take to get over a broken heart?"

Caleb glanced in Kody's direction before he answered. "You don't even want to know. . . . My best advice?" He jerked his chin to the opposite end of the hallway. "Distraction."

Scowling, Nick wasn't sure what he meant until Casey Woods threw herself against him so hard that he stumbled back and hit the lockers behind him with a resounding crash. He would complain, but having his arms full of the most popular cheerleader in school squelched any desire to be negative about how this miracle had come into being.

She looked up at him and smiled. "You're my hero, Nick!" She kissed him.

Stunned past any kind of rational thought, he didn't move. He couldn't. It wasn't every day the captain of the cheerleaders shoved him into the wall against school policy and lip-locked him. Even more shocking was the sensation of her long dark ponytail brushing against the bare skin on his arm.

After a second, she pulled back and gave him a hot look that melted him on the spot. "Call me later, 'kay?"

He tried to speak, but nothing would come out. Instead, he stood there like some gulping catfish with his mouth opening and closing and making no sound whatsoever.

Yeah, I'm so slick, teen models call me for dating advice.

Luckily, Casey didn't wait around for his brain to kick in and have him say something *really* stupid. She skipped back into the crowd after one of her friends. Still stunned, Nick pushed himself off the locker bank.

"I'm so glad I'm not you."

He blinked at Brynna's dire tone as she opened her locker beside him. "I didn't do anything."

"Yeah, but I caught the look on Kody's face when she saw Casey molesting you, then reversed course and headed the other way. Oooo, Nick, it wasn't pretty. Kody gonna have her some deep-fried Cajun mountain oysters for dinner . . . probably breakfast, too."

Nick let out a tired breath as his pain returned . . . with friends. "Nah, she won't. We broke up."

"Since when?"

"Ten minutes ago," Caleb answered for him.

"No!" Brynna gasped. "Say it ain't so, Gautier. You two were perfect together."

This wasn't helping his mental state. What next? Would some sappy breakup song start playing over the intercom to torture him? "Not perfect enough."

Brynna growled low in her throat. "What did you do?"

Her question offended him. "It wasn't me. Why does it always have to be the guy's fault?"

"'Cause it usually is."

Well, that was insulting. "Thanks a lot, Brynna. And for the record, *I'm* the victim."

"Then I'm sorry."

Nick inclined his head to her, grateful that she'd at least tried to sound sincere. "I appreciate it."

Rubbing his arm, she offered him a sympathetic smile. "For the record? I hope you two get back together."

"For the record, we won't."

She shook her head sadly and closed her locker door. "Well, if you need a friend, you have my number. I haven't forgotten what you did for me when I needed someone. You really are a great guy, Nick."

"Thanks."

"Any time." Brynna headed off to class.

Nick turned away and walked toward his next period. Thankfully, it was with Caleb and not Kody.

Caleb picked up his pace to walk beside him. "You do know Brynna was hitting on you just now."

Yeah, right. Caleb was shy a few bricks on his wall if he really believed that. "No, she wasn't. She thinks of me like a brother."

"You sure?"

"Positive. I tried to hold her hand once when I first started going here and she read me the riot act for it. I got the full we-are-just-friends-so-don't-make-me-call-my-older-brother-out-on-you-to-beat-you-to-a-pulp speech from her years ago."

Caleb laughed. "And that's why I only hook up with women who have sisters or, even better, no siblings at all."

"Got your butt whipped once, huh?"

"No." Caleb sobered. "But I know what I'd do for my sister if some idiot broke her heart."

That news floored him. Caleb never really talked about his family, and he'd never before made any kind of declaration of love toward them. "You have a sister?"

"Not full-blooded. But yeah, I have a number of them."

"Are they around?"

Caleb shook his head. "Even though I'd kill for them if they needed me to, we're not that close." He opened the classroom door for Nick to enter first.

"I'm sorry."

"Don't be. I'm not. I don't like personal entanglements or obligations. Gets you into too much trouble. But blood is blood. End of the day, if one of them needed me, I'd be stupid for them."

And that was why, even though Caleb was a demon, Nick respected him and called him friend. Caleb spent a lot of time denying his better nature, but Nick had seen it up close and personal enough to know that Caleb was cold-blooded decent. No matter how much the demon protested, you could always count on him in a fight.

Taking his seat, Nick pulled his book out and opened it to the day's assignment. Still, he couldn't get Kody out of his mind. Now that they were officially broken up, she would be coming for him for sure. The only question was, when?

Belam?

Nekoda looked up at the whisper of her real name that no one in the human realm used anymore. In the far corner stood the shimmery image of her guide, Sraosha. Only she could see him and he was definitely summoning her.

Could this day get any better? Really? Why couldn't Nick have set *her* on fire and ended her misery?

Sighing, she got up and walked to Mr. Raney's desk. "Mr. Raney? May I please have a pass to the restroom?"

"You know we don't—"

She lowered her voice and chose the one topic her male math teacher wouldn't argue with. "Sorry, but it's that time of month and—"

"Enough!" he snapped, reaching for the pad of passes on his desk. "I don't want to hear about anything that personal." He quickly scribbled in the form, then tore the sheet off. "Don't be long, Miss Kennedy."

"Thank you." Taking the pass, she ducked out of the room and headed for the bathroom. She would vanish immediately, but didn't want to take a chance on being caught by one of the school's hidden cameras. Though she knew where most were located, she wasn't sure about all of them, and her powers didn't play well with electronics.

Better safe than sorry.

She went into the bathroom and entered the first stall, then locked the door and flashed herself to Sraosha's less than friendly office.

Dark and dismal, it was a sad study in grays and browns. Not appealing in the least. But he seemed to like it that way.

Unlike his office, Sraosha was a thing of absolute beauty as he stood waiting next to the floor-to-ceiling windows that looked out onto nothing. Literally. It was absolutely dark . . . like they were lost in space. The only light came from the edges of a dim amber-colored tray overhead.

Tall, lithe, and extremely graceful, Sraosha was so beautiful it was hard to look straight at him. His long blond hair flowed around a body that was pure perfection. Every feature appeared to be carved with extreme precision to render him angelic and breathtaking. And for once, he allowed her to see his eyes. They were an eerie, iridescent green. Dressed in ancient battle armor, he commanded attention and respect . . . even from her.

"You summoned me?"

Sraosha blinked slowly before he answered. "It is time."

Those were the three words she'd been dreading most. Her final order. "We can't kill him. Not yet."

Sraosha arched a commanding brow that questioned her sanity for daring to contradict him. "What is your excuse today?"

"The senior Malachai still lives. If I kill Nick, Adarian will have no weakness whatsoever, and no reason to hold back, since nothing other than Nick can weaken him. And we both know I can't defeat Adarian on my own." She had the scars to prove it. "So unless you're harboring a weapon I know nothing about, or are willing to give me a hand in the fight, we have no choice except to wait for Nick to fulfill his destiny and kill his father."

"And then he will have his father's strength and powers in addition to the ones he already has. You think you can defeat him then?"

No. She'd be even more ineffectual against him than she'd been against his predecessors.

But death wasn't her only option. "He's not beyond redemption." Unlike his father and the others, Nick had a heart that felt and understood real love. Personal sacrifice.

Loyalty.

No Malachai before had even known those terms existed.

Sraosha sneered. "You're letting your feelings blind you. Just as you did before."

It was true. She'd had a perfect chance to slaughter Adarian when he'd first escaped the Nether Realm, and rather than take the shot, she'd felt too sorry for him to kill him. Even now, she could see his wretched state. His master, Noir, had tortured him well. Weak and battered, Adarian had barely been able to stand on his own, and she'd refused to kill in cold blood.

Like the warrior her father had trained her to be, she'd given him the chance to recover before they battled.

Her vital mistake.

Had she taken him out when he'd emerged, her brothers would still be here. . . .

Alive and whole. And she would be at home with her family, in her own time period. Not stuck in this purgatory.

"I've learned well and I won't make that mistake again."

Sraosha scoffed. "No? From where I stand that's exactly what you're doing. You think I can't feel the love you hold for a *demon*?" He spat that last word at her.

Ashamed, Nekoda looked away. "I have not forgotten my duties." How could she? She'd forsaken her real given name and taken on her sacred title so that she would never again be tempted by her emotions. Nekodas were marked servants who had no family ties to distract them. They lived for no purpose other than to serve the higher order and keep the balance of power intact. Unlike the Chthonians who had the ability to kill gods and were charged with overseeing them, nekodas weren't born to their positions.

They were chosen.

And unlike the Chthonians, they had very strict rules they had to follow, and beings they had to answer to.

She wasn't allowed to second-guess her guide, and yet, Sraosha was wrong about Nick. She could feel it with every part of herself. Nick wasn't their enemy.

Not yet anyway.

Sraosha stepped forward to tower over her. An act of supreme intimidation that might have worked on her had she been human or born of lesser stock. "Are you refusing to kill him, Belam?"

She faced him without flinching or cowering. "I'm refusing to unleash the senior Malachai onto this world, especially when we don't know if he'll ever father another child. Nick is the only one who can weaken him. And the only other being capable of killing Adarian at full strength is imprisoned in a place we can't free him from. Not without starting a whole 'nother fire that neither of us is ready to ignite."

Sraosha sucked his breath in sharply between his teeth. The expression on his face said that he was barely one second away from striking her. "Fine then. Get him to his father, then kill them both. Those are your orders."

Gah, he made it sound so simple.

"But—"

"No buts!" Sraosha snarled. "I am well aware that you no longer hold sway over the younger's emotions. Someone else is manipulating him. We can only assume that they work for the Atramentaceous Order, and before they take complete control of their weapon, we must destroy it."

Those words set her fury on fire. "Nick is a boy. He's not an it."

Sraosha cocked a disbelieving brow. "Is that insubordination I hear?"

"No, sir." It was indignation and extreme aggravation that he was being so obtuse about this. She'd been raised that you didn't slaughter the innocent on the chance that they "might" do something wrong.

"It better not be, and you'd do well to remember your place, nekoda. I took you in when you had nothing and no one. Have you forgotten how I found you?"

She swallowed the tears that rose up to choke her as they always did whenever she looked at the past. "I have forgotten nothing." Especially not the demon who had destroyed her entire family and left her alone in the universe. She'd vowed over her parents' graves that she would find the demon Malachai and destroy him before he had a chance to kill them.

No matter what, she would stop him.

"I will do my duty."

"Then you better hurry before Nick grows any stronger."

Nekoda lowered her head and pressed her fist to her heart in salute to her guide. But as she returned to the stall she'd left at St. Richard's, she couldn't stop the rush of emotions that tore her apart.

Sraosha was right. She'd fallen for Nick in the worst sort of way and now he wanted nothing to do with her. And judging by the look he'd given her earlier, he hated her passionately. And that hurt her a whole lot more than it should.

Who could have possibly told him what she was? She hadn't breathed a word to a single soul. She had no real friends. No family left.

No one should have known her true identity.

Someone was working against her. If she could find out who, then perhaps she could spare Nick from his death sentence.

Don't be stupid. You know Sraosha is right.

Sooner or later, Nick would go Malachai. The demon in him would devour every part of the human heart she treasured, and leave him nothing but a killing machine who had no mercy or compassion for anyone. He would become the monster they'd written legends about.

Reaching up, she touched the heart necklace he'd given her.

He was such a kind, giving soul. Respectful. Gentle. Things his father had never been.

Our births and bloodlines don't define us. The paths we choose to follow do. None of us have to be what we're born to be. We have more courage and power inside us than we know. Trust in yourself, kitten, and stay true to your own convictions, no matter what others say or do. They don't matter anyway. People will come and go from your life, but you will walk hand in hand with yourself forever. What-ever you do, don't choose to be something you hate. I walked that path for far too long, and it's an ugly place to live. I want you to be better, because I know for a fact that you are better than I ever was. Her father's words haunted her.

He had defied his birth and his parents. As had her mother and uncle. Each had chosen to be much more than they'd been born for. They had shown her strength and courage. What it meant to swim upstream through the deadliest waters and hazards.

There will be one Malachai born unlike all the others. He will know love and if you can keep him wrapped in it, grounded by it, he can be turned from the dark that spawned him. He will be the greatest champion this world has ever known. But should he lose anchor, he will turn into the one that destroys us all. For the very love that gives him good-ness is the love that will turn him to pure hatred when he loses it.

"I have to win him back," she whispered. It was the only way. She couldn't risk Nick hating her. If she could keep hatred out of his heart, he would stay as he was.

A hero.

Unlike Sraosha, she didn't think that killing him would solve anything. Another Malachai would come forward to replace him, and if it was the one she suspected, it would be even worse. Currently, the next in line to replace Nick was a god in full right, with full powers. No one would be able to stop a Malachai like that.

Ever.

Not even the Chthonians.

But Sraosha wouldn't listen to her. He wanted Nick's heart with a lust she didn't understand. If anyone should want Nick dead, it was her.

And part of her did. How could she not, given what all he'd taken from her. Over and over, she saw the demon Malachai—Nick's true form—killing her broth-ers. Her entire family had been slaughtered because of him.

Without reservation or hesitation, she had come

back in time so that she could stop his metamorphosis. This was her one and only chance to save everyone.

Even herself.

"I can't fail."

She would either save Nick from his true nature, or deliver his heart to Sraosha.

CHAPTER 3

Dang, boy, you drag that tail any lower and you won't be able to get across a parking lot."

Nick paused as he and Caleb entered the Triple B—the largest gun and computer store in the South, maybe even the world.

The owner, Big Bubba Burdette, was one of Nick's best friends and the closest thing to a father Nick had ever known. Standing over six feet tall, Bubba was well muscled and humongous—something that came from his days as an award-winning football player who would have gone pro had he not decided to give up glory to stay home with the wife and son he loved more than anything else.

A wife and son who had died tragically a decade back in a home invasion that had devastated Bubba, and made him the kind of extreme survivalist they featured on Doomsday documentaries and in gun magazines.

Not to mention, he was a firm believer that a zombie apocalypse was imminent. Hence the numerous zombie targets, undead paraphernalia, and the posters on the wall advertising his zombie survival classes he taught with his friend Mark. All over the store and shrunk down as small wallet-sized cards were tips on how to survive an attack.

Nick's personal favorite was the poster right behind the register that listed the number-one tip. Remember, you don't have to outrun the zombie. You just have to outrun your friends.

That didn't exactly warm his heart and make him want to put Bubba at his back in a fight. But then again, Bubba didn't really subscribe to that, and Nick had fought the undead, including zombies, enough with Bubba to know that in a fight, you could count on him and then some.

Bubba left no man behind, and his real philosophy in a fight was shoot first, double-tap the head, and then let God sort it out.

And since this was the anniversary week of his family's deaths, Bubba's mama was in town, visiting with him. Because of that, his dark hair was cut short and his beard had become a well-groomed goatee. He'd also dispensed with his ever-present zombie movie tees and red flannel shirts in favor of a black shirt with sleeves rolled up to his elbows. But his steel-toed combat boots were still his footwear of choice.

Mama or no mama.

Nick would tease him for his maternal fear, but given the fact that he towered over his own mother who kept him cowed and on a short leash, he had no room for mockery. He well understood the potent power of the mothership to quell even the fiercest opponent with nothing more than a glare and arched brow.

But the one thing about Bubba, aside from the fact the man was a total unpredictable lunatic, was that he constantly used Southernisms even Nick had a hard time making out.

"Do what?"

Bubba locked the case where he'd been putting away inventory, then slid the key into his pocket. He stood up to face Nick and Caleb. "You're blue, son. Practically glowing it, like some Mayan sacrifice, waiting to get your heart ripped out. What has you down so low?"

Caleb leaned against the long glass counter and gave Nick a snide grin. "Your Mayan analogy is amazingly astute, Bubba. He broke up with his girl."

Bubba tsked. "Ah now, that's a dang shame. I really liked Kody. She was cold-blooded decent."

Out of the corner of his eye, Nick saw Mark approaching him from the back room. With shaggy brown hair, he was about two inches shorter than Bubba, and was only slightly less muscled. Thinking Bubba's partner-in-crime was going to console him, he didn't react until Mark zapped him in the butt with a cattle prod.

"Hey!" Nick yelped as pain shot through him. "What are you doing?"

Mark, who had not cleaned up his usual rumpled clothing couture because Bubba's mama was in town, held the cattle prod like he might use it again. "Shocking some sense into you. Boy, are you out of your mind? You don't let a girl like Kody go without a fight . . . at least not until she sets fire to everything you own. Then you kick her out. But *not* before then." He moved to shock Nick again.

Nick jumped behind Caleb for protection. "Would you stop that?"

"No. I can't beat sense into you without going to jail for it." Mark closed the distance between them. "Ain't no laws against shocking a minor."

Nick continued to dance around Caleb, who was being derelict in his duty to keep the loon off him. "Isn't that tortfeasory or something? I'm sure there's a law against it."

Bubba let out a heavy sigh. "Unfortunately, Mark, he's right. It goes under the offensive touching laws."

"Offensive touching laws?" Mark drew up short to narrow his eyes at Bubba. "How you know that?"

"Don't want to go there. . . . Not one of my finer moments. Suffice it to say, I don't want to pay any more lawyer fees for a while. I'm about tapped out on them."

"Dear Lord, do I even want to know what y'all are getting into now?" Bubba's mama asked as she came through the black curtains that separated the back area from the front. Arms akimbo, she passed a menacing glare to Mark. "Do I need to call your daddy for more bail money, son?"

Mark straightened up instantly before the much smaller lady. Dressed in a no-nonsense black Armani business suit and low heels, she seemed substantially taller than her tiny five-foot-one stature . . . Mostly because you knew she wouldn't hesitate to take a stick to your backside if you needed it, no matter how big you thought you were in comparison to her.

A world-famed pediatric surgeon, Bobbi Jean Burdette took nothing from anyone, and that included lip from her only son and the best friend he'd grown up with.

And the instant Nick saw her, he grinned a warm welcome. In his head, he heard her favorite saying about Bubba and her hair, which she currently had put up in a sophisticated bun—*God gave me black, then Michael turned it gray, and L'Oreal made me a redhead.*

But the best part about Bubba's mama? She'd twice saved his life.

"Hi, Dr. Burdette," Nick said in greeting, then he gestured at Mark. "For the record, he was shocking me for no reason whatsoever."

Storms brewed in her hazel eyes as she turned her gaze back to Mark. "Markus Jethro Fingerman, you put that thing down. Right now! Good Lord, I barely got the boy patched up and now you threatening to undo all my hard work on him. Don't do something else to harm him or I'm going to turn his mama loose on you."

Mark immediately tossed the cattle prod so that it landed by Caleb's feet. He held his hands up as real fear entered his eyes. "Anything but Cherise. I swear I'd rather be naked in the swamp, surrounded by Madaug's super zombies and hungry gators, than be covered in Kevlar, fully armed with a live grenade in my teeth and flamethrower in my hands and face Cherise Gautier when she's in Nick-protection mode. I ain't never seen a scarier Chihuahua."

Mark was right. Forget his demon bodyguard, Nick's mom was a thousand times more fierce.

And deadlier.

"Besides, it ain't totally my fault, Dr. Burdette,"

Mark continued. "I was just trying to make him see some sense."

"Then, for heaven's sake, boy, try talking to him first. He is a bright child, you know? I'm sure he can see reason without electroshock treatments."

The look on Mark's face said he doubted it. But he didn't comment as he turned back to Nick. "So what'd you do to drive her off?"

Nick grimaced as Mark repeated Brynna's earlier assumption. "Why does everyone think I'm to blame?"

"Dude," Mark said in a patronizing tone. "Do you own a mirror? Guys like you don't get women that fine."

Now that was just plain rude. "Excuse me?"

Mark held his hands up again. "I ain't saying you're a bad-looking guy, not that I look at you that way, but . . . you got no fashion sense. At all."

Nick flicked the edge of Mark's jacket. "This from Dr. Camo?"

"I ain't the one who broke up with the hot girlfriend. I never did figure out how you rated with her anyway. So yeah, it has to be *your* fault."

Nick was aghast. "You know I am one of the most valuable players on my football team, right?"

Mark snorted. "So was I, and Bubba blew us all away in skill. So while that works in movies and TV shows, in real life . . . it ain't that big a thing. Really fine and decent women don't care what jersey you wear. And it definitely isn't what got a woman like Nekoda talking to you to begin with. So my advice to you, kid . . . piece of really nice jewelry and some expensive chocolates."

Dr. Burdette nodded. "I have to say he's right for most women. Shiny usually trumps stupid, and reminds a girl why she liked you in the first place."

Yeah, but he didn't want his assassin back in his life, which he had to keep to himself. Dr. Burdette could conceivably have him committed for rambling that kind of lunacy, even if it was the truth.

So he went with the part of the story that would keep him out of a straitjacket. "As a case in point, I'm the one who broke up with *her.*"

Mark looked at Caleb. "Hand me that cattle prod back. This boy's so stupid, I got to shock some brains into him."

Caleb laughed. "Don't tempt me."

Ignoring them, Bubba tsked. "Hope you had a good reason, Nick. From what I've seen, you two were golden together. And that don't come around often."

No, it didn't. And having lost the love of his life, Bubba knew that better than most.

"It wasn't stupid," Nick assured him.

Mark sighed. "I still think we ought to hold him

down and shock him till he gets over whatever's ailing him."

Dr. Burdette made a sound of deep aggravation in the back of her throat. "Try it, Mark, and I *will* tell his mama on you."

Mark deflated instantly. "Yes, ma'am." But the gleam in his eyes said that the minute Dr. Burdette left them alone, Mark was going for it.

Nick stepped forward so that his foot rested on the cattle prod. Better safe than sorry, especially whenever Mark was around.

"So what are you two doing here this early anyway?" Bubba asked, changing the subject. "Don't you have football practice?"

Nick let loose an evil laugh. "It ended early. Stone cracked the coach's wee-belows with a badly thrown ball. I'm sure we'll all be running laps for hours tomorrow. But today . . . Coach had to go ice himself."

Bubba and Mark sucked their breaths in sharply. "That'll ruin his weekend."

"Yeah, and then some," Caleb added.

Nick walked up to the counter and pointed to the RAM chips that were locked in the case next to boxes of ammo. "Kyrian wants to up his RAM."

"Ah . . . no problem. How much?"

"Max it out."

"You got it." Bubba pulled the RAM out while Nick reached for his wallet and credit card.

"How's it been at school?" Dr. Burdette asked as she went to lean against the counter not far from Nick. "Did they make that girl do her public apology yet?"

Nick flinched at the question. Dina Quattlebaum had been Brynna's best friend since they started school together. They'd always been close and inseparable until Dina got her feelings hurt over something ridiculous, and had conjured a demon that had wreaked havoc on the entire school. Dina had maliciously ruined several students' reputations, including Brynna's. But worse than even that, Dina had accused Nick of attacking her—something that had landed Nick in jail and then caused her father to go Babe Ruth on him . . . which was what Dr. Burdette had referred to earlier when she talked about patching him up. The man had almost killed him.

Luckily, the truth had come out before any real harm had been done, but the fallout was still a nasty thing they were all having to deal with at school. As the old saying went, lies traveled much faster than the truth and the truth never caught up with a lie. He was finding that out in a wicked way.

"She gave her apology first thing this morning, and then they took her to jail for all the stuff she did."

Dr. Burdette shook her head. "That's a darn shame. I hate to see someone so young ruin their life for something as stupid as jealousy."

"Yes, ma'am. Me, too." Nick paid for the RAM. But as he reached to take it, something painful stabbed him right between his eyes.

He sucked his breath in sharply.

Bubba frowned. "You okay?"

Nick nodded, then shook his head. "Got a weird feeling all of a sudden."

Dr. Burdette stepped around the counter to look at him. "What kind of feeling?"

"Dizzy and . . . I don't know. Just weird."

She cupped his chin in her hand and angled his head down so she could study his features while she pressed the back of her other hand against his forehead. "When was the last time you ate something?"

"Lunch."

"And a bag of chips about an hour ago," Caleb added. "Nick doesn't ever miss a meal or a snack."

Without responding to Caleb's dry tone, she pulled a penlight out of her pocket. "Come on to the back and let me take a better look at you."

"Ma, he's fine."

She cast Bubba an evil glare. "Michael, I have noticed that none of them fancy MIT doctorates you hold are in medicine. So if you don't mind . . . I don't tell you how to fix computers and do quantum physics or explain string theory, and you don't tell me how the body works and what I need to be looking at when a former patient goes pale for no apparent reason."

"Yes, ma'am," Bubba said, standing down.

Nick started for the back, then stumbled.

Bubba caught him and all but carried him to a chair. "Hey, boy? You all right?"

Nodding, Nick tried to get his bearings, but everything spun with a vicious frenzy. It was like time had slipped out of sync or something. Everything moved slow and fast at the same time. He heard the voices of the ether whispering all around him. Some were threatening and some were shrill. Together, they made a cacophony so confusing that it only made his dizziness worse.

All of a sudden, through the spinning haze, he smelled something absolutely foul. It was so bad, he choked and coughed. Hard.

But it brought everything into sharp focus. Bubba, Caleb, Dr. Burdette, and Mark were huddled around him.

Mark pulled his hand back from Nick's face. "See! Duck urine isn't just zombie cover, it doubles as smelling salts."

Nick coughed even harder, then cleared his throat. "That's the nastiest crap on the planet, Mark. Please don't ever do that again. I'd rather you shock me . . . or shoot me, even."

"Yeah," Mark said with a twisted laugh, "but it worked, didn't it?"

Nick screwed his face up in distaste while Dr. Burdette tilted his head back and passed the light over his eyes.

"You're a little clammy. What did you have for lunch?"

"Same thing Caleb did. Meat loaf, mashed potatoes, two bags of corn chips, a fruit roll-up, chocolate ice cream, and a Pop-Tart."

He was pretty sure she had the same exact expression that he must have worn when he smelled the duck urine. "I'm not even going to comment . . . oh yes I am. Boy, are you out of your ever-loving mind? What kind of boneheaded lunch is that? Is there anything even remotely nutritious in that lineup?" She looked at Caleb. "And you joined him with that?"

"It was good, Dr. Burdette."

"It was nutritious," Nick said quickly. "We had something from each food group."

She was aghast. "How you figure?"

"Meat loaf for protein. Fruit roll-up, the strawberry

in the Pop-Tarts, and mashed potatoes for my fruits and veggies. Corn chips for my grains and ice cream for dairy. It's all good stuff."

"I shudder at what they're teaching the youth of today. I can't believe the stuff you call food." She rolled her eyes. "It's as bad as the time I caught Michael poking holes in all my biscuits and pouring syrup in them for dinner, and drinking a six-pack of Coke while he did it."

"Hey, now," Bubba said defensively. "That was one of the best meals ever."

"Only if you want to go into a diabetic coma."

Nick laughed, then sobered the moment Dr. Burdette narrowed her gaze on him. "Sorry, ma'am . . . but I feel a lot better now."

She appeared less than convinced. "Are you just saying that so I'll leave you alone?"

"No, ma'am. I really do feel normal again."

Doubt clouded her eyes. "Let me call your mama to come get you. You don't need to be walking around right—"

"I can drive him, Dr. Burdette."

She frowned at Caleb. "You sure?"

He nodded. "I'll be glad to. That way Mrs. Gautier won't have to leave work and get upset."

"All right." She turned back toward Nick. "But if you start to feel anything abnormal again, call me immediately. Understand?"

"Yes, ma'am."

Nodding, she patted Nick on the shoulder and stood back so that he could get up.

Bubba handed him the small bag with Kyrian's RAM chip in it. "You sure you all right?"

"Yeah. Golden."

"A'ight, then. Be careful."

"I will."

Caleb led him out of the store and back to the sidewalk. The moment they were alone and the door was firmly closed, he faced Nick. "What didn't you tell them?"

Was that a trick question? "You know what I didn't tell them. It felt like something was clawing inside me, trying to get out and make a Nick-kabob. Kind of like when my powers take hold of me and I can't control them. But it wasn't the same as that. Not really . . . Ah heck, I don't know. It was just weird. You got any idea about what caused it?"

Caleb shook his head. "Could be a lot of things. Maybe a shift in the time sequence."

A chill went down Nick's spine as he thought about

Ambrose, who occasionally came from the future to help him. "How you mean?"

"Unlike most of us nonhuman entities, the Malachai can sense whenever someone tampers with time. While we have no clue it's been altered, Malachais will know. . . . Or it could be the manifestation of competing powers. Like a warning system to let you know that something's in town, and it has the ability to bleed you. Think of it like a Spidey sense."

Yeah, but he didn't want to think about *that* at all. "That's not comforting."

"Not supposed to be." Caleb started forward.

Nick caught his arm and pulled him to a stop. "Is that it? Are those the only two things it could have been?"

"No. It could be Noir trying to summon you to the Nether Realm. Or a Fringe Guard or other bounty hunter entering this plane, or walking past Bubba's store. It could have been a god popping into Sanctuary for a bite to eat . . . or a million other such things. Whatever it is, it's your powers attempting to charge so that you can face whatever threat might be heading your way."

Oh, goody. Just what he wanted. Someone else out to get him.

"Do your powers do that, too?"

Caleb nodded.

That gave him hope. "Then did you feel it a few minutes ago?"

"Nope, but all that means is whatever's after you isn't after me. Or it could be that it's not strong enough that I need to charge my powers to fight it. The warning system only goes off when *you* need to prepare yourself for battle."

Yah, me.

The moment Caleb finished, another foreign wave went through Nick and with it came clarity about his friend. Something he'd never known.

It was the reason Caleb's powers hadn't charged just now. . . .

"You're a demigod."

His features paling, Caleb stepped back. He narrowed his gaze in warning. "What did you say?"

Nick paused as he sought the source of that revelation. But there was nothing more tangible than a feeling of certainty deep in the pit of his stomach. He knew for a fact that Caleb was part ancient god, and a major one at that. "You are, aren't you? That's why you're stronger than other mid-level demons. It's why you were a general in the First War. You can siphon off your father's powers."

A shield came down around Caleb, preventing Nick from sensing anything else about him, even his mood. "You don't know what you're talking about."

"Yeah, right. You know better than to lie to me." Lie detection was about the only power Nick had that never failed him.

Caleb's eyes flashed bright orange in warning. "Drop the subject, Nick. Now."

Why? Why would that bother him? If Nick had the blood of a god in him, he'd dance around the block and tell everyone and their chickens. Loudly. Heck, he'd probably tattoo it to his forehead.

"Why didn't you tell me?"

"Don't ask questions you don't want to know the answer to," Caleb growled.

And in that instant, Nick saw the trigger of Caleb's rage in his mind as clearly as he saw the anger on Caleb's face.

Deep in the past, Caleb stood before his father, who looked so much like him that it was hard to tell them apart. But Nick knew Caleb's black battle armor that appeared to bleed on its own as camouflage so that no one would ever know if Caleb had been wounded in a fight. Caleb's black hair was longer then and fell in waves to his shoulders. A short, well-groomed beard dusted his cheeks as he confronted the god who had fathered him.

"What have you done?"

His father ground his teeth in an anger that rivaled Caleb's. "It's not what you think."

"Isn't it? You've sold out all of us . . . including me."

"I had no choice."

Caleb laughed bitterly. "We all have choices, old man." He raked his father with a sneer. "At least I finally know for sure where I fall in your affections. Not that I didn't before . . . Thanks for the rectal confirmation." With those words, his human skin transformed to that of a demon—as if Caleb no longer wanted to claim that part of himself at all. He jammed his helm down over his head and started away, but his father caught his arm.

"I do love you, *murahn*."

Caleb snatched his arm free. "I am no son of yours," he snarled between clenched teeth, "so don't pretend otherwise. I was nothing more than an unwanted byproduct of your lust for a demon who had no maternal instinct at all. You should have let her devour me the instant I was spawned. But don't worry. I won't shame you again by claiming you. As far as I'm concerned, I was born an orphan." With that, Caleb unfurled his wings and took flight, leaving his father behind to wince in pain.

Nick wanted desperately to know what his father had done to harm him, but his powers wouldn't cooperate. All he had was that tiny snippet of Caleb's past.

And if he understood anything, it was paternal conflict. His relationship with his own father made Caleb's appear normal.

But in the end, one thing was clear. He hated hurting his friend in any way. And nothing hurt worse than bad memories.

"I'm sorry, Caleb. I won't go there again, okay? Whatever is between you and yours is between you and yours. It's none of my business."

Caleb drew a ragged breath. "You've only just discovered what it's like to be born hybrid. To feel torn between two cultures and two warring parts of yourself. That's a battle I've had my entire existence, and honestly, it sucks. It's exactly like being torn between two women. The best thing to do, kid . . . decide which one you want to be and ignore the other."

"And if I can't?"

"Then you really are screwed and you will never know any kind of peace. Split loyalties work for no one."

As Nick opened his mouth to respond, another image flashed through his mind. It was one of Caleb and six other men who stood as a formidable wall against their enemies. Ferocious power emanated from them as they waited to confront whatever was coming for them. He didn't know who those other men were—if they were demons, gods, or some other group—but it was obvious they had been brothers, if not by blood, then by bond.

"Who were your allies when you fought against my father in the First War?"

Caleb snorted. "I never fought against *your* father, Nick. I led my army against the first Malachai."

That stunned him. "But I thought—"

"You are a direct descendent of the firstborn, but there have been several Malachais before your father. Adarian has lived the longest out of them all. Several only lasted a handful of years . . . long enough to spawn a replacement and then they were gone."

And the one thing that made those Malachais so different from Nick was that each had known who and what they were from the moment of birth. Nick was the only Malachai who'd been born thinking himself human.

It was hard to wake up one day and learn that everything you thought you knew about yourself was a lie. That nothing in your past was what it seemed or what you'd been told. That your parents weren't who and what you'd believed them to be.

He was still fighting hard to wrap his mind around it most days.

Gah, but it was impossible at times. Everything was changing so fast that it made his head spin even more than what it'd done inside Bubba's store.

Yesterday, he'd been a dirt-poor kid whose biggest concern was keeping his grades up and getting to school on time—walking his mom home whenever she worked late. Now he was two years from graduation with a job that carried a buttload of responsibility and secrets. And while he'd thought he was the man of the house when he was a kid, he now fully understood what taking care of his mother really entailed. How her safety hinged on every decision he made. One wrong move and her life would end . . . because of him.

Not to mention, his body was changing and growing faster than he could keep up with, and if that wasn't enough . . .

He was a dang demon half the universe wanted to hunt down and kill.

Including his girlfriend.

And the one thing on his side . . . stupid powers that were more of a detriment than help.

Thanks for that, universe. Glad you have me to pick on.

Closing his eyes, Nick sighed. "I'm too young to deal with all this."

Caleb snorted. "I know the feeling."

Yeah, right. "You're thousands of years old."

"I wasn't born this old, Nick, and because of my parents, I had a bounty on my head, too, when I was a kid. So I do know what you're feeling. And it's a hard place to call home. Trust me, I've had that address every day of my life."

Wow. Caleb could actually share. This was a first.

"How did you survive?" Nick asked him.

"I had an uncle who protected me. Taught me how to fight and shield myself and powers. Most of all, he taught me how to figure out when I should engage in war and when I should walk away and let it go."

"I haven't noticed you doing a lot of the latter."

Caleb laughed. "We have a lot in common, Nick. Stubborn and stupid to the core of our souls."

Yeah, but was what they called a friendship enough for Nick to be able to always trust Caleb at his back? Or would Caleb one day try to kill him, too?

Only time would tell.

Time . . .

Ah, crap!

Nick checked his watch and winced as he realized how late it'd gotten. "Can I catch a ride over to Kyrian's?"

"Sure." Caleb led him back toward their school, where his black Porsche 911 Turbo cabriolet was parked. It hadn't been all that long ago that Nick had been so intimidated by a car this expensive that he was scared to touch it.

Funny how fast things changed. Now, he was around expensive cars so much that he'd started thinking of them as normal. Who would have ever imagined that? Definitely not him.

Nick opened the car door to get in and paused as he caught sight of several classmates leaving the building. Two of them called out a greeting to Caleb, who ignored them completely, like he always did. Caleb hated having to play his role of Mr. Jock Popularity. Everyone at school thought he was a rich kid whose parents were always out of town.

If they only knew the truth. . . .

They'd probably burst into flames, or have a stroke and die from disbelief.

Pushing that thought aside, Nick got in and fastened his seat belt. "Try to keep it under ninety, okay?"

Caleb laughed as he started the engine, then floored it. Nick held his breath as they took a corner so fast, he was pretty sure two wheels came off the pavement.

"Thinking I should have grabbed a streetcar," he mumbled under his breath.

Caleb downshifted. "You fight armies of the damned

out to slay you, and my driving is what scares you? Really?"

"Have to say that's a big affirmative."

Caleb shook his head and laughed. "Don't worry, Nick. You're safe as a babe in my presence. I can't afford to let anything happen to you."

That would be more comforting if they weren't careening in and out of traffic in warp drive. What was it with immortals that they loved to speed and weave? Come to think of it, none of them had ever taken or passed a real driver's license test. . . .

Help me.

The good news was that it didn't take all that long to get to Kyrian's. Especially since they were traveling at the speed of sound.

Nick let out a relieved breath at his safe arrival. "FYI, I think I might have stained your seat. You'll probably want to clean that later."

Caleb stopped the car barely a millimeter from Kyrian's locked wrought-iron gate. "It's all right. I'll just buy a new one."

"All right, then. *Hasta mañana.*" Nick rolled out of the car and grabbed his backpack from the floorboard. He'd barely closed the door before Caleb peeled out.

He didn't know for sure what Caleb did when he

wasn't around. Caleb refused to elaborate on his free time. Then again, he refused to elaborate on most things.

Just like Nick's boss Kyrian and his friend Acheron. Another thing immortals had in common, apparently.

You don't talk much about yourself either.

True. He didn't like people getting all that close to him. That way, it didn't hurt so much when they left.

Maybe that was their problem, too. It made sense. An average human life was nothing when you lived forever. Kind of like owning a Great Dane. No sooner did you get good and attached, than old age claimed them and they were gone, and you were all alone again.

Yeah, that would be hard to deal with. Heaven knew Nick had a major death phobia anyway. He couldn't stand the thought of it.

Trying to put it out of his mind, Nick punched the code into the gate and waited for it to open.

As soon as it was wide enough, he headed up the curved driveway that led to the sprawling white antebellum mansion Kyrian called home. It was an impressive place with wraparound porches, up and down. The kind of house that reminded you of a wedding cake.

And as he walked closer, he had another weird sensation go through him—like some out-of-body experience. He saw himself from high above in the clouds.

There was no doubt that was Nick Gautier walking, yet it seemed like some unknown character on a TV screen. Like he was completely detached from his emotions and body.

What is going on with me today?

Thankfully, his phone buzzed in his pocket. That sensation slammed him back into his body and reality, and reconnected him with his emotions.

Nick pulled his phone out to see a message from Casey.

Hey, babe. I heard you guys got free early. Want to grab a bite to eat?

Nick scowled, then quickly typed a response. *I think you meant to send that to Stone.*

He'd just reached the steps when she answered.

Ha, ha, Nick. I know who I'm texting. So are you hungry? Want to hang out for a while?

Yeah, this day couldn't get any stranger.

Well, barring another one of Madaug's zombie attacks or a demon assault.

Have to work. Sorry.

He'd barely sent that before she shot back another text. Dang, that girl could hammer out words.

Call me when you get off. I'll be here.

Nick was so stunned that he would have walked

straight into the front door had Rosa not opened it first. About even in height to Bubba's mama, Rosa had black hair tinged with gray. In her early forties, she was Kyrian's housekeeper and more like another mother to Nick.

"You have a problem, Mr. Nick?" He always loved the way she said his name with her heavy Spanish accent. It was so cool.

"No, Rosa. I'm just trying to figure out a girl from school."

She laughed and stepped back so that he could enter the house. "There's no figure when you speak of women, *m'ijo*. We are mysterious creatures."

"Yes, yes you are." He slid his phone into his pocket. "Is Kyrian awake yet?"

She closed the door and pulled the cloth from her shoulder. "*Sí.* He is in the shower."

"Awesome."

Rosa scowled at him. "Do you feel all right, Nick? You look a bit pale."

That was another thing about Rosa, you couldn't get anything past her. "Yes, ma'am. Just had a bad day."

She gave him a sympathetic pout. "Would chocolate chips help you feel better?"

He immediately flashed a grin at her. "Ah, Ms. Rosa,

you are a godsend. Yes, that would help turn my day around exponentially."

Rising up on her tiptoes, she ruffled his hair. "They are in the kitchen, *m'ijo*. Still warm and gooey. Go grab yourself some."

"Muchas gracias!"

"De nada."

With quick steps, Nick ran to the back of the house, then paused as he felt a presence there that wasn't normal. "Rosa?" he called out. "Is Acheron here?" He always left an odd feeling in the air.

"No. Just you, me, and Kyrian."

Weird. "Okay. Thanks."

Still, he couldn't shake the sensation as he made his way to the kitchen counter to grab a handful of Rosa's delicious cookies. The smell was soothing, but he couldn't get over the odd tingling. It made the skin on the back of his neck crawl.

He swallowed a cookie and looked around the room, seeking the source of his discomfort.

What the . . . ?

You are going to die. . . . The disembodied voice that came from the hall was gender neutral.

His heart hammering, Nick searched everywhere, trying to find the source of it.

There was nothing. He was completely alone in the kitchen.

"Who are you?" he shot back in a low tone so that Rosa wouldn't hear it and think he was nuts. He backed away from the counter toward the door to his office, then slammed it shut.

I'm a harvester and you *are my bounty.*

CHAPTER 4

"Bring it home, punk," Nick snarled at the voice, dropping his backpack to the floor of the office he shared with Rosa. He braced himself for the fight. "This Cajun don't go down for nothing. You think you can take me, you better bring some friends."

The door behind him opened. Nick spun around, ready to battle whatever was there.

As soon as he saw who was entering, he sucked his breath in sharply. It was a giant of a man who stood almost seven feet in height. One who had on a pair of opaque sunglasses that concealed his eyes from view. Wearing black on black, and with long purple hair, he appeared at first glance no older than twenty, but the ferocity of his presence told everyone who came into contact with him that he was much more than what he appeared.

That he was badass enough to take down anyone dumb enough to challenge him.

And thankfully, he was one of Nick's best friends.

Nick growled at him. "Dang it all, Ash. You scared the crap out of me. Could you please knock once in a while?"

A knock sounded on the door that was open behind Acheron's gargantuan form. "Better?"

Not really. It was kind of creepy. But at least he knew about Acheron's unearthly powers and offbeat humor, so the disembodied knock wasn't that much of a surprise. As the leader of the Dark-Hunters and old-est member of their crew, Ash's psychic abilities were fierce and scary. The stuff people had nightmares about.

But Nick feared almost nothing, and Ash was defi-nitely no longer on that list.

Rolling his eyes, he sighed. "Little late there with the knock, buddy."

"Sorry. I didn't realize you'd be so jumpy. I forget that teenagers are like puppies. High-strung and ner-vous for no apparent reason. I guess we're all lucky you didn't soil the carpet, huh?"

"Ha, ha. More like you, T. rex, were born before doors were invented and don't know proper protocol. Just to clarify. You knock *before* you come into a room."

Ash let out an aggravated breath as he swiped his

brow with his middle finger. "For the record, we did have doors eleven thousand years ago. Like many other things you guys erroneously take credit for, you did not invent them."

Nick snorted. "Uh-huh. That's what all ancient people say. So what are you doing here?"

Ash tucked his hands into the pockets of his motor-cycle jacket that had a skull and crossbones painted across the back of it. "Responding to that wigged-out text you sent me from school. Why are you suddenly curious about demonology?"

There was something about Ash so trustworthy that Nick almost told him everything. But Ambrose had been emphatic that he keep Acheron out of his life as much as possible . . . for Ash's sake as much as his own. And while Nick didn't really trust his future self, he had no reason to doubt Ambrose's warnings. Especially since Ambrose knew the future and exactly what would happen to Nick if he didn't change things.

So he opted for a partial truth. "We had one loose in my school so I thought, given that I'm now in the middle of this oh-so-fun world of yours, I ought to educate myself on it in case another one decides to use St. Richard's or me for a playground. . . . So do you know any good books about it?"

Acheron laughed deep in his throat. "Now there's

something I never thought to hear coming out of *your* mouth. At least not unless it involved hentai or manga."

Nick slapped his knee in a grandiose, sarcastic gesture. "You're so hilarious. You know, if this whole Daimon-slaying gig doesn't work out for you, you should really consider being a comedian. The bright Barney hair color would just add to the overall entertainment factor."

Acheron smiled, flashing a tiny bit of his fangs. Over eleven thousand years old, Ash knew pretty much everything about anything. But unlike most of Nick's teachers, he wasn't arrogant or condescending about it. And when he explained the past to you, it was actually interesting, especially since you knew he'd lived through it and was speaking from personal experience.

"And one day, kid, that sense of humor of yours is going to get you eaten by something foul."

"So they keep telling me."

With an expression that said he was less than amused, Ash ran his thumb along the edge of his lips. "The best book I know is bound in human flesh and written in blood. Not sure you'd want it if I gave it to you, and even then, it's written in cuneiform."

"Cune-wha . . . ?"

"Exactly my point, Nick. . . . Cuneiform. Ancient

Sumerian. Not exactly something they teach in high school these days."

That figured. Nick scowled at him. "What good is it, then?"

"A lot. It's the definitive book on all subspecies of Eurasian and African demonkyn. There's not a breed on those continents that isn't well documented, right down to how to trap and kill them. But it has nothing about American, Australian, or Antarctican demons."

That last one floored him. Was Ash serious or joking again? "They have demons on Antarctica?"

"Yeah," Ash breathed. "It wasn't always covered by ice, that was just a precaution when they buried them. Not to mention, there are a few sunken small continents around it, such as Mu, Asmayda, Lumeria, Vlaanderen, and the aptly named Satanazes, which translates to the Isle of Demons. There's a really good reason no human wants to live on the South Pole. And why many have never returned from their trips there."

Nick narrowed his gaze at Acheron. "You're screwing with me, aren't you?"

"No. There's a lot of human history that wasn't written down. Sometimes for good reasons, and there are tons of things the powers-that-be don't want humanity to remember or rediscover. And even what's written

SHERRILYN KENYON

isn't always right. People skew things all the time to make themselves look better."

"Such as?"

"Well, if you ask the god Apollo what happened to Atlantis, he'll tell you *he* sank it. Plato, on the other hand, blames the sinking on Poseidon. The Keetoowah say it was a blond-haired demon who annihilated it."

"And the truth?" Nick asked.

Acheron shrugged. "Don't know. I was temporarily dead when my home was sucked into the ocean. I keep watching the History Channel hoping for enlightenment, but so far . . . nada."

Nick laughed at his dry tone. "You're lying to me."

Acheron arched a brow. "What makes you think that?"

"I don't know. It's a feeling I have that tells me you know exactly what happened to your homeland, but that you don't want to share."

Acheron's stance and expression gave nothing away. Man, to have those evil poker face powers. "What can I say? I have a long history of not playing well with others."

Knowing Acheron was even less likely to share than Caleb, Nick changed the subject. "So how many classifications of demon are there, anyway?"

"Thousands. Every culture has its own group."

"You can't be more specific?"

Ash shrugged. "If I thought about it, but really? Who cares?"

"I do. So what's the exact number?"

"Nine thousand, two hundred and twelve subcategories."

Now that was a lot, and Nick was one of them. No, Nick was the *king* of them, or would be one day.

But Acheron didn't know that. And Nick wasn't about to enlighten him. Especially since Acheron made a habit out of killing one particular demon class of beings.

Still, it was impressive that Acheron could pull the exact number out of the ether. His powers really were terrifying. "Do you know them all?"

"Not personally. Contrary to what you think, not all preternatural beings hang out at the local Supernatural Pub looking for humans and dates."

Nick let out an irritated breath. "That wasn't what I meant. Do you know all the different kinds?"

"Yes, and we've talked about this before. Would you like the list alphabetically, regionally, or chronologically?"

Nick rolled his eyes again. "I would accuse you of being sarcastic, but I have a feeling you actually could name them all in those orders."

"Yes, I can. But that being said, I don't know everything about all of them. Some of them aren't in the human realm so I've never had the chance to cross their path. Some are extinct and were so even when I was born. Others are major pains in my posterior more times than they should be."

A weird chill went down Nick's spine at that last bit. It was something Ash said about him. A lot. Could Ash possibly know what he was?

No, there was no way. Ash wouldn't have been so lackadaisical about it if he knew. In fact, given his devotion to humans, Acheron would most likely kill him if he ever learned Nick was a Malachai.

"Acheron? I didn't know you were still in town."

Ash turned as Kyrian joined them in Nick and Rosa's office. At six foot five, Kyrian didn't look up at many men, but Ash was one of the few. Blond, well muscled, and with features a cover model would envy, he had a presence every bit as fierce as Acheron's. His blond curls were slicked back and wet from his shower, but he was dressed in his usual all-black high-fashion designer style.

In his human life, Kyrian had been a renowned Greek prince and general. That aura of commanding nobility still bled from every precise gesture he made. Even his stance said, "bow down before me or get your throat cut."

Ash shook Kyrian's hand. "Given the strange vibe we encountered last night, I decided to stay on for a bit longer."

Nick frowned. "What strange vibe?"

Kyrian rubbed at his shoulder as if he'd been injured the night before. "We found a group of Daimons who actually fought back with a great deal of skill, instead of running away like they normally do."

"Did you get them?"

"No," Acheron answered before Kyrian had a chance. "Which is another reason I'm staying a little longer than planned."

Kyrian glared at Acheron. "You know, Acheron, I led entire armies up against Rome's finest. I think I can handle this without a babysitter."

"And when you were going up against Rome, I daresay you had more than you, Xander, and Talon in your army."

"I really hate it when you use logic against me." Kyrian crossed his arms over his chest.

"Xander?" Nick asked Acheron, wondering about the unfamiliar name.

"Another Dark-Hunter here in New Orleans."

Nick gaped. "There's a third Dark-Hunter and you're just now telling me this?"

"We actually have four here," Kyrian said. "But Rogue speaks even less than Xander does."

Nick looked back and forth between them. "And . . . why am I just now finding out about this?"

Ash shrugged. "Need to know . . . and you didn't."

Yeah, it said a lot about how secretive they were and the fact that as Kyrian's human Squire, Nick was supposed to be privy to all Dark-Hunter details, especially those that concerned or mattered to him. "Aren't you guys afraid I'd see one of them and stake them by mistake?"

"Nope," Ash said. "They're not blond. That's the only reason we told you about Talon. We figured if you ran across Xander or Kit, you'd think they were some other species."

That was the thing about Daimons, since they didn't intermingle with other species, they were all natural blondes.

"Who's Kit?" Nick asked with a frown. "Is that another one?"

Kyrian shook his head. "Rogue's real name isn't Rogue. His parents weren't *that* cruel. It's Christopher Boughy, or Kit."

"Why does he go by Rogue, then? Is he an X-Men fan?"

Ash sighed. "FYI, I wouldn't crack that joke around

him. I doubt his High Surliness would be amused and he tends to be fast with a blade to the throat. Back in the eighteenth century, he was an English highwayman known as the Black Rogue. Rogue for short."

"Oh."

"So, Acheron," Kyrian said, hijacking their conversation. "What happened to your car? I saw the busted fender on it. How unlike you to crash into anything."

Nick cringed as Acheron turned toward him with an arched brow.

"Hey now," Nick said, holding his hands up in defense of himself, "it was not *my* fault. I was minding my own business when that trash can went suicidal, came out of nowhere, and jumped in front of the car."

"It was on the curb, Nick," Ash said drily. "Along with a number of screaming pedestrians, running for their lives."

"That's *your* story. I'm sticking to mine. . . . And there ought to be a law about homicidal trash cans, and fines for the people who put them on the street. They're really dangerous. . . . Just saying."

Kyrian shook his head. "And you wonder why I haven't volunteered to teach him how to drive?"

"I know why you haven't volunteered. I, on the other hand, need a psych eval for being so stupid."

"No comment, for I have never been quite so stupid

as to intentionally insult *you*." Kyrian pegged Nick with a grimace. "So, kid, did you get—"

"Right here, boss." Knowing what Kyrian wanted without his finishing the sentence, Nick pulled the RAM out of his pocket. "I'm going to install it first thing. I also texted Kell about your boots and he said that his Squire mailed them back yesterday, but it'll be a week on your sword. He's waiting for a shipment of the titanium he uses to smelt the blades. So then, I checked with Liza to see what she had in inventory. She said that she has a smaller short sword if you want to try it while you wait for your replacement. If you're interested, I can pick that up before you head out tonight, and I asked Kell to make four more swords as backups so that you won't have to wait in the future should your primary and secondary get busted."

Kyrian inclined his head to Acheron. "Worth every penny of his salary."

"Yeah, I'm thinking about cloning him. We could make a killing selling Nick PAs."

Kyrian laughed, then gave a nod to Nick. "I shall leave you to your duties and go work out until the sun goes down. If you'd like to join me in a bit, I can show you more sword-fighting techniques."

And with that, he quit the room.

Acheron returned to their previous discussion. "So,

is there any demon you wanted to know about in particular?"

Don't do it.

But before his common sense could prevail over his stupidity, he blurted out the one thing he wanted to know most. "Ever heard of a Malachai?"

Acheron's jaw went slack, thus confirming he had more than a working knowledge of Nick's species. "Where did you hear that term?"

Yeah, okay, it was a touchy subject for Acheron, too.

"The demon at my school mentioned one. You know anything about them?"

"More than I want to."

"Meaning?"

Ash did what he did best—he diverted a personal question into a generic one. "A Malachai is one of the oldest demons in existence. There's only one left, so it's not likely you'll ever come across him."

If only he was that lucky.

Now to test exactly how much knowledge Ash had of Nick and his father. "Do you know where he is?"

Acheron shook his head. "No one does. He escaped from his master centuries ago and has been in hiding ever since."

Nick had to give his father credit. He might be a first-rate jerk, but he knew how to shield himself.

"Do you know how he came into being?"

Ash frowned. "You seem to be a little more than just passingly curious."

"I am. I want to know why the demon was talking about him. Is there something really special about a Malachai?"

"Yeah, if you want to seriously mangle people or end the world as we know it, he's the one to summon. He was the first of the demonic destroyers and his breed fathered many of the subsequent and best-known evil demons. Luckily, none of the children possess the powers of their fathers. Rather, they're all watered-down versions of the Malachai."

"Really?" That wasn't what Nick had been told.

Ash nodded. "The only exception is the original Malachai bloodline. The firstborn alone can father a child even more powerful than he is."

All right, that explained Nick's powers and why they were so dangerous.

"Do you know why?" Nick asked.

"Not really. But I suspect it has to do with the fact that he, unlike the others of his kind, was born from a goddess who had an affair with a Sephiroth."

"What's a Sephiroth?" Nick already knew, but if he didn't ask, Acheron might become suspicious again.

"They were consorts and soldiers of the primal gods. But they were never supposed to breed with them."

"Then why did they?"

Acheron shrugged. "The goddess wanted a baby and she wanted it to be powerful, but not torn by pantheon politics. So, she conceived a child with her Sephiroth, who was also a demigod."

"What made the Malachai evil?"

Ash paused before he answered. "While he was born from a mother who wielded dark powers, his father was born of light. So he had a fifty-fifty shot as to which side he'd fall on. Some say he was decent enough until the first war of the gods. To end that war and save the world, the original gods forged a truce that required both the light and dark powers to destroy what remained of their armies. Unwilling to kill her own son, the goddess struck a bargain to spare one Sephiroth and one Malachai. So all of them were put to death, except the Sephiroth who had betrayed his people and her son. Then her son became infused with hatred and turned psychotic when he was ordered by the light gods to kill the Malachai female he'd hidden from execution."

"He loved her?"

Acheron nodded.

That gave Nick hope. "I didn't think they could love."

"You can't really hate without it. And Monakribos worshiped his beloved Rubati. But when he refused to end her life, the gods tricked him into it. As she lay dying in his arms, she confessed to him that she was pregnant with his child and that by his own actions, he'd killed them both. He begged the gods and, in particular, his mother, to save them, but she couldn't do it without restarting the war they'd just ended. Instead, she made it so that he could have more children. But if they were born with his Malachai abilities, to keep with the truce she'd agreed to, he would have to die by their tenth birthday or whenever they came into their powers."

Man, it sucked to be a Malachai.

I am never *having kids.*

"How did he become a tool for evil?"

"He was tricked into killing the woman he loved, Nick. And his unborn child. The guilt and grief drove him mad and poisoned his blood with hatred and venom. And that's how you know a Malachai when you come across one. Unless they're using their powers to conceal what they are, they don't bleed red. A full-blown Malachai bleeds black."

That was something to remember. So far, he was red-blooded. . . . Good. There was still hope for him.

"Does it only turn black when they go evil?"

Ash nodded.

Now Nick knew what to look for. That actually helped a great deal. "Next question. Do they have to go evil?"

"That is the question, isn't it? Are we pawns to, or masters of, our own destinies? Every being has to make that choice for him or herself."

"So it's possible for a Malachai to be good?"

"In theory. As with all other species, it depends on his strength of character, and the decisions he makes."

For the first time in months, Nick had real hope. Ambrose was right. He could avoid the destiny that awaited him. He didn't have to become a cold-blooded killer, after all.

Awesome!

"But," Acheron continued, "it's not easy to go against your nature. Especially when you're a creature of destruction. One bad temper outburst, and you lose all humanity. You say and do things you don't mean to and it's too late to undo them. Creatures like the Malachai have a harder time than others keeping their noses clean and not giving in to the darkness that's forever seducing them."

Nick scowled. "You sound like you have personal experience with that."

"We all have demons inside us, Nick. The Tsalagi have an old saying—every heart holds two wolves. One is the white wolf, who is made up of love, kindness, respect, decency, compassion, and all the things that are good in life. The black wolf is born of jealousy, hatred, pettiness, prejudice, vindictiveness, and all the poisons of the human personality. The two constantly war with each other for dominance. And one day, one wolf will overtake and devour the other."

"Yeah, but which one?"

"Always the one you feed, kid. You feed good to it and the white one grows. You feed evil and the black wolf devours. But in the end, you alone make the choice of which wolf you nurture. And that's true of every species and race."

Nick nodded. *I can overcome.*

No, he *would* overcome. His father and birth didn't have to define him, after all. He was the one in control of himself. No one else . . .

"Thanks, Ash. You've given me a lot to think about."

"No problem. If you have any other questions, you know how to reach me." Ash turned to leave.

"Wait." Nick stopped him. "I do have one more. Have you ever heard of a harvester?"

"As in someone who pulls vegetables out of a garden?"

Nick rolled his eyes. "No, like something that goes after demons?"

"Not per se. There are all kinds of creatures who hunt demons for different reasons. It really depends on the demon and its country of origin, as well as that of the hunter. And of course, you have the bounty hunters, which are a separate species entirely."

Nick didn't like the sound of that. "How so?"

"If a demon breaks a law from its pantheon or another, or if someone or something wants to own it or control it, they can offer up a reward for either the demon's capture or death. At which point the bounty hunters come out in force."

Great. Just what he wanted to hear. More creatures out to kill him. Yee-flippin'-haw.

"Would someone ever hunt a Malachai?"

"Oh yeah. Everyone hunts the Malachai. He is the grand prize of all time. There's not a demon in existence that carries a heftier price on its head than he does. Not to mention, if you enslave the Malachai, you have absolute evil at your disposal, and there's nothing you can't conquer."

Oh great, slavery? And here Nick thought being Kyrian's Squire was inhibiting and degrading.

"How do you enslave a Malachai?" he asked, wanting to know what to avoid.

"With a really big army."

"I'm serious, Ash."

He flashed a taunting grin. "You'd have to weaken him first."

"And you do that, how?"

Ash scowled. "Why are you so intent on this?"

Nick didn't dare tell him the truth. "Scholarly curiosity. You talk about the ultimate evil. I want to know how to defeat it. 'Cause you know how my luck runs. And in case it goes south one night when you're not around to help me fight, I'd like to know how to hurt it."

Ash arched a shocked brow. "Well, since scholarly curiosity is such a novelty for you . . ."

Nick ignored his sarcasm.

"Easiest way is if he has a son destined to inherit his powers, put them together. The younger Malachai starts sucking the power out of him immediately. But the drawback to that is, once the father's dead, the child will then have his powers and his father's. So if you're smart, you'll kill one and enslave the other before the child develops fully. You might not have as strong a Malachai that way, but you will have one, and not die in the process."

Yeah, that definitely wasn't appealing. So whatever he did, he couldn't let anyone get him in the same room with his father again. No matter what.

"And the hardest way?" Nick asked.

"You go full-on and try to collar him. And good luck with that."

Nick frowned. "I don't understand. Collar him, how?"

"The three primal gods who once controlled him have a special collar that restricts his powers and it keeps him from harming them. That was the slavery he escaped. You get the collar, which the gods who own it have to allow you to do, and you place it on his neck before he kills you. That's definitely the hardest way." Acheron paused. "So are you writing a book with all of this?"

Nick laughed nervously. "No. But I think I will use it for my next D&D quest. How cool would that be, huh?"

Acheron shook his head. "Happy dragon hunting, kid. Don't get lost in the labyrinth."

As Ash left, Nick headed upstairs to install the RAM in Kyrian's computer while his thoughts churned over Ash's information. It was a lot to chew on and made him wish he had Acheron's knowledge base. What would it be like to have the brain of an encyclopedia?

Live long enough and you'll have that answer, too.

True. Ambrose was just like Acheron. He knew everything—past, present, and future.

SHERRILYN KENYON

As Nick reached the staircase, he hesitated. An odd electrical sensation went through him. It felt like someone was watching his every move.

"Rosa?"

She didn't answer, which meant it wasn't her.

"Kyrian?"

Again, no answer.

Nick took a step, then paused. "Harvester?"

Deep in his mind, he heard a sinister laugh that made him jump.

Yeah, okay, creepy didn't even come close to describing what he felt. There was a chill to his blood that rushed through him and made the hair on his arms stand up again.

"What are you?" he breathed.

Death. The whisper was so faint that at first he thought he imagined it.

"Yeah, right. I happen to be on a first-name basis with Death, and you're not him, buddy."

He's not the only one, and he's not the one who's come for you. Your life will be mine soon.

Instead of scaring him, that threat set fire to his temper. No one threatened Nick Gautier.

"I'm not afraid of you. You want to fight . . . bring it."

Something struck the wall by his face. Hard. It was so close to him that whatever it was grazed his nose.

In spite of his bravado, that actually scared him blind. Hard to fight something when you couldn't see it . . . Jack-rabbiting up the stairs, he went into Kyrian's training room instead of his office.

Nick slammed the door and threw himself against it, arms wide to keep it shut.

Kyrian looked up from his punching bag with a curious brow. He stepped away from it. "You all right, kid?"

No. But he had too much dignity to admit that out loud. "Question. Is this house haunted?"

With an even deeper scowl, Kyrian shook his head. "No. Believe me. Before any Dark-Hunter moves into a new location, it is thoroughly checked for any and all ghosts."

There was another thing Nick hadn't been told. How much were they holding back? "Really? Why?"

"We're soulless creatures, Nick. So those who have souls and no bodies tend to want to take up residence inside us. It's actually not hard for them to take over. That's why Dark-Hunters don't go into cemeteries. It's too dangerous for us, and no one wants a possessed Dark-Hunter on the loose."

That added another chill to him. "Can demons possess Dark-Hunters?"

"No. They're not the same thing as a human ghost.

Whenever they use those powers against us, it conflicts with ours and backfires on them. It was a safeguard Artemis put in place to keep the living Daimons from taking us over and controlling us."

"Ah . . . okay."

Kyrian returned to punching his heavy weighted bag. "Did you get my RAM installed?"

"No, not yet. I'll . . . uh . . . I'll go do it." But Nick didn't want to leave the safety of Kyrian's presence.

Unfortunately, he didn't have any choice. Not without looking even more ridiculous to his boss. And a total weenie, to boot.

Sighing, he forced himself to leave and head back down the hall, to Kyrian's office. As soon as he was inside, he locked the door . . . Just in case. Then rethought the action, since Kyrian would think him nuts if he found it that way. Nick unlocked it. And still the feeling of being watched stayed with him.

Whatever it is, it's still here.

Aggravated at himself for being chicken, Nick pulled the case off Kyrian's PC. He set the RAM on the desk, then reached into his back pocket to pull out his grimoire. The size of a small paperback novel, it'd been a gift from Ambrose to help him understand some of the madness that surrounded him, and to answer some of the "other" questions that came up.

"All right, Nashira," Nick said in a low tone. "Talk to me. What the heck is watching me?"

He slid his knife out of his pocket, opened the book, and pricked his finger, allowing three drops of blood to touch a blank page. *"Dredanya eire coulet,"* he whispered, waking the female spirit who lived inside the enchanted pages. The moment he finished speaking, his blood began swirling until it formed words:

> *Do not fear that which cannot be seen.*
> *For they are lost in between.*
> *'Tis the ones who come alive*
> *That your blood will allow to thrive.*

Nick snorted at the cryptic stanzas. "Not really useful, Nashira. Doesn't answer my question."

His blood crawled over to the next page.

> *Answer, answer, you always say,*
> *But it doesn't work that way.*
> *In time, the truth you shall find.*
> *And then you will understand my rhyme.*

"I'm such a masochist to even try talking to you."

Underneath the words, a picture of an obscene gesture formed.

"Oh very nice, Nashira. Very nice. Wherever did you learn that?"

In your pocket I reside.
Ever privy to your deride.
But more than that, I can see.
And that includes bathroom stall graffiti.

Nick screwed his face up in distaste. "Oh my God, no. Tell me you haven't been spying on me in the rest room. You perv!"

Calm yourself, you evil troll.
My job is not to console.
But if it is privacy you seek,
Leave me in your backpack so I can't peek.

Now he understood why other people got so aggravated with *his* attitude disorder. He wanted to strangle his book.

Or burn it. Where were Bradbury's firemen when you needed them?

"Thanks for the comfort, hon. 'Preciate it." Nick returned the grimoire to his pocket and finished sliding the RAM into Kyrian's PC.

But as he did so, he mulled over Nashira's words. *Do*

not fear that which cannot be seen . . . they are lost in be-tween. What did that mean?

Was the entity just messing with his head?

Kyrian had told him it couldn't be a ghost in the house. Which left a lot of other possibilities. None of which were good for his health.

Or sanity.

Stop dwelling on it. You're safe.

Determined to ignore the weird, icky feeling in his gut, Nick started for the door. Just as he reached the center of the room, he heard something snap. Pausing, he looked around for the source of the sound.

An instant later, the huge chandelier over his head fell down on him.

CHAPTER 5

Nick jumped back, narrowly escaping the chandelier arms. But his foot caught in the fringe of the Persian carpet, sending him to the ground as it crashed down beside him. Shards of crystal and glass showered his body and hair. He barely had time to turn his head away and shield his eyes.

The door burst open.

"Nick?"

Lowering the arm he had over his face to protect it, he opened his eyes to find a sweating Kyrian towering over him, pulling off his boxing gloves. Nick shook his head to loosen shards from his hair. "I'm all right."

With an expression that said he wasn't buying it, Kyrian knelt down to investigate Nick's condition. Gently, he took Nick's chin in his hand and examined him. "What happened?"

"No idea. I heard something snap and the next thing

I know . . . your light fixture tried to kill me. I saw my whole life flash before my eyes, boss. It was horrific. I haven't done anything to regret yet and it's been way too brief. I at least want a license before I check out, you know?"

Kyrian rolled his eyes. "Yeah, you're all right. Thank the gods. I'd hate to have your mother coming after me again because I let you get hurt on my watch." He helped Nick to his feet.

Then he went to study the chandelier remains. Nick paused at the sight of it . . . all over the room. He'd never seen anything splinter into so many pieces.

He was still dusting fragments off his clothes and hair. "I hope that wasn't expensive."

"Probably around sixty to eighty thousand dollars."

Nick sucked his breath in sharply. "I hope you mean Jamaican dollars and not U.S. Dude, seriously? It's a light fixture, not a supercar . . . or a house."

Kyrian picked through some of the broken pieces with the toe of his boot. "Quit hyperventilating. It came with the house, but it is an antique Waterford crystal chandelier. Back in the day, this room was a formal ballroom, and this was its showpiece."

"Oh." Still . . . who paid *that* for a light?

Kyrian looked up at the ceiling where the silk cord hung from the ornate medallion like a jungle snake. "I guess the chain wore out. I should have had it checked." He met Nick's wide-eyed stare. "Call for an electrician to look into it and see if any of the wiring poses a shock or fire hazard, and make an appointment for him to install another one as soon as he can, and to check the rest of the fixtures in the house."

He said that like they grew on trees. "Where do I get a chandelier?"

Kyrian gave him a dry stare. "We live in New Orleans, Einstein. You can't blow your nose on Royal Street that your germs won't land on a crystal chandelier in an antique store. Just pick one that's roughly the same size and design."

Nick returned Kyrian's stare with one equally insulting. "You know, boss, while I realize it wouldn't pose a problem for you, the cost of one of these definitely exceeds my card limit. How you want me to pay for it? 'Cause no offense, I ain't that good-looking."

Oh yeah, that was an awesomely vicious look. "I'll have you added to my AmEx account, and they'll overnight a card for you."

"Limit?"

"Not one. But don't go hog-wild. While your mother scares me, I do know how to bury bodies in places where they'll never be found."

Rosa rushed into the room and gaped at the mess. "*Madre de Dios!* What happened?"

Nick pointed at the chandelier remains. "It tried to turn me into a pancake."

She grabbed him into a fierce hug. "*M'ijo!* Are you hurt? It didn't hit you, did it?"

"It just assaulted my ego. Physically, I'm good."

"No," she snapped. "You're bleeding."

Nick's eyes widened. "Bleeding? Where?"

"You cut your cheek," Kyrian answered. "It's not bad, though."

Nick gaped at him. "Since when is bleeding ever a good thing?"

Kyrian made a sound of disgust.

Rosa ignored him as she draped her arm over Nick's shoulders. "Come downstairs, Nick, and let me tend you."

"Yes, ma'am."

"And don't bleed on my floors," Kyrian called after him.

Nick couldn't let that pass. He stuck his head back in the door. "Don't worry, boss. It's the counters and rugs I'm going for."

Dodging out of the room before Kyrian forgot about his fear of his mother, Nick followed Rosa to the stairs, but he couldn't shake the bad feeling inside him that the source of the disembodied voice had a lot of power.

Enough to almost drop a chandelier on me.

Yeah, that'd been a little too close. He'd report it to Caleb later. Maybe C might have some insight as to what could have done that to him.

Maybe I shouldn't walk home. . . .

If the harvester could get to him here, where Kyrian had all kinds of protection against supernatural beings, it'd be a thousand times easier to assault him on the street where there was nothing.

Rosa led him into the kitchen and sat him on a raised stool at the breakfast bar while she went to the cabinet that held Kyrian's first-aid supplies. She came back with an alcohol wipe, Neosporin, and Band-Aids.

As she tended him, his thoughts spun with possibilities about who would be after him with such viciousness. And no matter how he looked at it, he kept coming back to one name.

Nekoda.

Who else would have access to Kyrian's house when it was kept guarded and shielded? For all he knew, *she* was the harvester, and was using that just to screw with his head.

His mother had always warned him that there was nothing more lethal on the planet than a woman with a broken heart. Or one who thought a guy had done her wrong. They would use a guy's faults to justify any action they took against him.

Even handing the husband who adored them over to his worst enemies. . . .

And look at Mark. His last girlfriend had piled everything of his on the front lawn and torched it. Then she'd keyed his car and posted vicious things about him online.

Yeah. Who else would want to drop a two-hundred-pound crystal chandelier on him for no good reason?

That had crazy ex-girlfriend written all over it.

The more he thought about it, the more it made complete sense. This was how she was going to kill him, after all. Torture him until he was dead. Make him think he was crazy.

Figures. I would get the nutty girlfriend with the epic psychic powers. . . .

And he was sure she would make him pay dearly before she finished him off. *This is going to be so bad.*

Over the next few hours while he went about his job, Nick was extremely skittish. Any noise made him jump like a three-tailed cat in a rocking chair factory. Kyrian had a lot of chandeliers in his house. And the one in the foyer was truly frightening in size. Given how much the one that had almost squashed him weighed, he didn't even want to contemplate the weight of that sucker.

Insult to injury, he'd cut his hand while cleaning the mess of it up, too. Now he looked like a mummy reject with the bandage on his cheek and the gauze wrapped around his hand and fingers.

Thanks, Kody.

Paybacks sucked. And she was the queen of doling them out.

As Nick gathered his schoolbooks to head home, Rosa joined him in their shared office.

"*M'ijo*, there is a girl I do not know at the front door. She say she come to pick you up and drive you home."

Nick scowled. It wasn't Kody. To his knowledge, she didn't have a license. Or a car. Could it be Brynna? Was she old enough to drive yet?

Unsure of who was waiting for him, he slung his backpack over his shoulder. "Thanks, Rosa. Have a good night."

"You, too. See you tomorrow."

"*Hasta mañana.*" Reluctantly, Nick headed for the front door. He opened it slowly, dreading what might be standing on the other side.

To his complete shock, it was Casey.

She gasped as soon as she saw him. "Oh my God,

Nick. What happened to you? Were you in a wreck or something?"

"Um, hi, Casey. Not a wreck. Just real clumsy today." Yeah, so no one would ever accuse him of being suave and articulate, especially not around the female species. It seemed Kody wasn't the only one who could render him incoherent. Apparently it was all females of his age group.

Great, I'll die an old man alone. . . . By myself.

Awkward silence hung between them until Nick cleared his throat. "Uh . . . what are you doing here? You're not stalking me, are you?"

"Hardly. You said you were going to work tonight, so I thought I'd give you a ride home." She held her keys up to show him the pink furball key chain. "Surely you'd rather ride with me than on a streetcar, right?"

Not really. The streetcar didn't make him nervous. Nor did he feel like a loser geek there. But he wasn't about to tell her that and up his nimrod quotient for the day. If the captain of the cheerleaders offered to take you home, the correct answer was always "Sure. That'd be nice. Thanks."

She smiled, but the strange thing was, it didn't make his stomach flutter the way Kody's smile always did.

I am not right. . . .

Only a real idiot moron would pine for a woman who'd been sent to kill him. *Color me idiot moron.*

Truth be told, Casey really was the hottest girl in school. He should be thrilled she was even deigning to talk to him. But then, she was also the most screwed up. She had to be, to play ping-pong relationship all the time with Stone. One minute she was all over him, and the next she was chewing him out and storming off, then coming on to Nick. Only to go back to Stone. It was enough to make a man dizzy.

With bouncing steps, she led him down the stairs and out to the street where her car was parked. Nick slowed down as he saw some vintage something that reminded him of a mouse—it was even the same pink as her key chain. All it needed was ears and a tail to make the image even more accurate. Heck, the front end looked like it already had a set of whiskers.

"What is this?"

She grinned. "1972 Karmann Ghia convertible. Couldn't you just die? It's the cutest thing ever! I love this car. It's fully restored and like driving a time capsule or something."

It was pretty awesome. "I never heard of one before."

"It's a Volkswagen. Now get in and be careful with the interior. I don't want it damaged."

Wow, that was a first. A girl who treasured her car.

Maybe they had something in common after all. Not that *he* had a car, but he did love and appreciate other people's rides.

Reaching the side of it, he frowned in uncertainty. Awesome though it was, the car was a tiny two-seater that didn't leave a lot of room for his long legs and overloaded backpack. "You want me to put my gear in the trunk?"

"Sure." She laughed lightly as he headed to the back end. "But it's not in the rear, silly. The engine's there. The trunk's up front."

Nick reversed course. "Oh. Sorry." He'd had no idea it was like a Porsche. Must be a German car thing.

She opened the trunk for him, then invaded his personal space in a most distracting way. "Want to grab a bite on the way home?"

The seductive way she said that, he wasn't too sure she was talking about food. And it was making him *really* nervous. Girls who looked like her didn't usually notice him. Even though she'd been coming on to him off and on this last year, he still couldn't quite accept that it wasn't on a dare or something.

Nick took a step back. "I thought you were back with Stone."

She wrinkled her nose. "We broke up."

"Since when?"

"Since I found out you were available." Eyeing him like the last bone in a dog kennel, she ran her tongue along her bottom lip.

Nick's heart raced. He felt like a cornered fox surrounded by hounds. *Help me. . . .*

Before he realized what she was doing, she fisted her hands in his hideous Hawaiian shirt and jerked him toward her. Then she gave him the hottest kiss he'd ever had. One that set fire to his blood and stole his breath. Loosening her grip, she slid her hands around to his back and held him tight against her.

His body roared to life at the taste of her. *I am hallucinating. This isn't happening.*

It couldn't be.

She pulled back and nipped his chin with her teeth. *Gah, I hope I shaved close enough.* How horrifying to have her nip his three hairs and be grossed out by his lack of a real man beard.

"So how 'bout it?" she asked.

How about what? He'd totally forgotten whatever they'd been talking about.

It was food, idiot.

Oh yeah, that was it.

Nick licked his lips. "Um, I've already eaten."

She rolled her eyes, then laughed. "You are so wonderfully clueless at times. And I don't mean that as an insult. You are just so cute."

"Yeah, 'cause that's so what I was going for," he said sarcastically.

She laughed again. Slamming her trunk down, she headed for the driver's seat.

Unsure and, in truth, a little frightened of her, Nick headed to the passenger side and got in.

"So where do you live?" She started the car.

He was still getting used to not being mortified whenever someone from school asked him that question. Their former condo had been a dilapidated POS that wasn't fit to house the ten million families of cockroaches who called it home. "A couple of blocks away from school . . . over on Bourbon."

She gaped at him. "You really live on Bourbon Street?"

"Yeah."

"Isn't it loud at night?"

He wasn't sure if she was horrified or intrigued by his address. "Not where we live. Once you get past St. Ann's and head toward Ursulines, it's really quiet . . . except during Mardi Gras. Then, there's not much in the Quarter that doesn't shatter the eardrums."

She pulled away from the curb. "Tell me about it. . . .

Well, since we have to go down that way to drop you off, you want to stop for beignets at the Café Du Monde?"

This was probably the first time in his life that he was turning down food, but for the sake of his sanity, he couldn't bring himself to accept. It would just be too weird to be there with Casey. Not to mention, beignets were not first-date food since the loose powdered sugar topping made everyone who ate them look like a messy toddler. Really not the image he wanted her to have of him. Powdered sugar was the *only* thing on earth that could make his shirt uglier than what it already was. "I need to get home. My mom will be worried about me."

"You could call her and tell her we're stopping off."

"Yeah, but then she'd drill me on who you are and why we're stopping, and then she'd be offended that she didn't get to meet you first."

"Your mom's real strict, huh?"

"You have no idea."

As she drove, she dropped her hand to rest on his thigh. Nick almost came out of the car seat as a rush of adrenaline tore through him. Especially when she began trailing her small, delicate hand closer to his "no zone."

He caught her hand to stop it in its torturous path before it struck gold.

She scowled at him. "What's wrong? Stone loves it when I do that to him."

Yeah, and he would like it, too. But he wasn't that kind of guy. They barely knew each other. She hadn't even bought him dinner yet. . . . "I'm not Stone."

"And don't I know it. You're a lot more delish."

Nick's head spun. *This isn't real. I must have gotten hit by that chandelier after all.* Yeah, that made sense. He was in the hospital, in a coma, and this was some far-fetched reality conjured by . . . too many cookies or something.

But then he remembered what Ambrose had told him. *Getting girls will not be your problem. . . . Casey will be a good girlfriend in high school and you'll be friends long after that.*

Maybe this was how their relationship had started. *Yeah, and maybe I'm in that coma somewhere.* Swallowing hard, he watched the way her hair blew in the wind as they drove through traffic. It was a bit chilly to have the top down, but Casey didn't seem to mind. She had the heat blowing on maximum.

"You need to relax, Nick." She stroked his thigh beneath his hand. "And stop being so hard on yourself."

"I'm not hard on myself."

"Yes, you are. You're a great guy, you know? You deserve great things."

"I have great things." At least now he did. His past, not so much.

"You might have them, but you act like you're waiting for someone to snatch it all away. Like you're not worthy of anything, except table scraps and insults."

Was it that obvious? And here he'd always thought he had a pretty good poker face. Not as good as Ash's . . .

But he wasn't about to admit any of that to Casey. "I don't do that."

"Yes, you do. Case in point, yesterday at practice . . . The coach called your name as starter and you looked positively stunned. Like you couldn't believe it. When you ran your drills, even with your helmet on, I could tell that you were waiting for him to change his mind and bench you. You do that with everything."

He opened his mouth to argue, then realized how right she was. He did hold his head low. Too many years of bitter poverty, of people looking down their noses at him, had left its mark on his soul. Half the school was convinced he'd cheated his way into it.

Half?

More like ninety percent, or more. Even his teammates kept commenting on how the only reason he'd been let back on the team was because they'd lost so many of the their members to Madaug's zombies. That wouldn't hurt so much if Coach Devus hadn't told him that he didn't care if Nick played or not, he merely needed someone in a jersey to fill out their roster. So in the end, his teammates were right.

For that matter, any time he tried to have even a tiny scrap of ego, someone or something crawled out of the woodwork to mortify him in front of everyone and bash his ego on the nearest rock. So he'd given up on ever having any kind of self-esteem. Yeah, he pretended to be arrogant as a defense mechanism. But inside he knew the truth. He believed himself to be an even bigger loser than the rest of the world did.

She squeezed his leg. "You're a Ferrari, Nick. It's time for you to realize that."

He scoffed. "I might be a Ferrari, but I have four flat tires." And a rusted-out engine and no doors.

"See . . . there you go, putting yourself down. Why do you always do that?"

Before he could stop it, the truth came pouring out of him. "It's easier to take other people's insults and crap if I beat them to the punch. It doesn't pay to have delusions of grandeur when there are so many people in the world looking to take you down a notch every time you dare to try and have some dignity. Therefore, why I should try?"

"So what?" she snapped. "Screw them! They wouldn't be attacking you if *they* weren't pathetic. It's nothing more than their own admission that they are lesser creatures who envy you. Well-adjusted, intelligent people don't have to put someone else down in order to feel superior or good about themselves. Only massive losers do that. And you, Nick, contrary to what you think, are not a loser."

Funny, when she said it, he could almost believe it.

"We are young, Nick. Our time is *now* and there is no coming back to this place in our lives. You need to live it to the fullest. Grab the apple and take a big bite of it."

"Yeah, but that didn't work out so well for Adam."

Laughing, she moved her hand back to the gearshift. "Are you calling me a snake?"

"No. Just pointing out that sometimes caution is a good thing."

She blew a raspberry at him. "Here. I want you to memorize something for me. . . . *Digmus sum.*"

"Dig . . . how?"

She shook her head. "It's Latin and it means, 'I am worthy.' I want you to say it until you actually believe it."

Nick frowned. "I don't know. . . ."

"I'm serious, Nick. Say it over and over until it becomes a litany."

"I would, but I'm still stuck on the fact that you actually know Latin."

She gave him an irritated smirk. "I'm not as vacuous as you think I am."

"I never said you were vacuous."

"Your looks have."

Guilt consumed him. But honestly, he'd never thought of her as stupid. At least not until it came to one thing he couldn't figure out. "No, that's more my confusion about what you see in a jerk like Stone. And why you tolerate him all the time."

Shrugging, she turned the wheel and downshifted. "Life is lonely. Sometimes you just want to be with someone, even if they're not the best for you. They are better than nothing."

That was something he'd never agree with. "Now who needs a lecture in worthiness? Better to be alone than stuck with someone who treats you bad."

"And that's why I like you, Nick. You're not like other kids at school. You see the truth through the lies. You don't follow along like some sheep blinded by the butts of the herd in front of him."

That was definitely true, and it was something many of them didn't hesitate to rub his nose in. Being different was not easy, and it made him a constant, moving target for teenage hatred and ridicule.

Trying not to think about it, he guided her through

the Quarter to where their condo was. She parked out front and turned off the car.

"You really do live close to school," Casey said as she got out and then opened her trunk for him to retrieve his backpack.

"Yeah, I really like it here." It was a vast improvement over his last home where the guy across the street had been shot and killed in a drug deal gone bad. "Can't imagine living anywhere else."

She screwed her face up. "Don't you ever think about traveling?"

He shrugged nonchalantly. "Why should I? Everything I could possibly want is right here at home."

His comment shocked her. "You are extremely complacent, aren't you? Don't you ever want more?"

Nick looked up at the three-story building in front of him where his condo was one of nine. It was spacious and he had his own room *and* bath. Not to mention, all the neighbors were really nice and friendly. So her question baffled him. "I have more than I need, and that's plenty for me. There's nothing else *to* want."

Gaping, she crossed her arms over her chest. "You don't want to visit Paris? London? Tokyo? Is there really no place on earth you'd like to see?"

He glanced at the green shutters and steps, and thought about his mom. "I guess Rome."

That seemed to stun her even more. "Really? You like gladiators or something?"

"Nah. Not for me. My mother would love to visit the Vatican and maybe catch a glimpse of the Pope. It'd be the single biggest thrill of her life."

"Even bigger than when she had you?"

Nick stifled a shiver at the horror his mother must have felt over his birth. He hadn't even been born in a hospital—because they had no money. She'd delivered him on his aunt Menyara's couch. There was no way that could be a happy memory for anyone, except the cleaning company. "Having me was no picnic for her, I assure you. While she might not regret it, I know it's been hard for her. So no, I don't put having me in the same thrill bank as her meeting the Pope."

She tsked at him. "What am I going to do with you? Your mother is lucky to have a teenage son who talks to her, never mind one who respects her and doesn't back-talk her all the time. Trust me, that makes you the best son imaginable." She closed the trunk. "There's a whole world out there, Nick. One that's filled with adventure and sights the likes of which you can't imagine. I love New Orleans, too. But there's so much more to visit and learn about. Why confine yourself to one town for the whole of your life?"

Now that she mentioned it, that was what he'd done.

He really had never once considered leaving New Orleans, except during their evacuations during hurricane season. And even then, he couldn't get back home fast enough.

Maybe he should think about more. . . .

Casey sidled up to him. "So, can I meet your mom?"

He hesitated. "Why?"

"So that the next time I invite you out, you won't have an easy excuse to blow me off." She pressed herself against him, making him real uncomfortable again.

"You are very forward, you know that?"

She smiled a smile that turned his blood into lava. "There's nothing wrong with going after the things you want, and I want you, Nicholas Gautier."

Yeah, the devil is sitting on icicles today. . . .

And eating ice cream from his own hand.

Still, he couldn't believe what she was saying to him. "A little over a year ago, you didn't even know I existed and I sat behind you in four classes."

She made a sound of supreme annoyance. "How many times do I have to apologize for that? And don't forget, I was the one who saved you from getting caught when you were snooping around the coach's office. And . . . it was *I* who helped you gather the items you needed to keep you out of jail or the morgue."

Nick couldn't meet her gaze as the truth slapped

him hard. She had done all of those things for him. And just like him, she could have gone to jail or been killed had anyone caught her. Like it or not, he did owe her for taking those chances.

Casey walked her fingers up his chest to his chin, then she buried her hand in his hair and whispered in his ear. "Introduce me, Nick. I promise I won't bite or embarrass you."

It was hard to think clearly with chills all over his body and with her standing so close to him, breathing in his ear. Honestly, there was only one thing on his mind, and it wasn't introducing her to his mother.

"You could never embarrass me. My God, woman, have you seen my wardrobe? Dignity waved bye-bye to me a long time ago."

She laughed as she fingered his ear. "Ah . . . Nick. You are so funny and intelligent. The world is lucky to have you in it."

For the first time, he felt a degree of pride. It was so nice to be with someone who saw only the good in him. His mother, with her well-meaning intentions of trying to make him a better man, dogged the crap out of him all the time. Kody had been kind to him, but she'd never hesitated to be brutally honest, either, and he didn't even want to think about Caleb's and Ambrose's dire warnings about him becoming a monster who would one day devour the world. While they would compliment him from time to time, it was nothing like what Casey did.

She alone hadn't assumed his breakup with Kody had been caused by *his* actions. In her eyes, he was good and decent, and nothing else.

How refreshing.

"Okay." Taking her hand, he led her to the door and punched the keycode in. He opened the heavy iron door and let her enter first. "We're the first condo on the second floor."

He followed her up the stairs, digging his keys out of his pocket so that he could unlock the door when they reached it.

Casey stood back while he opened the door. He went in and dropped his backpack by the couch.

"Hey, Ma?"

"In my room, Boo," she called from down the hallway. "I'll be out in a second."

He shut the door while Casey looked around their place, and he tried to imagine it through her eyes. Her dad was a surgeon and they lived in a really humongous house that made his whole building look small. Her bedroom was probably bigger than their living room and kitchen combined. "I know it's not much, but—"

"Nick," she chided. "It's beautiful. I love the bright

colors. Your mom has good taste, and whatever she's cooking smells incredible."

He dropped his keys on the table by the door. "It's catfish gumbo. She always makes it on Thursday nights so that we can eat on it all day Friday."

She scowled. "Why's that?"

He pointed first to the crucifix next to the door, then to the shrine of Mary and Jesus in the corner of their living room that came complete with saint candles and a small St. Michael font of Holy Water. "Catholic. We can't have meat on Fridays, only fish."

"I thought the Church stopped doing that?"

"Church might have, but not my mom. She's really old-fashioned that way. Heck, she still won't even enter the church without something covering her head. And if you're not Catholic, please don't tell her. It'll break her heart."

Casey laughed. "Okay then. Thanks for the warning."

His mom came down the hall and slowed as she caught sight of Casey. Tiny and blond, his mother looked a lot younger than her thirty years. Most people assumed her to be his older sister until he called her Mom, then they were stunned.

She barely reached the middle of his chest these days and even Casey was several inches taller. Still, his mother was absolutely fearless, especially when it came to protecting him.

"Mom, this is Casey Woods. She goes to school with me."

"Hi, Mrs. Gautier."

His mom didn't seem to hear either of them. Rather, she gasped at Nick and cupped his cheek in her hand. "What in the world happened to you, boy?" Scowling, she tried to peek beneath the bandage on his cheek.

"Nothing, Ma. Ms. Rosa fixed me up. I just cut my hand and scraped my cheek."

That didn't seem to placate her in the least. "Doing what?"

Dodging death, but that would only make her worse than she already was. So he defaulted to another half-truth. "Some glass broke and I was cleaning it up."

His mom sighed. "Nicholas Ambrosius Aloysius Gautier . . ."

Ooo, she broke out the full Catholic confirmation name. That was never a good sign.

"You are trying to shorten my life, aren't you?"

"Never, Mom." In fact, he was doing everything he could to make sure she lived well into old age.

His future self had even come back in time for it.

Growling at him, she slid her gaze over toward Casey.

"Hi, Casey. I'm sorry. I wasn't ignoring you. I was just worried about my boy . . . which seems to be my full-time occupation these days." She smiled, but the gesture didn't quite reach her blue eyes. "You should have warned me we were having company, Boo."

"I didn't know. Sorry. She picked me up from work and drove home, then I thought you'd like to meet her since you're weird that way."

His mom narrowed her eyes at him, then spun around to Casey. "You have your license, I take it?"

"Yes, ma'am. I passed with flying colors."

Her glare intensified. "How long have you been driving?"

"A couple of months."

"And you feel competent to drive with other teenagers in the car?"

Gaping, Casey looked at him.

Nick held his hands up in surrender. "I warned you she'd play Ask a Thousand Questions."

Finally, a real smile broke across his mother's face. "I'm just messing with you, Casey. Sorry . . . So what do your parents do?"

Casey relaxed a degree. "My father's a surgeon and my mom's a philanthropist."

"A what?" his mom asked.

Nick leaned toward her and whispered loudly, "It's

rich-people code, Ma. It means they have so much money that they look for ways to give some of it away."

Her jaw went slack, then she turned toward Casey. "Is that true?"

Casey screwed her face up in discomfort. "Kind of. But she helps a lot of good organizations with her work . . . including Catholic Charities."

That succeeded in changing his mother's entire demeanor. One thing about Cherise Gautier, she was a virulent defender of the Faith and Church. "That's wonderful. How very kind and decent of her."

"Yes, ma'am."

"Well, I need to go check on the gumbo to make sure I don't burn it. Would you like to stay for dinner?"

Nick cringed at the question. While he liked Casey, she did make him really uncomfortable at times.

But for once, Casey gave him a reprieve. "Thank you for the offer, Mrs. Gautier. Unfortunately, I have a lot of homework I need to get started on. It was a pleasure meeting you, though."

"You, too." His mom headed for the kitchen.

Alone with Casey, Nick fell into his usual awkward silence.

She wrinkled her nose at him. "Don't worry, hon. It's all good. I really like your mom. She's great." Rising up on her tiptoes, she kissed his lips. She pulled back and bit her lip as she scanned his body with a hungry look. "Tomorrow, you will belong to me, Nick, and after work and practice, we're going to have some real fun."

Before he could recover his senses, she left.

Nick stood there for a full minute in complete stupefaction. What was going on? Had he gotten sucked into an alternate universe or what?

Forget whatever was after him . . . *this* had to be a sign of the Apocalypse.

He was going to meet his death, all right. Only it would be death by pleasure. And it would come from the hands of their head cheerleader.

CHAPTER 6

Ignoring the men who turned to stare after her, Zarelda sauntered through the crowded tables at the Café Du Monde until she found Grim waiting in the far corner, eating beignets. She sat down in the empty seat that was opposite of him.

He gestured toward the extra cup of café au lait in front of him. "I took the pleasure of ordering for you."

She scoffed at his generosity. "No offense, but I'd rather order for myself. Only a fool partakes of what Death has to offer, and my mother drowned all her stupid children."

He laughed out loud. "You don't trust me?"

"Not a bit. I've known you too long." She motioned a male waiter over to her and ordered her own drink and beignets.

As the waiter left, Zarelda glanced around the crowded coffee shop to the sugar-laden chairs that showed a bit of wear and the tables that were strewn with even more messy powdered sugar.

While the large area they were seated in was covered with a green-and-white-striped awning, it was still open and exposed to the elements . . . and to insects, to say nothing of the birds that hopped between human and metal legs, scrounging for scraps.

She arched a brow at Grim. "This is not the place I would have imagined *you* frequenting, given your fear of germs and dirt. Not to mention your aversion to people who breathe."

He pulled a large container of Purell out of his pocket and set it down next to her. "Best invention since toilet paper. Except for the fact that it cuts down on the unseen things that can kill humans . . . that part sucks for me, but I have to say that I do so love using it. While it may not save my life, it does wonders for my sanity . . . such as it is."

And now that she noticed it, Grim had the entire tabletop covered with white paper napkins until there wasn't a bit of it showing. "I find it so odd that Death is a potent germ-a-phobe."

He shrugged. "Only because I know how many people die every year from bacterial infections caused by undercooked food and a lack of basic hygiene."

"But you're immortal."

He curled his lip. "No excuse for nastiness. I may be immune, but I still have no desire to touch human filth or have it touch me, never mind something I'm going to ingest."

I am not going to win this argument. Death was emphatic about the subject.

Crazy, but emphatic.

Grim wiped his lips. "So how's your mission going? Better, I trust."

"Your little trick with the girlfriend was just what we needed to push him forward. I have to congratulate you on that."

"It pays to know people and nonpeople. I was very lucky to track down the nugget of her origin and nature of her assignment."

She didn't comment on that. "Nekoda still might be a problem, though. If she hasn't killed him yet—"

"I wouldn't worry about her. She's weak and stupidly sympathetic to our Malachai. Most likely, she won't kill him. So let's not waste time talking about her. Nick is the one we need control of. Fast."

"And I will deliver him to you." She paused as the waiter returned with her order and she paid for her food. Picking up the plain white coffee mug, she narrowed her eyes on Grim. "But I want to make sure that our bargain is still in place and that you don't have a nasty surprise waiting for me. You *can* and *will* free my brother, correct?"

"Absolutely. I've already been in touch with the necessary party, who says while she's not thrilled about it, she isn't opposed to the possibility. You turn Nick to our cause and Zavid will be freed, I promise you."

Hoping she wasn't being lied to or tricked, Zarelda glanced away as a wave of guilt consumed her. Centuries ago, Zavid had taken her place in a hellhole to keep her safe. She didn't even want to think about what he'd been through there. If he'd be the same brother she'd known so long ago.

Torture and misery changed people. . . .

One dreadful bargain that had been made out of fear.

And both their lives had been forever ruined, and all because she hadn't paid attention to the small print. Hadn't looked ahead to see all the repercussions of her selfish desires.

Gods, how she wished she'd been the one to suffer for it. She should never have agreed to let Zavid be so selfless. In retrospect, it would have been much easier to endure his prison herself than to know he was being tortured because of her stupidity, and his love and protection of her that had made him so altruistic.

Idiot.

But no matter what, she had to get him out of there. And after all these centuries of trying, she finally had a way to do it.

Provided Grim wasn't as backstabbing as the last vicious creature she'd bargained with.

Never trust a jealous goddess, especially not where a man was concerned.

"So how are you enjoying your new body?" Grim asked. "It must be weird for you to have one again after all this time."

Swallowing her drink of coffee, she wrinkled her nose at the bitter taste. She reached for the sugar. "It took a little getting used to and it chafes a bit. But I think I've adjusted to it." That only after she'd bitten a giant hole in her tongue the first time she'd tried to eat. Truthfully, there were many things about being locked inside a corporeal body that she'd forgotten. Bad breath. Hair tangles. Hot liquids. Scalding bath water. Furniture lurking in dark rooms, and that so misaptly named *funny* bone.

Not to mention the interminable hours spent looking for a semi-clean public rest room. She shivered at that dismal memory.

"Tell me something, Grim . . . how do humans get through high school without becoming raving lunatics? Uh! I'm so glad I was born before schools were invented, and I'd give anything to bypass this misery I'm forced to endure."

She set her plain white mug down. "I have got to kill her parents once all of this is finished. They are . . . ridiculous." She deepened her voice to mock them. "Clean the dishes, take out the trash, do your homework, you're going to be late. Why are you still up?" She grimaced. "On and on, they rant. Just the sound of her father's voice makes me want to blast him into oblivion. No wonder you want to end the world. When did mankind get so whiny about every little thing?"

He laughed, then changed the subject. "Is she fighting you for control?"

Flexing her hand to make sure she had one hundred percent of the control of her body, she sighed wearily. "Sometimes, but she's weak. Still, I have got to have my brother suck her soul out of me as soon as he's released. I hate how she's always crying and begging. She's so needy and cloying. I'll be so glad when I won't need her memories anymore and can do away with her, once and for all." She glanced over three tables to a group of giggling teenaged girls who made her cringe.

Gah, how she despised all of them.

Turning back to Grim, she released another heavy sigh. "But, the little twit has her uses right now. I turn her loose whenever I have to have private time with that dullard she dates." She curled her lip in repugnance. "I'll never understand why women put up with animals like Stone."

Or any man, really.

"No accounting for taste."

She saluted him with her mug, wishing she could go back in time and settle a score with one man in particular. . . .

Leaning back in his chair, Grim crossed his arms over his chest. "How much longer do you think it'll take?"

She sipped her coffee slowly as she considered it. "Hard to say. As you know from your own dealings with him, he's very strong-willed. But for all his braggadocio and posturing, he has no confidence whatsoever. And that, my evil friend, is the weakness I'm attacking and exploiting. He doesn't think he deserves anything so it leaves him wide open . . . no matter how strong his opinions are."

"Sneaky . . . I like that."

"Well, you know the old saying. Build them up to tear them down. You tell them what they want to hear until they stop listening to those who tell them the truth. Then they're yours."

Human ego and jealousy. The two most potent weapons for destroying any human.

And they worked pretty well on gods and demons, too.

Grim stroked his chin as he thought over her plan. "I should warn you that I've already taught him about the powers of persuasion."

"This isn't persuasion, sweetheart. It's about the power of the human ego and its voracious need to be fed."

Grim let out a wicked laugh. "Remind me not to get on your bad side."

"Don't worry. You uphold your side of the bargain and don't betray or trick me, and I will be your eternal cohort to ruin and/or enslave anyone you send my way."

So who was that girl?"

Nick looked up from his backpack with a frown. "I told you, Ma. Casey Woods."

She paused in her cleaning to glare at him. "I caught that. Why was she bringing you home? You shouldn't let a girl do that while you're going with someone else. Kody would have a justifiable fit if she found out."

Here it comes. . . .

Rising to his feet, he tucked his hands into his pockets and lowered his head in expectation of her reaction. "We broke up."

His mother sucked her breath in sharply as she stopped cleaning, mid-swipe. "What did *you* do?"

Nick sighed in disgust. "Really, Mom? You, too?"

"Me, too, what?"

His jaw ticcing, he met her gaze. "Why do I have to be the one who screwed up? Huh? Couldn't *she* have done something wrong?"

She dried her hands on a dish towel. "Did she?"

"Yes."

"And what was it?"

How could you tell your mother that your girlfriend was a preternatural assassin out to kill you and not get locked in a psych ward?

He had no idea, and no desire to test her maternal loyalty to someone she thought was a paranoid schizo. Nick shifted his feet uneasily. Since he didn't want to lie to her, he had to come up with some seriously creative truth.

I should be writing fiction. . . .

"She had divided loyalties, and I don't want to have to watch my back every time she's around." There. Truth.

His mother walked over to him and brushed her hand through his hair. "I'm so sorry, baby. Are you all right?"

Nick shook his head. "Not really. I miss her." *'Cause*

I'm a flaming idiot who can't let go of a woman out to kill me. "But that which doesn't kill us . . ."

"Will only require years of therapy," she finished with her favorite spin on the old saying. "You want a chocolate-chip sundae to cheer yourself up?"

Nick made a face at her. "Not a girl, Mom. Case you haven't noticed, your daughter comes equipped with outdoor plumbing."

Laughing, she ruffled his hair again. "But?"

"Yeah, okay. I'll take some. Thanks."

He followed her to the kitchen and stood back while she went to the freezer to dig out the chocolate-chip ice cream container. "Is it always this hard, Ma?"

"I don't know, Boo. At this point, you've had more girlfriends than I ever had boyfriends."

And that was definitely his fault. Because of him and his father, she'd never once dated anyone. She didn't want to take a chance on bringing some guy into the house who would yell at or hit him. For that, he was forever grateful . . . and extremely guilt-ridden.

His mother was a beautiful woman who could have any man she wanted. One who would treat her like a queen. Saddest part? He was the only one she'd ever loved, and the only one she thought worth keeping.

The woman was definitely crazy.

She placed the bowl of chocolate-drenched ice cream

down in front of him, along with a can of whipped cream. *"Bon appétit, mon fils."*

"Merci." He took the bowl and can to the kitchen table and sat down.

She placed a kiss on the top of his head while he loaded the bowl up with half the can. Wrinkling her nose, she shivered. "You got enough there, Sparky?"

He took the spoon from her hand. "I'm not the only person here who drowns their sorrows in Reddi-Wip."

"Just don't take shots directly out of the can without warning me to buy a new one."

"Okay." He dug in.

His mom lingered by his side until he looked up with a frown. "What?"

She hesitated. "Do you want to talk about it?"

Nick cringed at her offer. "Again, not a daughter."

She cupped his cheek in her hand and smiled down at him. "Men have feelings, too. I know . . . I raised you, and I know that hurt look in your eyes. It breaks my heart to see it, baby. Please tell me what I can do to help."

Nick laid his hand over hers as he fought down a sudden wave of tears. She was right. It hurt. Bad. Like an unexpected kick to the stones. It was so stupid, but he'd seen a future with Kody. He'd wanted to be with her forever.

And her betrayal cut him to his soul.

At least I'm not alone in this. Kody might reject him or try to kill him, but his mom was one woman he knew would never betray him or let him down. No matter what, she would love him regardless.

He gave her hand a light squeeze. "You're doing it, Mom. Besides, I'll get over it eventually. Right?"

"Definitely." She leaned her head down on top of his and gave him a fierce hug from behind. "Ever my strong little soldier. I love you, Nick. More than my life. I'd do anything for you."

"I know. I feel the same way."

She kissed his head, then released him. "Don't worry about doing your chores tonight. I'll get them."

He gaped. "Really? Dang . . . remind me to get a broken heart more often."

Laughing again, she put away the ice cream. "I was going to watch some reruns. I'd love to have you join me . . . if you feel like it."

Strangely, he did. In fact, he couldn't think of anything better than putting his head down in her lap and having her baby him a little tonight.

You're too old for that.

Maybe, but no one would know, and it would mean a lot to his mom. And it would go a long way in making his stomach not hurt so much.

As far back as he could remember, his mom had said that no matter how old he got, he'd always be her baby. Now he understood what that meant. It wasn't just for her. There were times when men and women needed to be kids again. Needed to know that there was someone out there who did love them, no matter what they did. Someone they could turn to for a hug whenever life coldcocked them. While girlfriends would come and go, his mom would always be with him.

Until I do something stupid that causes her to die. . . .

He winced as he remembered that one detail that Ambrose had dropped on his head.

I have less than ten years to stop it.

While that might seem like a lot of time, he knew it wasn't. Time moved quick. Too quick most days.

Not wanting to think about that tonight, he finished off his sundae and rinsed out the bowl before he took the trash out for her even though she'd told him he didn't have to. He never liked her going outside alone this late at night. For all her ferocity, she was still a tiny woman who would be an easy mark for someone like the animals he once ran with. They wouldn't hesitate to mug her.

After putting a fresh bag in the can, he joined his mother on the couch. She was already curled up under the thick, fluffy pink blanket he'd given her for Mother's Day last year. For some reason, she was forever cold. Nick sat down, then leaned over, onto his side so that he could place his head in her lap.

His mom immediately put her hand in his hair and stroked his scalp. Something that went a long way in making him feel better. "I'm very proud of you, Nick."

"Thanks, Mom . . . for everything."

She kissed his head, then handed him the remote. "I know you can't stand my girl shows. Just don't find us something scary or bloody. You know how much I hate anything to do with the supernatural."

Gee, thanks, Mom. He wondered how she would feel to know what she'd really given birth to.

Would it matter? Would she hate him, too?

No. He knew better.

But again, he didn't want to chance it. Ambrose had already warned him that when he'd told their mother the truth about his birth in a former life, she hadn't handled it well.

Not that he blamed her. There were times when he faced it that he wanted to run into a corner and cry like a kindergartener himself.

And unlike her, there had been a time when he'd hoped vampires and shapeshifters were real.

Let's hear it for my stupidity.

All of a sudden, he felt something in the air. He

glanced up as the sensation spread through his body like a harbinger, stirring his powers so that whatever it was didn't catch him unawares.

The invisible protection symbols Menyara had painted above their front door started glowing. His mother couldn't see them. But he did and he knew exactly what that meant.

Something inhuman was trying to get to him.

Thank you, Menyara. . . . He didn't want to contemplate what would happen to him tonight if his godmother wasn't a Voodoo priestess. The symbols were really bright overhead. As if the being was testing them for a weakness it could exploit.

Was it the same thing he'd heard earlier? The harvester out to get him?

Or was it Kody trying to finish him off?

He had no way of knowing for sure, and never had he been more grateful to Menyara for her overly cautious ways. In fact, he was going to sleep tonight with his little bag of gris-gris she'd made for him around his neck, clutching it tight.

Closing his eyes, Nick used what little powers he'd learned from Grim and Caleb to push against whatever was trying to get in. For a full minute, the glow turned so bright, it was like the sun was shining in the room.

Then it went away as quickly as it'd come.

His heart pounded. *What are you?*

Times like this, he'd give anything to have Kyrian's or Ash's abilities. They didn't have to take crap from anyone.

And one day, I will have those powers, too.

No. Not true. His Malachai abilities would make a mockery of theirs. . . . He couldn't wait to wield them when they no longer backfired on him.

But no sooner had that thought finished in his mind than he heard someone whisper in his ear.

Be careful what you wish for. . . .
You just might get it.

CHAPTER 7

"Nick!"

Walking down the hall toward his English class, Nick barely had time to brace himself before Casey latched on to his arm like Velcro.

"Hey."

She scowled at him. "Hey? Is that the best you can do? Really?" She tsked at him. "You look awesome in your football jersey, by the way."

Man, he hated compliments. They always made him feel strange, especially when they came from people who shouldn't be deigning to speak to him. "Thanks. You look good in your uniform, too."

She grinned at him and swished her hips to show off the white panels on her pleated black and gold cheerleader skirt. "I know, right?"

No one could ever accuse her of having low self-esteem. Not that he blamed her. She was gorgeous.

Out of nowhere, Stone grabbed the front of his shirt and body slammed him into a bank of lockers. "What do you think you're doing, Gautier?"

Nick shoved him back. "I ain't your 'ho, boy. And you ain't my pimp. You don't knock me around. I know you're attracted to me and all, but—"

Stone swung at him.

Nick ducked and came up with a punch that would have laid the punk out cold had Caleb not grabbed Stone and jerked him back one nanosecond before Nick's fist slammed into his jaw.

Caleb planted himself between them. "Have you two lost your minds? You want to get suspended from the team *and* school?"

"I was minding my own business," Nick growled. "He accosted me first."

Stone grabbed Casey by her upper arm. "C'mon, baby."

She pried his hand off her. "I'm not going anywhere with *you*."

Stone glared at her. "You want to go off with a rapist? Fine. Don't come crying to me when he violates you."

Nick's gaze darkened. "Dina lied and she admitted it . . . *publicly*."

Stone sneered at him. "Yeah, right. Like we don't know your boss paid her off."

Was he insane?

His anger spurring him to violence, Nick started for him, but Caleb caught him and pushed him back two steps.

"Let it go, Gautier," Caleb growled in his ear.

"What's going on here?"

Nick calmed down as their principal, Mr. Head, stopped next to Stone and raked the two of them with a curious stare.

Nick caught the flash of red in Caleb's eyes as the demon released him.

"Nothing," Nick mumbled to the principal. "Nothing at all."

Head looked to Stone. "Is that true, Blakemore?"

Stone curled his lip at Nick. "We have a predator in this school, Mr. Head, and I was trying to protect my girl from him."

Casey gaped, then scoffed. "I'm not your girl, you knuckle-dragging Neanderthal." She moved back to Nick's side. "Stone attacked Nick for no reason whatsoever, Mr. Head, and Nick is being kind enough to not get Stone into trouble, even though he deserves it."

Nick gaped. *Dang, Casey . . . did anyone happen to get the license plate of the bus you just threw him under? Remind me not to ever do anything wrong around you.*

Disloyalty, thy name is Casey Woods.

Head turned to Caleb. "Is she telling the truth?"

Caleb passed a meaningful glare at Nick before he answered honestly. "Yes, sir."

"All right, then. Stone, my office. Now." Head hesitated, then turned back to Nick. "I better not see you in another fight in my school, Gautier. You got me?"

"Yes, sir."

To Nick's complete shock, Head actually left him alone and took Stone to his office.

Wow, this was a first. Always in the past, whenever Stone started something with him, Nick paid for it and Stone danced away scot-free. It actually scared him that he wasn't headed to the office to be given detention instead of Stone.

The earth poles have reversed. The entire world is upside down. Houston, we have some kind of weird problem, 'cause this just doesn't happen to me.

I'm in an alternate reality.

Yeah, that made sense. He met Caleb's dark gaze. "The world is coming to an end, isn't it?"

Caleb snorted. "Not that I'm aware of, and I would probably know if it was."

"You two are so funny." Casey kissed Nick's cheek. "I'll see you after class." She darted off into the crowd.

Nick was still shell-shocked over what had happened.

"I swear, this really has to be a sign of the Apocalypse."

Caleb clapped him on the back. "Take the good and let's get to class before you rack up another tardy."

Yeah, but it was hard to take the good when he'd been fed a steady diet of bad from as far back as he could remember.

As he reached the room, he saw Kody heading for him. Against his will, his heart skipped a beat. Then it headed straight to his stomach when he saw that she no longer wore his necklace.

Well, why should she? Not like you didn't break up with her or something.

Yeah, okay, she had no reason to wear it anymore. So why did it hurt so bad that she didn't?

Trying not to think about it, he headed into the room and took his usual seat next to Caleb. Kody sat in the front and kept her back to him.

He glanced to the empty desk on his left. The desk that had been Kody's up until today. His throat tight, he tried not to glance at her. But his eyes kept betraying him. He couldn't help it. She was so beautiful. And today her perfect body was wrapped in a pink sweater that had been strategically designed by some sadistic jerk who wanted to make sure no mortal man could focus on anything except her.

Or in his case, semi-immortal demon.

What's going on, Nick?

He slid his gaze to Caleb. For once, he welcomed Malphas in his head, since it distracted him. *I didn't sleep much last night. Something weird has been happening.*

Caleb arched a brow. *Define weird.*

Good point. In their world, weird had many connotations. None of which were usually healthy for Nick. *Menyara's symbols lit up like Bourbon Street on Mardi Gras. And I kept hearing a voice telling me that it was going to get me.*

Kody?

Against his will, he glanced over to her again. *While I am sure that it is her current and constant occupation to kill me, it wasn't her voice I heard.*

Did you recognize it?

Nick shook his head.

Why didn't you call me when it happened?

I figured I was safe so long as the symbols glowed. Right?

Caleb growled at him. *You don't make that call with your safety, Gautier. In the future, when you get death threats from disembodied voices, call me. Night or day.*

Why? All you do is complain whenever I bug you.

Caleb glared at him. *Bug me anyway.*

Fine. Whatever. Caleb could be so testy for no known reason. At times, it was like dating a woman with irritable bowel syndrome.

Or rabies.

Finally, he felt Caleb's cranky butt retreating from his head. Alone with his thoughts, Nick tried to focus on class. But it was hard to care about English when he had an unknown hit man and an ex-girlfriend out to kill him.

It was a thought that hung heavy in his mind all through the day.

When the final bell rang, he let out a relieved sigh. He'd survived another school day without death, zombie attacks, or massive ego annihilation.

Or so he thought.

Nick slowed as he neared his locker to get his homework. Someone had written RAPIST PIG across it in giant letters with a black magic marker. A muscle ticced in his jaw as his fury mounted.

He was so sick of dealing with the blowback caused by Dina and her redonkulous, petty jealousy. *Let it go, people. Get a life.*

And let me have one again.

"Don't feel so bad, Nick," Brynna said as she came up behind him. "They got me, too." She pointed to her locker, where someone had written SLUT and drawn obscene images. "I already told Mr. Head about it, and he promised they'd paint over them before school tomorrow."

Yeah, great. *After* everyone had seen it all. What good was that?

Hey, kid, sorry they shot you in the head. But here, let us stick a bandage on your finger so that you'll feel better about that missing frontal lobe.

Nick let out a low, deadly breath. "I'm really getting sick of this, Bryn. It's ridiculous. They made her apologize to us publicly, for God's sake, and admit to everyone she was lying about it all."

"Doesn't matter. People believe what they want to, truth be danged. It kills me, too. Take my cousin, Kim, for example. When she was in middle school, she was voted homecoming queen two years in a row. The second year, the mother of one of the other girls in her class calls up my aunt in hysterics, complaining how unfair it is that no one likes her cow of a daughter. And how wrong it is for Kim to get to be the homecoming queen twice, even though everyone in class voted for Kim and not the cow, or another girl. . . ."

Brynna shook her head. "God love my aunt, she's just like your mother, Nick—the kind-heartedest person ever born. Not wanting any drama, and not wanting to hurt the feelings of a homely fourteen-year-old girl, my aunt convinced Kim to share her crown that second year. And because Kim's such a sweetie, too, she took pity on the girl and agreed to it. Then, four years later when they're both seniors, that hag, who can't hold a candle to Kim on her best day, starts telling everyone that Kim's mother was the one who called up in hysterics and made *her* share *her* crown. As if . . . And here's the kicker. The homecoming queen was announced publicly to the school when the votes were first counted. It wasn't until the very next day that they went back and added the cow as co-queen. Everyone knew Kim had won it, free and clear, and still some of them believed the hag four years later when she lied about it. Ridiculous, right? One lie . . . and an eternity of pain. I think it's why those soulless creeps do it. They don't care what lies they tell or who they hurt."

Wanting blood from all of them, Nick shook his head. "There ought to be a special place in Hades for them all."

"There is," Brynna said emphatically. "They have to live their miserable lives trapped with themselves. I can't think of any worse punishment."

Nick scoffed. "I can. A mouth full of busted teeth."

Brynn tsked at his suggestion. "Violence begets violence."

"And sometimes violence begets satisfaction."

She sighed heavily. "You don't really believe that, do you?"

He looked at his vandalized locker as another wave

of indignant anger consumed him. "Let's just say if I knew who did that, they'd be limping home."

She patted him on the shoulder to soothe him. "Do you remember what you told me when I allowed the jerks in this school to almost drive me to suicide over Dina's lies?"

Of course he did. He'd been terrified that he'd lose her friendship over something as stupid as human cruelty. "That you were worth more than all of them combined."

"Yes, and you said that I should never let them steal my day. That they weren't worth it. And you were correct. They're not."

Yeah, but right now, he couldn't find that decent part of himself. All he could feel was pure, stone-cold hatred. It infected him to the bone level.

Brynna opened her notebook and pulled out several sheets of paper. She handed them to him. "LaShonda and I are starting a new initiative . . . the Anti-Bully Brigade. That's the poster and manifesto we're handing out and posting everywhere they'll let us. They're even going to print it in the school paper."

Nick smiled at the logo they'd come up with. It was a fanged cat-looking key with *ABB* forming a butterfly-like design. In big white letters over the red key were the words, *It's Easy to Make the Grade. Join the Anti-Bully Brigade.*

He pulled the other pages to the top so that he could read them.

Dear Tormentor,

Today, you made me cry. You made me feel like the lowest piece of dirt that has ever walked this earth. You stole a piece of my heart and soul, and my self-esteem. Just when I had finally managed to convince myself that I wasn't quite the ugliest or dumbest person alive, you came in and reaffirmed that never-ending playback in my head that insults me even when you're not around. The same playback that tells me, over and over, life sucks, and it's never going to get any better no matter what I do, because I don't deserve anything better. I am nothing, and nothing is all I'll ever be. Even when I try my very best, like I did today, it's not good enough to make me human or worth something in the eyes of the world. I don't need you or anyone else to reaffirm something I already know about myself.

My hurt didn't show on the outside because I learned a long time ago to make sure that you couldn't take that pleasure, too, that you and the others who think you're funny or witty or cute, or are too afraid of you to do anything more than follow along, couldn't see how much pain you've caused me. The times in the past when I made the mistake of letting you see my tears, all of you laughed at me over them, and you made it worse. You made me choke on my dignity, and hate that which had been a source of pride for me . . . until you mocked it.

You have kicked me in my heart, and ravaged what little self-worth I had managed to scrape together.

But that's okay, because that is what makes me stronger than you and your followers. I don't have to point out someone else's flaws. I don't need to put someone else down or mock someone in order to feel better about myself, or to prove my worth, authority, power, or intelligence. The mere fact that you do proves that we who refrain from such cruelty are a superior species. We are the ones who have evolved beyond simple animal behavior that makes a base creature attack something it doesn't understand, something that is different or not as strong.

It doesn't take superior intelligence to tear down someone and/or their hard work. To mock their best effort or a physical trait that can't be helped. It doesn't prove that you're more intelligent or better in any way. A stick of dynamite can level a building, but it can't build one.

You have made me afraid to go to school. You've made me sick to my stomach whenever I think about going to work. You've made me afraid in my own home. You have needlessly insulted me in stores, on the phone, or wherever I accidentally stumbled upon you. You have ruined my past, my present, my day, and stolen a part of my soul.

Like the rest of us, you come from all kinds of backgrounds. Some not very happy, and cruelty is all you've ever known, so you lash out in an effort to ease your own pain. Others have no excuse whatsoever. Your background is above reproach. Rather, it's a vicious need inside you that we don't understand, and it's why it's so hard to identify you at times, because you blend in like an undetected poison.

You've been my teachers, clergy, my fellow students, coworkers, bosses, principals, sometimes you were a former friend or even family I once trusted.

You've taken things I told you in utter confidence, and twisted them into lies to be used against me. Without cause, you have told lies against me. You have refused to see me as a human being. You have kicked me when I was up, and you have kicked me when I was down.

But today, you will kick me no more. I will no longer be your verbal or physical punching bag. Today, I discovered the secret that will never allow you or your friends, who will one day turn on you too, to hurt me again.

Today as I lay broken and bleeding in that dark place I crawl into when I think I can't take it anymore, I found something extraordinary.

My humanity.

As my soul screamed in bleeding agony and I wanted to die rather than live one more day in a world where you exist, I realized that my tears and ability to feel pain without lashing out to return that hurt to someone else makes me human.

I find my pleasure when someone smiles over something I've said or done. When I make them feel better about themselves and their lives. When I look at an okay drawing and tell the artist that it is a work of art, worthy of hanging in a museum. The smile on their face, the pride that glows in their eyes, the happiness I see inside them makes my heart swell. It gives me a joy you can never understand. Just as I will never understand your need to hurt.

Kindness costs nothing to give, but to the person who receives it, it could be the one thing that saves their life. The one thing that gives them hope in their darkest hour. No act of charity or kindness, no matter how small, is ever wasted.

In the immortal words of Maya Angelou . . . people will forget what you said, people will forget what you did, but people will never forget how you made them feel.

Whenever they think of me, I want them to smile and feel good inside. . . . And I will never allow you to take that from me or from them.

No matter how you taunt or beat me, I will not become you, and pay your cruelty forward. In time, you will be gone from my life, and I will move forward to become even stronger and smarter than I am today. Because I can celebrate with others and applaud their efforts with an open heart capable of love and acceptance, I will evolve to an even greater level of happiness while you stay mired in your petty hatred and bitterness.

More than that, I discovered the best secret of all. I don't care what you think because I don't think enough of you to listen. You're not worth the energy it would cost me to hate you. There is nothing about you that I want to be. I don't want your clothes. I don't want your friends. Your job. I don't want your life, and I definitely don't want to live an existence where I have to hurt someone else in order to feel good about myself.

I will not let you steal my humanity. You will not teach me your hatred or intolerance.

Not today. Not ever.

In spite of what you think, you're not anonymous. You're ubiquitous.

No matter where you come from, or the clothes you wear, or the computer screen you hide behind, you are just like all thieves. Rather than work and create something yourself, you prefer to steal from someone else. Even your emotions are stolen.

And while I might not be able to see the future today or any light whatsoever, I know it will come through this darkness and free me from the ugliness you've caused. If I hang on with both hands, my strength will save me. My life is a gift and I will not let you take that from me, too. You're definitely not worth it.

I am here and I am important. Maybe not to you. But to those I make smile, to the ones who see the beauty inside me, the ones who seek me out because of who I am and because of the positive emotions I give to them, I am irreplaceable.

You are not. Should you die tomorrow, no one would weep. I've been to your funeral and I've seen that truth, too. When you die, there will be another bully, just like you, spewing the same cruel lies and lines that never change, to take your place.

As I said, you are all alike.

But we are not. We are individuals. We do matter, and to those closest to us, we are the entire world. Our loss would cut them to the core of their hearts and they would weep forever. Our death would leave a hole inside them that never closes. We are the fragile flowers that spill our fragrance into the world, and bring beauty whenever we're spotted by those capable of seeing us in all our glory.

And so I finish my letter with this. Go ahead and laugh at me. Mock me. Insult me. Tear me down. Do your worst. Because through it all, I will do my best in spite of you and your cruelty. From this day forward, I will never hear your ugly words again. I will live my life for me and those few who love me just as I am, the ones who cannot imagine a world without me in it. From now on, I will laugh at you when you start in on me, because I now know the simple truth.

Animals attack what they fear. And you, in spite of all your bluster and bragging, fear little old me. If I truly were insignificant and worthless, you wouldn't bother tormenting me. So I will continue living my life for me with the happy knowledge that I threaten you.

Meanwhile me and the rest of my real friends won't bother talking about you. You don't matter enough to us to take up time better spent on preparing for a future where you don't exist. Time changes everything and everyone. Today you're the bully. Tomorrow someone will bully you. And when that happens, unlike you, we will reach out to you in sympathy and love, and try to make you feel better. Because that is who and what we are—

Intelligent and beautiful human beings.

Forever yours,

The Anti-Bully Brigade

Frowning, Nick looked up to see her eager expression as she waited for his response. "You wrote this?"

Her face fell instantly. "You don't have to sound so surprised, you know?"

Nick sputtered. He wasn't surprised. Rather, he was highly impressed. "I didn't mean to offend you, it's just so . . ."

"Honest? Blunt? That's because I wrote it right after you left my house. Your words and kindness in my darkest hour touched a place deep inside my heart. I know how far away I live from you, and yet you dropped everything and ran over to make sure I was all right. There aren't many boys in this world who would do what you did for a friend. So thank you for being you, Nick. It meant everything to me that day."

He was too stunned to speak as she kissed his cheek.

She took the pages back from him and then handed him an ABB button with their logo on it. "You're our first official member." Her hand lingered on his as she passed it over. She squeezed his fingers, then let go.

How very odd. She'd drained every bit of his anger out of him. He was so calm now. So at peace. Only his mother and Kody had ever had this effect on him.

"Whatever you do, Nick, don't ever change." She started away.

"Hey, Bryn?" he called.

She paused to look back at him.

"I wasn't surprised. I was very impressed. You're a great writer."

Her face turned bright pink before she mumbled a low "Thank you," and darted off.

"It's amazing, isn't it?"

He scowled as Caleb moved in behind him. "What is?"

"The impact a single person can have on another.

What might be a passing pleasantry to you could be a lifeline to someone else. . . . You saved her life, you know?"

Nick shook his head. "I just went to her house to make sure she was all right."

Caleb leaned in closer to him to speak in a low tone. "And that's what gives me hope that you won't become Adarian. You have no idea how rare a gift it is to put others before yourself. It's not an easy thing to do."

He scoffed. "You put my safety above yours all the time."

"Only because my continued health depends on yours."

"I don't believe you."

Caleb shrugged nonchalantly. "You don't have to. I believe me, and in this, I'm the one who counts." He grabbed Nick by the jersey and pulled him toward the doors. "C'mon, slick, we've got to go before we're late to practice. I'm not running laps because you dragged your butt, and, thanks to you, Stone's not here to coldcock the coach today, and get us out early."

Kody hesitated as she approached Sanctuary on Ursulines. Not because the famed bar and grill housed a menagerie of lethal shapeshifters and was owned by a family of bears, but because Nick's mom worked there. In the past, Cherise had always been friendly to her. But she had no idea what Nick had told his mother or how Cherise would greet her today.

Still, this had to be done, and she was not a coward.

Summoning her courage, she headed for the doors that were guarded by a massive blond werebear named Dev. He had his long, curly blond hair pulled back into a ponytail, and he smiled at her approach.

"Afternoon, Miss Kody. How you doing?"

"Pretty good. You?"

Flashing her a dazzling smile, he brushed his hand over the double bow-and-arrow tattoo on his biceps. "I can't complain, but I always do."

Kody laughed. One thing about Dev, aside from the fact that he was extremely gorgeous, he had a wicked sense of humor. "Is Cherise working?"

"She is. But her evil spawn isn't with her."

If Dev only knew how close to the truth those words were. "I know. I was hoping to catch her here without him."

"Then you're in luck. She's on kitchen duty today. If Remi gives you any lip for being back there, let me know and I'll reorient his attitude for you." Remi and Dev made up half of a set of identical quadruplets. And while the four of them might look alike, Dev,

Remi, Cherif, and Quinn had very different personalities. Remi was the grump of the bunch. Quinn the bashful one. Cherif Mr. Serious, and Dev the eternal charmer.

"Thanks, Dev."

"Any time, sweetie."

Kody walked inside and scanned the tables that were clustered around the entrance. A smile curved her lips at the coffin in the far left corner that had a sign draped over it. Written in what appeared to be blood were the words *Aimee's last boyfriend*.

Aimee Peltier was the only daughter of the bear family, and she was a knockout with a body Kody would have to pay a surgeon to get. As such, Aimee's eleven brothers and giant father tended to be a little overprotective of her.

Kody winced as that thought reminded her of her own family. Her brothers had made her every bit as crazy with their incessant interference and overprotective lunacy. Back in the day, they'd line up to inspect any guy she was interested in. Then they'd threaten him with horrific images of what they'd do if her would-be guy even so much as made her frown.

And they were angels compared to her father, who couldn't stand anything male, other than him, his brother, and her brothers, coming near her.

Gods, how she missed them all. What she wouldn't give to have them make her crazy one more time. . . .

Trying not to think about it, she headed for the bar in back. The door to the kitchen was beside it.

She nodded at Cherif, who was drying glasses and putting them away as she pushed the kitchen door open. This time of day, it wasn't too busy. Cherise was standing at one of the steel tables, pressing out hand-made biscuits.

Kody didn't see Remi and she was more than grateful for it. The only person in the back with Cherise was the other cook, Jose, who was busy chopping vegetables.

Jose smiled at her. "*Hola*, Kody."

"Hi, Jose."

Cherise paused as she caught sight of her. A veil came down over her face, hiding her emotions and thoughts. "What are you doing here?" They could use that tone to ice down sodas.

Kody reached into her pocket and pulled out the box that held the necklace Nick had given her. Closing the distance between them, she set it on a clean area of stainless steel table next to Cherise. "I wanted Nick to have that back. I'm hoping he can get a refund for it."

Cherise scowled. "That's very decent of you, Nekoda. Thank you. There aren't many girls who would be so considerate, especially not with something that cost as much as that did."

Kody reluctantly let go of the box. Not because the necklace was valuable—she couldn't care less about that—but because it signified the broken trust with Nick. And that she hated with every part of her. "My parents raised me better. You don't use people, and you don't take from them."

She saw the sympathetic pain in Cherise's eyes. . . . And the respect. "I'm sorry things didn't work out between you two."

"Me, too. But it is what it is." She turned to leave.

"Kody?"

She looked back at Cherise with an arched brow.

"Nick is very hot-tempered . . . like me. It's that spicy Cajun blood that flows thick in our veins. Give him a few days and—"

"He won't change his mind, Mrs. Gautier. You and I both know he's too stubborn for that. Once he makes his mind up . . ."

"Another thing he comes by honestly. I'd so hoped he wouldn't inherit some of my less than desirable traits."

Kody smiled. "Obstinance has its place, and there's nothing wrong with being passionate about things."

"Passionate," his mom said wistfully. "I like that." She went back to rolling out her biscuits. "You take care, honey. If you need anything, I'm still here for you. Nick or no Nick."

Those words touched her deeply. And they made her ache for her own mother.

Cherise Gautier had the biggest heart that Kody had ever seen. She was an easy woman to love.

"Yes, ma'am. Thank you." As Kody reached the swinging door that led back into the public area, she looked back at Cherise.

She had flour smeared across one cheek and her blond hair was pulled up into a bun. Even so, she was incredibly beautiful. In the back of her mind, Kody saw Cherise's alternate life. Had his mother put Nick up for adoption as her parents had wanted, she would have gone on to Tulane University and would have been married to a lawyer now, living the life of a rich socialite. Instead of an only son, she would have had three daughters who looked just like her. Cherise would have never known the degradations and poverty she'd faced with an infant and no place to call home.

But to Cherise, Nick was so worth every bit of it and then some. You could see it in her eyes every time she looked at her son. She loved him completely, and there were no regrets inside her at all.

And if I kill him, it will destroy her.

Cherise wouldn't be able to function without her son. Not after she'd suffered so much to keep and raise him.

Kody looked up at the ceiling and pushed her thoughts from this realm, into Sraosha's so that her Guide could hear her words. *We are never to harm or cause the harming of innocents. My orders contradict each other.*

Sraosha's response was cold and brittle. *His life or yours. It's that simple.*

Simple? Please. It was the most complicated thing she'd ever had to contend with.

But there was no need to keep postponing the inevitable. No matter what, Adarian had to die. He was too dangerous to live with the powers he'd amassed. No Malachai was ever to have grown this strong.

And once he was gone, she'd have to deal with his son. Nick could never turn into the monster who'd fathered him. She couldn't allow that. Not if she was to save her own family.

One way or another, Nick would have to be stopped. And she was the only one who could do it.

CHAPTER 8

Sitting on a locker room bench, Nick tied his regular shoes and moaned in utter agony. After tackling him with a vicious blow, Mason had discreetly stomped him hard in the ribs—done in retaliation for Stone's detention that had kept him off the field today and out of the upcoming game. And with every minute that passed, it ached more.

At its current rate of expansion, he should be fully incapacitated within an hour.

Maybe ten minutes.

"You going to live?" Caleb asked as he stopped by Nick's side.

Nick glared at the bulging black backpack on the floor at Caleb's feet that he really didn't want to pick up. "Probably not."

Caleb snorted. "Well, if you plan to die, give me a

little heads-up so I can either save you or go into hiding to save my skin."

Oh, that just warmed the cockles of his heart. "Yeah . . . Roger that." Nick's phone started ringing again. Sighing, he glanced down to see who it was. . . . As if there was any doubt in his mind.

"Casey?" Caleb asked.

He cut the sound. "Who else?"

Caleb flung his towel over his shoulder and shut his locker door. "Dang, Nick, she's like some crazed celebrity stalker."

"Yeah, well, I said I wanted a normal girlfriend who had no real problems."

"Be careful what you wish for. You just might get it."

A chill went down his spine. He snapped his head up to meet Caleb's gaze. "What'd you say?"

"Be careful—"

"Yeah, no, I heard you. It was just . . . eerie. I've been hearing that a lot lately."

Caleb pitched his towel into the laundry basket. "Well, you know what they say . . . *Echriana verti yana.*"

Nick scowled as he gingerly rubbed his injured side. "Um, yeah. I hear that one all the time. . . . What crack are you on, buddy?"

Laughing, Caleb picked the backpack up with an

ease Nick envied and set it on the bench beside him. "It's my language. It means, when the universe speaks, listen. It's common in demonkyn lore to believe that the gods send us omens and signs all the time. Once you learn to recognize them, it can save your butt a lot of agony."

"Do you really believe that?"

"Honestly? I think they just like screwing with our heads. But there is something to be said for monitoring anything in your world that's redundant."

His phone rang again.

"Ugh!" Nick silenced it.

So she texted him.

He actually whimpered. "Do all girls do this?"

Caleb shrugged. "How would I know? I don't hook up with girls."

"T-M-I, Cay. T-M-I. I don't want to know what, if anything, you hook up with."

Laughing again, Caleb pulled his car keys out of his pocket. "You want me to take you to work?"

"If you don't mind. I definitely don't want to hike with that right now." Nick got up and stared at his evil five-hundred-pound backpack.

"Really, Nick?" Caleb's tone was drier than the Sahara. "You want me to carry that, too?"

Nick batted his eyelashes at him. "Why, you're such

a strong, handsome brute, Caleb Malphas," he said in a thick, overexaggerated Southern drawl. "Why, it'd just mean the entire world to me to have my suitor be so thoughtful and kind."

Caleb shoved at him, causing him to groan in pain. "Don't say shit like that out loud. I'll kill you if someone overhears you and thinks you're serious." He jerked the backpack off the bench, tossed it over his shoulder, and headed for the door.

"Caleb, baby, wait! Honey, I didn't mean to make you mad!" Nick started after him, then had to stop as a wave of pain racked him across his ribs. He cursed Mason under his breath.

You better hope I don't ever catch you off campus, dickweed. Next time he set someone on fire, it could very well be Mason . . . and it might not be an accident.

"Nicky? Baby? What's wrong?"

Nick pulled up short the instant he left the locker room and came face-to-face with the Queen of the Multiple and Annoying Texts.

"Hi, Casey."

She arched both brows as she noted his arm across his middle and his slumped stance. "Is something wrong, sug?"

"Took a bad hit during practice."

"Is that why you've been ignoring me?"

Nick cringed as he ran through a list of possible responses that wouldn't cause her to do further harm to his body. The only problem? He couldn't think of a single one that wouldn't get him jack-slapped.

"He wasn't ignoring you, Casey," Caleb said as he backtracked to Nick's side. "It was my fault. I took his phone away. I didn't want him distracted after he'd already been hurt. Sorry."

Score one for the fast-thinking demon friend. *Thank you,* Nick shot over to Caleb's thoughts.

Caleb inclined his head to him.

"So are you done?" Casey asked Nick.

"Not yet. I've still got to go to work."

She flashed a mischievous grin at him. "No, you don't. I already talked to Mr. Hunter, and he agreed that you could use a night off. So it looks like you're mine tonight."

Nick feigned a smile over the sudden lump in his stomach. "Goody." He glanced past her to Caleb. *Help me.*

Caleb gave him a wicked grin. *Not on your life, amigo. Your girl. Your problem.* He handed Nick the backpack so hard that it caused Nick to grunt. "You kids have fun," he said with an evil gleam in his eye. "I'll see you tomorrow."

Caleb!

He ignored Nick's desperate call as he headed out of the building.

Coward.

I heard that.

Of course he did. And then the rat chose to ignore it. *Fine, I'll remember this, Malphas.*

Casey rose up on her tiptoes and kissed him. "Finally, we have some alone time."

"Yeah, but I've got a lot of homework."

She nipped his chin. "You'll get it done. You always do. Besides, you're number one in the class ranking. Let a night slide and give Brynna some hope that she might actually snag valedictorian away from you before graduation." She took his hand and pulled him toward the door. "I have a surprise for you."

That really made the knot in his gut tighten to the point he'd probably pass a diamond later tonight. "I've learned to really hate surprises."

"You won't hate this one."

He wasn't so sure about that. Last time he'd heard that, he'd almost been eaten by a demon.

Casey pulled him to her car, then put his backpack in her front trunk.

"Where are we going?" he asked as they got into the car.

"You really don't like surprises, do you?"

"Not even a little."

Sighing, she started the car and waited until they were on their way before she answered. "Did you hear that Alex Peltier is starting a band?"

"Yeah, I heard him say something about it. Why?"

"They're looking for a drummer."

He still wasn't following her train of thought or overly perky attitude about it. "Okay . . ."

She turned her head to pin him with a pointed stare.

That didn't help him guess at all. His telepathy only worked with other telepaths. And since Casey was normal, he was clueless. "I'm apparently missing a vital clue. Can I buy a vowel, Pat?"

To his utter relief, she turned her head back toward traffic before they crashed and became a hood ornament for a semi. "They're looking for a drummer, Nick. You're a drummer, right?"

Was she insane?

"Uh . . . no. No, I'm not."

"You played in band. I remember it."

So did he, even though he'd tried his best to forget it. "Three years ago for six weeks, and then I had to drop out."

"Why?"

He clamped his jaw tight before he admitted to her

that they hadn't been able to afford drumsticks. How embarrassing was that? Drumsticks were only a couple of bucks, and until Kyrian had hired him, they hadn't even had a buck and change left over for him to stay in band.

Sadly, the whole reason he'd picked drums was because it was the only instrument he didn't have to buy or rent. He'd used his schoolbooks as practice pads. And even that had been more than his mother could afford.

But he would never admit to that poverty out loud. He had too much pride for that.

"I didn't have time for it," he lied.

"You still learned how to play."

"Not well," he added quickly. "You know, there's a really big difference between learning what a note is, and being Tommy Lee."

"Yeah, but I bet you remember a lot more than you think you do."

He appreciated her confidence in him, but at some point, common sense had to make an appearance in this conversation. "No, Casey, I don't. I barely learned anything."

"Seriously, Nick? You need to learn to believe in yourself. There's nothing you can't do if you put your mind to it. That's why I'm taking you to the audition."

He glanced at the road and actually considered jumping for it. He'd rather be a stain on the pavement than endure the horrors of what she had planned. "I tell you what I believe. . . . I believe I'm going to highly embarrass myself . . . which is something I can do without."

"No, you won't." He heard the deep aggravation in her tone as she snapped at him.

Even though his ribs protested it, he raked his hand through his dark hair. "Why are you doing this to me? What did I do to you to make you hate me like this?"

She gave him a peeved glare. "I don't hate you, baby. And I'm not doing anything to you. You said just the other day in class that you'd love to be in a band."

"I also said I'd love to be an astronaut. I hope that don't mean you're going to throw me in a rocket and launch my butt into outer space."

"Stop being ridiculous."

Nick wanted to beat her. He wasn't being ridiculous. She was. And unreasonable too.

I don't need this crap. He really didn't. The day had been bad enough, and after barely escaping death yesterday—twice—he didn't want to go through anything horrible today.

Was it really too much to ask for a twenty-four-hour

period of normality? His stomach heaved as a wave of terror consumed him.

That feeling didn't get better as they pulled up in front of Madaug St. James's house and she parked her car on the curb. She turned in the seat to face him. "They're auditioning in Eric's garage. Eric and Alex are the guitarists . . . or one's a bass or something. I can't remember. But you know Eric, right?"

He nodded. Eric was Madaug's older brother Nick and Bubba had helped to save from zombies last year. "Casey—"

"Shh! No argument." She got out, then literally pulled him from the car and up the driveway with him dragging his feet the whole way. He hadn't been this big a baby since he was ten years old and his mother had pulled him into the lacy panty section of Walmart in front of one of his teachers and her daughter who was in his class while the two of them had been shopping for Tina's training bras.

Oh the humanity and degradation of *that* nightmare!

Nick felt like he was going to hurl. *Why couldn't Mason have killed me during practice?*

As they neared the garage, he heard someone attempting to play . . . a song he couldn't even begin to identify. It reminded him of a two-year-old with an overturned pan. The poor kid was hitting the drums very deliberately while counting the beat out loud. He'd stomped the bass pedal with his foot, then counted and hit the snare and floor tom. . . .

And the serious torture that was going on with the hi-hat and crash cymbals made the hair on the back of his neck rise.

Yeah, okay, Nick could probably play better than *that*. But the kid didn't seem to care as he kept going in an awkward style that froze Nick to the spot as soon as they came into view of the drummer. Nick didn't recognize him from school, but since Eric didn't go to St. Richard's with him, Alex, and Madaug, he could be from Eric's high school instead.

To the credit of the band, none of them laughed or jeered at the guy's poor skills. Of course, their expressions basically said they were too horrified or shocked to move, never mind speak.

Except for Alex, who had one hand over his mouth while his blue eyes were wide and round as he watched the kid play. Tall and blond, Alex Peltier was a member of the bear clan that owned and ran Sanctuary on Ursulines, where Nick's mom worked. He and Nick had been cursory friends for a couple of years, and in all honesty, he liked the bear.

Nick really only knew Eric through Madaug and his ritualistic bitch sessions about how much Madaug hated his older brother and the emo stage that Eric seemed to be locked into.

A lot on the odd but extremely brilliant side, Madaug was the certifiable genius who'd created the Zombie Hunter game that had turned half their football team into zombies almost two years ago. Luckily, they'd stopped it, but it hadn't been easy.

The other two guys who sat in stunned silence with Eric and Alex, Nick didn't know at all.

Screwing up her face, Casey pressed her finger into her left ear and shuddered.

Finally, the kid stopped abusing the drums. He got up and made a grandiose, formal bow to Alex and company. "Thank you. Thank you very much," he said, even though no one was applauding. "For the record, I can practice any day but Sunday." He came forward and handed each band member a card. "That's my name and number for your convenience. I know, to be fair, you'll want to hear everyone else audition for the band. Once they're done and you realize how great I am, you can reach me there until nine. I'm not allowed to take calls after nine or else." He smiled at each of them. "I can't wait to hear from you."

Alex's mouth opened and closed several times before he finally spoke. "Thanks . . ." He looked down at the card. "David. We really appreciate you coming by."

"See you soon." David drew near Nick and raked him with a sneer. "You should go on home. They already have a drummer. . . . Me."

Nice ego there, buddy.

But Nick didn't say anything out loud. Who was he to hurt someone else's feelings? Honestly, he envied the kid that kind of confidence. God knew he'd never had a drop of it.

"Hey, Nick," Alex said, rising to his feet as he realized they were there. "Casey. What are you doing here?"

"I have no idea," Nick mumbled.

Casey scoffed at him, then she stepped forward, dragging Nick in her wake. "He's here to audition."

Alex's eyes widened. "You play drums?"

"Play the radio, mostly."

"Stop, Nick," Casey chided as she pushed him closer to Alex. "He plays incredibly well. He's just bashful about it."

Still, he kept fighting her. "Really don't. I suck, big time." He gestured over his shoulder to the tiny Chihuahua who wouldn't get her teeth out of his heinie. "Casey hit her head earlier when they dropped her off the top of their cheerleader pyramid, so I think I'll take her for a CAT scan and—"

"Nick!" she snapped. "Stop it! Now get over there and play."

Alex bit back a laugh. "I don't think she's going to let you escape until you play something."

"Yeah, 'cause I have not been embarrassed to my bones enough times today. Thanks, Case."

Alex gestured to Eric. "I know you know Eric already."

Dressed black on black, Eric had a blond streak in the middle of his dyed black hair that he wore spiked all over his head. He jerked his chin in greeting. "What up, Gautier?"

Not my dignity. That's for dang sure. "Eric."

Next, Alex indicated a guy who looked closer to Eric's age than Nick's. "Our lead singer is Marlon Phelps."

He stood up to shake Nick's hand. With dark skin and black eyes, Marlon was several inches shorter than Nick. And as he drew close, he raked a hungry look over Nick that quickly told him they were on entirely different teams when it came to pursuing prom dates.

"Hi," he said in a wispy voice as he extended a hand toward Nick. "Please, call me Marla or Marls."

"Hi, Marls." Nick shook his proffered hand.

Alex continued his introductions. "And the silent,

moody one over there, with the sunglasses he won't take off, is our bass player, Duff Portakalian."

Duff had short, jet-black hair and an aura around him of a street punk who'd rather rip your head off than shake your hand. But as he gave a nod toward Nick, Nick saw his real form flash through his mind. Like Alex, he might appear to be a guy in his teens, but in reality, he was in his early thirties . . . and a werepanther. One of the most peculiar things about Were-Hunters was that they aged a lot slower than humans. Their adolescence hit them in their late twenties and early thirties. At which point they were put in human schools to help them learn how to interact with nonpreternatural beings.

Something that didn't always work out to everyone's benefit.

"Hi, Duff."

Duff ignored him completely.

Alex sighed. "You'll have to forgive him, Nick. He has perpetual PMS."

"Hey!" Casey snapped indignantly. "That's a sexist thing to say!"

Alex laughed. "Not your PMS. His PMS. Premeditated Mental Sickness."

Scowling, she looked back and forth between them. "What's that?"

"He's pretending to be clinically antisocial. Right, Duff?"

Duff flipped him off.

Ignoring the gesture, Alex turned back to Nick. "Anyway, we've been asking everyone to play 'Wipe Out' if they can . . . or whatever else you might know that's rock."

"Okay . . ."

Wipe out. How apropos, since that was what he was about to do.

Nick looked to Casey, still wanting an out, but she wasn't about to give him one. She appeared even more determined than before.

Thanks, Case.

Nick scratched nervously at the back of his neck. "You wouldn't happen to have an extra set of drumsticks I can borrow . . . would you?"

Duff curled his lips. "He doesn't even have his own sticks? C'mon, Alex. This is a complete waste of my time."

"Oh shut up," Casey snapped at him. "Like you have anything better to do than feel sorry for yourself." She reached down and snatched a set of sticks from the guitar case at Eric's feet.

Nick wasn't sure which of them was the most stunned by her actions. He didn't know if he should apologize or run.

She pressed the sticks into his hands. "Show them what you can do, baby."

Nick still wanted to vomit. But what the heck? He'd suffered far worse humiliations in his life than this one. At least she wasn't bra shopping with her mom while his mother oohed and ahhed over lacy panties in public while he held her pink purse.

Wanting a giant black hole to suck him out of this, he went to the standard five-piece red drum kit and took a few minutes to adjust the throne and pieces for his height. He put his foot on the pedal and took inventory of what he was working with. One floor tom, two rack-mounted toms, the snare and bass. Hi-hat and cymbols—two crash and one ride.

All right. Everything he needed to fully embarrass himself. Cool beans.

This too shall pass. . . .

And unfortunately, he *would* live through it.

With a sigh of dread, Nick closed his eyes so that he wouldn't have to see their horrified faces, and searched his memory for something he could play that wouldn't be too mortifying for any of them.

All of a sudden, in the back of his mind, he heard the sound of crashing thunder, then a freaky laugh, and someone saying *wipe out. . . .*

The next thing he knew, he was playing the song. No, not playing . . .

He was *owning* it. Without missing a single beat . . .

What the heck? How could he do this? He'd never really played this song before. Only heard it a few times on the radio. Yet his body went through the movements and notes as if he'd played it a thousand times.

Alex came to his feet with a cheerful whoop, then reached for his guitar and joined in with the riff.

Yeah, okay, not to sound egotistical, but it was pretty epic. Nick smiled as he tasted real pride for the first time in his life. And when Duff joined in and started jamming with them, he really felt like something other than a stone-cold loser.

Even Madaug's little brother Ian came outside to listen to them play. Though why Ian was dressed as a box was anyone's guess. . . .

But at least the little box liked Nick's music. For that alone, he might be willing to adopt a younger brother the next time Madaug tried to give Ian away.

Two minutes later, Nick finished with a flourish. Ian jumped up and down, cheering along with Casey. At least until he lost one box arm that he had to quickly pick up and attempt to reattach.

Nick wasn't sure who was more surprised by his lack of suckage. The guys or him.

Duff tucked his pick into the strings on the neck of his bass. "You're good, Gautier. *Real* good."

Coming from his surly personality, that had to be a giant compliment. "Thanks, Duff."

Duff inclined his head to him, then set his bass aside.

"Well?" Alex asked the group.

"He's got my vote," Eric said.

Marlon nodded. "Definitely fine by me." A slow smile broke across his face. "In more ways than one."

Alex beamed. "Then it looks like we have a band. All we need now is a name."

"Pokemon Live!" Ian shouted.

Eric curled his lips at his brother. "We're not across the river, Ian. Go inside and leave us alone."

Ian glared at him. "I hope Madaug turns you into a zombie again, you freak, and this time the principal eats *you!*"

Eric took a step toward him. Ian let out a yelp and jack-rabbited for the house, shedding pieces of his box costume in his wake.

With a sound of disgust, Eric shook his head. "I knew I should have traded him for a sister when I was a kid."

Ignoring Eric's family drama, Duff leaned forward on his chair to put his elbows on his knees. "What about Vexed?"

Eric shook his head. "We don't want a name people will have to look up to understand."

"Vexed?" Duff asked in a disgusted tone. "Really?"

"Hey, have you met the average student at our schools?" Eric asked.

Duff backed down. "Point well taken. Vexed is out."

Casey exchanged a frown with Nick, who had absolutely no idea what to name the group.

Eric tapped his long black nails on the speaker in front of him. "What about Five Angry Guys?"

When the others started to agree, Nick spoke up fast. "Uh, no. Never."

Duff frowned. "Why not? I like it."

"Yeah, me, too," Alex said.

Nick held up his hands. "Fine, but when people shorten it, and they will, we'll be known as F-A-G."

Eric, Alex, and Duff were mortified by the acronym.

Marlon laughed. "Oh, I like it even more."

The other members exchanged uncomfortable grimaces.

"Oh c'mon, y'all," Marlon said, still pressing for it. "We'll be like Queen, with Freddie Mercury."

Nick draped his arm around Marlon's shoulders.

"While that will help you with your dance card, Marls, it will leave the four of us relegated to tundra status at school. Please have mercy on us. We beg you."

He sighed wearily. "Fine. But we could change it to Five Angry Men. 'Course *I'm* not angry, but I'm willing to learn."

Nick laughed as Alex chimed in with approval.

Duff nodded.

"Five Angry Men, it is." Eric went to clap Duff on the back.

"Don't touch me!" he growled like the panther he was.

Eric jumped back.

Casey leaned against Nick and smiled at him. "Told you you could play the drums."

Something in her tone set his inner warning system off. "How did you know?"

She shrugged. "You look like a drummer."

He also looked like an idiot in the tacky shirts his mother insisted he wear, but that was definitely untrue.

He hoped.

Suddenly suspicious of her, Nick handed the sticks to Alex, who refused to take them back.

"Keep them. We're going to be practicing here in Eric's garage three nights a week. If you want extra time, you can use Damien's practice kit in the club room at Sanctuary. The Howlers usually practice really late at night or early in the morning. So the kit should be free for your use during after-school hours."

Nick was touched by Alex's generosity. But then that was one thing about the bears, they were all kindhearted and had been stone-cold decent to him and his mom.

"When's the first practice?" Nick asked.

Alex zipped his guitar into a black gig bag. "Day after tomorrow. Four to six."

Nick sucked his breath in sharply. "That conflicts with football."

Alex considered it for a minute, then looked over to the others. "Can we do seven to nine?"

Duff shrugged. "I don't care."

"Fine with my schedule," Marlon said.

Eric nodded. "Tabby might be a little nuts since it'll cut into her vampire stalking time, but that shouldn't be too big a deal. She prefers I play in a band, anyway."

Nick had to bite back a laugh about that. He'd met Eric's girlfriend, Tabitha Devereaux, before he'd met Eric. While she was sexy on a level unto herself, she was a bit touched in the head.

"Seven it is," Alex said, dragging Nick's thoughts back to them. "We'll see you then."

"All right."

Casey wrapped herself around him and walked him back toward her car. She beamed at him the whole way. "How do you feel, Nick?"

He hated to admit it, but . . . "Unbelievably good about myself. Thank you for making me do this."

"No problem. Sometimes we don't know what our talents are until we try."

Maybe. Still, he would never have listed this on his résumé. Of course, he was sure it was his powers that gave him this ability. Like the answer in chem class . . .

He was growing stronger every day.

"I'm in a band," he breathed, unable to believe it. He'd always wanted to be in one. The dream had been so strong that he'd never really spoken about it to his mom. Mostly because he didn't want to upset her over the fact that they couldn't afford it.

Now that they could . . .

He was going to rock the house down, and use his powers for something other than evil.

Inside Artemis's temple on Mount Olympus, Ambrose stumbled as a fierce pain ripped through his skull. It was a familiar agony he'd learned all too well these last few years.

Nick had changed something in their past that had affected their future.

Closing his eyes, he tried to see what it was that had altered. But before he could, another wave of misery consumed him. And this one drove him to his knees.

"What are you doing, Nick?" he breathed, trying to push the pain away enough so that he could focus.

It was useless. The agony pulled him under and refused to let him go.

"Ambrose?"

He winced at Artemis's voice that resonated inside his aching skull.

She knelt beside him, then gasped. "Your nose is bleeding."

That he already knew since he could taste it. She cupped his face in her hands.

"I'm all right, Artie."

Artemis shook her head in denial. "You don't appear to be all right. You look rather sick and pale."

Worse, he was shaking. "I need blood."

She pulled the curly red hair back from her neck in an open invitation. The sight of her alabaster skin made him salivate. But her blood wasn't what he needed right now.

"The demon's blood."

Color faded from her cheeks. "You're almost out. You told me not to let you use it anymore."

"I have no choice. Something's wrong." He panted as he felt his powers grow even stronger. More fierce. His skin began to turn from tawny to the red and black swirling skin of the Malachai.

Artemis shrank back from him.

Ambrose wrestled with the demon that was kicking inside him, demanding release. Growling, he fought for control with everything he had. But it wasn't easy. The beast was so much more than it'd been.

What have you done, boy?

His memories were shifting and rearranging so fast that it left him sick to his stomach.

For a moment, he saw his mother on that fateful night when she'd been killed, and thought that maybe, just maybe, this time they had saved her. But it was a false hope. Artemis's bow-and-arrow mark was still on his face and his mother remained dead.

Yet the most frightening realization came a second later. Instead of them pushing the Malachai into eternal submission, Nick had just released him.

Ambrose felt his humanity leave as his vision turned from human to the red haze of rage. He no longer cared about anyone or anything. All he could taste was blood.

All he could feel was hate. Enough with humanity and their disease. It was time for them to yield their world to their masters. . . .

He rose to his feet as his wings unfurled.

Artemis screamed.

Laughing, he lunged for her.

CHAPTER 9

Nick barely recognized himself as he stared into the full-length store mirror in front of him. Casey had all but strong-armed him into a frou-frou salon that smelled way too much like perfume to get his hair cut, and then forced him into Saks Fifth Avenue to shop for something less hideous to wear. All his life, he'd walked past the Shops at Canal Place and wondered what it'd be like to have enough money to shop here.

His first excursion had been a few months ago when he'd bought a shirt for Kyrian's birthday. As strange as it sounded, it hadn't occurred to him to buy clothes for himself.

Now . . .

He grinned at the sight of the expensive black pants, belt, and black silk shirt he wore. Yeah, this was definitely the life. "I make this look *good*."

Casey laughed. "I love it when you flash those dimples at me."

That landed like a punch to his nose. Nick stopped smiling immediately, and cleared his throat.

She tsked at him. "How on earth did I upset you by complimenting you?"

"I hate my dimples," he said in a low but emphatic tone. "They're girly."

She made a loud sound of total disagreement. "They are not. They're girl magnets, maybe, but definitely not gir*ly*. Why would you think that?"

He wiped at his cheeks where the dimples were hiding, wishing he could remove them forever. "There was a woman in church when I was a kid who always said I smiled so pretty that I should have been born a girl. It wouldn't have been so bad had I not always had a feeling that my mother would've preferred a daughter over me."

She appeared aghast at the comment. "How can you possibly think that?"

Nick shrugged as he remembered the unguarded expressions on his mother's face when he caught her wistfully touching tiny ruffled dresses in stores, or the way her longing gaze would follow after little girls with their mothers. But he didn't want to share that with Casey. "I don't know."

"Has she ever said that to you?"

She'd made jokes about it from time to time. And he didn't want to admit it out loud either. "Nah, I guess not."

Casey leaned up against his back and wrapped her arms around his waist. She smiled at him in the mirror. "Trust me, Nick. You look hot in this. Completely edible."

That caused his right eyebrow to shoot up all on its own as heat scorched his cheeks and his thoughts burned with images he was still too young to have in his head. They made him even more uncomfortable than being in an expensive store where he felt like a fraud, and kept waiting for the security guard to come throw him out.

"So what do you think?" the clerk asked as he joined them.

"He'll take it," Casey said before Nick had a chance to speak.

Nick hesitated, knowing his mother would never approve of an all-black outfit. She'd have all manner of fits.

But he did like it. . . .

"Ooo, Akri-Nick, looking spiffy like the Simi in your all-black clothes. Except you're a boy and not a Simi, but you know what the Simi means. You finally coming into the demon world in all your finery. Now all we needs is to get you some barbecue sauce, and a big ole plate of Cajun *boudin rouge,* cracklin' and hog's head cheese. Yum. Yum. Yum!"

Laughing at the unique singsong accent that was unlike anything else he'd ever heard, Nick turned as Simi came up on his right and paused to look into the mirror over his left shoulder.

A little odd . . . no, take that back, a *lot* odd, Simi was another good, demonic friend of his. Today her ever-changing black hair had a purple stripe on the left-hand side that matched the short, frilly skirt and Doc Martens she wore. A matching purple corset peeked out from beneath an ornate black lace jacket that reminded him of an anime drawing. She was absolutely breath-taking and always good for a laugh. "Hey, girl! What are you doing here?"

With a wide smile, Simi lifted her arms to show him two wrists full of bangles that she jangled. "Buying the Simi some new sparklies. I was feeling kind of low 'cause of that heifer goddess Akri won't let me eat, and thought some good eats would cheer me right up, and I know they will." She snapped her teeth together.

Nick still had no idea who the heifer goddess or the Akri was that she spoke about all the time. She acted as if he knew, and if he asked her, she'd say as much. Which really didn't help him figure out their identities.

Simi pursed her lips. "What you doing here all alone, by yourself, with no one else?"

Casey wrapped a possessive arm around his waist and tugged him away from Simi's grasp. "He's not alone . . . By far."

Could her tone be any icier?

But Simi was undaunted and uninsulted as she glanced around the store in sharp, short head gestures that reminded him of a bird. "Where's Akra-Kody? I know she didn't leave you alone, by your lonesome. She know better 'cause Cajun boy get into all manner of trouble whenever he's left on his own, by himself."

Her words returned the lump of sadness to his stomach. Simi was right. He and Kody had been basically inseparable.

Until now.

"We broke up."

Simi made a tsking noise that sounded strangely like someone typing on a keyboard. "Now why you want to go and leave a perfectly good akra for something else?" She passed a less than complimentary glare over Casey's body. "And here the Simi thought men traded up, not down . . ." She dropped her voice to a deep baritone. "Like way down. Bottom of the barrels."

Casey came around him with a snarl.

Nick caught her and pulled her back. He'd seen

Simi in a fight and Casey was no match for an angry demon with mad Simi skills. And if Simi had her customary barbecue sauce in that coffin-shaped purse she always carried, she'd make really short work of Casey.

"Maybe we should talk about this later, Simi?" he asked pointedly.

Simi hissed at Casey like a cat. "We can talk later, but the Simi say you not gonna listen 'cause you hearing something else right now and it ain't got nothing to do with your boy ears or brains but rather your boy parts." She held her hand up imperiously to keep them from interrupting her. "But mark the Simi's words, Mr. Gautier. Some counsel . . ." Hesitating, she pressed her finger to her lips in thought. "Or is it council?" She waved it away with a flounce. "Oh who cares? Some things ain't worth listening to. So don't let them things into your head, Nicky, where they," she lowered her voice to where he could barely hear her, "whisper, whisper, whisper." She straightened up and pinned Casey with a gimlet stare. "Ticked-off demons are hard to exorcize and get out of your skin. Trust me on that 'cause the Simi know *her* demons . . . and *their* demons, too."

With one last nasty hiss at Casey, Simi turned and stalked off.

Nick started to go after her, but Casey stopped him. "You need to pay for your clothes, Nick."

Oh yeah . . . dang. Last thing he wanted was to be arrested for shoplifting in Saks. How could he have forgotten so easily? The soft, well-fitting clothes felt very different from his usual hand-me-down wear.

Still, he turned his head to look past Casey, trying to see where Simi was going. But it was too late. She'd vanished completely.

Dang, that demon could motor. . . .

Sighing, he left Casey's side and returned to the dressing room to change into his old clothes, then he went to the register where he almost choked at the price of his shirt alone. But the clerk didn't take mercy on him or his wallet as he rang Nick out. The cost of it all made him hyperventilate. Holy cow and beef jerky . . .

Really?

To his credit, he didn't show his mortification, even though he wanted to cradle his wallet to his chest and run for the door before he bought things he really didn't need. It was so hard to act nonchalant over something tantamount to two months' rent. Thank goodness his mama wasn't here. She'd beat him for the waste.

Good lord, when did it get so expensive to buy a pair of shoes, socks, one black T-shirt, and three outfits? No wonder his mom shopped at Goodwill. Those ugly shirts weren't so ugly after all.

Don't think about it, Nick. You make enough money now, and besides, their cost is the least of your current problems.

True, he still had Kody out there, wanting him dead.

And if you have to die, go out well dressed.

Yeah, right. His happiness completely vaporized by the mere mention of Kody's name, Nick reached for the bags.

"Wait." Casey turned back to the clerk. "He wants to wear the last outfit home. Cut the tags for us, please."

Nick almost whimpered when the clerk obeyed. There was no way to return them now. Once he walked out, they'd never take the items back. His stomach shrank at the thought.

Even more upset than before, he took his new clothes to the dressing room to swap them out.

I am so whipped. He'd stood up to zombies, demons, and a deranged coach out to steal his soul, so why was telling one pretty cheerleader that he didn't want to go broke on a pair of jeans so hard?

Because I'm tired of being a loser. Just once in his life, he wanted to look like somebody. Feel like somebody.

He tucked his tacky Hawaiian monstrosity and threadbare jeans and worn shoes into the bag, then went to meet Casey, who bit her bottom lip when she saw him. Her entire face lit up.

Yeah, okay, the price *was* worth it. At least that was the thought until another memory cocked him hard.

Kody had always looked at him like that without his having to go broke for it. *I like your Hawaiian shirts, Nick. They're your signature.*

Signature tacky, maybe . . .

But Kody had never once been embarrassed or made uncomfortable by his mother's insistence on his fugly clothes.

Unlike Casey.

Nick bit his lip as he tried not to go there. *Change was good, right? Everyone needed to shake things up. Defy the norm. Try something new . . .*

But if that was true, then why did he feel so bad right now? It was stupid. Yet he couldn't shake the funk that had him in a fierce headlock. While he liked the clothes, he didn't really like the reason he was wearing them.

Casey stopped him as they passed by a mirrored column and forced him to look at his reflection. "Who is that handsome, refined gentleman?"

But Nick didn't see himself. Instead, he saw a female clerk behind them who was staring at him with a hunger in her eyes that matched Casey's. More heat exploded over his face. He wasn't used to women paying him much attention, unless they were insulting him or laughing at something stupid he'd done.

Without commenting on Casey's question, he started for the doors, but she reached out and stopped him. "Not so fast. You need sunglasses to go with your new posh image."

"I've got a pair already."

She rolled her eyes. "Not those cheap things you wear. The right pair of sunglasses can make or break the man."

He would argue that point, but he had to admit that the ones Kyrian and Acheron wore were exceptional. And while he didn't think it would break the man, it did lend an air of coolness to them that he was sadly lacking.

So he allowed her to haul him over to the sunglasses counter where designer eyewear was laid out like a bright, shiny banquet Simi would most likely cut a swathe through with her barbecue sauce.

Yeah, okay, these really were a lot better-looking than the scratched-up pair he'd bought in a gas station clearance bin three years ago for a buck. Honestly, he'd never known that there were this many kinds or colors.

A female clerk beelined for them. "Can I help you?"

Nick had a compunction to look behind him to see

if someone else had walked up. It'd taken the other clerk ten minutes to acknowledge them in the men's department. And even then, he'd been reluctant to help until he realized Nick had a platinum credit card and Casey wasn't afraid to use it.

"Which ones do you like?" Casey asked.

Nick shrugged. How could one mere mortal, or in his case, semi-immortal man choose from so many? "What do you suggest?"

The clerk pulled out a pair of yellowish Oakleys. "These are really popular. A lot of guys go for these."

Yowza! Nick had to bite back profanity at the price tag. But he was sure he'd gone bug-eyed when he glanced at it. Were they out of their ever-loving minds? Who paid that for something you were going to drop in the driveway and possibly back over? Or worse, sit on them and crush them or leave them in a restaurant somewhere?

Grimacing, he shook his head and moved away from her. "Do you have Predator sunglasses?" He had no idea what they cost, but that was what Acheron wore, and Ash, in all his Goth glory, didn't strike him as someone who would give over a body part for fashion.

"Of course." When the clerk started to hand them to Nick, Casey intervened and pulled the tag off before he had a chance to see it.

Casey set them in his hand. "They'll be my present to you if you like them."

Nick hesitated. "I don't know about that, Case. . . ."

"Shh." She put her fingers over his lips, causing his body to erupt again. Dang, he should have bought a longer jacket. . . .

"Don't think, Nick. Just try them on." It was definitely hard to think straight when she looked at him like a Victoria's Secret model.

His throat dry, Nick did, and froze as he saw himself in the mirror on the counter. With his new haircut and the stylish glasses and clothes, he looked grown. There in the mirror, he didn't see the scared kid who normally stared out at him, afraid he was going to accidentally cut his throat while he shaved and bleed out before his mom came to find his body.

He looked like a man. Confident. Sophisticated.

Rich.

Was that really him? He turned his head to verify it. Yeah, it was definitely his reflection. . . .

But it didn't look like him.

Casey arched an expectant brow. "Well?"

"I like them," he said before he could stop himself.

She smiled and dug out her own pink Visa card. "We'll take them." She handed the card to the clerk.

Still, Nick hesitated. It was one thing to have her

buy him a Coke. Another to take something that could very well be a hundred bucks or more. "Casey, I really can't—"

"Yes, you can," she said, cutting him off. "Just say thank you."

He wanted to argue, he really did, but she had that unique girl expression that said, "Boy, don't you dare argue with me or you *will* regret it." His mom and Kody had tutored him well on what happened to any male dumb enough to try their luck when that look was present.

Submit . . .

Taking a deep breath, he inclined his head to her. "Thank you."

She kissed him. "You're very welcome."

"They really do look good on you," the clerk said as she handed Casey the receipt to sign. "You wear them like they were custom-made for you."

And that caused him to be even more uncomfortable. *People, stop complimenting me.* He really didn't like it. "Um, thanks."

Casey handed the signed receipt back while the clerk gave them the case and bag for the sunglasses.

Nick couldn't explain it, but he did feel different. Much more confident. Was this what Kyrian, Caleb, and Acheron felt like all the time?

It was kind of cool not to be self-conscious. To have clothes you knew didn't come from a thrift store sale rack.

Lifting his chin with a newfound pride, he followed Casey out of the store.

Casey watched Nick very carefully as they headed to the lot where she'd parked her car. While he'd been cute in his regular clothes, in his new ones, he was absolutely stunning. She'd had no idea when she started this little confidence-building game what the Malachai really looked like.

Dang . . .

Full grown, Nick would be stellar. In fact, it was taking everything she had not to take a bite out of him now. But he was still very skittish. Every time she reached toward him, he jumped as if she were a high-voltage wire about to wrap around him and zap him hard. While it had been cute in the beginning, it was starting to wear on her nerves.

She had to get him to relax if she was to open the channel for his powers. "Are you hungry?" she asked as they put his new clothes in her trunk.

"I'm always hungry."

That had been true of her brother at Nick's age, too. She'd never seen anyone pack away more food than Zavid.

She ran through her mind the restaurants that were nearby that would appeal to a teenaged Malachai. "Hard Rock?"

She saw the hesitation in his eyes before he mumbled, "Sure."

What was that? "Would you rather eat somewhere else?"

"Nah. Hard Rock's fine." He frowned as she moved to unlock the doors to her car. "We're driving?"

"Of course."

He actually scowled at her. "Why? It's just on the other side of the Westin. It's what? Half a mile, if even? We're just going to move from this parking lot over two? It'd take us longer to navigate traffic than hoof it."

Was he serious? Zarelda didn't walk. She'd never been a pedestrian.

"C'mon," he said, flashing those adorable dimples at her. "We can walk along the river. It'll be fun and scenic. That is why you have a convertible, right? To embrace nature and the fresh air?"

No, but she couldn't tell him the real reason—it made jumping out for human victims a lot easier. Biting her lip, she glanced up at the evening sky. "It's getting dark."

He scoffed at her argument. "It's early still and there's

plenty of lighting along the way." He winked at her. "C'mon, Casey, I'll be your protector."

If he only knew the truth. . . .

He was the one who needed a protector.

From her.

Humans definitely weren't her predator. They were her food. "All right." She locked, then closed the door and walked around to his side of the car.

He held his elbow out to her so that she could take it. Zarelda almost declined, but Casey wouldn't do that. She'd be flattered and thrilled to walk arm in arm with a boy this fine. And in truth, so was she. It'd been a long time since anyone made her feel like this. Like she was desirable and normal.

She hated him for that.

Worse, he placed his hand over hers and walked as if she meant something to him. That alone made her want to claw out his eyes and eat them for hors d'oeuvres. . . . Because she knew it was a lie. If he had any inkling as to who and what she really was, he'd be fighting her or trying to kill her.

Just like all demons did.

She'd already been lied to and betrayed once, and her brother was paying the price for it.

Trust no one. Every thing betrays.

And the Malachai in particular was one nasty, treacherous beast.

Unaware of her hatred, Nick took her to the back side of the parking deck that looked out onto a large cement wall that blocked them from the huge bank of transformers.

Casey cut an unamused smirk at him. "Nice wall, Nick. Love the *danger high voltage* signs."

He laughed. "Only the best for you, baby. Only the best for you." Still smiling, he led her across the parking lot toward the streetcar tracks. And the closer they got to them, the more tense he became. Did he sense something she didn't? Were they about to be attacked by an unseen threat?

She glanced about nervously, well aware of the fact that even a half-formed Malachai had a much more heightened alarm system than she did. "Are you all right?"

"Yeah." He loosened his hold on her as if he would need to start running any second. "Pavlovian response to how many times in the past I've had to run to catch a streetcar."

She snorted until she realized he wasn't joking. "How much have you had to do that?"

"Let me put it to you this way . . ." He checked his watch. "The next car that's heading to the French Mar-

ket station from here will arrive in just under six minutes."

"Oh my God, you have the whole line schedule
memorized? Are you serious?"

"As heart failure. Before we moved, I used to catch
the French Market stop to Dumaine every morning for
school."

She wrinkled her nose as she remembered those
days. "No wonder you were always dripping sweat when
you got there. Why didn't you ride a bus?"

He shrugged. "Bus would have taken longer and it
wouldn't get me any closer than Ursulines or the Square.
The streetcar was quicker and more direct."

That only confused her more. "But the Market to
Dumaine is even shorter than our little jaunt here.
Wouldn't it have been easier and closer to get off at Ur-
sulines on either the bus or streetcar?"

"Yeah, but after I ran to catch the streetcar at the
Market, I needed that extra stop to catch my breath.
And with morning traffic, the streetcar was still quicker
and much more reliable."

That confession stunned her. Why would anyone
put themselves through that kind of misery just to get
to a school where he was a pariah? "You really aren't
joking?"

"No, I'm not."

Nor was he complaining. That was the hardest part to believe.

He never did, for that matter. He merely accepted people and things as they were.

How refreshing.

And stupid.

Arm in arm, they walked up the stairs behind the Bienville station, to the brick walkway that ran mostly parallel to the Mississippi River. The water glistened from the setting sun and provided a nice tranquility to the cool evening. Off in the background was the picturesque suspension bridge that connected the city to Algiers Point.

Nick was right. It was very pretty, and at this time of day, semiprivate. There was almost no one over here with them. Only a few stragglers or hobos off in the distance.

For the first time since Grim had assigned her duty here in New Orleans, she saw the city as something other than a nuisance, and Nick as something other than a target.

"Okay, I'm glad you talked me into this. I do like it."

He flashed those dimples. "I told you."

Slowing down, she laughed as they neared the beautiful Monument to the Immigrant where a muse of hope looked out over the river while protecting a Victorian family of four that bravely faced the city with nothing more than the clothes on their backs. She didn't know why, but the carved little girl and boy reminded her of her and her brother.

Unwilling to remember those days, she slid a teasing glance to Nick. "Yeah, yeah. You're the man. What can I say?"

Before Nick could answer, a shadow stood up from where he'd been crouching on the hidden benches in front of the monument and pointed a gun at them. "You can say nothing, bitch, if you want to stay alive."

Another armed man stepped out from the tree on the left and pinned Casey and Nick between them.

Sucking her breath in sharply, she froze. While she was an immortal creature, the body she was in wasn't. One shot into Casey's flesh, and she could be trapped between worlds forever. . . .

CHAPTER 10

What were the odds of this? Nick ground his teeth until he tasted blood as he recognized the guys holding guns on them.

Alan and Tyree.

Oh yeah, this was karma of epic proportions. He owed both of them a payback large enough to get the country completely out of debt. They were the whole reason he now worked for Kyrian Hunter. Back in the day when he'd stupidly called them friends, Alan had duped him into almost mugging two tourists.

What kind of "friend" would do that to another, right?

Hey, let's all go to prison together, shall we? Forget college, Nick, and a future with a beautiful wife and kids. Angola prison and baggy orange jumpsuits are so much better for you and your ego, too. We'll all get big hairy boyfriends and never be eligible for a decent job again. C'mon, let's go!

Boo-yah!

When Nick had refused to jeopardize what little future he had to go along with Alan's "brilliant" scheme, they'd turned on him with relish and had almost killed him.

But for Kyrian intervening at the very last second, they would have. And they'd have done it with a gleam in their eyes that he had yet to forget. His childhood "friends" who had claimed to be his brothers from another mother had relished beating him into the ground.

Now as he stared at them in their natural gangsta habitat, he wondered how he'd ever seen them as anything other than the selfish animals they were. How had he ever called them friends and not seen the cruelty they were capable of? Yet back then that cruelty had never been directed at him, only other people Tyree and Alan had judged deserving of their hatred.

At the end of the day, Nick hadn't wanted to judge them for things they couldn't help, the way the rest of the world had wrongly judged him. But sometimes, just sometimes, those judgments were warranted and necessary survival skills. And instead of summarily saying they were wronged by circumstances beyond their control, Nick should have looked closer at them and seen what part of their situation was exactly their fault and no one else's.

Right or wrong, everyone made their own decisions and should be held accountable for them.

Trying not to be obvious, Nick scanned the shadows for the missing member of their merry criminal band. But for once, he was nowhere to be seen.

"Where's Mike?" Nick asked, putting Casey behind him as he calmly faced them. This kind of cowardly scum didn't frighten him at all. They just pissed him off. "Did he finally wise up and move on, or is he lying in a gator's belly down in the bayou 'cause he caught a clue and told you where to stick it?"

Alan gaped as he recognized Nick's voice. "Go-chay? Nah, dog, that ain't you. That *can't* be you."

Tyree curled his lip as he ran his covetous gaze over Nick's new clothes. "Nah. It don't look like Go-chay at all. He's not wearing them gag-ugly shirts."

"Go-shay," Nick said from between his clenched teeth, correcting their mispronunciation of his last name—something they knew he couldn't stand.

Alan sneered at him. "Who you roll to get them threads, boy? I know you can't afford them with what your whore of a mama makes taking off her clothes for pocket change, and that old lady you work for sure ain't paying that kind of money for you to take out her trash at night."

Tyree laughed. "If she is, I think we ought to pay her a visit one night after she closes her shop."

Casey started crying hysterically. "What's going on, Nick? Who are these people?"

He spoke to her over his shoulder. "It's all right. Stay calm."

Alan let out a low whistle. "That your woman? Day-am." He tilted his head to see her better. "Nah, can't be. She too fine for a piece of ignorant Cajun gutter trash like you. Now be a good boy and pass her purse and your wallet over to us, and we might let you live through the night."

A slow smile spread across Nick's face as he broke into a thick Cajun accent. Something that should have warned them how hot his temper was right now and the fact that they ought to be running away as fast as they could. The more Cajun he sounded, the more lethal his actions. *"À présent, cher.* What say we pass a *bon temps* instead, *n'est pas?"*

Alan cocked the .38 he held sideways and aimed it at Nick's chest. "How many times I got to shoot till you learn better than to mess with me, boy?"

Payback's a b—

And she was about to come over with friends to collect rent with interest.

Nick held his hands up and splayed his fingers to lure them into thinking he was passive.

Yeah, right. Nick Gautier passive . . .

They really were too stupid to live.

"*Ça c'est bon, capon.* Ain't no need in getting hos-tile. *Bon rien.*" Nick moved slowly while Casey's wails picked up tempo. He held one hand out to her. "Let me have your purse, *bebelle.*"

Tears streamed down her cheeks, streaking her makeup as she obeyed without question . . . something Kody would have never done. Heck, Kody would have already yanked out a sword and cut one of their heads off.

But Casey was *not* Kody. She was meek and helpless.

Nick wrapped his hand in the strap of her purse while he fished his wallet out of his back pocket. Then he whispered to Casey, "When I move toward them, I want you to drop to the ground, okay? And stay there until I tell you to get up." Louder, for the benefit of their muggers, he said, "Just do what they say, Boo. It'll all be all right."

Her hands visibly shaking, she nodded.

Tyree licked his lips as he skimmed Casey's body with interest. "I think we ought to keep his girl and have some fun with her before we let her go. What do you think, Alan?"

Alan grinned. "Yeah. I think we might do that."

Like heck you will. . . .

Nick held the purse out to Alan, making sure to keep it just a hair past his reach. "I think that would be a very unhealthy thing for you to do, *tchu*," Nick said, his voice dropping an octave as his hands began to heat up. "Kind of like smoking two packs a day, only much more lethal and quicker to kill you."

"You don't scare me, dog, and you damn sure don't tell me what to do." Alan snatched at the purse, thinking Nick would loosen his grip and let him have it.

Instead, Nick jerked it forward, bringing Alan into his range. Before Alan could catch his balance, Nick ripped the gun out of his hand and aimed it at Tyree. He fired it.

Screaming, Tyree ran for the parking lot.

Nick would have pursued him, but Alan punched at him and tried to get the gun back. In that instant, Nick felt his powers surge forward with an audible rush that filled his ears with a fierce, drumming beat.

The smell and taste of blood permeated everything.

Kirast kiroza kirent. Conceived in violence to do violence and to die violently. That was the promise written in the first language that wrapped around Nick's Malachai symbol. It was the Code of his breed.

Alan's hatred and propensity to hurt others fed the

Malachai inside Nick, making him all the stronger. It was why Nick's father chose to live in prison when there was no human power in existence that could hold Adarian.

Hatred, prejudice, jealousy . . . all the negative emotions around a Malachai were like handing a can of supercharged spinach to Popeye. The more violence that was directed near them or to them, the more power and strength they could draw from it.

Heat engulfed Nick's hands, burning both him and Alan.

With a fierce cry of rage, Nick caught Alan a hard punch to the jaw that sent him straight to the ground. Nick fell on top of him, raining fiery blow after blow on Alan's body as he sought to make some kind of peace with the past where Alan had intended to kill him.

Over and over, he saw that fateful night in his mind when he'd been a scared fourteen-year-old boy, and the three of them had stomped, beat, and shot him while he tried only to protect himself from their unwarranted brutality.

And for what?

For refusing to traumatize and rob an elderly couple whose only mistake was walking down the wrong street at the wrong time?

Scum like them needed to die. Alan and his crew were a disease on this earth and it was time to cure it.

"Kill him, Nick!" Casey shouted. "Kill him! It's what he deserves!"

The smell of blood thickened in his nostrils as Alan begged for a mercy he hadn't shown Nick, meanwhile Casey continued to scream for him to end Alan's life until their two voices mingled like some kind of macabre duet.

Inside his mind, he heard his Malachai demonic voice laughing. Saw his skin starting to mottle with its true black and red tone.

A thousand sounds assaulted him, but one voice rang out loudest.

We sleep soundly in our beds because rough men stand ready in the night to visit violence on those who would do us harm. Winston Churchill . . . Kyrian quoted that so much that it perpetually rang in Nick's ears. It was so common a mantra for the Dark-Hunters that many of them used it as the tagline in their e-mails or had it tattooed on their bodies. It was second only to the Spartan motto: *È tàn è epì tâs. Return with your shield or upon it*, i.e., victory or death.

And Alan definitely deserved to die for all his sins against this world. All his crimes against the innocent people he'd victimized. Nick had promised himself retribution for his own gunshot should they ever meet again.

Fate had brought Alan back into his reach. Who was he to argue with what was obviously a God-given gift?

I have to keep my word. Gautiers were known by the oaths. It was the one thing his mother had drilled into him. *You never break a promise, especially when it's to yourself.*

He held the gun to Alan's temple, and in his mind, he saw a clear image of Alan standing over him while Nick lay beaten and helpless on the street. Saw the eager gleam in Alan's eyes as he'd looked forward to blowing Nick's head off.

"Say your prayers, Gautier." Those had been his words to Nick. *"You're about to become a statistic."*

The coldness of Alan's actions that night spurred Nick as he pulled the hammer back with his thumb to cock the gun.

He tightened his grip on the trigger.

Just as he was about to do it, his brain kicked up a voice that drowned out both Alan and Casey.

Kody's . . .

Every person is born with feelings of envy and hate. If he gives way to them, they will lead him to do violence and crime, and any sense of loyalty and good faith will be aban-

doned. Then he is forever lost. He is forever damned. Not by the world or the circumstances of his birth, but by his own free will.

All of a sudden, his vision cleared and it felt like he slammed back into his body. Hyperaware now, he saw the bloody mess he'd made of Alan. The horrific sight sickened him. He barely recognized Alan's features. Blood was splattered all over both of them. The new clothes he'd been so proud of were now ruined.

How could I have done that to another human being? He wasn't an animal.

No, you're worse. You're the Malachai.

"P-p-please," Alan begged through his swollen, bleeding lips. "Don't kill me."

Releasing him, Nick stumbled back.

"What are you doing?" Casey demanded as she closed the distance between them. "He was going to rob you and rape me. He's an animal! Kill him before he harms someone else. You owe it to the world to make it safe and end his life."

At her incessant nagging, his rage started rising once more. . . . Everything faded until he was again focused only on making Alan suffer.

I'm going Malachai. . . .

And there was nothing he could do to stop it.

CHAPTER 11

Caleb looked up from the Sumerian text he was reading as a chill rushed over his skin. It was an ancient stirring in the ether that he hadn't felt in centuries.

And it was one that made his hackles rise and his molten blood run cold.

Somehow Nick was quickly pulling his father's powers into his body.

This was *not* good. Nick wasn't used to the power *he* had, never mind the greater power of a full Malachai. "What have you done, kid?" He rose and started to go after Nick, but before he could, he felt another deep, undeniable ripple.

Adarian summoning him to his side.

As Adarian's personal slave, Caleb had no choice except to do as he was told. And there was no missing the franticness of this summoning. Adarian was panicked.

Maybe he's finally dying. . . .

A bolt of white-hot hope shot through him. He'd been praying for Adarian's death for so long that he couldn't remember the last free breath he'd enjoyed.

Die, already, you worthless POS.

Transforming into his raven form, Caleb flew out of the open upstairs window and headed upstate for Angola prison where Nick's father hid in plain sight among some of the most dangerous criminals in the country. It was the one place where Adarian could keep his powers fully charged without even trying. The one place his enemies would never dream of seeking him. After all, who would voluntarily incarcerate himself after he'd broken free of the hellish otherworld prison Adarian had spent most of his life in?

Obvious answer—the Malachai. But other creatures didn't think like them. The Malachai breed was a special kind of twisted that defied most brains and moral codes.

Reaching the famed prison, Caleb flew to the window where Adarian's solitary cell was. But the elder Malachai wasn't there. Caleb cocked his head. It was too late for Adarian to have one of his yard breaks. . . .

Since he was on death row for one of the most heinous killing sprees in Louisiana history, he was supposed to be kept in his cell twenty-three hours a day.

He's finally dead.

For one half heartbeat, Caleb rejoiced.

Until he realized that he was still being summoned by his master.

Crap. *It lives. . . .*

Disgusted with his luck, Caleb followed the sensation until he reached the R. E. Barrow Jr. Treatment Center, where inmates went for medical care. Returning to his human form, he flashed himself into the building and stayed invisible as he searched for his master.

He knew he'd found Adarian when he came to the most secured room in the facility. Something that was really laughable since Adarian could get in and out of the building as easily as Caleb did.

Without slowing, he walked through the guarded door and into the sparsely furnished room where Adarian was strapped down by all fours to the hospital bed. . . . Yeah, right. That would really stop Adarian if he wanted to kill someone.

But that being said, Adarian looked awful. The elder Malachai was pale and gaunt in appearance. Weak. Caleb had never seen him like this. Adarian even had a bandage over his head and dark, deep bruises covered his exposed skin.

Yet that wasn't what stunned Caleb the most. It was

the color of the blood that seeped through Adarian's gauze dressing.

Dark red. That could mean only one thing. . . .

"Are you dying?"

Adarian curled his lip at Caleb's stupid and obvious question. "Take the joy from your tone, *slave*. I'm not dead yet and I still have enough power to end your pathetic existence." But the death rattle in his chest mocked that threat.

Caleb moved closer to the bed to examine the numerous wounds marring Adarian's body. "What happened?"

His breathing labored, he licked his dry, cracked lips. "Riot. At first, it strengthened me. Then . . ." He lifted his strapped hand to show his bleeding skin. "What is going on, Malphas? I should not be weakening while the humans are fighting each other here. I should be growing stronger than ever. How can this be?"

Caleb had no idea why Adarian would be losing power like this. In the past, it'd always been simple. The elder retained his full strength until the younger Malachai came into his own. Then the younger would confront his father and drain him. Once the elder was weak enough, the younger killed him and assumed his rightful place as the sole Malachai.

A perfect blood exchange and inheritance.

Well, not perfect if you were the Malachai who died. . . .

But Nick hadn't been near his father since Adarian had gone to Nick's hospital room and tried to kill him first and absorb Nick's fledgling powers before Nick learned how to kill him.

"Was it a demon that attacked you?" Caleb asked, thinking it was one of the many predators pursuing Adarian who'd landed a lucky shot on the beast.

"Human, of all disgusting things. I was wounded by a mere mortal!" He had a right to be indignant. Caleb would be highly offended, too, had a lowly human reduced him to Adarian's current state.

Adarian's jaw quivered. "Find whatever has done this to me and kill it."

"And if it's Nick?"

"Bring him here so I can kill him myself."

Ah, paternal love . . .

How he loathed it. Like Nick, he'd never known what it was like to have a real father. His father had plotted against him and used him just like Adarian had done with Nick. But one point in his father's favor, the bastard hadn't tried to kill him.

Yet.

"I'm running out of time, Malphas. Do not betray

me in this. Know that if something kills me, you will *not* be freed."

Caleb scoffed. "That's not the way it works."

Adarian laughed cruelly. "It is when you bargain for it." He glared smugly at Caleb. "I know your ilk, and I know you wouldn't lift a finger to save me unless your own ass was on the line, too. So I have tied your geist to mine. Whoever takes my powers takes your servitude with them. Forever."

Caleb cursed as that cold, brutal reality racked him. Only the Malachai had the ability to bond demon geists. It wasn't easy, but . . .

"I have no way to gain my freedom? Ever?" he snarled at Adarian.

"You can only control who holds your leash."

Well, wasn't this all hunky-dory? Just what he wanted to hear. It ranked right up there with *Sorry, you were accidentally turned into a eunuch while you slept.* . . .

In that one moment, he wanted to kill Adarian more than he ever had before. But the laws of his people would drain his own powers and kill him if he even attempted it. And if he died in bondage, his geist would be trapped in a grisly nether realm where he would never have any kind of peace or rest whatsoever.

Eternal hell that made mockery of the one mortals feared.

Impotent rage clouded his vision. "I hate you."

Adarian closed his eyes as if he savored those words, and why shouldn't he? Caleb's hatred only fueled Adarian's power and made him stronger.

After a second, he opened his eyes to glare at him. "Go, Malphas. Find my attacker."

"As you will it, my burning external hemorrhoid." Caleb withdrew as fast as he could before his hatred fed Adarian more. He didn't want to do anything for the beast he didn't have to.

How did I become this pathetic a wretch?

His fury and grief mixed inside him as he remembered the fierce, undefeated demon he used to be. Gods, how he despised his memories. All they did was show him the mistakes he'd made. The faces of the past that haunted him to the point he could no longer sleep through any given night.

Before he could stop himself, he manifested his most prized possession into his palm. An ancient gold locket, it contained a single precious lock of white-blond hair that he hadn't seen in centuries. He was too afraid to open the locket and chance losing his last link to the only thing that he'd ever deemed valuable. Tears welled in his eyes as he ran his finger over the engraving on the outside that was written in his native language. . . .

Teria assim.

Forever yours.

In his mind, he saw the most perfect human woman who had ever been born. Gentle and kind, she had turned him from an instrument of absolute destruction into a noble hero who had been willing to risk everything to save her race and protect them all, no matter the personal cost. When every living creature had been out to take his life and had driven him mad with his need to survive and conquer them, she had tamed him with her tenderest touch. She had never once seen him as a rabid monster to be destroyed or enslaved.

While others had feared and cursed him, she had reached out and offered him innocent friendship. In all the centuries he'd existed, she alone had loved him. And the agony of her loss was every bit as profound and cutting now as it had been the moment she'd drawn her last breath in his arms.

I would give anything to have one more moment with you. . . . To smell the sunshine on your skin . . .

Hear my name on your precious lips.

"I miss you so much, Lilliana," he breathed, his voice breaking with the weight of his pain.

He had lived solely for her beautiful smile.

And she had died protecting his worthless life.

The injustice of it was enough to drive him insane. But the gods wouldn't allow him even the comfort of madness to escape this hell he was trapped in. And he was no longer the creature who had loved her to distraction. She had taken his nobility and love with her into eternity, and left him forever bereft and aching for her.

I am sorrow.

My name is Hatred.

Disease.

Wrath.

A single tear slid down his cheek.

Infuriated by that weakness, he wiped it away so hard that he bruised his skin. The searing pain brought him back to the present and to the task Adarian had given him. The elder Malachai was about to die, and since Caleb didn't know what was killing him, he had no idea who his next master would be.

But the one thing he could guarantee, who or whatever was coming for Adarian wouldn't hesitate to use and abuse both Caleb's physical being and his powers. And as bad as Adarian was, for the most part he had left Caleb alone.

His next master might not be so neglectful.

A tic started in his jaw. Slavery sucked for anyone, but for demons it was so much worse. If their masters wanted to torture them, they couldn't even die and escape it. And most everything that knew how to enslave demonkyn possessed a cruel streak that made the Marquis de Sade look like a Buddhist monk flower child.

Grinding his teeth, he used his powers to return Lilliana's locket to his room where it would be safe from harm or loss. His hand turned cold immediately from the sudden emptiness, and the hole in his heart ached all the more.

When he'd looked into her kind, blue eyes, he'd seen a future with her by his side forever.

Instead of an eternity of happiness and love, he'd only been granted three precious years with her. Or more precisely, twelve hundred and four days.

A mere blip on eternity.

Closing his eyes, he tried to forget that her life had been the only thing he had ever begged for.

But even now, he could see himself covered with her blood as he screamed out for his father to help him. For someone, anyone he'd served to breathe life back into the only person who had ever made him feel whole. Needed.

Loved.

His precious Lilliana had lived and she had perished by her convictions.

. . . Damned is the soul that dies while the evil it committed lives on. And the most damned of all are those who see the evil coming for others and refuse to confront it. For it

is not out of fear that heroes are born, but rather out of their selfless love that will not allow them safety bought from the torture, death, and degradation of others. It is better to die in defense of another than to live with the knowledge that you could have saved them but chose to do nothing.

And to those who think that one person cannot make a difference, I say this . . . the deadliest tidal wave begins as an unseen ripple in a vast ocean. Live your life so that your integrity will motivate others to strive for excellence long after you've passed on, and know that no good deed or sacrifice, or offer of sincere friendship or love, is ever forgotten by the one who receives it.

Lilliana's words haunted him. She had taught him that it was far better to be alone than to be surrounded by people who were morally bankrupt. People who sought to bring him down with jealous words and barbs they couched in humor, thinking he was too stupid to recognize the insults they thought they'd so cleverly hidden.

He'd given up his lead role as a fierce, conquering warlord to live in a tiny hut where Lilliana had made him the king of her small, precious world. And she had been right. He had never, for even one nanosecond, forgotten the warmth of her love that had taught his dead heart how to beat.

To this day, even though he hated it, he still strove to be the man she'd seen him as.

Yeah, he understood exactly the brutal cold hatred the first Malachai had borne for his mother over the death of his wife and child. It was the same hatred he bore for his own father, who had ignored his pleas to spare Lilliana's life. To take his life in exchange for hers.

How could you, you worthless bastard, when you knew full well that she was all I had?

His nostrils flared as more anger filled him.

Stop, Malphas. Don't think about it. There was nothing he could do to change the past.

It was the future he needed to focus on. That was the only thing he could alter.

Whoever was killing the Malachai was an evil force to be feared. And if they could kill Adarian while he was in a place where nothing other than Nick should be able to weaken him, then they would be able to control Nick, too.

That was truly chilling.

While Caleb might not like this world he was forced to live in, he knew how much worse it would be in the hands of something *that* powerful, and he would not dishonor his wife's memory by putting his hands in his pockets and turning away from the battle to come.

Not when he knew how to fight and how to win.

This wasn't about following the orders he'd been given. It wasn't about saving his own worthless existence . . .

he was already in hell. It was about doing what was right.

Fighting for those who couldn't fight for themselves.

Adarian was lost to his hatred and there was nothing Caleb could do to salvage him.

But Nick . . .

Hope is that tiny light that the gods have given us so that we can find our way through our darkest hours. And while we might stub our toes and bruise our knees, if we keep moving forward, even when our progress is slow and painful, we will overcome and be made better by our journey. . . . No misery or bad situation is ever infinite or final until we make a conscious decision for it to be so.

Caleb had scoffed at Lilliana's naive idealism. *So basically what you're telling me, little one, is that hope is a human's way of flipping off the gods and saying "ha, ha, you lose and I have no intention of quitting?" Take it from someone with a lot of personal experience, they tend to react badly when you do that.*

But in the end, he had surrendered his battle flag to his wife. Mostly because she'd kissed him until he'd lost the ability to form any rational thought. At least that was the lie he told himself to keep from admitting that in spite of all the horrors he'd seen and utter agony he'd survived, he still had hope inside his heart. Whether it originated as more torture or as divine inspiration, something always happened to carry him forward through every dismal ordeal.

And while he might not win this latest fight, he would go down battling the whole way, with everything he had. Not for himself or for his own vainglory. Not because he'd been ordered to do it.

He would stand strong and fight to the bitter end for the simple reason that it was the right thing to do.

Yeah, even he admitted it was stupid.

Caleb glanced back at the building where he'd left Adarian and let out a bitter laugh. "We are so going to die."

CHAPTER 12

With the barrel aimed right between Alan's eyes, Nick pulled the trigger and felt the recoil in his hand.

A mere instant before the bullet left the chamber, something hard slammed into his wrist, knocking the gun free and sparing Alan's putrid life. The gun landed a moment later with a solid thud on the concrete. His fury exploding, Nick turned on his new attacker, intending to kill them.

But just as his hand flew back for a punch, warm, soft hands cupped his cheeks and then a pair of tender lips touched his.

The shock of being so unexpectedly kissed drove all the demon and anger out of him. A sweet, feminine essence filled his nostrils, making his head spin as he breathed her in. It was neither Kody nor Casey he tasted.

And the kiss she gave him was so hot that it awoke every male hormone in his body.

Growling deep in his throat, Nick lost himself to the wonderful sensation.

Until someone hit him on the shoulder. Hard. His anger renewed, he turned with a curse to find Casey glaring at him.

The stern expression on her face told him she wanted to carve his heart into pieces. *"What* do you think you're doing?"

Shocked and confused, Nick glanced back to the woman in his arms. The instant he saw who it was, his stomach hit the ground. No, it couldn't be.

Simi?

Saint merde!

With a tender smile, Simi moved in to kiss him again.

Nick jumped back three feet. The one thing that his future self had all but beat into him was that he had to stay away from Simi. She was to be kept off his menu for all eternity. No matter what.

Simi passed a hungry look over him. "You know, Akri-Nick . . . you taste good even without barbecue sauce."

Oh, someone shoot me. . . .

From the look on Casey's face, he would say she was about to.

But before she had the chance, another gunshot rang out. Simi tackled Nick to the ground, filling his arms with her warm curves again.

Yeah, this was nice, but . . .

He rolled with Simi to see Alan on his feet, aiming the gun for another shot. Reacting on pure instinct, Nick conjured a fireball and shot it at Alan. It caught his arm and engulfed it in flames. Alan went down screaming while Nick jerked his head toward Casey, who hadn't made a single sound since the gun had gone off.

She lay on the ground a few feet from him in a crumpled heap. Unmoving.

No . . .

Sirens filled the air as the police finally came toward them. Nick paid no attention as he headed for Casey to see if she was still alive. "Simi? Make sure he doesn't get that gun again."

Her eyes lighting with joy, Simi licked her lips. "Can the Simi eat his arm? You already toasted it. It just waiting for dinnertime."

"No, Simi. Don't."

She made a sound of utter irritation as she picked up the gun and glared at Alan. "You are so related to akri.

No, Simi, no. That's all I hear. You know, *'bon appétit'* is a perfectly good phrase, too. And it's one that makes the Simi a lot happier than 'no, Simi, don't.'"

He ignored her irritated monologue and Alan's cries of pain as he rushed to Casey's side. *Please don't be dead.* He'd never forgive himself if he'd let her die because he was stupid and hormonal. He skimmed her body, but didn't see any blood.

"Casey?" he breathed as the police descended on the parking lot, filling the darkening sky with bright, flashing lights.

She didn't respond at all as car doors opened.

"Freeze!" someone shouted. "Put down the gun!"

Nick glanced over to see Simi holding it on Alan, whose arm was now smoldering instead of blazing. Panic made him sick to his stomach as he feared what the demon might do to the police. "Simi, drop it fast and hold your hands up so they can see that you're not armed." Not that it mattered. She was actually a hundred times more lethal without weaponry than a battalion at full arsenal.

Luckily, Simi obeyed him.

Still kneeling beside Casey, Nick lifted his arms and laced his fingers behind his head, so that some nervous rookie didn't accidentally shoot him. "We need an ambulance. Please!"

The police swarmed them.

"What happened?" a female officer asked as she squatted beside Nick.

"We were walking to the Hard Rock for dinner when he and another guy pulled guns on us." He pointed to Alan, who was telling another officer that Nick had jumped him after he asked Casey for her name. "Not knowing we were being mugged, my friend Simi showed up and startled them. The other guy ran away while I fought that one for the gun and it went off. I dropped it, he picked it up and fired. I think he shot my girl-friend, but I can't tell. Please, get her help!"

"Don't worry. An ambulance is on the way."

Nick nodded as a male officer came up and jerked him to his feet. "What are you doing?"

"He says you attacked him for no reason and that he was protecting himself from a homicidal lunatic. Since he's the one bleeding the worst and your girlfriend was holding an unregistered gun on him when we arrived . . . We'll take you all down to the station until we get this sorted out."

"He mugged us!" Nick growled, indignant that Alan might skate free after all.

It didn't matter what he said. The cop slammed a handcuff down hard on his wrist and jerked his arm behind his back to lock it to his other hand. He yanked

Nick to his feet so hard, Nick was amazed it didn't tear his arm out of the socket.

"He's crazy!" Alan shouted as the cop dragged Nick toward the parked police cars where a large, curious crowd had formed. "Don't get him near me. He's on drugs or something. I ain't never seen nobody act that way. He even set me on fire!"

Nick had to bite his tongue to keep from saying Alan deserved it.

As they reached one of the cars, a deep voice rumbled next to them. "Hey, Lenny, what's going on?"

Thank God, it was Acheron.

The cop paused next to Ash, who, courtesy of his black biker boots, was almost seven feet tall. "I don't know, Ash. We got a call about multiple gunshots and now we've got this guy," he jerked Nick's cuffed hands, "claiming to be mugged and that one over there saying this one attacked him for no reason."

Ash shook his head, then leaned down to speak in a low tone. "You know you're arresting Kyrian's Squire, right?"

The cop paled instantly. "He's one of us?"

Ash nodded. "Fully inducted into the sacred council."

"Son of a . . . No. I had no idea."

"I have my Squire's card in my wallet," Nick said over his shoulder. "It's on the ground back there where

I dropped it while trying to hand it over before he shot at us . . . first."

"Kyrian's been training him to protect himself from our natural enemies." Ash jerked his chin toward Alan. "Looks like Nick's been a good student."

"Yeah, I'll say. He beat the crap out of him."

"What was I supposed to do? He threatened to rape my date and kill me."

The cop reached down and unlocked the cuffs. "Sorry about that, but you have to appreciate what we saw when we got here."

Turning to face him, Nick curled his lip. "Yeah, I know what you think you saw . . . Cajun trash."

The cop looked away, shamefaced.

Ash folded his arms over his chest. "You okay, kid?"

Nick didn't answer as he saw the paramedics pushing Casey's stretcher toward the ambulance that was parked a few feet from them. He ran over to see how she was doing. She was conscious and they had an oxygen mask over her face.

"Casey?"

She reached for him. "Nick? Are you okay?"

"Yeah, you?"

She nodded.

"We're just taking her in as a precaution," the EMT explained as they stopped to open the back doors.

Casey squeezed his hand. "Can you get my car home for me?"

"You sure you don't want your dad to get it?"

"I'm sure. My keys are in my bag."

"Don't worry. I'll take care of it. You just get better."

She smiled at him as the EMT broke their hands apart. They lifted the stretcher and slid her inside.

Nick didn't move as they shut the doors and took off with her.

Ash came up and put a comforting hand on his shoulder. "So what really happened?"

"I don't know what you mean."

Ash arched a bitterly amused brow. "I'm an eleven-thousand-year-old warrior, Nick. I can tell the difference between someone fighting back to protect himself, and when someone beats the crap out of someone he has a personal grudge against. What'd he do to you?"

"He's the one who shot me the night I met Kyrian."

"And you didn't kill him?"

Nick shrugged. "Police got here first and they looked a little trigger-happy."

Acheron nodded as he dropped his hand. "Good call." All of a sudden, his phone started ringing. "Excuse me." Ash pulled it out and moved away to answer it.

Nick left him to check on Simi, but there was no sign of her. He walked over to the woman officer who'd been so nice before Lenny roughed him up. "Where's my friend?"

"They just took her off in the ambulance."

"Not Casey. Simi."

"Who?"

Was the woman blind? Simi was a hard creature to miss. "The tall, Goth girl who was here a minute ago?"

She screwed her face up. "I didn't see her. Hey, Tim? Was there another girl here?"

"Nah. Why?"

Nick opened his mouth to respond, then snapped it shut. Now to most people, it would be weird for no one to remember seeing a six-foot-tall Simi holding a gun on Alan.

For him . . .

Business as usual.

Simi had some impressive psychic powers and obviously amnesia for others was one of them. Man, to have those awesome Jedi mind tricks. That and the Force choke . . .

Two things every teenage boy could use to make his life a lot easier.

Wishing for what couldn't be, he walked over to the officer who was bagging Casey's purse and his wallet. "Um, can I have my stuff back?"

The officer hesitated before handing his wallet over, but he kept the purse.

Really? Nick sighed as he braced himself for a fight. "Her car's over at Canal Place. She wanted me to get it home for her. Kind of hard if I don't have her keys."

He screwed his face up in doubt.

"Give the kid the keys, Leo."

"You sure?" he asked Lenny, who was heading over to the woman officer.

"Yeah, but I'll take her bag to her at the hospital."

Nick rolled his eyes. "What? You think I'm going to steal it?"

"It's just protocol." Lenny handed him the car keys, then moved away.

Still irritated, Nick went back to where he'd left Acheron, who was just finishing his call. "Can I ask a favor?"

Ash slid his phone into his back pocket. "Sure."

"Casey wanted me to take her car home and since I don't have my license yet . . ."

"Your mom's still holding that card over your head, huh?"

Nick made a sound of profound disgust. "Yeah. She says I don't have enough time behind the wheel. Whatever, I guess."

"Your mom loves you, Nick."

"I know, Ash. I really do. But there's a difference between love and ownership and suffocation, you know?"

"Better than most," he mumbled under his breath. There was so much sincere sympathy and anger in his tone that it made Nick pause.

"Your mom, too?"

Acheron laughed, flashing a tiny bit of fang. "No. My parents weren't around when I was a kid. I was raised by strangers."

Those words startled him. Ash rarely spoke about his past to anyone. "What was *that* like?"

Ash shrugged. "It was like being raised by strangers . . . People who don't care what happens to you and who never have your best interests at heart. Mostly, it was really lonely."

Yeah, he supposed it was. "So you never saw your parents at all?"

"Nope."

"Did they die?"

Ash snorted. "It's a long story, Nick, and not a happy one, which is why I try not to talk about it. And it's why I have a hard time whenever you bitch about a smothering mother I'd have sold my soul to grow up with. I know Cherise is hard on you at times, but there's a difference between someone who's genuinely worried about you and your future, and someone who's punishing you for their own interests and perverse pleasure. Trust me."

He'd never thought of it that way. "I'm sorry, Ash."

"Don't be. No matter how bad you think your life is, there is always someone out there with a story to make yours look grand in comparison. At least the people who were cruel to me weren't really family. In my opinion, it would've been a lot worse if they had been the people who were supposed to love and protect me from harm."

Nick nodded. "Sometimes, Ash, you irritate me. But honestly, I really appreciate the way you put things in perspective. It helps, you know?"

"That's the one good thing about living so long . . . it definitely gives you time to reflect and see things you miss when you're being assaulted with problems and are trying to get through a very finite life span." Ash stepped back. "So where's her car?"

"Canal Place."

Ash fell in beside him as they walked over to the parking lot where he and Casey had left the car.

"This was not the way this was supposed to turn out," Nick said as he unlocked the car doors.

"That's true of most days. So are you driving or me?"

Nick laughed. "I've had enough excitement for one day, Ash. I don't think my heart could handle a trip through evening traffic with you behind the wheel."

Grinning, Ash folded himself into the car while Nick got in and started it.

As he drove toward Casey's house, the day's events kept replaying in his head. But the one thing that he fixated on was how close he'd come to really killing Alan and Tyree. Yeah, he'd killed zombies, but they weren't living people, and he'd banished demons, but . . .

"What's it like, Ash?"

"What's what like?"

Nick swallowed hard as he forced himself to ask what he needed to have an answer to. "Killing someone."

Acheron hesitated as if reliving something brutal in his own past. "It sucks. For both of you. Especially the first time." He paused for a second before he continued. "Savitar has a saying . . ."

Nick had never met Savitar, but from the way Acheron talked about him, he assumed the ancient being had been some kind of mentor to Ash over the centuries. And an extremely powerful one at that.

"When you first take someone's life, two people die. The person you just killed and the human being you used to be. You're never the same after that—it changes you forever and not in a good way—and no matter how hard you try, you can't go back to the innocence you had. Ever."

Nick turned left as he considered that. "So who was your first?"

"My brother."

Nick gasped at that most unexpected answer. Ash? Fratricide? Had he heard that correctly?

Surely not. Ash was a good guy. He would never take his own brother's life. Would he?

No, not unless there was a *really* good reason for it.

"What was that?" He glanced over to Ash, whose face was completely stoic. "Why? How? Was it an accident?"

Ash let out a long, tired sigh. "Not an accident at all. Purely and ruthlessly meditated. I stabbed him while he was asleep in his bed."

That hit Nick like a punch to his breadbasket. "How old were you?"

"Not much older than you are . . . Just a baby with a bad temper."

Chills ran over him at the harshness of killing someone while he slept. Man, that was cold, and it was so out of Acheron's character. "Why would you do something like that?"

Ash made a bitter sound before he answered. "You wouldn't believe me if I told you. . . . Luckily, even though he died, they brought him back. But it didn't matter. What I did was inexcusable. And in my heart, I knew I had killed my own brother for what was basically my own selfish reasons and jealousy. That I had looked right into his eyes when he awoke in pain, and I saw the shock, fear, and horror he felt as his life drained out of him and his warm blood covered my hand. I can still feel it sometimes . . . along with the shame and disgust I had as I realized I wasn't the person I thought myself to be. In that one awful moment, I saw myself for what I really was—a heartless animal who deserved nothing but hatred. The reasons didn't matter. They still don't. And death, even when necessary and justified, will haunt you forever."

Nick tried to imagine the emotions Ash was talking about, but really he couldn't. And honestly, he was grateful for that mercy. There were some experiences no one needed to have.

"What about the Daimons you kill?" They were the demons who stole human souls to elongate their lives. If a Dark-Hunter didn't find and kill the Daimon, the stolen human soul would die and be lost forever, giving their victim eternal torment. The only way to save the human soul was to kill the Daimon before they totally devoured it. "Surely you don't care about killing them."

"Nick . . . they are still living, breathing people and they don't deserve the curse Apollo gave them over something their ancient ancestors did. They have families and friends they love, who love them back. People who will be torn apart by grief when they're gone. Every sentient creature has plans and hopes for their future. And every one of them will look at you with terror in their eyes as they realize that the life they cherished is over and that they will never again see the people they love. It doesn't matter how warranted their death is, you will still feel like shit afterwards, and wonder what kind of monster you are for doing what you did."

Ash ground his teeth. "Whatever deserved hatred or indignation you hold toward them, or the heady rush of adrenaline that comes when it's self-defense and you have no choice . . . it will wither beneath the tsunami of your guilt and self-loathing. In time, if you're lucky, you will make peace with your actions, and while you're awake, you might even convince your conscience that your actions saved others and were completely justified and sanctioned. But at night, when you're asleep, or any time your unguarded thoughts travel without you, you will be haunted by their eyes and faces, and by the knowledge that your life was bought at the expense of theirs. . . . And *that*, little brother, will eat at you forever."

"Is that why Kyrian seldom sleeps?"

"It's why none of us sleep for very long."

Nick gripped the wheel as he tried to come to terms with everything he'd learned and everything that had happened tonight. But what disturbed him was the fear that he wouldn't always have the same humanity Acheron spoke of once the Malachai took him over. He just couldn't see his heartless father being haunted by anything. "Do you think that's true of demons, too? Of the Daimons who kill humans?"

"I know it's true, Nick. And while there are rare exceptions of barbaric creatures who are truly without conscience or compassion, most are not."

"But what if you're born broken? What if your genes are so tainted that you have no choice except to be a killer?"

Ash shook his head wearily. "You have got to quit fixating on this, Nick. We all have a choice. Believe me. I was born out of the darkest corner of hell and inside me lives a vengeful beast that wants to lash out and destroy everything it touches, without hesitation or prejudice."

That news floored him. Was it true?

"But you're always so calm and relaxed."

"I've learned to hide it well. But it doesn't mean that it's not there, just below the calm surface, salivating for the nearest jugular. . . . You are not your father, little brother. You will never be like him."

If only he could make Ash's conviction his own. "You're the only one who thinks that."

"It doesn't matter what other people think. The only opinion that really matters is yours. We are all the writers of our lives. We can make our stories comedies or tragedies. Tales of horror, or of inspiration. *Your* attitude and *your* fortitude and courage are what determine your destiny, Nick. . . . Life is hard and it sucks for all. Every person you meet is waging his or her own war against a callous universe that is plotting against them. And we are all battle-weary. But in the midst of our hell, there is always something we can hold on to, whether it's a dream of the future or a memory of the past, or a warm hand that soothes us. We just have to take a moment during the fight to remember that we're not alone, and that we're not just fighting for ourselves. We're fighting for the people we love."

"Do you really believe that?"

Ash laughed bitterly. "Most of the time. But, admittedly, there are many other times when I think I'm as full of bullshit as you do."

Nick grinned even though he hated the way Acheron could see into his thoughts. "I appreciate the honesty."

"Anytime."

He paused as he let Ash's words play through his thoughts for a minute. But for better or worse, he kept coming back to one basic fear. . . . "Ash, do you know what keeps me up at night?"

"At your age, I'd imagine thoughts of scantily clad women."

Nick snorted. "How very stereotypical of you."

"Hey, I was your age once, and I've known a lot more of us over the centuries. But honestly, I do know what you're thinking. And I know what you hide from others. Deep inside, in places we don't want to admit to owning, those of us who have sperm donors instead of fathers wish that once, just once, they would look at us like a father is supposed to look at his kid. That they would be proud to call us their children. And alongside that bitter desire we hate ourselves for feeling comes the fear that we're going to be just like them one day, and that our children will hate us the way we hate them."

"Yeah. Exactly. I don't want to be my father."

"You don't have to be . . . there's a scene in *The Iliad* that—"

"The what?"

"I weep at the modern educational system," Ash said under his breath. Then louder, "It's a story written by a man named Homer about the Trojan War."

"Oh, I know that."

Ash inclined his head to him. "There's a scene in *The Iliad* when Hector is about to leave for battle where he's talking to his wife, Andromache, and he reaches for their son, Scamandrius, who recoils from him because he doesn't recognize his father while Hector is dressed in his armor. Hector laughs, then removes his helm and puts it on the ground so that Scamandrius can see his face. Then he soothes his son and prays aloud for him. . . .

"*'Zeus, all you other gods, grant that this child, my son, may become, like me, preeminent among the Trojans, as strong and brave as me. Grant that he may rule Troy with strength. May people someday say, as he returns from war, 'This man is far better than his father.'*

"*That*, Nick, is what everyone should strive for . . . not to be the same as our sperm donors, but better. Your father has shown you what you don't want to be. Now it's up to you to take the lessons he's taught you and use them to do better. We should all try to leave the world a better place than what we found when we got here."

Nick fell silent at those words for several minutes. That was what he wanted. When he died, he didn't want the world to be glad to have him out of it. "Is that what happened with you?"

"That is for the world to decide. But I can tell you this. I try and I do my best every day. In the end, that's all we can do."

Nick considered that for the rest of the way as he navigated traffic.

He parked the car in front of Casey's house. There wasn't a light on inside the sprawling mansion at all. It looked completely deserted. "Do you think her parents have been notified?"

Ash went still as if he were listening to the ether. After a few seconds, he nodded. "They're on their way to her."

Good. He knew firsthand how awful it was to be alone in a hospital. No one should be stuck like that.

Getting out of the car, he locked the door, then retrieved his stuff from the trunk.

Nick hesitated. "Where do you think I should put the keys?"

"Under the mat on the front porch. You can text her and let her know where they are."

"You're brilliant."

Ash broke out with a cocky grin. "I know."

Laughing, Nick did what he said. He was on his way back to the street when a weird wave went through him. He thought he'd imagined it until he saw the way Ash stood on the pathway, tense and alert.

Completely still.

"You felt that, didn't you?" Nick whispered.

Ash gave a subtle nod.

"What is it?"

"I'm not sure." Ash moved closer to Nick as if to protect him. "And honestly, Nick, that's what concerns me. It's not often I don't have an answer."

You should have killed him. . . .

Those echoing words came like a subtle breeze that was so light, Nick wasn't sure it was real.

You have to take your place. . . .

"Do you hear that?" he asked Ash.

"Hear what?"

The air around them went perfectly still. Like standing in the eye of a hurricane.

Before Nick could react, Acheron used his powers to teleport them from Casey's house, into Nick's bedroom in his condo. The quickness of it disoriented Nick to the point that he thought he'd hurl.

Choking on bile, he forced his stomach to back

down. "Next time, warn a brother before you snatch him around, Ash. That stuff's harsh and I'd hate to barf on your expensive boots."

"Yeah, and I'd hate to have to kill you for it, too."

Nick started to respond until he looked up and realized that for once Acheron wasn't wearing his opaque sunglasses. He was immediately assaulted by two simultaneous and shocking truths about his friend.

One . . . without those sunglasses on, Acheron was absolutely beautiful. His every feature was perfectly sculpted like a major work of art.

But what really slapped him hardest was Acheron's eyes. There was nothing human about them. They swirled with a deep glowing silver . . . like mercury in a centrifuge. Nick had never seen or heard of anything like them. Those weren't the black, light-sensitive eyes of a Dark-Hunter.

They were the eyes of something far more powerful and ancient.

"Dude," Nick breathed. "What's the deal with your eyes?"

The sunglasses returned immediately to cover them. "Sorry about that. You okay?"

No, he wasn't. "What are you, Ash? Really?"

"The last of my kind on this earth. You know that."

Yeah, but . . . "Did all Atlanteans have eyes like yours?"

"No."

"Why do they swirl?"

A tic started in Ash's jaw, letting him know that Ash was extremely self-conscious about them . . . which must be why he always kept them covered no matter how dark it was.

"Why are your eyes blue, Nick? Bad genetics. Your eyes are as much an anomaly as mine. Just more people happen to share your mutation."

Suddenly, he felt bad for saying anything. "I'm sorry, Ash. If you want the truth, though, I think they're cool as all get-out. Can I see them again?"

"I'm not a specimen in a museum, hung on a wall for your amusement."

"I didn't mean it that way."

Ash held his hand up in irritation. "I know, Nick. I do. But I've taken a lot of grief over them through the centuries. You've no idea . . . and it is a serious hot button for me."

And Ash wasn't as calm as he appeared. Nick made a mental note of what he'd said in the car about his temper. Whatever he did, he didn't want to push Ash over the edge.

"I still think they're awesome."

"That's because you haven't had to deal with the negative aspects of a deformity people have never understood."

In that moment, Nick had an epiphany of what Ash's childhood must have been like. Ancient societies had been even less tolerant of people who were different than modern-day high schools. And for whatever reason, Ash had been raised without his parents to protect him.

Oh yeah, his past s-u-c-k-e-d.

"Did your brother have eyes like you?"

Ash shook his head. "His eyes were the same color as yours . . . it was how people told us apart at a glance."

Oh yeah . . . That's right. Ash had told him that he was a twin, but Nick had forgotten that. "Is that why you hated him?"

"No, and I'll let you in on a secret. I never really hated my brother. I hated myself, and I took that out on him, and I blamed him for things that weren't his fault any more than they were mine. When you're in that kind of extreme mental anguish and absolute agony that you can't escape no matter what you try, you turn your hatred outward, because it's a lot easier to focus your hatred on someone you don't have to look at in the mirror. And my brother was just an easy person to blame since he was everything I wanted to be—respected, intelligent, skilled, a natural leader—and I couldn't stand that I walked in his shadow as a lesser being."

Nick scowled. "You tell me these things and I just can't wrap my head around them. You're Acheron Parthenopaeus—the baddest of asses . . . the feared and beloved leader of an army of immortal protectors. You're wealthy beyond dreams and you have the most epic powers of anyone I've ever heard of. I'd kill to have one tenth of your looks and build. How could you *ever* look at yourself and find a flaw? Seriously?"

"Because I'm not the same person now that I was when I was human. I've changed in ways you can't begin to imagine, and in the end, what I've learned is that childhood is what you spend your entire adulthood trying to get over. And when it's a bad one, no amount of success or wealth will ease the vicious, hating voices that linger long after your tormentors are dead and buried. You carry that hate with you everywhere you go. It's why I keep telling you not to listen to the ones who attack you. Don't get that never-ending soundtrack started. It's the most self-destructive thing you can do to yourself."

Those heartfelt words withered something inside Nick, but not in a bad way. They reached him in a way nothing else ever had before. "Ash?"

"Yeah?"

Nick cleared his throat. "Do not . . . and I mean *do . . . not . . .* take this the wrong way, okay?" He wrapped his arms around Ash and hugged him. "I will always be your brother," he whispered in Ash's ear. "And I won't ever hate you."

Only then did Ash hug him back, and it was awkward enough to let him know that Ash had neither given nor received many hugs in his extremely long life. "You're such a strange kid, Nick."

Laughing, Nick released him. "So everyone tells me. But I like being strange and different . . . most days anyway."

Ash gave him a sad smile. "You have a great heart. Don't ever let life change that."

"I don't plan to."

But even as he spoke those words, Nick had a bad feeling that his change wasn't ultimately in his hands. That fate would move forward whether he wanted it to or not. Ambrose had tried and tried to keep him from morphing into the Malachai.

Each time he'd failed.

According to his future self, this was their last shot to save all of them. No more do-overs.

If Nick screwed up again . . .

His mom, Bubba, Caleb, Kyrian, and everyone he

held dear would die. He and Ash could become bitter enemies.

And Nick would destroy the entire world and everyone in it.

That thought had barely finished before he heard a blood-chilling scream echo from the living room.

CHAPTER 13

N<i>ick!"</i>

That scream shredded Nick's nervous system like an electrical torture device as he ran from his bedroom to the living room with Ash one step behind him. From the shrill tone and raw panic in it, he was expecting to find blood on the walls and at least ten or twelve dozen armed men attacking his mother.

So the sight of her wailing alone in the living room brought him to a stop so sudden, Ash collided with him. Terrified he'd missed something in his haste, he turned around frantically, trying to find the demons or whatever had her so torn up.

But they were the only ones in the room.

Without warning, she grabbed him into the tightest hug he'd ever had. Dang, for a tiny woman, she was strong.

"Ma, you're killing me. I can't breathe."

Instead of her loosening her hold, she tightened it more as she cried against his chest.

He looked helplessly at Acheron.

To his credit, Ash didn't react at all to his mother's insane hysteria. With a nonchalance Nick envied, Ash tucked his hands into his jacket pockets. "Call me crazy, but I'm assuming by all of this that she heard about your little incident tonight."

Stepping back, she cupped Nick's face in her hands and turned his head from side to side to inspect it. "Are you hurt at all, baby?"

"I think you might have bruised a rib or two just now."

She rolled her eyes irritably. "Not from me, boy! When that animal attacked you. Did he hurt you?"

"No. I'm all right."

She glared at the blood on his clothes. "Who was bleeding?"

"Not me. Promise." Much, anyway.

Only then did she release him and go to Acheron. She grabbed him in an equally fierce hug even though she barely came up to his waist. "Thank you so much for seeing my baby home and staying with him until I got here."

Wow, Ash looked even more uncomfortable and un-certain with Nick's mom holding him than he'd been when Nick hugged him a few minutes ago. That man really wasn't used to open affection. He reminded Nick of a puppy being held by a small child. While he tolerated it, it was obvious he'd rather be getting a root canal or colonoscopy.

With a ragged breath, she let go of Ash and turned back to Nick, who stepped away before she seized him again in that tight anaconda grip. "That's it," she snapped. "Tomorrow you're getting your license, and I won't hear any argument from you about it. I'm not having you walk anywhere else, ever again. From now on, you drive my car anywhere you need to go and that includes school, you hear me?"

Was she nuts? It would take him twice as long to drive to school, and then he'd most likely have to park even farther away than what their condo was. "Ma, it's just around the corner."

"I don't care. It's not worth the chance." She broke down into more tears.

Cringing, but knowing he had to do something to calm her down, Nick forced himself into her anacondic hug range and held her against him so she could squeeze all the blood to his head. He looked helplessly at Acheron.

Ash shrugged. "Don't cut those pernicious eyes at me, kid. Kyrian's the one who had the mom and all the sisters. Maybe he can tell you what to do for her. I'm clueless."

"Oh stop. Both of you." His mom stepped back and pressed her hands against her face as she finally calmed down. "I'm well aware of the fact that I'm a basket case, okay? I can't help it. Neither of you has any idea what it does to a parent to find out something bad happened to your baby when you weren't there to help them. It's like the universe sucks all the air out of your lungs and you can't breathe again until you see for yourself that they're okay. It's an unimaginable hell."

"I'm not saying anything, Mrs. Gautier. I have no problem with your mothering at all. More power to you."

Nick held his hands up in surrender. "Stupid ain't on my forehead and I don't want to get grounded. Cry all you want, Mom. Anytime."

She let out a sound of supreme irritation and then scowled at Nick's new clothes. "What are you wearing?"

Nick looked down as a bad feeling went through him. With all the crap that had happened, he'd completely forgotten to change.

I am screwed. . . .

"Clothes," he said hesitantly.

Not his smoothest comeback. It was like throwing a grenade in a nitroglycerine factory. "Whose clothes?"

"Mine."

"And where did you get them?"

"Store."

She hissed in anger, making his stomach shrink tight in Pavlovian expectation of her overreaction. "Nick, you look like some lowlife hoodlum up to no good and out to get into trouble! Good boys don't wear solid black on the street. For that matter, why don't you just grow your hair down your back and pierce your ears and other body parts so that everyone will think you're nothing but no-account trash with no one who cares about you?"

Horrified by her tirade, Nick cut his eyes to Acheron, who was swathed in black from head to toe and whose hair fell to the center of his back. Not to mention the earring in his left lobe and the small stud in his right nostril.

Ash was the poster boy of what his mom had just condemned. . . .

His mom's entire face flamed as she realized what she'd inadvertently said and implied about his friend. She turned to face him. "I didn't mean it that way, Ash."

Ash gave her a kind smile. "No offense taken, Mrs. Gautier. I've been called a lot worse and that was just a couple of hours ago."

Still, his mother was mortified by her insensitive comments. "I have never, ever thought that about you. I know you're a good man and I did not mean to imply otherwise."

"Really, it's fine. I'm not offended in the least," he reiterated. "I dress like I do because I want people to leave me alone and cross the street when they see me coming. Everything you said to Nick about other people's perceptions is correct and I back you one hundred percent."

"It was still thoughtless and cruel, and I would never hurt you that way, Ash."

"I know."

Her features sad, she reached up and pulled Ash's face down to hers, then kissed his cheek. "I think the world of you, and I'm glad you're Nick's friend."

"Thank you . . . and on that note, I'm going to make myself scarce so that you can finish reaming your son without worrying about feelings I don't have." He grinned at her, then looked over to Nick. "I'll see you tomorrow, slick. Try not to get into any more trouble between now and then."

"Later."

His mom didn't speak until after Ash was gone, then she turned on him with a look that made him want to hold a crucifix up in front of his face to banish the evil coming toward him. "Now explain those clothes, boy, and what's this I heard at work from Alex Peltier about you joining a band? A band, Nicky? Really?"

He shrugged. "It's harmless, Mom. I thought I'd try something new."

"Then try taking out the trash without me having to nag you for it. Make up my bed for me in the morning. Scrub out the tub and lower the toilet seat. I can think of a thousand things new you can do that wouldn't make me want to spank you even though you dwarf me."

"Mom . . . c'mon. I don't mean to be rude, but you're really overreacting to this. You know Alex and his entire family. He's as clean-cut and upstanding as they come. I'm just playing the drums for him. It's no big deal. As for my clothes . . . I hate those tacky used Hawaiian shirts, and I've told you that for years. Ash, Caleb and Kyrian, and Dev and dozens of other people wear black all the time. No one thinks anything about it. Really."

She narrowed her gaze on him. "I want better for you, Boo. I spent my entire youth with people looking down on me and calling me trash."

"I was there with you for it, Mom. I heard them, too. And I know exactly how you felt, and I promise you that those god-awful shirts you've forced me to wear have not spared me the wrath or insults of my fellow morons. If I have to be insulted, please let me do it in Dolce and Gabbana, and real suede loafers, rather than backyard tacky wear."

Biting her lip, she nodded. "Okay. You're right. You're sixteen, and you have your own job that pays good money you work hard for. As much as I hate it, you are a man and not my little baby boy boo anymore. I just . . ." She broke off into a small sob.

He pulled her into his arms and held her tight. "It's okay. I'm still your baby boy boo, but I don't want the rest of the world calling me that. Just you."

She laughed and squeezed him tight. "We're a pair, aren't we?"

"Two peas, you and me, as snug as bugs in a rug," he said, quoting one of her favorite sayings from his childhood. Anytime he'd been sick or had felt bad about something, she'd scooped him into her lap and whispered that to him while she made him feel better.

God, he loved his mom so much. . . .

She sank her hand in his hair, then let go. "Have you eaten anything?"

"No, ma'am. I was on my way for food when . . ." He stopped as he realized what he was about to say. The last thing he wanted to do was start her crying again.

To his relief, she held it together. "I'll go warm up something good for you."

"Thanks, Mom. I'll be in there in a second. First, I'm going to change into something without blood-stains."

She growled at him. "You're *not* funny."

Without commenting on that, he returned to his room to find Caleb standing just inside his closed window. Sucking his breath in sharply, he quickly shut the door before his mom caught a glimpse of their home invader and had another hissy. "What are you doing here, C?"

"Checking on you."

Nick scowled. Surely Caleb didn't know about the mugging . . . did he? "Why?"

Caleb pushed himself away from the window and went to Nick's desk. He pulled out the chair and straddled it. "Something weird is happening. . . . Your father's dying."

While he didn't have a lot of feelings for his dad, that news shocked him. "What?"

Caleb nodded slowly. "He's in bad shape. Are you the one killing him?"

"No!" he said emphatically. "What kind of fool question is that? Why would you let that thought even enter your head? Jeez!"

Caleb leaned forward to prop his arms across the back of the chair. "Because the only thing I know that can kill him is *you*." He paused and then frowned as he noted Nick's rumpled clothes. "Why are you covered in blood?"

"Real swift on the uptake there, Sparky. Glad I wasn't hemorrhaging on the floor, needing help. With those keen powers of observation you possess, I'd have died ten minutes ago."

Caleb snorted. "Don't worry, punkin. I'd have cauterized the wound for you long before you bled out."

"And you'd probably enjoy it, too."

Caleb flashed a grin. "Not as much as I'd enjoy drinking your blood, but . . ." He sobered. "What really happened?"

"I got mugged at the Riverwalk."

He let out a low whistle. "By a demon? A Daimon? Couch potato?"

Nick shook his head. "Humans. Alan and Tyree. They didn't recognize me until after they had dropped a bead on me."

Both of Caleb's eyebrows shot north. "Are they still alive?"

"Alan is. Not sure about Tyree. I shot at him with Alan's gun, and he ran off."

After rising from the chair, Caleb closed the distance between them and grabbed Nick's jaw in a fierce grip.

"Hey!" he snapped, trying to push him back.

He wouldn't loosen his hold at all. After a minute, he sighed in relief and let Nick go. "He's alive."

Yeah, okay, that was a little creepy.

Nick rubbed at his now sore jaw. "How do you know?"

"You're still yourself. If you'd killed a human, even by accident, and especially with malice, the Malachai would be in the process of devouring all your humanity."

Nick gaped. "You're just now telling me this?"

"It hasn't been an issue until now. But with your father weak, it wouldn't take much to convert you over."

Nick was sickened by the thought. But at least it clarified one thing that had worried him. "So that's why my blood turned blackish in the fight. . . ."

Caleb snapped to full attention. "What was that?"

Nick lifted his hand to show him his busted knuckles. "While we were fighting and I wanted to kill Alan, my skin changed and my blood darkened. It was really creepy and gross."

Caleb cursed under his breath. "We have a *bad* situation here."

"How so?"

He saw the hesitation in Caleb's dark eyes. After a minute, he let out a slow, tired breath. "I'm not going to lie to you, Nick. Your father has royally screwed me, and I have no idea why I'm surprised by it. . . . But you remember when I told you that I'd have my freedom when he dies?"

"Yeah?"

"He's bound me to his powers."

Bemused, Nick wondered why Caleb was so upset about that. "I don't understand."

Caleb returned to his chair. "When a demon is enslaved, we are tied to our master's life force. But a Malachai is a different kind of beast. Unlike others, their powers and life force are two separate, living things, so a Malachai can bind a demon to his lifetime or to the life of his powers. When he does the latter—"

Nick sucked his breath in sharply as he caught up to Caleb's ire. "You will be enslaved to whatever takes over my father's powers."

Caleb touched his finger to the tip of his nose in a silent salute to Nick's correct answer. "And because he has charged me with watching over you these past few years, I know who you are and where you live and sleep."

"Yeah, so?"

"Nick . . . Think about it for a second. Go that extra step, past the obvious. If my next master bids me to bring you to him so that he can drain you, too, I will

SHERRILYN KENYON

have no choice but to follow his orders and hurt you. . . . I will never again be free, and so long as I live, I am a *huge* threat to you. Now do you get it?"

He considered Caleb's predicament a second, then came up with another alternative. "But if I take my father's powers, I can free you, right?"

Caleb shook his head. "It doesn't work that way. Because of what Adarian did, I am and will forever be enslaved . . . unless the creature holding his powers is utterly destroyed."

"Even if you die first?"

There was no missing the thick bitterness in Caleb's dark eyes. "You know how Dark-Hunters turn into Shades when they die and live in eternal hell and misery?"

"Yeah?"

Caleb inclined his head. "Bingo. They're not the only ones."

Nick groaned in sympathetic pain for him. How awful. "Why would he do that to you? What'd you do?"

"He's the Malachai, Nick. He's completely incapable of caring about anyone or anything. I'm his tool and he did this to motivate me to find whatever is weakening him and kill it so that I won't become their property. . . . *But* if *you* kill him while he's weak, I won't stop you from it."

276

He made it sound so easy, but Nick knew better. "Caleb—"

Caleb lifted his hand to cut his argument off. "I know, Nick. It's a risk for you. But either way, we're both screwed. You cannot afford for whatever is killing him to get his powers and then come after you. You won't be able to survive their attack."

Raking his hands through his hair, Nick tried his best to think of something else, but he couldn't. More than that, he kept coming back to one simple truth. "I'm not ready to be a Malachai."

Caleb laid his head down on his folded arms. "We could try to bind your father's powers as he dies. To lock them down so that they don't hit you all at once. That way, we could take our time training you and expose you to them individually."

Nick was highly suspicious. "Can it be done?"

"In theory."

He let out a high-pitched half laugh. "Theory, Caleb? Are you high? I don't like that word. What if something goes wrong?"

"What if it goes right?"

"Oh yeah, that's helpful . . . thanks, Cay. Throw some optimistic possibility into my face, why don't you? 'Cause as we both know from much experience, nothing I try *ever* goes wrong."

"Cut the sarcasm, Gautier." Caleb sighed. "You're right. Everything you touch goes nuclear in ways we never foresee."

Nick nodded in agreement. But in the end, he knew that Caleb was right. If, God forbid, something else took control of Caleb's slavery, Nick wouldn't stand a chance against him.

And it wasn't just that. Caleb was his friend. The demon had bled for him, multiple times. There weren't many people Nick would put at his back.

Caleb was about it. And he wouldn't hesitate to trust him. Ever.

"All right, Cay. Let's say we try this your way. What would we have to do to bind my powers?"

A light of hope shined in Caleb's dark eyes. "Don't play with me, Nick. Not about this."

Nick was aghast. "You know, we are friends. At least that's how *I* think of *you*. Do you honestly believe I would be able to live with myself if I let someone hurt you after all you've done for me? Gee, thanks for the love, Malphas."

Caleb rose slowly from the chair and moved to stand in front of him. The expression on his face said that he couldn't even conceive of real friendship. That in his world, it was the most alien concept he knew. "I don't know what to say to that . . . I haven't had a friend since before human time began. At least not one who wouldn't hesitate to betray me to save their own skin. And with you being a Malachai . . ."

"I'm not just a Malachai, Caleb. I'm a Gautier first and foremost, and Gautiers take care of their family. Always. And until you give me reason to think otherwise, we are brothers."

Caleb froze as he heard a word no one had applied to him since the day he'd buried his wife.

Family. In his world, with the exception of Lilliana, family had just meant they were the first to offer you up as a sacrifice for whatever selfish thing they wanted.

And as he stared into Nick's sincere gaze, he realized that he considered Nick a brother, too. That he would die to protect him. Not because Adarian had ordered it.

Because he finally believed Kody was right.

Nick wasn't like the others before him. He had a soul and a heart. He cared about other people.

Against all odds and genetics, Nick was decent.

Caleb held his hand up to him. "Brothers in arms?"

"Brothers in arms," Nick said, taking his hand and shaking on it. "Now, what do we need to do this?"

"Honestly? One hell of a miracle."

Nick actually laughed at that. "Hey, boy, what are you? Blind?" He tapped at the religious medallion he always wore around his neck. "I'm Catholic. Miracles are our specialty."

Caleb wished he shared Nick's optimism about that. But as Nick had pointed out, everything they touched together blew back on them. And while he was grateful Nick was at least willing to try, there was a really good chance that they both could die while trying to bind a Malachai's powers.

To his knowledge, there had never been a Malachai who was half human. In the past, they had always bred with demons, gods, and other preternatural beings. Creatures who had the strength and the stamina to withstand the weight of a Malachai's preternatural strength. At least in the beginning.

But in time, one by one, they had all gone insane with it and become the worst sort of monster.

"Nick?" Cherise called from the kitchen. "Your food's getting cold, baby."

"Coming, Mom," Nick said before he turned to face Caleb. "When do we do this?"

"As fast as we can. I don't know how soon the creature who's draining Adarian's power will strike. We have to kill him before they do."

Nick swallowed at those words, especially after what Ash had told him about killing someone.

And they had been talking about strangers then. . . .

Would Nick *really* be able to execute his own father? Granted, they weren't close, but . . .

It was his dad.

His doubt was swallowed by the memory of what had possessed him when he'd confronted Alan. He'd not only been capable of it, he'd been relishing Alan's pleas and cries of pain. Something that truly sickened him.

Conceived in violence to do violence.

Afraid of the destiny he was about to willingly step into, Nick reached up to rub his mother's St. Nicholas medallion that she'd given him for Confirmation. The saint he'd been named for. While most folks only knew St. Nick as Santa Claus, Nick's mom had made sure that he well understood why she'd named him for the medieval bishop. The name itself meant *victory of the people.* And St. Nicholas was the designated patron saint and guardian of children, women, innocents, and those who sought justice, and refuge from storms, as well as safe passage home.

May St. Nicholas hold the tiller.

Through the darkest nights and most dangerous of storms, St. Nicholas guide me safely back to the light and security of my family. . . .

And he would find his way home. There was no way he'd allow his father's powers to corrupt or change him.

Nick clenched the medallion in his fist. *I will not fail in this.* While he might be a Malachai, he was also a guardian. Somehow, he was going to defy the odds that condemned him. And he would save the lives of those he loved.

He would.

Demonic laughter filled his head. *Believe your lies, Malachai. But I will feast on your heart and use your powers to slaughter the very things you're trying to protect, starting with your mother.*

You don't stand a chance. . . .

CHAPTER 14

"You ready for this?"

Nick jumped at the sound of Ash's voice in his room. He'd expected Caleb to be waiting for him after dinner. Instead, it was the Atlantean. "Jeez, you scared the crap out of me! What are you doing here?"

Ash held his hand up. There was a small piece of plastic between two fingers that he wiggled back and forth. "Didn't think you'd want to wait."

Nick frowned. "On what?"

Laughing, Ash held the card out to him. "You don't play this game right."

Nick took the plastic, then glanced down. He did a double take before he gaped at Ash. "No way!"

"You're a Squire, slick. We tend to pull a few strings for you guys, and there's no chance on this planet that I'm going to spend hours waiting at the DMV for you to get called and then possibly fail. I've done my time in hell. No more."

Still, Nick couldn't believe it. He held the license up to check it against the light. It looked authentic. . . . It even had a bad picture of him in a tacky shirt. "Is this real?"

"Absolutely. But the one drawback is if your mom changes her mind about you driving, it will be revoked. Until then, welcome to the world of grown-up responsibility."

Nick could shout he was so excited. "This is so awesome. Thank you!"

"No problem." Ash turned as if he was going to leave, then stopped. "By the way, you probably want to meet me outside for a few minutes."

"Okay. I'll be right out."

Ash vanished while Nick went to ask his mom if he could run a couple of errands.

"Don't be gone too long."

"Won't. Promise." Nick left her on the couch and headed down to the street.

It took him a second to find Ash, who was a little ways down by a set of parked cars.

"So what do you need me to do?" Nick asked.

Ash handed him a set of car keys. "Just don't hurt yourself, or anyone else."

Nick scowled. Ash talked in more riddles than Nashira did. "Huh?"

Laughing, Ash shook his head and stepped back. He indicated the silver Jag he'd used for most of Nick's driving lessons. "It's all yours, kid. Enjoy."

No way . . .

Nick couldn't have been more stunned had Ash pimp-slapped him. In fact, he'd have expected that over this. But there was one small problem. . . . "You know my mom won't let me accept this, right?"

"It's a company car, for your personal use. Kyrian's name is on the lease, but you're listed as the primary driver on the insurance. When you graduate, we'll sign it over to you."

Letting out a loud whoop, Nick threw himself against Ash and hugged him. "I love you, man! You're the best!"

Ash clapped him on the back. "I'll see you later, kid." He headed for Ursulines.

"Hey, Ash?"

He turned to look back at Nick.

"Really . . . thank you!"

"Anytime. Just stay out of trouble."

A sick feeling settled in his stomach as he watched Ash vanish into the darkness. *Stay out of trouble. . . .*

That had always been his plan, but trouble kept tackling him to the ground and sitting on his chest.

"Hey, what's going on?"

He jumped at the sound of Caleb's voice behind him. "Ash just gave me the keys to the car he's been training me on." He grinned like a moron. "I can drive!"

"It's not all it's cracked up to be."

Nick slid the keys into his pocket, along with his license. "Now I get to find out, don't I?"

"You do, indeed." Caleb inclined his head toward the street. "You ready to do this?"

"Yeah, just don't kill me tonight. I've got places to drive to later."

"Like where?"

"No idea."

Caleb laughed, then led the way over to Royal Street. They stopped in front of a store with long green shutters. Caleb had assured him that this store would have everything they needed to bind Nick's powers so that they didn't overwhelm him. . . . Erzulie's Authentic Voodoo. His first impression of it was that it looked incredibly pink and purple, and extremely mainstream.

Frowning, he turned his head to Caleb. "How long has this store been here?"

Caleb shrugged. "It was here when I arrived in New Orleans."

How weird. "So it's been here for years. . . ."

"Yeah, why?"

"I've never seen it before." And it was less than a block from Bubba's Triple B and just down the street from his school. Not to mention, it was right next door to Sean Kelly's Royal Street Deli where he'd eaten so many times, he couldn't even begin to count them all. He must have walked past this place millions of times. So how had he not known it was here?

Caleb's eyes widened.

That look didn't bode well. "What?" Nick asked as a wave of trepidation filled him.

"Just thinking . . ." Caleb skimmed the street and buildings around them. "If you've never seen this place when it's basically on the corner of St. Ann and Royal where we walk almost every day . . . something had it shielded from you."

"What does that mean?"

"It means that this place will be important to you one day, and that something was trying to keep you away from it."

"Is that a good thing or a bad one?" Nick asked.

"No idea, which is what concerns me most."

Not half as much as it concerned Nick. Unlike Caleb, he had no doubt it would be something bad. That was just the way his luck ran. "Should we leave, then?"

Caleb shook his head. "Can't. I have to have the right supplies for the binding, and some of the ingredients are really rare . . . this is the best place to get them." He stepped past Nick and opened the door.

Nick entered with a great deal of reservation, not sure what to expect of a store the universe hadn't wanted him to see. Part of him expected to burst into flames the minute he crossed the threshold. But somehow he got inside without dying on the spot. He'd been to several Voodoo stores over the years. It was hard to live in New Orleans and not go in one at some point, if for no other reason, mere curiosity.

And this one was both similar and, at the same time, very different. On his left was a large Voodoo altar that encompassed the fireplace and was topped by a purple mantel. On top of the mantel was the typical warning not to touch or photograph the altar as it was a real place of worship.

Over bottles of wine, candles, beads, money, and flowers that people had left on the top shelf as offerings was a huge painting of a light-skinned woman who had a purple snake crawling up her left arm. The sign below identified her as Erzulie—the lwa of love and beauty that the store was named for.

Ah . . . now Nick fully understood the decor. That was why the store was so girly in appearance. . . . The whole place that bore her name paid homage to her. Made sense.

He turned to look around more. The wall on his right was lined with shelves of merchandise. Bottles of oils, spells, poppets, perfumes, lwas, soaps, fetishes, and all other manner of ritual items. There were small round tables with more oils, soaps, and perfumes lined up in the center. The back of the store had a screen and empty table along with two chairs for those people who wanted readings or other private Voodoo services.

A tall, brown-haired woman came out of the back, carrying a corrugated box of new merchandise. Beautiful and filled with grace, she was dressed in a pair of jeans and a purple sweater with bell sleeves. Her blue eyes lit up with joyful friendship as she saw them. "Caleb . . . it's been a while, sweetie. How are you doing?"

"Hey, Ana. Pretty good." He took the box from her hands and carried it to the counter so that he could place it next to her register for her to unpack.

"Thank you so much for the help." Ana paused at the sight of Nick. "Can I help you?"

"He's with me." Caleb gestured between them. "Nick, meet Ana. Ana, Nick."

"Hi," Nick said quietly. There was something about her that was really familiar, but he couldn't place it.

"Bashful. How cute." She turned back to Caleb. "So what can I do for my favorite knowledgeable loon?"

Smiling at her teasing, he indicated the shelves with his thumb. "I need a few things. Mind if I help myself?"

"Go for it, sug. Just let me know if you need any help."

"Will do."

Nick picked up one of the baskets by the altar and handed it to Caleb, who took it to the wall and started filling it with things Nick knew nothing about. While he was trying to learn all of this, there was just so much, and what with school . . .

He one day expected his brain to explode from all the necessary and trivial information he was attempting to cram into it.

As he looked around while he waited for Caleb, he saw a couple of photos near the register. Some were of Voodoo priests and priestesses. But others were of an all-girl family. A *huge* all-girl family. And while he glanced over them, he caught a familiar face.

Was that . . . ?

He stepped closer to make sure it was who he thought, and then his jaw went slack.

Yes . . . yes, it was.

Nick frowned at Ana. "You know Tabitha Devereaux?"

"Of course. She's my niece."

"Really?" He had to catch himself before he said "but you look so normal." After all, the woman did own a Voodoo store, which by its very existence knocked her out of the realm of normality. Still . . . owning this store was a far cry from Tabitha's special breed of scary intensity.

All of a sudden, Nick felt an odd sensation run over his skin. He had no idea what it was, but it made him turn around to see a girl not much older than him coming out of the back. Her brown hair was almost the same color as Ana's and she had a pair of big blue eyes.

"We need more paper towels," she said to Ana. She straightened her top and then slowed her approach as she realized the two of them weren't alone in the store. She looked at Ana curiously.

Ana jerked her chin toward him. "His name's Nick. He knows Tabby. Do you two know each other?"

The girl shook her head before pinning a suspicious glare on Nick. She had a gleam in her eyes that said she was trying to decide what category to put him in.

Scary. Insane. Or friendly.

"Are you one of Tabby's zoo crew?"

Nick had no idea what she meant by that. "Zoo crew?"

"The insane lunatics she runs around with at night,

looking for vampires to stake?" She shook her head at Ana. "I don't know where she gets that from."

'Cause she definitely couldn't get it from the Voodoo side of the family.

But Nick refrained from stating the obvious and having her hex him for it. "No. I'm not a zoo crew loon."

That appeased her. "Ah, good. I'm her older sister, Tiyana, by the way. Nice meeting you."

"Yeah, you too." Sort of. Though to be honest, he was beginning to think their entire family tree was deeply rooted in the lush swamp of weird, idiosyncratic, and insane.

"Hey, Ana?" Caleb asked, intruding on a conversation that had been going nowhere. "Do you have some unused blackberry, thistle, and papoose root in the back?"

"Of course. Do you need valerian, too?"

"No, thanks. We're trying to bind evil, not invite it out to party."

"Glad to hear that. Last kid we had in here . . . Let's just say, people who don't understand the powers they're courting should play Parcheesi in their spare time."

"I couldn't agree more." Caleb dropped another small container in his basket. "I also need at least ten ounces of your 7 African Powers oil and a huge vat of black salt."

She exchanged a wide-eyed stare with Tiyana that said Caleb's order was excessive. "What are you into, boy?" Oh yeah, there was no missing the castigation in her tone or question.

"Not at liberty to say. But don't worry. I really do know what I'm doing."

"I hope so, C. 'Cause I don't want to have to go rescue you from something that requires that much binding." She let out a low whistle before she looked back at Tiyana. "And if you ever mess with something like this . . . both your mother and I will get you."

Tiyana rolled her eyes. "I'm not Tabitha or her twin. Or the psycho named Karma. Please don't confuse us."

Laughing, Ana headed to the back to get what Caleb needed. Nick froze as he reached the end of the high counter and saw a large crystal ball unattended. It pulled him toward it with a lure he couldn't resist. The one power he had that worked best was scrying, and anytime he saw something that reflective, he had to look into it. He placed his hand on the back of the cool surface to help direct the light.

There in the center of the ball, he saw an image of a

slightly older Tiyana having dinner with Ambrose inside a really nice restaurant.

No, not Ambrose . . .

Him. They were laughing and talking in such a way that he knew they were good friends. Or maybe even something more. Was that why the store had been shielded from him?

"Do you go to school with my sisters?" Tiyana asked as she started pricing the items in the box Caleb had carried for her aunt.

It took him a second to break contact with the ball and understand her question. "Um, no. I go to St. Richard's."

She narrowed her gaze on him as if trying to pry information out of his brain without words. "Then how do you know Tabby?"

"Bubba Burdette."

That relaxed her instantly. She wrinkled her nose, then laughed. "I love Bubba . . . he's . . ."

"Unique?"

"Good word." She leaned forward onto the counter and gave him a view down her shirt he was sure she didn't mean to. He quickly averted his gaze to hers as heat crept over his entire face and made his ears burn. "You have the most beautiful pair of blue eyes I've ever seen. I bet girls at your school go crazy all the time over them."

And she would lose that bet. Good thing the girl didn't play poker. "Not really."

She laughed, then, to his instant relief, straightened. "You know, Nick. If I was a few years younger . . ." She winked at him.

Feeling really awkward now and a bit scared by her cougar ways, Nick stepped back, closer to Caleb. *What the heck's going on lately?* he asked Caleb in his head. *Girls are coming on to me everywhere.*

Relax, kid. It's the glamour that comes with your powers. They do that to most of us.

So that was it. Now he understood what had happened with Simi and it made him feel a lot better.

Until he kept thinking about it . . .

He should probably be grateful he had come-do-me powers with women, but he honestly didn't like it at all.

Well, that stinks, Cay. How will I ever know if a woman really likes me?

Easy. It'll be the woman who's immune to it. She won't come on to you. She'll tell you off.

Great. Just what he needed. Someone else criticizing him. *I think I'd rather stick with the ones who are awed by my demonic yet sweet powers of persuasion.*

Caleb snorted at him.

"All right," Ana said as she returned with another box full of stuff. "I think—" She stopped mid-sentence as all the lights went out in the store, bathing them in utter darkness.

Caleb stepped closer to Nick while Ana beelined to her niece to protect her.

"Ana?" Tiyana asked, reaching for her aunt's hand. "Do you feel that?"

"I do. Caleb?"

He set his basket on top of the counter and lowered his head in a way that told Nick he was listening to the ether around them. "Yeah, it's some seriously dark powers and they are looking for someone."

Was it him? Nick knew it had to be, but he was hoping and praying that maybe someone else might be on the menu for once. Ash was in town. . . . It was possible he could have angered something with massive grudge capabilities.

Right?

"I swear it feels like Noir," Ana breathed.

Nick went cold at a name he seriously didn't want to hear. Noir was the ancient god who owned the Malachai—the same god his father was currently hiding from. He glanced to Caleb and pushed his thoughts to him. *I thought he*—Nick couldn't even think Noir's name without feeding the dark god's powers—*was locked down in his realm and couldn't leave.*

He is. His servants aren't.

Oh goody. That meant they could easily be here for him. And he could only imagine what kind of playmates Noir would send out to recover the missing Malachai embryo. Nick had met a couple of them already and had no interest in getting acquainted with any more.

His panic rising, he swallowed hard as the sound of rustling . . . legs or wings or some other ominous body part echoed on the street outside. It made the hair on the back of his neck stand on end.

Caleb ran to the shop's door and locked it tight. All around them, various objects in the store began to glow bright. Like Menyara's symbols in his condo, Ana had thrown protection spells up to keep her store safe from the creatures who would do her or her customers harm.

"Will that hold it off?" Caleb asked Ana.

Ana and her niece exchanged a concerned frown. "It should. But . . ."

I hate buts.

A tic started in Caleb's jaw. "Now's not a good time for a but."

Ana didn't respond verbally. Her eyes, however, grew so wide, it was a wonder they remained in their sockets.

Turning to see what had her so horrified, Nick stepped back as his own terror seized him. The doors and windows began to move like they were breathing. In and out, over and over, with such force that the wood whined under the strain of it. The glass began to crack. The sound went down his spine like nails against a chalkboard.

Then, faster than he could react, the windows blew out, showering them with glass shards. Insane laughter echoed. And out of nowhere a rabid herd of animals—cats, dogs, birds, insects, and such—ran past the store like a pack of baying hounds after a fox.

Nick let out an elongated breath of relief. Since they weren't stopping, maybe they weren't after him after all.

At least that was his thought until one large, mangy brown dog doubled back. Covered in a white frothing sweat, it stood before the windows on its hind legs to look in at them and growl angrily.

Nick crossed himself and started praying.

"Mara," Tiyana said in a breathless tone.

Nick scowled at her. "Who the heck's Mara?"

"Not a who, Nick," Caleb explained. "The Mara are Norse spirits who use animals to hunt down an assigned target."

"What are they after?" Ana asked.

Me. It was the safest bet. But Nick didn't say that out loud. He was afraid if he did, the dog might attack. Although judging by the way it was eyeballing them, it was about to open business on them anyway.

It backed up on its haunches.

Nick crouched low, bracing himself for the attack.

All of a sudden, out of nowhere, fire burst across the opening of the store, lighting up the dark street and sending the dog and its friends running away as fast as they could.

A jubilant rebel yell rang out, bringing a smile to Nick's face as he recognized the lunatic sound. And he was grateful he was too far away to smell the duck urine.

An instant later, Bubba and Mark, both armed with military-grade flamethrowers, swept the street free of the Mara. In unison, they covered every inch of the pavement without setting anything on fire.

That in and of itself was a miracle. Especially for the two most accident-prone people Nick had ever had the misfortune of calling friend.

"Yeah!" Mark shouted in a deep tone, shaking his fist after the dogs. "That's right, bitches, run back to whatever hole you crawled out of and stay there!"

Bubba stopped on the stoop outside of Erzulie's to look through the broken-out windows. "Y'all all right in there?"

Ana laughed at him. "Depends. Are you planning to burn down my store?"

"Not planning to. But . . . I wasn't planning on having

to stop my zombie survival class tonight to run after some ancient Slavic demon bloodhounds neither."

Ana saluted him. "Touché."

"Bubba!" Mark shouted from down the street. "I could use a little help here. Cujo's fighting back and he's got a lot of angry friends with him."

Bubba stepped backward to glance down the street where Mark had gone. "Nah, you appear to be doing all right by yourself."

"I hate you, fat man!"

"Fat?" Bubba said indignantly. "Your head weighs more than I do, and don't get me started on your ego that has its own zip code." He turned back toward them and saluted them with the pilot light on his flame-thrower. "Y'all have a good night and stay alive."

Just as Caleb took a step toward the raised counter, Bubba reappeared in the open windows. "Hey, Nick? You got a minute?"

Unsure how wise that would be given the weirdness of this night, he glanced at Caleb to see what he thought.

"Ain't nothing going to eat you while Bubba's around," Caleb said with a laugh. "They might screw with him for fun, but he won't let them through. You go on and see what he needs while I check out. I'll be there in a few."

Nick wasn't sure he liked that idea, but he left in spite of his common sense. Carefully, so as not to get hurt, he picked his way through the glass fragments until he was outside on the sidewalk beside Bubba.

Car alarms rang out up and down the street and there was hardly a store left with its windows intact. At the sound of approaching police sirens, Mark came running down the street with the backpack portion of the flamethrower bobbing while he cradled the tube with the pilot light in his arms to protect it.

Now there's a sight you don't see every day.

Unless you befriended lunatics.

With lightning speed, Bubba took his flamethrower off and held it out with one arm. In a perfect handoff, Mark grabbed it as he ran past them, toward the Triple B. The man didn't even slow down or miss a single step.

Nick was impressed. Horrified and amused, but really impressed. "Should I ask?"

Bubba wiped his hands off on his jeans. "The commissioner stopped by a couple of weeks ago and told us that if another police officer caught either me or Mark out in public with the flamethrowers again, they'd haul us in for arson and keep us there until we're too old and feeble to lift a weapon."

"Ah . . . so what did you need?"

Bubba rubbed at his neck in a gesture that always

signaled he was nervous about something. A wave of fear shot through Nick. It wasn't often that anything rattled Bubba. And when it did . . .

It was biblically bad.

"Is something wrong?" Nick asked.

"Nah . . . I just . . ." His voice trailed off as various expressions played across his face.

An awful feeling went through Nick. *Please let me be wrong. This night has already sucked enough.* He couldn't stand for it to get worse. "Please, God, Bubba, tell me you're not about to ask me out, are you?"

Bubba made a rude sound at him. "Hell, nah. I'd date Mark first, provided he took a bath so I wouldn't have to fumigate my truck or store."

That was a relief.

"But," Bubba continued, "now that you mention it . . . that is what I wanted to ask you about."

"Dating Mark? Really?"

'Cause the kid with a brand-new license was such an expert on going out with others.

Bubba gave him a dry, irritated stare.

Then after a few seconds, he inhaled a deep breath and rubbed his hand over his chin. "Look, I'm just going to blurt this out, so bear with me. I wanted to ask you if you'd be opposed to me asking out your mama? I've been thinking about it for a while now and I didn't want to go behind your back and do it. If it bothers you at all, just tell me and I'll never mention it again. But your mama's a fine woman and I would never do anything to dishonor her or upset you."

For a full, solid minute, Nick couldn't breathe as that question hit him like a kick to his groin. Had he really heard that? Was it possible?

Bubba wants to date my mother. . . .

The mere concept threw him straight into shock.

Bubba snapped his fingers in front of his face. "Nick? You all right?"

No. The world was suddenly upside down. . . . Total pole reversal, and it wasn't from the demons and other things out to get him.

Bubba wanted to date his mother.

Bubba . . .

His mom. His blessed, sainted mother who never even looked at a man that way. She was so uptight and staunch about that, that Nick had half convinced himself she'd turn into a pillar of salt if she even contemplated talking to the opposite sex, never mind actually touching one of them.

But then, Bubba never looked at women either. Not once since his wife died. Mark had told him that. Heck. Bubba didn't even talk about women. It was as if his heart was so broken by the loss of Melissa that he couldn't bear the thought of spending even a minute with another woman, other than his own mama.

Yet once the initial shock of the question settled and Nick had some higher cognitive functioning again, he stopped looking at it like an infant who thought he'd been born through immaculate conception.

His mother was a sweet, beautiful woman who was barely thirty years old.

And Bubba, while a bit on the crazy side, was a great man who wasn't that much older than her. . . . He was also the closest thing to a father Nick had ever known.

His mind whirling, he went back in time to that afternoon he'd first met Bubba. It'd been a particularly bad day his first month at St. Richard's. Stone had punched him so hard during first period that his nose had still been stinging that afternoon, and his eyes hadn't stopped tearing up.

Worse, he'd been given an assignment in English that required him to have a computer and Internet connection. Since they couldn't afford either, Nick had spent over an hour trying to find an Internet café or computer store that would rent time to him when he didn't have an ID or parent with him. Most had run him off three seconds after he entered the building.

By the time he'd stumbled into the Triple B, he'd

been so frustrated, he'd wanted to throw himself into the Pontchartrain.

Bubba, in all his humongous rippling muscled form that made the Hulk look like a pigmy, had stood at the counter of his store, staring right at him. Back then, he'd had a thick black beard, shaggy hair, and was wearing a black glow-in-the-dark KILL THEM ALL AND LET GOD SORT THEM OUT tee covered by a red flannel lumberjack shirt.

Frozen in terror at the sight of Bubba's stern glower and arms the size of a tree trunk, Nick had wanted to run, but he was afraid to move lest he wet his pants. And he'd been convinced that Bubba would kill him dead if he wet the floor.

"Can I help you?" Bubba's thick drawl had rumbled out of his massive chest like low-lying thunder.

It'd taken a few seconds before Nick's own voice could rise above a whisper. "Um, I need to rent a computer for homework."

That scowl had darkened before Bubba broke into one of his famous crap-eating grins. "You don't have to look so scared, boy. I've already filled up on snot-nose at lunch and don't got no more room in my belly for another one for a while." He'd reached under the counter and pulled out a laptop, then set it up with a chair for

Nick in the front of the store. "I don't normally rent computers, but I do have one right here you can use till you get finished with your homework. Just take your time and don't worry about the cost."

"I can't take charity. My mama won't let me."

"Fine then. You can take out some trash in the back when you get done."

The next thing Nick had known, he was working on his paper at the counter near the register, laughing at Bubba's stories of his scary adventures with Mark, and splitting a pizza with him after Bubba had heard his stomach rumbling.

By the time he had his assignment finished, with a lot of help from Bubba, he'd thought the world of the man. They didn't make many guys like Big Bubba Burdette.

And his mother was a lady in a category all her own. . . .

If she were ever going to have a relationship with a man, Nick couldn't think of anyone else he'd rather have her with than Bubba.

"Dang, Bubba," Caleb said as he joined them. "What'd you do to him?"

"I just asked a question. But I think it sent him into a coma or something."

"What was the question?"

Nick held his hand up to interrupt them as he finally had a rational thought again. "You know what, Bubba?" He met Bubba's gaze levelly. "I'd be fine with you dating my mama. I don't know if she'll say yes. She's never been on a date before, but if she agrees, I'm all for it. She needs someone to make her happy. But I just have one question."

"Yeah?"

"If you two were to get married, would Mark be my irritating stepbrother or my mentally challenged uncle we don't talk about in public?"

Bubba laughed. "You better be glad he's not here to hear that, boy. He'd kick your butt."

Probably so. "Seriously though, I'm all good with it. May the Force be with you when you ask her. You can never tell how she's going to react to things like this. And don't hold it against me if she says no."

"Don't worry. I won't." Bubba inclined his head to him. "Thank you, Nick. I appreciate it. And I promise I won't do anything to make you uncomfortable or dishonor your mama." Then he nodded to Caleb and headed for his store at the same time the police began arriving.

Nick met Caleb's gaze. "It's a sign, isn't it?"

"What is?"

"Bubba wanting to date my mom. . . . The world is coming to an end."

Caleb laughed at his dire tone. "No, Nick. Not if we can help it."

Nick wanted to believe that, but as they started back toward his house, a bad feeling went through him. A feeling that only got worse as they were passing a police car and he overheard an officer talking on his radio.

"What was the name of that escaped prisoner again?"

"Adarian Malachai. And they're pretty sure he's headed our way. He's already killed six people who tried to stop his escape. So he is definitely armed and dangerous. Do not attempt to apprehend him alone. We're getting information now about any family he might have in the area and will pass that along once it comes in."

Nick felt the color draining from his face as he met Caleb's wide-eyed stare. While he knew he'd be the primary target his father would want to kill, there was one other person his father would prey on.

"We've got to get to my mother. Now!"

CHAPTER 15

Caleb caught Nick's arm and pulled him to a stop. "Hang on. Something's not right."

"Yeah, my bastard father's escaped and—"

"No!" he growled through clenched teeth. "Listen to me, Nick. I saw your father right before I came to you. He's not in any kind of shape to fight anyone. Not even a human. He didn't get out of there on his own. He couldn't have."

Wanting to kill Caleb for holding him back, Nick tried to break free of Caleb's iron grip. "Then he has a helper. What else is new?"

Caleb's fingers bit harder into his arm, keeping him in place in spite of Nick's struggles to get free. "Your father has no allies, Nick. I'm it. Do you understand me? The Malachai is the King Shit of our universe. All preternatural creatures, including the majority of the gods who remain in power, exist in a state of absolute fear of him. Even Noir. He might have held your father's leash, but he knew he was holding his death in captivity, which is why he kept your father weakened and chained. . . . That being said, everyone covets his power, and if they can ever get to a weakened Malachai, they can take those powers and use them."

"Then why does he trust *you*?"

"I'm his slave. There's no way I can hurt him and he knows it. So long as he lives, my powers are his to command. If I tried to use them against him, they would rebound on me and I could conceivably lose mine entirely or die myself. I'm the only creature alive he can turn to right now who can't kill him for his powers."

Nick shook his head. "I don't understand what you're saying."

"I'm saying that if your father is really out of jail, something went in and got him for a reason, and if he's still alive, that creature is holding him prisoner. And whatever those reasons are that they haven't killed him, they are not for your father's benefit, and especially not yours. The Malachai is the most cursed creature ever born. They can know no love of any kind, and that includes friendship. They can't even trust their own mothers at their back."

Nick calmed a degree as he considered that and came to the conclusion that his mother wasn't in immediate danger from his father. She should be at home, safe. "Who would have taken him, then?"

Caleb finally let go of his arm. "*That* is the right question. Now let me really taint your Corn Flakes by reminding you that if something has found him and they manage to take his powers, they alone will have the ability to kill *you*. That's why I said we had to get you to him immediately, before something like this happened or he dies."

"Wouldn't you know if they'd killed him? Wouldn't they have control of you now?"

"Not necessarily. It could just mean they haven't summoned me yet. They may not even realize that they have a slave. But you are right about one thing. We need to secure your mom until this is over. Not because of your father, but because she's *your* weakest link. Whoever has her, has you by the stones."

Nick glanced down to Bubba's store. His first thought was to put his mom with him. Bubba would protect her with his life. He knew it. But the cops were all over the Triple B, and were interrogating both him and Mark about what had happened.

That left him with only one other person he could trust. Pulling his phone out, he called Kyrian, who answered on the second ring.

"What do you need, Cajun?"

"Can you meet me at my house? I just heard from the police that my dad escaped jail and I'm afraid he might come after my mom."

Kyrian didn't hesitate with his response. "I'll be there in five minutes."

Nick hung up and slid his phone back into his pocket. He met Caleb's bemused stare that silently asked if Nick had heard a word he'd said about his father's real situation. "It's the only thing we can use that will get my mom to cooperate," he explained. "Otherwise, she'd refuse to stay at Kyrian's. But if she thinks my father might show up at our doorstep and hurt *me* . . ."

"Good thought."

"Yeah, I know. Some days I'm not totally stupid." Nick headed for home with a sick feeling in his gut. Was all of this the harvester playing havoc with his life or was this something else?

Someone new?

Every day seemed to bring a more powerful enemy out of the ether to screw with him. It was worse than playing the ultimate level of a video game with no more spare lives.

And no cheat codes.

"I'm too young for this crap," he said under his breath.

"If it's any condolence you handle it like a man, and better than anyone I've fought beside in a very long time."

Caleb's rare praise stunned him. Unsure what had motivated it, he frowned at his friend. "Will it ever get easier?"

"I could lie and say yeah, but honestly? Life isn't supposed to be easy. Ever. But with the hardest challenges go the greatest rewards. And every incredible moment of my life came only after I did something that made my gut clench with fear."

Nick scoffed at his words. "You're full of more crap than a sewage plant."

Caleb laughed. "I know it feels like everything in the universe is out to get you, and in your case it's actually true, but—"

"No offense, Caleb, pep talks are *not* your forte. Please stop. Any more and I'll be knotting a noose around my throat."

"Let me finish, jerkweed. We all have moments when we're sure the gods in power have chosen us to be their personal whipping boys, but if you take a step back, you'll see the way out, and years later when you look at it with some perspective—"

"If you tell me it won't seem so bad, I swear to God, in the mood I'm in, I'm going to punch you."

"I wasn't going to say that. There will be many an event in your life that no amount of time will ever take the sting out of it. Days when you know your heart has been brutally ripped out and thoroughly stomped. But every one of those events is a defining moment in our lives that, for better or worse, changes us forever and carves a scar on our souls. They will leave us angry, bitter, shell-shocked and bleeding—that is a guarantee from a cold, brutal universe that hates us."

Nick really didn't want to hear this.

But there was no stopping Caleb when he was on a roll. "We don't have a choice in how or when our bad days will blindside us. But what we do choose is how we allow them to leave us once they're gone. You can use those moments as a catalyst to spur you on to greater things or you can let it be the event that breaks you and leaves you shattered and forever lost in darkness. *That,* my friend, is the curse of free will. You can blame it all on fate and the universe, but in the end *you* alone decide if you're going to lie down and let hell take you under, or if you're going to stand strong in defiance of it all with your middle finger raised."

Caleb stopped on the sidewalk to pierce him with a fiery gaze. "If you muster that courage to stand under fire and not go down, you will amass an inner strength that no one can touch. You won't be another faceless, nameless, forgotten human in a long historical line of the defeated. You will be a steeled warrior, and a force to be forever reckoned with. And beneath the pain that lingers, you will have the comfort of knowing that you are strongest of all. That when others caved and broke, you kept fighting even against hopeless odds."

Nick scoffed. "And that's really supposed to make me feel better? Seriously?"

"No one can take your dignity or hold you down, Nick, unless you let them. I was once the most feared commander in an army of demons and am now a slave to a creature I would rather gut than look at. Every morning when I get up and have to ready myself to face the horror of putrid human high school, condescending teachers, and hormonal teenagers so that I can protect your worthless hide, is a morning I want to paint the walls behind me with my brain matter."

"Thanks, Cay," Nick said bitterly. "Way to motivate. You should think about charging admission."

"But . . ." Caleb held his finger up in front of Nick's face to silence him. "I don't pull that trigger because I know that even though I don't see an end to my hell right now, nothing is ever final or eternal. Not success, and definitely not failure. High school will pass and we'll move on to the next phase. I can't guarantee what's going to happen or what crap the universe will decide to gut me with, but I do control whether I'm a fighter or a victim . . . and I will *never* be a victim."

"Neither will I."

"And that is why I fight for you, Nick. Even when I have an urge to kill you."

Nick shook his head at the surliness of that last comment. "You really do suck at this."

Caleb laughed. "But I don't suck at everything, and we need to get to your mother and secure her safety."

As they started forward, Nick heard a deep, low growl. He searched the darkness for the source. "Is that the Mara again?"

Caleb picked up the pace and pushed Nick to walk directly in front of him. "No. It's something worse."

"One day you need to write down the hierarchy of spooky crap for me."

Caleb didn't comment as he shoved his bag into Nick's hands. "Get to your mother and send her with Kyrian to his house. You don't leave that condo until I come for you. Understood?"

"Yeah, but I don't—"

Caleb pushed him with both hands. "Run!"

Nick hesitated as a huge black wolf that was the size of a horse launched itself for his throat. Right before it would have bit Nick, Caleb caught it by the neck and tackled it to the ground. With glowing purple eyes, the snarling wolf sank its teeth into Caleb's arm.

Caleb cursed in pain.

Nick started forward to help, but Caleb's orange eyes flared in the darkness as he summoned his demon powers. "Get to safety, Nick. Dammit, boy, move!"

Even though the very idea of running stuck hard in his craw, Nick turned and did what Caleb ordered, knowing that if he stayed, he'd only be a distraction that could get Caleb seriously hurt or killed. He clutched at the bag so he didn't lose anything, and didn't slow down until he reached the locked iron door of their condo. As he punched in the code, he felt a stirring in the air behind him.

Please be Kyrian. . . .

He turned to see a giant black shadow closing in.

Definitely not his boss. The pungent scent of sulfur choked him. It was so dense he could taste it. *Get in, get in. . . .*

Why was it anytime you needed to hurry, electronics slowed down to a crawl and lagged? How did they know?

He finally heard the light beep, followed by the whir of the lock opening.

Just as he grabbed the door handle, the blackness seized him and threw him to the side of the building.

SHERRILYN KENYON

Nick hit the brick so hard, dancing lights clouded his vision. Caleb's supplies scattered everywhere, rolling across the sidewalk. The creature grabbed him by the throat, cutting his air off.

His eyes widened as his gaze focused on her perfect, translucent features. Ethereal and ghostly, she floated above the ground like some graceful angel with tendrils of ribbon spiraling around her. But her stark white eyes were pitiless as she leaned in to kiss him.

Only it wasn't a kiss. The instant she placed her lips to his, he felt her pulling his breath out of his body with the force of a full-blown hurricane. Her laughter echoed in his head as his very soul was ripped from its foundations.

Nick tried to fight her off, but since she had no real form, there was nothing to hit or push against. No way to stop her from suffocating him. How she was holding him down without a body made no sense, yet he couldn't escape her. He tried his best to breathe, yet no air would fill his lungs. It only left them.

With no choice and growing weaker by the heartbeat, he fell to the sidewalk. Still, he fought on, crawling his way back to the stairs so that he could get inside to where Menyara had painted her symbols of protection. They would get this thing off him. . . .

They had to.

After what seemed like an eternity, he reached the door again, only to discover it'd relocked itself, and jammed shut. There was no way he could stand up under her onslaught to reach the keypad.

His head spinning, he knew was dying.

And there was nothing he could do to stop it.

CHAPTER 16

W

e have a serious problem."

Grim opened his eyes to see Wynter Laguerre in front of him while he sat on his cold throne that was made from the bones of fallen heroes. Even now, he could hear their whispers as they'd tried to barter with him for their lives.

Mmmm, how he loved the sound of hopeless misery. No matter how brave the soul, they all had a tendency to turn craven when they knew their death was imminent.

When they learned firsthand that Death didn't negotiate.

But that wasn't what he needed to focus on. "You have nerve waking me from my slumber, War. Of all creatures, you should know better." Because he very seldom slept, Grim was never a happy morning person. Rather, he woke up with bloodlust and rage.

War, however, had no natural fear of him since they

were ancient allies, and he relied on her to feed him a steady diet of victims. "Oh . . . well then," she said nonchalantly, "return to your sleep. It'll wait." She started to leave.

Her frigid tone told him that whatever it was, it was urgent. "What will wait?"

She tossed her long dark hair over her shoulder. Even though it was pitch-black in his study, he saw her perfectly because nothing could ever hide from death. "You said you wanted your rest. Far be it from me to disturb you."

Grim rubbed at his eyes and squashed his natural inclination to snap at her. She was trying to pick a fight with him. It was what she lived for and he had no intention of giving it to her. "I'm awake now. The damage is done. Tell me what brings you to my humble abode."

She cast her gaze around his massive throne room where he'd amassed some of the world's greatest treasures. "Yeah, your shack is such a dump. You should hire a maid."

He sighed irritably. "Are you really here to discuss my spring cleaning?"

"No . . . I'm here to warn you that Thorn knows someone freed his pet from his pit, and is furious over it. He's already summoned his army to go after it, and return Holler to his hole immediately."

Grim cursed under his breath. Thorn was an aptly named pain in his nether region. Much like the Dark-Hunters Grim loathed, Thorn helped the humans by leading a group called Hellchasers—damned souls Thorn had bargained for so that they could earn their redemption by returning the worst preternatural escapees to whatever hell or prison realm they'd escaped from. . . . He was an even bigger bleeding heart than Acheron.

But what stung the most was that Thorn had once been Grim's biggest ally. Until the day, during the greatest plague of all time, the beast had turned against Grim and snatched Holler from his side, then imprisoned Holler in Thorn's dungeon and dared Grim to release him.

They'd been at war with each other ever since.

He glared at War. "How did he find out?"

"Do I look like a crystal ball?"

Oh to relive the past when he'd been able to take an ax to her for that kind of snark. Such fond memories he had, but they were worthless right now when he had to deal with her and her quirks.

"Then how do you know he knows we freed Holler?" he asked, letting the full weight of his agitation taint his tone.

She stepped aside to show him the shimmery ghost form that had been hiding behind her back.

Zarelda swallowed in fear as she faced him. "Holler cast me out of the girl's body tonight, and I can no longer get into it."

Really? Did he have to do everything for them? "Sacrifice another victim and return."

"I tried."

"And?"

"I was stopped by a huge male Hellchaser who then interrogated me for Holler's whereabouts. He marked me with some kind of device, and now I'm noncorporeal no matter what I try."

"But wait," War said, her eyes gleaming with perverse pleasure. "It gets better. . . . After your little chitchat with Hel about freeing Zarelda's brother from her custody in exchange for Holler's slavery, our favorite Norse death goddess got curious, went digging, and found out you were after the Malachai. Since she doesn't trust you, Grim, she has called out her Mara and Hel Hounds to fetch him to Helheim."

Zarelda sucked her breath in sharply at the mention of the Hel Hounds. "Is Zavid among them?"

War shrugged. "Again, I am not a crystal ball and I really couldn't care less about your brother."

"Then how do you know so much?" Zarelda snapped.

Grim leaned back with a slight smile, waiting for War to tear the stupid little chit apart.

To his great disappointment, she didn't. Her voice was almost kind when she answered. "I unleashed one of my harvesters on the junior Malachai, hoping to help you season him up for his conversion. My agent has been watching and terrorizing him ever since, and she happens to know a Hel Hound and Mara when she sees one. She was just about to move in when they tore past her."

Grim closed his eyes and hissed in anger as he sorted through this latest development. His plan had been flawless. Borrow Holler from Thorn to weaken Adarian while Zarelda strengthened Nick and tied his heart to her. Once Adarian was dead and Nick was firmly in their camp, he'd planned to trick the goddess Hel into releasing Zavid to make Zarelda happy, and keep her around to pacify the younger Malachai so that Nick didn't turn on them.

Not to mention the bonus round of having Zavid kill Caleb for them. The Norse god, Holler, was only a nugget to get Zavid free. After that, Grim would have gladly returned Holler to Thorn's dungeon and then dealt with Hel's wrath over his little lie. Since she wasn't nearly as powerful as Thorn, he hadn't been concerned about duping her at all.

Now . . .

Disaster.

Damn Hel for being smart enough to know he was lying to her.

War met his glower without flinching. "So, genius. What's your plan now?"

"Where's your harvester?"

"On standby, awaiting orders."

Grim stood up and descended his dais. "Then by all means, let's unleash her."

CHAPTER 17

Caleb slowed as he neared Nick's condo and saw his supplies scattered all over the ground in front of it. "What the . . . ?" Closing his eyes, he reached out with his powers to contact Nick.

No one answered.

His heart pounding, he punched the code into the door at the same time Kyrian pulled up to the curb in his black Lamborghini and got out. Caleb held the door open until Kyrian joined him on the stoop.

The ancient Greek general scowled as he came close enough to see the blood, bruises, and scratches the Hel Hound had given Caleb as a memento of their lovely time together. "What happened to you?"

"Dogfight." Caleb snorted. "New Orleans definitely needs stricter leash laws."

Kyrian didn't respond to that. "Is Nick inside?"

Caleb glanced back at the mess that littered the

ground and squelched the fear that gripped him. "I hope so."

Trying not to panic prematurely, he led the way in, and then upstairs to the condo. Knocking on the door, he waited, but no one answered.

C'mon, give me a break. Let the kid just be his usual slow-to-react self.

Kyrian pushed him aside. "Nick?" he called, banging on the door himself. "Cherise?"

Still no answer.

Of course not. 'Cause that would just make his crappy life a hair better. . . .

Gods forbid.

Grimacing as his own panic and concern rose, Kyrian pulled the keys out of his pocket and unlocked the door. The minute they stepped inside, all doubts that something had happened dissipated. Caleb cursed. A major fight had gone down here. Pictures were knocked off the walls. The side table was upturned and the lamp that normally rested on it was shattered. But even worse was the blood on the floor.

And on the ceiling.

No . . .

They were too late. Kyrian quickly searched the rooms, but Caleb knew that there weren't any bodies here. Whatever had nabbed them had taken them out of the human realm. There was absolutely no sign of Nick on this earth. Had there been, he would have felt it and been able to locate him.

The same was true of Adarian. Caleb couldn't find him, either.

Kyrian came back to the living room with a fierce growl. "Call the cops. I'm going to look for them."

Lot of good that'll do. But he was happy to have Kyrian occupied with a wild-goose chase. The Greek general had no idea that Caleb was anything other than a normal teen boy and he wanted to keep it that way. He'd never been real chatty about himself anyway and the fewer creatures who knew who and what he was, the easier he breathed and the longer he lived.

Enemies kill. Friends betray.

He not only believed that, he had the words tattooed across his back beneath his demon's mark.

"Call me if you find anything," Caleb said.

As soon as he was sure Kyrian had left, he rushed outside to gather up the ingredients for his binding spell. If Nick and his mother were still alive, it was even more important now that they get Adarian's powers into Nick.

Don't be dead. The pain that thought caused was not something he wanted to examine. *I don't care about him. It's my own butt that concerns me. . . .* Over and over, he tried to convince himself that the only reason it mattered was because he didn't want to be enslaved to an unknown dickhead.

Yeah, that was it. Otherwise he wouldn't care at all. But deep inside a place he didn't want to admit to, he knew he was lying.

Caleb found the last dropped container buried in a crevice by the next house. Now he could start the spell. Rising, he sighed as he scanned the dark street. "Where are you, Nick?"

What had happened to him?

He had no way of knowing, but he knew someone who could find out. Fast. If she'd speak to him . . .

Caleb would probably have to do some serious begging to get her back on their side.

I hate swallowing my pride.

But sometimes it was a necessary evil. And this was definitely one of those times. Hoping he could pull off a miracle, he flashed himself from Nick's condo on Bourbon over to Kody's home on Burgundy Street. He had no idea if she'd be there or if she'd even open the door.

It didn't matter. He had to try.

That being said, he was unprepared for what awaited him when he appeared on the sidewalk outside of her building. Unlike Nick, he'd never been here before. He'd had no reason to visit.

He only knew the address because he'd added it to his phone in case of an emergency. Course he never thought the emergency would be this. . . .

Nor did he think he'd want to kill Kody the way he did right now as he rolled his eyes at her salmon-colored house with dark green panels that was a long cottage style similar to quite a few others in town.

"Really, Kody? C'mon. You've got to be kidding me."

The problem? Because of past tax laws, many of the homes in New Orleans were narrow in front and long down the back. They were termed shotguns because you could literally open the front door and shoot a straight line through them to the back door without hitting a wall. The other big historical tax had been on front windows. So the crafty citizens who refused to be taxed on something so ridiculous had decided to put doors along the front of the homes instead.

Kody's little fortress had four of them and not a single window in it. Worse, all four "doors" were bolted shut and had the same small stone stoop under them. There was no way of knowing which one was the door and which ones were windows. It was like playing a bad game of *Let's Make a Deal*, or the lady and the tiger.

I ain't got time for this crap.

Caleb curled his lip. "All right, Monty. Let's see

what's behind door number two." Growling in frustration, he pounded on it.

Door number four opened a few seconds later to show him one ticked-off Kody. "What are you doing here?"

"Getting seriously pissed off."

"Well, you can do that somewhere else. I suggest over at 809 Bourbon." She moved to close the door.

Ignoring the fact she'd just told him to go back to Nick's, Caleb flashed to the door and blocked it before she could slam it on him.

Her green eyes blazed with indignant fury. "Desperate to lose an arm, are we?"

"No. Desperate to save Nick's life."

She paled instantly as the furious light in her gaze turned to concern. "What's wrong?"

"In case you can't tell by the bloody bruises on me, he was attacked, and now both he and his mother are missing."

She opened the door and let him into her quaint house that was way too ornate, pink, and feminine for his personal taste. "Elaborate."

Caleb set his bag down on her lace-covered end table. "Adarian summoned me earlier to let me know that he was dying."

"Nick's killing him?" That would be the obvious question. Too bad nothing with Nick ever went the way it was supposed to.

Caleb shook his head. "Adarian didn't know who had weakened him and I still don't. The plan was for me to get Nick to Adarian so he could kill him and then to lock down Adarian's powers until Nick's ready for them."

She gestured toward his bag. "That explains your groceries."

"Yeah, and while I was getting them a short time ago, we were violently attacked."

"So I heard and saw."

"And you didn't think to come help?"

"I was told I wasn't welcomed or allowed. I figured if I went, either you or Nick would blame me for it."

He hated to admit that she was right.

"Anyway," he said, continuing. "As we were heading back to Nick's we heard on the police radio that Adarian had escaped jail, but he was too weak to do that. The demon could barely blink when I left him. So I'm thinking that whoever it was who got him out has kidnapped all three of them and is planning on becoming the next Malachai."

Kody screwed her face up in distaste. "I just got wicked indigestion."

"Good, 'cause I've had it all night. Can you locate Nick?"

"All I can do is try."

Nick came awake to find himself facedown in a small cage inside what had to be the coldest cave on the planet. Shivering, he blew air into his hands to warm them, but all it did was form a cloud that quickly dissipated and left him even colder than before.

Am I still alive?

He wasn't sure. This place definitely wasn't heaven, and if hell was this cold, he had a major beef to make with his priests on their misinformation.

But that at least made him remember his latest power that could really come in handy in this barren hole. Closing his eyes, he summoned the fire. His hands instantly lit up.

Oh yeah, *much* better.

Until it ignited high and almost set his head on fire. Great, just what he needed. Singed-off Terminator-style eyebrows. That would get him an awesome prom date . . . never. Cursing, Nick shook his hands until they went out, then tried again.

This time, he managed a little better control over the size of the flame. Lifting his hand so that he could see more details about his prison, he scanned the empty ice cave. His cage was in a corner and there was nothing except crystalized stalactites and stalagmites all around him. Something about it reminded him of a video game. Maybe because it looked like a really good place to get bodied.

Was this one of the Antarctic demon realms Acheron had told him about? That would definitely explain the biting cold and the nasty smell that made his stomach knot in disgust.

Off in the distance, he could hear dogs barking and wolves howling. Or maybe it was wolves barking, too.

Did they do that?

He wasn't sure.

And speaking of, he heard the low rumble of a deep growl on his right. Whatever it was making that noise sounded massively huge. Nick scooted back in the cage, hoping whatever it was, it couldn't bite through steel and that it kept walking past his area.

After a few seconds, the beast entered through a small opening in front of the cave. Black as the darkness around them, it was a giant wolf. And the moment it turned to look at him and Nick saw its luminescent purple eyes, he realized it was the same one that had attacked Caleb.

Oh, this can't be good. . . .

Limping and bleeding, it approached his cage so that the beast could sniff it. Worried about Caleb, Nick bit his lip. While it appeared Caleb took a chunk out of the wolf, the fact that it was here and alive, and Caleb wasn't, didn't bode well for his friend.

It bared its bloodied, sharp teeth, then growled and snarled at Nick as if trying to reach him through the bars.

"Get back!" A loud whip cracked across the wolf's back, causing it to recoil and howl, then snap at the leather cord. "Back, I said!" Two more lashes landed on it before the wolf backed down and limped over to a steel post that was embedded into the cavern wall.

Nick stared at the trail of smeared blood staining the ice in the wolf's wake. He'd feel bad for the creature had it not eaten Caleb.

At least that was his thought until the wolf collapsed and then turned into a guy who didn't look all that much older than him. He had thick, wavy dark hair that fell to his shoulders and a couple days' growth of beard. Completely naked, he lay with his back to Nick. Scars marred almost every inch of him. Most were from a whip, but many others were bite marks, knife wounds and bullets.

Ignoring Nick and his cage, the woman who'd beat the wolf down approached the wolf slowly as if expecting him to get up and attack her. When she was almost within arm's reach, she transformed her whip into a long, bladed staff. A blade she used so that she could poke him. She even went so far as to lift his face up with it.

He didn't move.

Finally satisfied that he wasn't playing opossum, she raised her hand toward the post. A chain materialized and then crawled over the ice to the man and looped itself around his neck to keep him there.

Only then did she turn to face Nick.

His breath caught in his throat. Around his mother's age, she was exquisite and ethereal. Long, white-blond hair fanned over a body that should be gracing magazines that would have him grounded for life if his mom ever caught him reading them. But from the waist down, she had the legs of a rotting corpse. One that came complete with the smell of the back end of an unwashed yak.

"So you are the Malachai. . . ." She sounded disappointed.

Good. Maybe she'd let him go. "Who are you?"

"Hel."

Not quite afraid of her, but rather apprehensive, he arched a brow. "Isn't it a little cold to be hell?"

She laughed at that. "Not your hell, moron. I am the goddess Hel and this is my realm, *Hel*heim."

Helheim he knew from playing Dungeons and Dragons with Madaug and his friends. Hel . . . he'd never heard of before. But Madaug would probably be able to recite an entire dissertation on her, her family, and any insect she'd ever met. Even better, Madaug would most likely know what, if any, weakness she had. *Remind me to never make fun of him again for his bank of useless information.*

Nick stood up to face her. "Why am I here and what have you done with my mother?"

"I know nothing of your mother. I care nothing about your mother. Just as I care nothing for you. You are only a means to an end for me. And as soon as I get what I want, I don't care what they do to you."

He threw one of his fireballs at her.

She stopped it with a blast of ice that shattered it midair. "Instead of attacking me, boy, you should be grateful."

"Grateful for being locked in a cage?"

"Grateful you're alive. According to my hound, you were almost dead when he pulled the harvester off you."

Nick's pulse quickened. Finally someone who knew what one was. . . . Though to be honest, he'd have rather found the definition online. "Harvester?"

"Soul-eaters. They are sent to destroy anyone who is born of evil." She walked a small circle around his cage.

"Hard to believe something as puny as you is worth the life of a captive god."

Before he could respond to that, she vanished.

"I'm not puny!" Nick shouted after her. While he might be thin and gangly, he was over six feet tall. Not puny by any standards. . . .

Much.

Sitting down, he turned his attention to the passed-out wolf, who was still bleeding all over the place. So the thing that ate his best friend had saved his life. . . . Nick wasn't sure what to think about that.

Not that he really cared. While he didn't like the thought of Caleb being hurt or dead, the one thought that scared him the most was his mother. What had happened to her?

Maybe Kyrian had made it in time and was now keeping her safe. It was his only hope, and he intended to latch on to it with both hands.

And his teeth.

Hours went by as Nick tried every power he could to escape his cage. Nothing worked. As usual, the universe mocked his attempts with a dose of ineptitude that made him wonder why the heck he kept trying when he should just lie down and think of porn princesses like a normal teenage boy.

Dang you, Caleb, for your twisted pep talks. They kept him going even when it was stupid.

Frustrated, he fire-blasted the door again with both hands. The flames hit it, then rebounded back and singed both the hair on his head and that on his arms.

Beautiful. I smell like a burned sewer rat.

Hey, Casey, want to go eat dinner with me now?

"You're wasting your time."

Nick jumped at the deep, heavily accented voice. Turning, he saw that the wolf was awake and staring at him with those luminescent purple eyes.

"I thought you were dead."

Ignoring Nick's comment, the wolf lifted up a corner of the thick, warm blue blanket that covered him. "You?"

"Yeah, I was going blind from the sight of your naked hairy butt."

One corner of his mouth twitched as if he started to smile then caught himself. "And the pillow?"

Now it was Nick's turn not to comment. No need in letting him know that even though he'd most likely eaten Caleb, Nick had felt sorry for him. Not to mention, the wolf was really lucky Nick's powers had worked and not turned him into a goat or something.

But now that the wolf was awake, there was one question Nick was desperate to have an answer for. "Did you kill Caleb?"

"The daeve you were with?"

"Yeah."

"He lives."

Nick's relief came out as a sharp burst of breath. He hadn't realized just how upset he'd been at the thought of Caleb dying while protecting him until just this second. "Looks like he got a pretty good chunk of you."

The wolf glanced away, then ran his hand through his dark, wavy hair. He grimaced as he saw the blood on his hand from an injury he must have had on his head. To his credit, he was handling the pain really well.

"I'm Nick, by the way."

The wolf wiped the blood off on his leg. "I know."

He waited for the wolf to offer his name in turn, but after a few minutes he realized that the wolf had no intention of it. "You have a name?" Nick prompted.

"I don't remember it."

Scowling, Nick snorted. "You're joking, right?"

He shook his head, killing every last bit of Nick's humor. Wow . . . Did he have amnesia or something else?

A really bad suspicion went through him. "How long have you been here?" Nick asked.

He cast an irritated frown in Nick's direction. "Why do you talk so much?"

"I'm Southern."

The deepened scowl on his face said that he had no idea what Nick was talking about. Which meant he'd been trapped here for a minimum of several hundred years.

"You don't get out much, do you?"

That went right over the wolf's head. Without a word, he dragged himself over to the wall and licked at the ice.

Yuck. Nick shuddered. "What are you doing?"

He licked for a few more seconds before he wiped his hand over his mouth. "I'm thirsty."

"Dude, really? Couldn't you have just waited until they brought us water?"

"They don't bring water to us in here. You get what you scrounge for."

Nick's jaw went slack. "They don't bring us food?"

He shook his head.

Uh-uh. No way . . . He refused to believe what the wolf was telling him. "Dude? Seriously?"

"We are immortal. We don't have to eat." The wolf's rumbling stomach denied that. It was so loud, Nick could hear it from across the room.

It made his own stomach cramp for food. "Oh no,

no, no, no. This ain't gonna work. I have to have three squares a day. *Comprends?*"

"I don't know that language."

Nick frowned. It'd been English but for one word. "Food. I'm talking about food. What do we do when we're hungry?"

"Sometimes animals wander in. If they get close enough, we have food."

Nasty . . .

"Dude, why you live there, then? Tell you what . . . You get me out of here and I'll buy you the best meal you've ever had. We're talking etouffee, andouille, and gumbo so good you'll slap ya mama for it."

"Do you think I'd be here if I had a choice?" the wolf snarled viciously.

That baffled him. The wolf had been free in New Orleans and no one had been holding his chain when he came in here earlier. "You were out of here and free, why on earth would you come back?"

He scowled at Nick as if he didn't understand the question.

But his confusion enlightened Nick, who finally understood. "Oh . . . you're like Caleb. You're enslaved."

"No. Not enslaved. I made a bargain. I am here so that my sister is not."

"Then get up and leave, and take my butt with you. . . . Please."

The wolf shook his head. "My sister would have to serve in my stead, and she is not as strong. She wouldn't last a week here."

"While I admire your devotion, that is whacked, and it makes me really glad I'm an only child. But since you love her so much, then you'll understand that I have to get out of here and find my mother, okay? I'm pretty sure she's in bad danger."

The look on his face said that he had no idea what Nick was talking about. It was like the concept of a mother was completely alien to him.

"Beast!"

A deep, frightening level of ferocity came over him at the male shout that cut through their cavern and rebounded off the walls. He immediately transformed back into the wolf. Crouching low, he backed up against the wall, ready to pounce on whatever was coming toward them.

"Where is he?" another male voice demanded.

Nick frowned as a giant man came storming into their corner. He drew up short the instant he saw Nick. "Who are you?"

"Nick. You?"

"Not Nick."

"Balder? What's taking so long? I have a wager to win."

"Coming." Balder went to the chain that held the wolf captive and jerked it from the wall.

The wolf went crazy, snarling and fighting against him as Balder jerked and dragged him toward the entrance. "Save your energy for the ring, dog."

Nick wasn't sure what they were about to do with him, but he had a pretty good idea. And judging from the way the wolf did everything he could not to be dragged out of here, he knew exactly what was waiting for him.

Poor guy. It had to be terrible.

But the one thing that event rammed home with vicious clarity was what would be done to Nick if Noir ever got ahold of him, and what Caleb's fate could be in the hands of another master.

It was a sobering thought. And it spurred Nick to renew his fight to get out of this cage as fast as possible. These people were nuts and the last thing he wanted was to be a part of their sick, twisted world.

"I've got to get home . . ." Nick glanced around, then decided to go for broke. "Ambrose!" he shouted, trying to summon his future self. "Boy . . . answer me! I don't care how crazy you are. I need your help and I need it now!"

Always in the past, Ambrose had come when he called. If not physically, he'd talked to Nick in his head. But Nick hadn't heard from him in days.

What the heck was going on?

CHAPTER 18

Mount Olympus
The distant future

Terrified and shaking, Artemis hid in the same crevice she'd once used to play hide-and-seek with her brother Apollo, countless centuries ago, when they'd been young and naive. . . . Back when theirs had been the most powerful pantheon that ruled. Never in those long-ago days had she dreamed that she'd be hiding here to save her own life.

Her precious Nick was completely lost now. There was no part of him or Ambrose left. After all this time of his fighting his true nature, only the monster Malachai inhabited his beautiful body.

Tears streamed down her face as she fought for self-control. She couldn't make a sound or he'd find her and kill her, just as he'd done the rest of her family.

Pressing her trembling hand to her lips to keep herself silent, she wanted to scream in horror and grief as her guilt mounted. She was a goddess. Why hadn't she been able to help him maintain his control?

"Artemis?"

She gasped at the low whisper of someone she'd thought was long dead. She glanced behind her to see an ancient god of Order. "What are you doing here?"

"Trying to save the world."

"You're too late."

"In the most hopeless of hells, there is always one thing that remains. One thing that cannot be killed unless *it* decides to die on its own and is surrendered by the one who possesses it."

The indomitable human spirit. Mankind's greatest gift and its worst curse.

It was the only thing that not even the gods could defeat. . . .

Order offered her a smile. "So long as one human has it, we can stop any evil. No matter how strong and powerful we think it is."

Artemis wanted to believe that . . . she wanted to have hope again, but she knew better. "There are no humans left."

"Never underestimate the survival of man or his capacity to sacrifice himself for what he loves most."

Order held a hand out to her. "We still have one small chance to stop the Malachai. Are you with me, little sister?"

Artemis hesitated. The one thing Acheron had taught her . . . Even the most minuscule of chances could be turned into a great victory. All you needed was to find the courage inside to try for it.

But she was so scared. What if she failed? Right now, she was alive. If she stuck her head out of this hole, she could die.

She could lose everything.

No, she'd already lost everything. What she had in this hole wasn't living. And while survival had its place, sooner or later every creature deserved to have more than just meager, fearful survival.

They deserved to live.

If only it was as easy as it sounded, but life took courage. *And I am not courageous.* She'd never been such. Acheron had been right about that. She had always put her own well-being over those she loved. And what had it gotten her?

Misery. Solitude.

You are alive.

Yes, she had her life, but at what cost? She couldn't even face herself in mirrors anymore, because every time she met her own gaze, she knew what she'd done, and she couldn't hide from her conscience.

You can't change the past. But she could change the future. And she could change the present.

For the first time in her existence she found the one thing she'd never known she had.

Bravery.

Taking Order's hand, she nodded. "Let us undo what has been done."

Nick growled as he tried again to break free. "I won't be held by you!" he screamed out, hoping Hel could hear him. And he meant every word.

Gautiers didn't back down. They didn't give in.

And no one would ever defeat him. Not even a goddess.

He kicked the bars even though it bruised his feet and legs and jarred every inch of him.

It's hopeless.

"Shut up," he snarled at himself. "I don't want your negative crap! If you can't help, get out of my head."

All of a sudden, he heard someone approaching. Crouching low, he prepared himself to fight who or whatever it was.

"Bring it, punk."

A huge dark something lumbered slowly into his jail, casting a massive shadow on the wall. That was enough to make a half-grown demon wet his pants.

Nick backed up, tense and alert.

As quickly as it'd grown to the size of the Empire State Building, the shadow shrank down to show it was the wolf returning. Nick expected him to head for his post. Instead, he limped on three legs, dragging his forward left one, toward Nick's cage.

Panting hard and covered in foamy white sweat, blood, and scratches, the wolf paused outside the door to stare at Nick. There was a gash above his left eye and the pain in his gaze was searing. It held Nick spellbound. And as they continued to stare at each other, the wolf turned back into his human form. Nick grimaced at the depth of the cut that ran along his brow. He needed stitches. Badly. The entire left side of his face was horrifically bruised, and his nose and lips were bleeding like crazy. His left arm was broken and twisted. He appeared so worn-out and defeated that Nick couldn't understand how he kept from collapsing on the floor again.

Before Nick could recover from his shock at seeing him like that, the wolf opened the door.

"Go," he whispered, gesturing toward the back side

of the cave. "There's a small, narrow path that will lead you through the mist of shrills. They cannot hurt you unless you listen to them. Ignore whatever it is they say and stay on course. Move as quickly as you can. At the end of the path, you will emerge into a room that contains several doors. There you'll have to choose your way home. But beware, the easiest is the hardest and the hardest isn't as bad as you think. . . . And one of those doors will lead you to your death."

"How will I know which is death?"

The wolf winced as if a wave of pain went through him. "The paths are different for each of us. And you won't know if you've picked the right one until it's too late. But only you can decide which one takes you home." He stepped back and fell to the floor.

Nick went to him, but the wolf shoved him away with a snarl.

"Why are you helping me?" he asked, trying to understand the wolf's sudden turnaround.

"I have no idea. I guess Hel and the others are right. I am stupid."

No, he was a hero. "C'mon," Nick reached for his right arm, "we can get out of here together."

He shook his head. "You have to travel alone. It's the only way you'll make it. Besides, if I go with you, I can't hold Hel and her hounds back from your trail."

"Bud, no offense, but you don't look like you could hold a caterpillar back in your current condition."

He met Nick's gaze and the fire in those purple eyes belied the pain that also burned there. "I'm stronger than I look. Now go before it's too late."

"What will happen to you when she finds out you've freed me?"

He laughed bitterly. "Look at me, kid. What more can she do?"

Kill him. Torture him. With the gods, there was no telling.

Guilt reared up and bit Nick hard. "I can't leave, knowing you're going to be punished for helping me. What kind of dickhead do you think I am?"

"Sometimes we have to make hard choices, and I am nothing to you."

"You're not nothing. You're a hero to me. The man who saved my life."

The wolf scoffed. "Definitely not a man. I'm just a stranger and you have family who needs you. Go save your mother, and remember, so long as you follow your true heart, you will never make a bad choice."

Just as the wolf stayed here to save his sister. He understood family the same way Nick did. "Thank you."

The wolf didn't respond.

Reluctantly, Nick headed for the small opening. Just as he reached it, the wolf called out, "Nick?"

He paused to look back to see the wolf lying on top of the blanket. "Yeah?"

"Thank you for your gifts."

"Anytime." Inclining his head to the wolf, Nick wedged his body through the narrow slit.

As he stepped onto the path, he considered their last exchange. The wolf was right. He was a complete stranger. Nick knew almost nothing about him.

Except for one all-important thing.

The wolf had given Nick a chance when no one else had. For that, he would always owe him. And he wouldn't squander the wolf's sacrifice. He promised himself he would make the most of this.

More determined than before, Nick started down the dark, terrifying path. The air here was so cold that it set his teeth to chattering. It was so freezing even his bones ached. Who would have thought that there was something that could make his cage look desirable?

Leave it to Hel . . .

Closing his eyes, Nick used his powers to set fire to his hands.

It didn't work. Not even a tiny spark . . .

Ah, man, this sucked. For one heartbeat, he actually

considered going back so that he could at least see something other than the oppressive darkness that made his
eyes ache. But he knew what waited for him there. And
it was neither pleasant nor desirable.

Yeah, and what's in front of you might eat you.

True. If his standard luck held, it would most likely be
a whole lot worse. Whoever had come up with the saying
"out of the frying pan and into the fire" had definitely met
him in a former life. They must have been best friends.

With the hardest challenges go the greatest rewards. He
scoffed at that thought. Caleb's words offered about as
much comfort right now as a good eye-gouging. And yet
as stupid as they were, Nick clung to them and trudged
forward, hoping with everything he had that Caleb
hadn't been lying about that.

That maybe once, just once, fate would work in his
favor and not against him with a grudge match that
seemed to take every breath he drew as a personal insult. Holding his hands out in front of him, Nick tried
to feel for a wall or something solid, but the only thing
was the ground beneath his feet.

As the wolf had warned, he was completely blind
about where he was heading. He could see nothing at all.
Just an unending hall of darkness that smelled like the
underbelly of a turd monster. There was also a strong
popping sound that he couldn't identify.

Suddenly, something caught against his toe and tripped him. Nick belly flopped on the ground so hard that it knocked the breath out of him. For a moment, he couldn't move as the pain racked him hard.

When he went to stand, his foot slipped on the ice and he slid sideways. . . .

Into absolute nothing.

Nick grabbed on to the ground as hard as he could while his body dangled over a cliff. Crap! His right hand slipped and he almost lost his left-hand grip. Terrified, he scrambled to get both of his arms on the correct side of the ledge. Finally he managed to stop sliding, but he was still dangling over the edge of . . . sudden death?

The wolf had neglected to warn him about *this*.

His heart thumped against his breastbone so hard it felt like it might come through it. He knew he needed to pull himself up, but honestly he was terrified to even try. What if he slid again and couldn't catch himself?

How far away was the ground?

A few inches, not so bad. A few feet, doable. A few yards?

Not pretty.

His arms ached from the strain of holding his body's weight. He wouldn't be able to hold on much longer. Scared or not, he'd have to try.

Bracing himself, he remembered the chant for strength Nashira had given him from his grimoire.

Sacred light.
Sacred night.
Give me strength . . .
Beyond my sight.

He whispered the words, over and over, focusing on those instead of his fears and doubts. Grinding his teeth, he swung his leg up and caught the edge of the path with his heel. It took every bit of strength he had to lift his body up and roll back onto solid ground.

Weak, panting, and shaken, Nick lay on the walk and listened to the darkness while his heart continued to pound hard in his chest. That had been a lot closer to death than he'd wanted to come. Determined not to repeat that fall, he felt along the darkness until he found a small rock. At least he hoped that's what the smooth round object was.

Crossing his legs to make sure he didn't accidentally stumble, he remained seated and threw it over the edge where he'd fallen.

For several minutes he heard nothing.

Not until it finally hit the bottom. The instant it did,

lightning flashed all around, illuminating the entire cavern. *Holy mother of God . . .*

He was sitting on an extremely narrow ice walkway with giant stalactites suspended over him by the narrowest of bases. Bases that were melting fast and cracking . . .

That was the source of the popping sounds he heard. If one of those were to fall, it would impale him like a sharpened stake.

In the water far below were ugly, humongous reptilian sea monsters that glided along the black surface. Nick couldn't breathe as he realized just how much danger he was in, from everything around him.

"I'm going to die."

You didn't really think the journey would be easy, did you? Nick cringed at his mother's favorite taunt whenever things got bad for them.

"Get out of my head, Mom. I don't have time for your lectures right now."

Yet he heard her voice loud and clear in his mind. *Why do you think there's only a single stairway to heaven, but an entire highway to hell? Because it's a lot easier to slide down than climb up, and it takes a whole lot less energy to boot. But the one thing about us Gautiers is that we never do anything that's easy when there's a major butt-kicking to be had.*

"I get it," he snapped at himself. "Nelly is dead. You can stop beating her."

He had to keep going and not let anything stop him.

And as tempting as it was to turn around and run back to the caged safety he'd left behind, he'd have to cross just as much dangerous ground to return as he would to move forward where who knew what was waiting for him.

Why did I throw that rock?

'Cause he'd wanted to see what was there. And whoever said curiosity had killed the cat must have watched it walk off this precipice and get eaten by the monsters swimming below.

Okay. Focus. Got to keep going. And he couldn't do that until he got back on his feet. He bit back a whimper at the mere thought.

Over, under, around, or blasting through like Bubba and Mark. There was always a way to get through any obstacle. You just had to find the right explosive.

Letting out a deep breath, Nick braced himself to stand up and move forward. *I'll just pretend I don't know there's a five-hundred-foot iguana in a sea below waiting for me to fall.*

Or huge swords dangling over my head about to break off and plant me to the bridge . . .

It could be worse.

Yeah, right. Why did people say that when it was obvious bullshit? Really, it could *not* get worse.

At least that was the thought. But no sooner had those words gone through his mind than he heard the strident voices the wolf had warned him about.

You are going to fail. Who are you to think that you won't? What makes you so special? Nothing. Nothing at all. You're just like your worthless, selfish father. Everyone hates you. No one would care if you died right now. No one would miss you. They wouldn't even send a card to your funeral.

Who do you think you are to venture here like somebody? You're nothing but a pathetic waste who should never have been born. Your mother weeps over your birth and every time she thinks of you. The world would be much better off without you in it. Loser. Stupid. Retard. Moron.

Every horrible thought he'd ever had about himself . . . every doubt . . . every insult and harsh word that other people had leveled at him echoed in the dank darkness. Their cruelty and his own shouted until he could hear nothing else. Not even the pops of weakening ice.

Whoever said that words could never hurt you was a flank rank moron! 'Cause every one of them tore through him and shredded what little ego he had. They left his soul bleeding in agony. He felt like he was walking barefoot over a glass meadow with his heart strapped to the bottom of each foot.

Those words hurt so much more than any physical blow and they voiced all the inner doubts about himself that constantly flogged him.

I am a socially awkward mandork. No girl is ever going to want to be seen in public with someone as ugly and stupid as I am. Why should they? I'm never going to be anything more than a piece of ignorant, backwoods trash eking out a sorry existence where I barely make rent. . . .

You don't belong here with decent people, Gautier. You belong in a dump with the rest of the garbage.

Tears filled his eyes. Acheron had been right. It wouldn't matter if he became president and ruled the entire world, if he led an army to save all of humanity, he'd always hear that hatred. It was forever carved into his soul.

The weight of it all drove him to his knees. He covered his ears, trying to blot it out and not hear it anymore. But no matter what he tried, it wouldn't stop. If anything it seemed to get louder.

Nick screamed out in utter agony. "I hate all of you!" But that wasn't really what hurt him. It wasn't even the truth and he knew it.

He hated himself. He always had.

You will destroy the world. No matter what you do or try, it won't be enough. You will kill everyone you love. . . .

Everyone believed that. Caleb. Kody. Ambrose.

Him.

You should just throw yourself off the edge and let the ugly iguana have you.

Mocking laughter rang out.

Tears gathered in his eyes as he considered the future Ambrose had told him about. As he saw Ambrose's scarred face and angry, bitter eyes.

His eyes.

His face.

You should just lie down and die. . . .

Everything was so overwhelming. If he were to die, his mother would be safe. Kody could return to wherever she'd come from. . . .

The world would be a better place.

Do it.

More tired than he'd ever thought he'd be at sixteen, Nick started to fall. *I just want the pain to end. . . .*

What are you doing, Gautier? Nick frowned as he heard Caleb's growl in his ear that drowned out all the words of hatred. *When did you turn into a punk?*

It was enough to slap him hard, and when it did, the lyrics from his favorite song spilled out of his lips as a breathless whisper.

If you're looking for trouble, just look right in my face.
Yeah, this Cajun don't run. Not for nothing.

And definitely not today.

He rose up in the darkness and glared straight in its face. "You want a piece of me? Then c'mon, bitches, and get some. But you better not come alone!"

In that moment, he felt the heat of perseverance inside him rise up and take hold. It flamed so bright that he no longer felt the cold at all. Oh hell no . . .

Lowering his head, he moved forward with determined steps. He had things to do and people to save.

Starting with himself.

He paid no attention to his haters. No attention to the dangers. He stayed focused on moving in a straight line as fast as he could. The voices became louder, but he did to them what he did whenever his mom started on one of her Olympic bitch sessions.

Ignored it for everything it wasn't worth.

He had sixteen solid years of selective hearing training. And his teachers thought it was worthless.

Ha!

And in the end, the wolf was right. The mists faded harmlessly away without hurting him, and he finally found himself in the room with multiple doors.

All right, we're here.

Each door had a small window in it. Nick went to the nearest one and glanced through it. The second he did, a monster jumped up and snarled in his face.

Screaming, Nick jumped back.

The monster pounded on the door, trying to get to him.

Nick panted in terror. Thank God no one had seen him act like a girl. Well, not Simi or Kody. He would have done that a lot sooner than either of them. But Casey would have screamed like he did, and then some.

"At least I didn't wet my pants." But that was as close to spontaneous loss of bladder control as he wanted to come. Ever.

He approached the next door with a lot more respect and caution. Looking in slowly, he frowned. It looked like a sunny beach. Water rolled against perfect snow-white sand. He could even hear birds singing.

Nice. Gorgeous. Inviting.

Definitely certain death. That had to be a trap. He'd seen this movie enough to know it.

Narrowing his eyes, he tried the next contender. But it was too dark to see anything at all. Since the dark had brought him here safely, maybe he should choose this one?

I was born from darkness.

Might have the right symmetry.

Still, he hesitated. Better to check out the other two doors before making a decision. No need to rush this when his life was on the line.

Frowning, he stepped over. The next one was what appeared to be a meadow at dusk. Woods surrounded it. Since it was neither appealing nor scary, it might be a safe bet.

Definite maybe on this one.

Scratching his ear, he went to the last one and froze. Instead of a window, it was a mirror that reflected his image back at him.

This was the right door.

It made total sense. His biggest enemy was himself. Kyrian said that all the time. *We know instinctively what to do and still we don't. Whatever you do, Nick, don't get in your own way.*

Nick put his hand on the knob, then paused. *What if I'm wrong?*

"I have to trust myself to do the right thing." And every journey began with a single step. Opening the door, he stepped through it and took a moment to get his bearings while the door closed.

The instant the latch clicked, the sunny sky above rumbled with thunder. Dark clouds rolled in and boiled, turning the sky into a deep, dark red. Bloodred.

Undaunted, Nick moved forward, across the vacant field that faded until it turned into New Orleans. . . .

Looking around, he scowled. "I know this place."

It was where North Robertson ended near the North Claiborne bridge in the Ninth Ward. When he'd been a kid, he and Tyree and Mike used to play here. Tyree's grandmother lived in the little white shotgun at the end of the road where the pavement stopped abruptly just short a few yards from the levee. Tall and heavy-set, Tyree's grandmother used to sit on the front porch in her rocker, shelling beans or knitting, or fanning herself with the big old Jesus hand fan she'd gotten from church so that she could watch them, and, as she so often shouted, "keep you godless heathens out of trouble."

They'd play ball near the levee or pretend to be wilderness explorers in the vacant, overgrown lot across the street. It had a cement pad where either a house had been and was destroyed, or where someone had planned to build one and never had. Either way, it'd been a great place for them to sit and eat the cookies Tyree's grandmother would bake for them on Sundays. And every time she brought them a batch, she'd say, "Now y'all boys be careful and don't get bit by some hungry gator coming up over the levee 'cause it smell rotten boys with cookie sugar in them. I'd hate to have to tell your mamas you done got eat now." They would exchange bug-eyed stares and keep watch for a gator that never came. Or tell each other they'd spotted one in the brush, and then they'd have to run for it or get eaten.

Even in the hot, sweltering, mosquito-infested summers, those had been good times. How he missed being that innocent and carefree. Back then he hadn't even known they were poor. Hadn't understood what his mom did for a living. No one in their neighborhood had looked down on them.

Pity life couldn't always be like that.

As Nick came up to the back of the house where Tyree's grandmother would hang her "unmentionables" and they'd chase lightning bugs, he smiled at the memory of a woman he couldn't have loved more had he been related to her.

He hadn't thought about this place in years. The last time he'd been here, he was eight years old and they'd come to pay respects to Tyree's family after they'd entombed his grandmother in St. Louis #1 with her husband he'd never met.

Nick paused as his heart broke all over again for the loss of such a wonderful woman. He could still hear Tyree's mother and aunts singing their mother's favorite hymns. "Will the Circle Be Unbroken" . . . A chill ran over him as he saw a ghostly image of her still at the clothesline, fussing at him for slinging mud too close to her laundry.

His throat tight, he cleared it. "Miss you, Miss Mabel."

Now don't you be sad for me, little Nicky. One day, I'm gonna be up in heaven with them angels. But don't you worry none. I'll still have time to look down on my boys and smile with pride at the men y'all become.

His eyes filling with tears, Nick reached a hand toward the image of her, knowing he couldn't touch her, but still feeling a need to try.

The image vanished instantly.

Blinking back his sadness, he glanced around. Why was he here? What was the point?

Was it because he was trying to find his way home, and this had been one of the first places where he'd learned to understand that word?

With no clue, Nick headed for the bus stop on Claiborne at Tennessee. At least he knew how to get back to his condo from here. It wouldn't take him long.

But as he turned to walk down Tennessee Street, he heard something strange overhead. It wasn't a plane or helicopter. He couldn't place the sound. Not until he heard a loud screech. Looking up, he saw a huge bird coming straight at him.

No, not a bird.

It was a winged, armored demon. One that swooped down, blowing fire at him. Nick dove toward a parked SUV, but instead of landing beside it, he went through the door.

He rolled across the ground several times before coming to rest on his back. Aching all over, he stared up at a ceiling instead of the sky.

What the . . . ?

No longer out in the open, he was in school between classes.

"Are you okay, baby?" Casey knelt down beside him.

Scowling, Nick looked around. Everything seemed normal. Just another day at St. Richard's.

Was this real?

"Gautier?" Coach Heffron snapped as he paused next to him and glared down at the floor where Nick was spread out. "I hope you don't stumble like that during the game. Get up, boy, you're blocking traffic and embarrassing yourself and your team."

Caleb stopped by his side and held his hand out to him. Nick took it and let his friend pull him to his feet.

"You all right?" he asked.

Nick wasn't sure. He glanced from Caleb to Casey to the other students he knew so well. Brynna was at her locker, talking to LaShonda about shopping. Stone and Mason were glaring at him from their lockers. Madaug walked past, his nose buried in a notebook with pages spilling out of it.

It appeared to be right. Everything as it usually was. Nothing strange, other than how he came to be here.

"Yeah."

Casey reached up to rub his head. "I don't know. You took a bad fall."

"Not hard enough," Kody mumbled as she walked past them and the light caught against the heart necklace he'd given her. She cast a malevolent glare at him that added credence to this being real.

Maybe that was how the doorway worked. It just threw you right back into a normal day.

Casey snarled in Kody's direction. "Jealousy doesn't become you, bitch!" Then she leaned into Nick. "Ignore her. You've moved up in the world."

Yeah, this felt normal.

Caleb handed him his nine-thousand-pound backpack.

Nick leaned in to speak to him so that Casey couldn't overhear anything. "What happened with my mom and dad?"

He blinked innocently. "What about them?"

Opening his mouth to elaborate, he snapped it shut.

The busy hallway filled with nosy ears was not the place to have this discussion. "Nothing."

Maybe the door had reset the past?

Maybe everything had been a dream. How would he know?

Stone "accidentally" bumped into him as he headed for class. "You look even more like a freak in those clothes, Gautier. You should go back to your trailer trash wear."

Caleb shook his head. "Ignore him, Nick. He's just jealous you're the hero and he's a loser."

Nick scowled in confusion. "Hero?"

"The game? You scored the winning TD Friday night after Stone fumbled the ball. Don't you remember?"

Okay, it must have dumped him forward in time.

Caleb arched a brow at Nick. "Maybe you ought to go to the nurse."

"I'm fine." Sort of. Since he wasn't sure which period it was, never mind the day of the week, Nick walked with Caleb, who didn't seem to think it odd that Nick was with him. Hopefully this was one of their shared classes. But since they were in the back hallway of the school, there was no clock for him to check the time.

Caleb went into Richardson's stark, bland room. Great . . . Couldn't the dimensional doorway have dropped him back later in the day? No, he had to be in the hag's class. *Figures*. But at least it was study hall and lunch.

Richardson narrowed her beady eyes at him and his new clothes. "What are you wearing, Mr. Gah-tee-aa?"

Nick bit back a caustic retort at her deliberate mispronunciation of his last name. She hated Cajuns and in particular she hated Cajun French, especially if you mixed it with English. Which was why it was a moral imperative that he break out his most charming grin and thickest accent. *"Pourquoi, cher, je voulais pas m'obstiner avec toi. Ça me fait de la peine that you take issue avec mon linge. Je fais le mieux que je peux."*

Why, hon, I don't want to argue with you. It pains me that you take issue with my clothes. I do the best that I can.

Oh yeah, she was madder than the devil now. Her face was so red, it matched her tacky eyeglasses. "Sit down, Gau-tee-yah, before I write you up."

Nick winked at her. *"Je t'aime, itou."*

"Stop baiting her," Caleb mumbled under his breath.

"Can't help it."

"For my sake, try."

Nick sat down and opened his books to do homework. He'd just started when someone threw a wadded piece of paper at him. Scowling, he looked to see Ben, another friend of Stone's, glaring at him.

"What pimp did you shoot for that outfit, Gautier?"

Letting out a breath in frustration, Nick didn't comment as he returned to work and saw the riddle they wanted him to solve for English:

It can be stolen, but never bought.
It can be given, but never taken.
It can be stepped on, but cannot walk.
It can fly, but has no wings.
It can sing, but has no voice.
It can be broken, but still it works.
It can be left, even while it follows.
And though it's easily commanded, it can never, ever be demanded.

What was any of that crap supposed to mean? Gah, how he hated homework.

As usual, class dragged on until he was ready to scream. The twenty minutes he had to wait before they could go to lunch seemed like an eternity.

He didn't relax until they entered the cafeteria. But his relief was short-lived as other people started making comments about his new non–Hawaiian shirt look.

"You think he went gay?"

"Nah, I think he was always gay."

Nick batted his eyelashes at the all-male table of Stone's cronies as he stopped after their comment and pursed his lips. "Why, I know all y'all looking for new boyfriends. But I'm happily taken." He looped his arm in Caleb's and prissed off with him toward the food line.

Caleb gave him a stoic stare.

"What?" Nick asked innocently.

"Since I'm your boyfriend, the least you could do is buy my lunch."

Nick scoffed at him. "Chivalry is so dead. *You* should buy mine."

Caleb rolled his eyes as he plopped a wad of mashed potatoes onto his tray and moved down the line.

Once they'd paid, Nick headed for Casey, who was at a table with two of her friends.

She scowled as he sat down beside her. "What are you doing?"

He exchanged a confused stare with Caleb. "Having lunch with my girl?"

Frowning even more, she looked at her friends. "Which one of you is dating the loser?"

"Ew! Not me."

"As if!" Stephanie raked a sneer over Nick's body. "I'd go all-girl school first."

Stone shoved Nick from behind. "What do you think you're doing?"

Even more confused, Nick stared at Casey. "What game are you playing?"

"Stone!" she snapped. "Do your job and get this stupid dork away from me."

Stone and his friends fell on Nick so fast and furiously that he didn't even have time to swing a single punch. One minute he was standing, the next they had him on the ground, stomping him like Alan, Tyree, and Mike had done.

"Caleb?"

For once, he didn't come to his aid. Instead, Nick's entire being changed. He went from his current self back to the day he'd started at St. Richard's.

Barely five two, he was gawky and scrawny as Mrs. Pantall introduced him to the class. "This is Nick Gautier. He's a new student."

"What'd he do?" Stone had laughed. "Cheat to get in? I know he didn't bribe anyone. He can't afford shoes that fit, he dang sure can't afford to bribe somebody. And what Dumpster did he steal that 1985 backpack from?"

Laughter erupted.

"Loser! Go back to the trailer park!"

"Is this really what you want?"

Nick turned around, scanning the room for the source of that voice. "What?"

A shadow manifested beside him. "You don't have to go back to this. It's your life, you control it."

How easy the voice made it sound. "I don't control other people."

"Don't you?"

Well, he did have the power of persuasion . . . when it worked, which was rare. "Not really."

"Yes, you do," she whispered in his ear. She placed a dagger in his hand and pushed him gently toward Stone. "Kill him and put your past to rest so that you can move into your future."

Nick's heart pounded at the unexpected order. "What?"

"You want to go home . . . it requires a blood sacrifice. Cut his throat. He'd never hesitate to cut yours."

Nicky? He heard his mother calling for him. *Where are you? I need to you to help me. Nicky, come home!*

"Your mother will die if you don't get to her."

Nick gripped the knife tight and stared at it. He wanted to go home more than anything. And he had no love whatsoever for Stone.

He took a step forward, then stopped. Something wasn't right about this. It felt wrong.

Real wrong.

Turning, he ran for the door and jerked it open. But instead of exposing the school's hall, he found Ambrose in the doorway, glaring at him. His eyes blazed that evil demon red that Nick despised.

"You have failed me," Ambrose growled.

"How? I'm trying."

"You are failing . . . again." Ambrose seized him and turned him around in his arms so that he could keep Nick from moving.

One moment, they were in the classroom, and in the next, they stood high atop the Jackson Brewery that looked out over a burning New Orleans landscape.

"Embrace your destiny. We are the end of all things."

Horror filled him as he watched the things he loved most perish. Ambrose's wings unfurled and flapped around them.

"There is nothing we can do. The harder we fight, the sooner it comes. Give in . . ." Tightening his grip, Ambrose launched into flight with Nick in his arms. "Say the words, Nick, and we will be one."

"No!" Nick punched him hard, causing Ambrose to drop him. Winds rushed over his body, tearing at his hair and skin, as he plummeted toward the ground at a frightful pace.

I'm going to die. . . .

The ground came closer, faster and faster.

Nick kept waiting for Ambrose to return and save him, but he didn't. There was no Caleb. Nothing.

No one was going to save his life. It was over.

Closing his eyes, he waited for impact.

CHAPTER 19

Caleb paused as he left Kody's bathroom and a flash of something caught his eye. Her bedroom door was slightly ajar. Pushing it open more, he skimmed the frilly pink room in search of what had called out to him.

It must be my exhaustion.

He stepped back, then froze as it happened again. It was a symbol she'd painted into her wall. Barely discernible, it only flashed in response when he touched the perimeter of the room. That was normal since he was a demon. It was how protection symbols and spells worked.

What wasn't normal was the design of it.

Or the ancient bow that was fastened above her headboard.

His breath left his body as he was thrown back in time to when he'd last seen those items. It was impossible for Kody to have them. The lady who'd owned them would never, ever have allowed another to use either. . . .

"What are you doing?" Kody snapped, moving around him so that she could shut her door.

But Caleb was in no mood for her attitude. Stepping past her, he entered the room, causing the emblem to blaze like fire on the left-hand wall. A stylized woman, she had her long hair flowing back while she held a bow and arrow aimed for the skies. It was the symbol of Dexaria Belam . . . the huntress. The same emblem that had adorned his battle shield.

His hand trembling, he reached for the bow. Just as his fingers brushed the wood, it flew from the wall, into Kody's grasp.

"No one touches my bow."

"*Your* bow?" he asked incredulously.

She lifted her chin in defiance. "Yes."

Fury set him on fire and he closed the distance between them. It took every piece of patience he had not to grab her and shake her until she answered his questions. "Where did you get that?"

"None of your business."

He gestured to the black feathers that were attached to the top of it by a thin leather cord. "Do you know what those are?"

"Tributes."

"From?"

"None of your business."

Caleb felt his eyes change to his demon's vision as she awoke the dangerous part of him with her repetition of the same useless answer. "There you're wrong. And if you want to live another minute, you will tell me what I want to know or we will go to war until one of us is dead. Where did you get Bathymaas's bow?"

He watched indecision play across her face as she debated if she was going to answer or fight.

After a full minute, she drew a ragged breath. "My mother gave it to me, and I invoke your most sacred oath that you pledged to her when you offered her your tribute that you will *never* tell another being who and what I am."

Stunned to silence, Caleb couldn't move as those words sank in. It wasn't possible. How could Nekoda be . . .

"You're her daughter?"

"I am."

And then he saw it. Before his eyes, Kody changed from her current pink tee and jeans into the leather armor the women of her mother's army wore. Her hair was lighter than her mother's and she was shorter. But the features were the same. Especially the shape of her eyes and lips. The shapely build of her body.

No wonder Kody had been so fearless in their fights. Her mother was the original goddess of Order and Justice.

Clasping his fist to his shoulder, he fell to one knee before her and lowered his head. "I pledged my eternal troth to your mother . . . and I would die for you."

Kody felt tears sting her eyes at Caleb's sincerity. "Out of my mother's generals, you were the one she prized above all others. The one she trusted most."

He rose up to tower over her again. "Then why didn't *you* trust me?"

"Too many centuries have passed. You've spent a long time in captivity to a monster who still holds sway over you. Both of those can change even the strongest and most steadfast heart."

"It hasn't changed mine."

"I know. I should have told you sooner. But I didn't dare. Not while my orders conflicted with yours."

Caleb turned suspicious at that. Bathymaas had always been about right and justice over murder. She would never condone the murder of even an innocent Malachai. "Your mother sent you to kill him?"

"No. The powers I serve did. It is because of my mother that I haven't."

That made sense. "You're judging him."

She nodded. "I don't see the monster yet. Therefore I can't justify taking his life."

"And your love of him has nothing to do with it?"

Her face turned bright red.

"Don't deny it," he said, cutting her off when she opened her mouth to speak. "I can see it as plainly as a flare over an open sea at midnight."

She sighed wearily. "When I was sent to kill the Malachai before he took all of his father's powers, I wasn't expecting to find Nicholas Gautier."

"Yeah, me neither." Caleb narrowed his gaze at her. "So what do we do?"

"Right now? We find him and save him. Then we will see."

Such sweet ambiguity with life, death, and fate . . .

Kody was definitely *not* her mother.

Instinctively, Nick threw his arms out as he was about to slam into the ground. The moment he did, his wings came out and spread themselves wide, lifting him up and away from the pavement.

Oh my God . . .

I'm flying!

Forget driving, *this* was the most incredible thing

he'd ever done. Until his wing clipped a wire and he careened sideways. He caught himself an instant before he stained the side of a building.

"This is awesome!" he shouted, then glanced around to make sure no one had seen his outburst. The last thing he wanted was to look stupid while doing something so very badass.

Ah yeah . . . this was living.

"Come get me now!" he dared his enemies.

The words had barely left his lips before someone shot a ball of fire at him. He jerked away from the blast, too fast and too far. Unused to his wings, he didn't have the best control. So he ended up slamming into another building.

Yeah, that was going to leave a mark.

I've got to get away from these things.

Nick headed out for the Mississippi River. There, he'd only have to avoid bridges.

Why do you choose to suffer?

Nick slowed as the voice rang out in his head. "I don't."

"Then why do you not join us? You are a Malachai. You don't have to put up with anyone insulting or belittling you. Ever. You have the power to be anything you want. To *have* anything you want."

"Fine, then. If that's true, there's only one thing I desire. I want to go home!"

"Why? Explain to me the mind of someone who chooses to go where no one wants them. I have seen how they treat you. What makes you desire that?"

Nick slowed even more as those words hung in his head. *You know, the freaky voice has a point.* Why did he want to be put down by others? Was he not abused enough as a kid?

But that was childish, he suddenly realized. *There are two sides to everything.*

It was Ash's wolf story. . . .

"What you are focused on are my nuisances," Nick told the voice. "And I have no desire to see them."

"Then stay and never be insulted again."

"I can't."

"Why?"

Nick laughed as he finally understood the point of this journey . . . and the way home. The wolf had given it to him. . . . "You know the answer. You wrote it in my notebook.

"It can be stolen, but never bought.

"It can be given, but never taken.

"It can be stepped on, but cannot walk.

"It can fly, but has no wings.

"It can sing, but has no voice.

"It can be broken, but still it works.

"It can be left, even while it follows.

"And though it's easily commanded, it can never, ever be demanded."

The shadow fluttered in front of him with an arched brow. "Do you know the answer?"

Of course he did. "My heart."

The shadow appeared impressed. "In all these centuries, you alone have learned our riddle."

"Does that mean I can leave?" Nick asked hopefully.

The scenery faded until they were again in the dark cavern. But this time, there was only the one door that had no window. The phantom lowered itself to the ground to tower over him. "When you are ready, you may go."

Nick headed straight to it. "Don't have to tell me twice."

"But . . ."

Hesitating, he looked back at the spirit. *I seriously hate that word.* "Yeah?"

"You can stay here where you will be respected and feared by all. Where no one will ever dare to mock or belittle you. The choice is yours."

"I already gave you my choice. I want to go home."

The door opened. But instead of being elated, Nick was duly cautious.

Was it another trick?

With your luck? Why should you doubt it?

Yet for once, he decided to go with faith and to follow his heart like the wolf had said. Bracing himself, just in case, he walked through the door and ended up right where he'd started.

Outside his condo.

You're messing with me, right?

Nick scanned the street. It was a lot darker now and so quiet it was downright spooky. But that didn't matter. He had to let his mom know he was safe.

Opening the iron door to his building, he rushed in and sprinted up the stairs. When he got to their condo, the door wasn't quite pulled to. A wave of furious fear rushed through him.

His mom would never leave the door ajar. Not for anything. She was so paranoid, she even locked her bedroom and bathroom doors.

"Ma?" he called, pushing it open cautiously.

Stopping dead in his tracks, he surveyed the damaged living room. But it was the blood on the floor and ceiling that he couldn't stop staring at. Was it his mother's?

That very thought terrified him.

"Mom!" he called, running to her bedroom, hoping she might be safely locked in there.

She wasn't. It was as empty as his heart. And it was just like Ambrose had warned him. He had put his mother in harm's way and when she needed him most to protect her, he hadn't been here.

How could I do this to her?

How?

Unable to stand the pain and guilt, he turned with the intention of finding Caleb and then hunting down his mother's whereabouts so that he could kill who or whatever had taken her.

CHAPTER 20

Summoning Caleb to his side, Nick knew he'd changed somehow. He could feel it with every molecule of his body. He was stronger and more confident now. More sure about his powers. That cave and his walk home had done something strange to him. Like some inner cosmic switch had been flipped into overdrive.

But he didn't have time to investigate it. Not while his mother was missing.

"Caleb!" he shouted.

To his relief, Caleb finally appeared in Nick's living room by his side.

His gaze suspicious, Caleb raked a slow stare down his body. "It *is* you. Right?"

What kind of question was that? "Who did you think was calling you?" Nick asked sarcastically.

Caleb shrugged. "Had no idea. I knew it wasn't your

father, and though I suspected it was you . . . you've been missing, I didn't want to pop into a bad situation, blind. So I dragged my feet a little."

Nick could forgive him that, especially after having seen the wolf and what real captivity could mean for demonkyn. Caleb had a right to be cautious.

Sliding closer to him, Caleb cocked his head as he gave Nick a piercing stare. He looked like he was ready to bolt or fight if Nick made any wrong or sudden move. Part of Nick wanted to say "boo" to see how high the demon would jump in fear. Only respect for Caleb's quick and deadly overreactions kept his impulse under control.

"What has happened to you?" Caleb asked.

Had his skin turned green? While Nick could feel an inner change, he wondered what Caleb saw on him that made his friend so skittish and hesitant. "What do you mean?"

Caleb took Nick's chin in his hand and turned Nick's head so that he could examine him carefully. "You look the same, but you're different. I can feel it in my gut. You're more powerful than you were before. Where did you go?"

"Hel," Nick said bitterly.

Caleb started to roll his eyes, then caught himself as if he realized Nick wasn't being a smartass for once. He let go of him immediately. "You mean Helheim?"

"You know it?"

"Not personally, but I've met a few of its residents over the centuries. Wonderful creatures . . . if you don't mind lunatics and serial killers."

"Yeah. Definitely not a place I'd recommend for a vacation, unless you're into gruesome and royally screwed up . . . kind of like high school, only colder."

Caleb ignored that last bit. "Why were you there?"

"Hel had me Nicknapped so that she could use me as a bargaining chip. Good to be me, eh?"

Caleb ignored his thick sarcasm. "With whom was she bargaining?"

"I don't know. She didn't say, and I wasn't there long enough to find out. I figured it didn't matter who wanted me, it was better to get away and think about the other later."

Caleb laughed. "Wise choice. But how did you get free? And don't you dare tell me it was because you're too cute to keep."

He'd been around him too long when he started knowing Nick's stock sarcastic retorts. But Caleb was right, they didn't have time to waste on it. "One of her servants let me go."

Caleb frowned. "Why would one do that?"

"I really don't know. Didn't care. Wanted to get home, but if I had to guess, I think it was more an act of defiance on his part to get back at her and to piss her off."

He laughed. "Then he must have been a demon."

"Why?" Nick asked.

"We're the only ones stupid and strong enough to defy our masters so blatantly."

That explained a lot about Nick's congenital birth defect—smartmouthitis. *Thanks, Dad.*

"You might be interested to know he was the same loup-garu who attacked us earlier on Royal."

Both of Caleb's eyebrows shot up as his face drained of all color. "I wasn't attacked by a loup-garu, Nick. That, I would have killed. What I fought was an Aamon."

Just what Nick loved most. More vocabulary to learn. And unlike the crap from school, not knowing these words could get him killed. "A what?"

"One of the first and highest order of warrior demons."

That didn't sound good. "As in one of the few who can kick *your* ass?"

Caleb gestured toward the bruises on his face and neck that said the wolf had cleaned the street with him. "I assumed he was after your father's powers. I had no idea someone had sent him to kidnap you. Did he give you his name?"

"No. He said he couldn't remember it."

"What do you mean?"

Nick shrugged with a nonchalance he didn't feel. "From what I gathered, he's been locked in Hel for a number of centuries. And I think they cock fight him. But the only thing I know for certain is that they don't hold him with any kind of regard. They have him tied down like a rabid animal and treat him like one."

He saw his own horror mirrored in Caleb's eyes, and while Caleb hadn't seen the abuse, there was something Nick picked up on that said he'd either seen or experienced something very similar in his past.

"I can't believe you stumbled onto an Aamon." A tic worked in Caleb's jaw. "They're even less people- and demon-friendly than a Malachai. . . . And there weren't that many of them to begin with, and even fewer of them who could still be alive today. Amazing."

"I'm assuming from your tone of voice, they weren't on your side of the war."

"No. They were definitely on yours and I'm lucky I got away from him intact tonight. He must have wanted you badly to let me go before ripping my throat out."

Nick laughed nervously. It was so much fun being the brass ring for hellmonkeys and jerks. "Here lately, everybody does." Except for supermodels and hot babes.

Dang, if he had to be pursued and locked up, couldn't it at least be by people he wanted chasing him? Women whose beds he wouldn't mind being chained to for eternity?

Oh well. Life sucked and then they billed you for it. Kind of like how airlines charged you money *before* you got on a plane so that in the event they screwed up and killed you, they were already paid, and they wouldn't have to give you a refund.

Nick sighed, then jerked his chin to the mess in his house. "So what happened here? Where's my mom?"

Caleb visibly cringed. "You know as much as I do."

And he should have cringed for giving that answer. Nick's vision darkened as his fury coursed through him, and demanded Caleb's heart for not protecting his mother. "What have you been doing while I was gone?"

His lip curling, Caleb raked him with a sneer. "Watching soap operas and picking belly lint out of my toes. . . . What the hell do you think I've been doing? I was making preparations to keep your sorry butt alive."

"And to the devil with my mother and her safety?"

"Yeah, Nick. That's *exactly* what I was thinking." Caleb's voice dripped with sarcasm. "'Cause I knew just how unhinged my lack of action would make *you*. My whole entire thinking process was how I could piss you off and make you go Malachai sooner rather than later. Ah, man, you so busted me." With a grin that should be worn by a psychotic clown, Caleb clapped him on the back. "So tell me, Nick, did my brilliant thinking work?"

"You better be glad I don't know how to Force choke you."

Caleb actually took a whole step back from him. His anger wilted under a wave of actual fear. Now there was something Nick had *never* seen on Caleb's face before. At least not where he was concerned.

"What happened to you?"

Nick calmed at the wary note in Caleb's voice. What was he seeing when he looked at him? "I have to find my mother."

"And you're the only one who can."

Nick scowled. "What do you mean?"

"It's why I didn't try to find her, Nick. She's been taken out of this realm. . . ." He shot back another step as Nick lunged for him, then turned sideways, out of Nick's immediate range. "She's not dead. Sheez!" Caleb raised his hands and put an energy shield around himself to keep Nick from beating him. "Calm down and listen. She's not *my* mother. I have no connection to her, which means no way to track her. Just as I couldn't track you into Helheim. But now that you're back, we can get her."

Nick smacked his fist against the invisible wall protecting Caleb—who should be on his knees in gratitude that Nick couldn't reach him right now. "Swear to me you're not lying."

"If I didn't think we could get your mother back alive and whole, I wouldn't be here. I'd be on my way to another hell realm 'cause I know her death would send you off into a massive piranha-style killing frenzy. And the longer you keep trying to rip my head off, the longer she's staying gone."

That succeeded in calming him. "Okay. How do we find her?"

Caleb visibly cringed.

Nick's gut tightened instantly. "What?"

"Take a deep breath. Ride herd on your temper and don't freak."

Yeah, that really helped his temper. Like a kick in his head and a stomp to his stones. "What?"

"We need help to do this."

The sick knot in his stomach twisted even tighter. "I'm seriously not going to like it, am I?"

"Nope. But we have to do it."

Growling deep in his throat, Nick raked his hand through his hair. "Fine. What is it?"

Caleb's gaze went over Nick's shoulder to focus on something behind him.

Curious and suspicious, Nick turned, then froze. Dressed in a black turtleneck and jeans, Kody stood there, holding a small vial. His stomach shot south as bile went north.

"Oh hell to the no!" Nick snapped as he faced Caleb again. Furious, he gestured toward her. "She's here to kill me. *That* is your solution? You're like one of those generals who wants to put a house fire out with a nuclear bomb, aren't you?"

"Nick—"

"Don't you Nick me, Malphas. You're not my mother. I—"

"Nick!" Kody shouted, interrupting him.

Enraged over a tone of voice only his mother could get away with using, Nick spun toward her. "What!"

She closed the distance between them. "Breathe," she said with a calmness he couldn't fathom. "You have to let go of everything negative inside you. If you want to find your mom, you have to track her with your heart. You can *only* track her with your heart. Hatred destroys everything it touches—it will never allow you to build any kind of bridge from this realm to whatever one she's been taken to. Your love of her is what will allow you to connect and find her."

He looked back at Caleb.

"I don't know how to use those powers, Nick. Like you, I was born for malice. It's what feeds me."

Nick swallowed as he finally brought his emotions

under control. For his mom alone, he was willing to trust his enemy. "What do I need to do?"

She held her hand out to him.

His first impulse was to slap it away and curse her. But his mother was more important to him than his hatred of Kody. Forcing himself to stay calm, he took her warm hand. The sensation of her flesh touching his sent a heated wave through him. He'd forgotten how soft her skin was. How much she smelled like sunshine and roses.

Kody smiled up at him.

That and her touch succeeded in driving out his hate and anger. The loss of it was so sudden that it left him exhausted. Drained.

Kody pulled him against her and sank her other hand into his hair. Even though he wanted to hate her for what she'd come to do, he laid his head on her shoulder and allowed her to hold him against her. Ever so slowly, she rocked with him in her arms.

"*Pax tecum,*" she whispered in his ear, sending chills all over his body. *Peace be with you.*

"*Et cum spiritu tuo,*" he responded automatically. *And with your spirit.*

And when she placed a light, tender kiss to the side of his head, he found a realm of warm serenity that he'd never known before. It was like all was right in the world. Like nothing could harm him or upset him.

She stroked his back. *"Ora pro nobis . . ."*

With those words a dam inside him burst open. In one instant, he could see the fabric of the entire universe and everything in it. He heard the voices of millions of people who had lived and who were alive. It hit him so hard and fast that had she not been holding him, he would have fallen. Instead, her strength kept him balanced while her warmth kept him anchored firmly right here.

The ether screamed out as it did anytime he tried to access it for information. But where it was normally too overwhelming for him to navigate, tonight he fully understood how to find his way through it all. How to focus until he only heard the one voice he sought.

His mother's.

And yet he couldn't find her. Nowhere . . . She was completely silent to him. His anger and panic started mounting, but Kody tightened her arms around him.

"Shh," she breathed against his ear. "Stay calm. *Sicut erat in principio, et nunc, et semper, et in saecula saeculorum."* As it was in the beginning, it is now and will be to the ages of ages. . . .

Once more, his anger dissipated. He heard the

sounds of horrendous fighting coming hard and fast at him.

Afraid for his mother, he followed it. Only it wasn't a battle for or about her.

He saw himself in his demonic form. His armor glistened in the dull light of a fading sun while he fought against an army that was determined to destroy every last bit of him and his troops. His soldiers pulled back to protect him. But it was too late.

He was about to be defeated.

Dumbfounded, he couldn't understand how this had happened. No one had ever equaled him. Not even the Sephiroth. He'd killed his archenemy in a matter of minutes.

And then he saw his true nemesis. The one who had bled him and his men the most . . .

Their leader emerged from the midst of their number. Drunk on his impending victory, he called out to rally his soldiers and push them forward for the last attack.

Nick knew instinctively that if he killed their leader, they would scatter like frightened roaches. The humans would fall.

His eyes flashed red, then the same swirling silver as Acheron's before he launched himself at the fool who'd left the safe shelter of his army. Focused solely on him, Nick ignored everything else.

He came down on top of the leader with his sword raised. Their weapons rang out as they clashed against each other. His enemy rained acid blood and fire down on Nick, who used his own powers to drive his enemy back. He met him stroke for violent stroke. To his credit, the man stood strong and he fought longer than anyone else had ever lasted.

The man might have even defeated him, but for one thing . . .

A sudden feminine cry of pain. His enemy's attention turned from their fight to the smaller soldier several yards away. He kicked Nick back, then ran to her.

Assuring him she was safe, she ordered him to return to their fight.

He refused to go. "There is nothing I will not do to protect my family," he said with a determination so raw, it reverberated all the way through the Malachai.

Fascinated by it, Nick watched the leader cradle her in his arms as if she were unspeakably precious . . . as if she weighed nothing at all. He picked her up and carried her, trying to get her far away from the danger. She clung to him as her blood ran down both their armored pieces.

It'd been so long since Nick had loved someone like that, that he tried to remember the emotion. But while he watched the two of them, it ignited his fury. How dare his enemy turn his back when there was a war to be fought!

Nick headed for him, dodging through the combatants around him, slaying any who dared to charge his path.

Unaware that Nick was coming for him, the soldier handed her off to another of his men. "Get her to safety. Do not let her die!"

He turned back to fight, but it was too late. Nick was already on him. He stabbed their leader straight through his worthless heart and drove him to the ground, where he planted his enemy with his sword pressed all the way through his weak human body. His enemy kicked and squirmed, but there was nothing he could do except die.

The woman screamed out as she fought against the man holding her. Stunned by it all, the soldier released her. Disregarding all danger, she ran to the fallen soldier.

"No!" she sobbed over and over again as she exposed his face. She laid her hand to his cheek and wept as if her entire world had been shattered.

He was dead and there was nothing she could do.

With the battle cry of a thousand Furies, she took the leader's sword and ran at Nick to kill him.

He raised his arm and caught her blow, then shot a blast at her that knocked her helmet free.

Dazed but undaunted, she jerked her head back to glare at him. A pair of sharp, green eyes telegraphed her hatred from a bruised face he knew all too well.

Kody.

Nick pulled back, wanting to flee a war he didn't want to see anymore. Was it past or yet to be fought?

He didn't have enough control of his powers to know for sure.

I killed what she loved.

Turning back to the scene, he looked down at the soldier he'd stabbed, and total shock floored him.

He'd killed himself. . . .

He was their leader. It was his face. . . .

Panic tore through him as he began to hyperventilate from the images that made no sense whatsoever. How could he be both people?

Safe in the present, Kody held him fast while her voice continued to offer him comfort and warmth. She laid her cheek against his. Her breath teased his ear and electrified his body.

He felt his powers sharpen.

"Don't cry, Cherise. I won't let them hurt you."

Still raw from what he'd seen in that last battle, and with his very foundation shaken, Nick jerked at the last thing he expected to hear. His father's bitter tone promising protection to his mother.

What the . . . ?

He drifted back from them so that he could identify where they were.

Ice-blue walls surrounded them with a shiny surface that cast distorted images all around them. In some ways, it reminded him of a warehouse. But it wasn't the same. He'd never seen anything like it. And after a few seconds, he realized those weren't reflections in the wall.

They were demons trying to break through.

In the center of the empty room, his mother was terrified and sobbing while his father walked an angry circle around her, daring the wall demons to try for him. In response, the swarming demons salivated for the elder Malachai's powers.

And Nick knew what all of them did. Soon Adarian would be weak enough to be killed by them. No matter how much fight his father might have, he wouldn't be able to last long against that number.

The demons slammed against the cage, simultaneously trying to break it open and drain his father.

Nick pulled away from Kody with a jerk. His brain

was on lockdown from everything he'd seen, to the point that he couldn't speak.

"Did you find her?" Kody asked.

Dazed, Nick nodded, then looked to Caleb. "I'm such an effing idiot."

"We knew that," he said drily. "We definitely didn't have to throw you into a coma for that little-known nugget."

Nick shoved at him.

"What did you see?" Kody asked as their ever-present voice of reason.

Nick returned his attention to her. "She's in a place I can't identify. It's like nothing I've ever seen before. It was just a room with demons inside the walls." He winced as an image of her terrified face cut through him. "I should *never* have left my mom alone tonight. How selfish am I?"

"Preoccupation with your own survival isn't selfish. It's human."

And that was what he'd missed most about not having Kody around. She had an incredible knack for taking the sting out of his stupidity. But tonight, he wasn't going to allow her to make him feel better. He didn't deserve it. "It was selfish, but the only real question is, how do we find her location and get her out?"

Caleb crossed his arms over his chest as he pinned a

smug look on Kody. "I have an idea. What do you know about summoning an Aamon?"

Her expression said Caleb had lost his mind. "That it's a really bad idea."

"Then I'm out. I got nothing."

Nick gave him a pained, droll stare. "Way to participate, Malphas. Thanks."

Kody held her hand up to interrupt them. "There might be another way."

"Yeah?" Caleb asked.

She smiled at both of them. "We could summon the Malachai."

Caleb scowled. "A Malachai we got." He pointed to Nick.

"I know. . . . And a Malachai can trace those of his kind. Even into another dimension."

"Cosmic doorway," Caleb breathed, then turned his attention to Nick. "I like it."

Nick had no idea what they were talking about, but from the intensity of those stares he had a feeling it wasn't good. Especially not for him. "What is a cosmic doorway?"

Ignoring the question, Kody tapped her finger to her chin as she continued to ponder her suggestion. "It's risky."

Caleb shrugged nonchalantly. "So's living."

"Entities, please," Nick said, getting their attention. "What are we talking about?"

Kody took a deep breath before she explained. "Failsafe. The younger Malachai can always go to the elder. There is no place in existence that he can't hide from his son."

Nick finally understood. "So that I can kill him when I come of age."

Kody nodded. "But it's risky. If you're not ready to kill him, he can kill you, and, knowing your father, he won't hesitate. Just like in the hospital."

She would bring that up. Not one of his finer moments by a long shot. Yet in his defense, he'd been unconscious and seriously hurt when his father had come into the room to kill him.

Before Kyrian and Acheron had driven him out and saved Nick's life, his father had promised to kill Nick the next time they met.

Let's hear it for paternal concern. . . .

Even so, Nick wasn't so sure about his father's ability to carry out his threat. Not so long as his mother was with him. Alone . . .

Yeah, his dad would be toast if he tried anything.

He cast them a smug grin. "Weird as it sounds, I don't think he's going to touch me with my mother in the room."

Caleb considered it. "He did back down from the mighty Chihuahua awful fast . . . not that I blame him. Cherise's pretty intense when it comes to you."

She was indeed.

"So what do we need to do?" Nick asked.

Kody held her hand out for him to take it.

Nick hesitated. She had been sent here to kill him. She'd admitted it.

Yet no sooner had that thought gone through his mind than he saw the image of her clutching his dead body in her arms and weeping at his loss. Since he'd been the man fighting by her side in his vision, he knew it couldn't be from her past.

Nor did it make sense that it'd be from their future. But even if it was, the future wasn't set in stone. Ambrose had taught him that. Any little thing he did could change it. However, if that vision was a glimpse at his future, in at least one alternate time and place he and Kody were together.

Which meant she wouldn't necessarily kill him in this life, this time.

Maybe.

He glanced to Caleb and remembered what his friend had said about making decisions that made his gut clench. This was definitely one of those times.

Hoping he wouldn't live to regret this, Nick took her hand. "When this is done, we need to talk."

"Nick, I can't—"

"Shh," he said, cutting her off. "Let's get through this first." He looked at Caleb.

"I might be your boyfriend in school, but I'm not holding your hand. Ever." He placed his fist on Nick's shoulder.

"Homophobe."

"Snotwit."

Nick tsked at him. "Cay . . . you disappoint me."

Caleb popped him on the back of his head. "Tell him how to do this, Kody, before my hostility escalates."

"Think of your father, Nick. Then imagine all of us together with him."

Adarian paced the room, trying everything he could to break out.

It was useless.

Damn you, Grim! You backstabbing dog.

He should have known better than to ever trust Death. What had he been thinking?

But then he knew. Death was supposed to be his ally in all things.

Since when has a Malachai ever had anyone to trust? Are you mad? It was true. His breed was only known to make enemies. Never friends.

Everything hated them.

Behind him, Cherise broke into another round of sobs as she huddled on the floor in terror of their situation, and the demons who wanted to kill them both.

Adarian winced at the sound. Her tears ripped at a heart he hadn't even known he'd possessed until the fateful day when she'd walked past him on the street. He had been on the trail of a demon he wanted to kill and absorb. But that desire had fled the moment her sweet scent hit him.

She had been shopping with her friends, whose faces he couldn't recall. They were completely unimportant. His attention had been solely on her. Her blond hair had been the color of sunlight and her big blue eyes the same as a perfect sky.

But it had been her precious laugh that chipped away the ice inside him. So full of life. So very sweet. She had captured him in an instant and left him helpless against her.

He'd been so enamored of her that he'd even enrolled in her school and posed as a student. All so that he could watch her from afar.

For over a year, that was all he'd done. Sat in mind-numbing classes just so he could be in the same room with her, like a desperate flower reaching for sunlight through the jagged cracks of a broken wall. He hadn't even tried to converse with her. He hadn't been worthy.

And then one day, miraculously, she'd noticed him as he sat behind her in a history class. Every day after that, she'd flounce into the room and talk to him before the bell like he was a normal boy. For the first time in his existence, he'd craved friendship. So he sought her out for no other reason than to laugh with her. He'd meant her no harm. Ever.

But because of his lack of human contact and ignorance of their world and customs, he hadn't even realized just how young she was at the time. That it was her naive innocence that lured him when he should have left her alone.

Even then, he would never have touched her had she not innocently kissed him. It'd been the first time in his centuries of living that anyone had shown him such tenderness. Or any tenderness at all.

She had opened emotions in him that he'd never known before. That he couldn't understand. Born to kill and destroy, a Malachai was a basic creature. They felt absolutely nothing except total hatred. There was no other anything. Just a void.

And that wonderful, beautiful kiss . . .

It alone had taught him regret and sadness. Misery. To this day, he would give anything if he could take back that afternoon and leave her as pure as he'd found her. In one thoughtless, selfish heartbeat, he'd killed the very thing he loved most.

I am a destroyer.

It was all he'd been born for. And he had destroyed the only woman in the universe that had ever meant anything to him. *Damn me for it.* And well he should have been.

His heart broken, he reached for her now. "Please don't cry, Cherise. I swear I won't let anyone hurt you again."

Her cold look pierced him. "Why should I believe you?"

"Because I mean it." He reached to brush away her tears. She cringed from his touch, and his stomach lurched. *Please don't do that to me. . . .*

All he wanted was for her to smile at him the way she used to.

You ruined it. Just as you ruin everything.

"What do you want from me, Cherise?"

She wiped angrily at her tears. "I want nothing from you. I want nothing to do with you, either."

His throat tightened with unfamiliar sadness. *Very well, my precious . . .*

He would leave her alone. But he would make sure no one else put a light of sadness in those celestial blue eyes.

Nick did his best to conjure the room he'd seen his parents in.

Nothing happened. He kept running the image over and over in his head, but with every second that passed, he lost hope. *I can't do it. I am worthless.*

I can't even save my own mother. . . .

Kody rose up on her tiptoes and whispered in his ear. "I believe in you, Nick." She tightened her hand on his.

In that moment, a bright white light shot through his skull and exploded. When it did, it felt like a blitz tackle against his abdomen, one that lifted him off his feet and shot him toward the sky.

One second, they were in his living room. In the next . . .

They were at the end of Canal Street? Really?

How could I have screwed this up?

Scowling, Nick turned around in the center of the neutral ground where Convention Center Boulevard intersected Canal at the World Trade Center.

Even worse? That gross, creepy Mardi Gras clown

statue that was the stuff of horror movies and bad childhood memories stared right at him, mocking his incompetence. He'd always hated the Batman/Joker lunatic smile it had.

In daylight it was disturbing. At night with the shadowy lights on it . . .

"Hello, little boy with your itty-bitty friends," his mind created a demonic falsetto for the statue's voice. *"Would you like to play with my shrunken head on a stick? Don't be afraid, he only wants a small bite of your flesh. And I only want your soul. . . ."*

Yeah, what sicko had thought *that* was a great landmark when ninety percent of the population shared his clownphobia?

"Why are we here?" Nick asked his friends as he eyeballed the jester lest it move and do something evil, as all clowns eventually did.

Caleb cursed in a low tone. "I should have thought of this place."

Nick was even more confused. "Why? The ferry doesn't run this late and the Riverwalk's been closed for hours."

"No, not those." Kody let go of his hand and checked her watch. "You think we can still get in?" she asked Caleb, who shrugged.

Nick was getting really irritated. "In where? Trouble? Synch? Between?"

They exchanged an amused look with his last guess.

"You're warm," Caleb said with an evil twist to his lips.

Yeah, that clown was definitely possessing him. . . .

"Le monde au delà du voile," Kody said.

Nick scowled. "The world behind the veil?"

She nodded. "Why do you think they call this neutral ground?"

"Because the Creoles in the Quarter," he pointed to the left side of Canal, "and the Americans in Uptown," he pointed right, "couldn't stand each other. So they let weeds and crap grow up to be a barrier between the two parts of the city. Later, they started meeting here to do business and sell things. Since they were conducting a form of cold war, they started calling all the medians where they met neutral ground."

"Yeah . . . you keep on believing the lies our kind feed to the humans." Caleb clapped his hand against Nick's shoulder. "Haven't you ever wondered about the Spanish Plaza behind this place?"

Was he on demon crack? "Um, no. Not really. Other than it was a cool place to get my feet wet when I was a kid."

Kody jumped in on Caleb's lunacy. "Ever notice that from up high, the fountain in the center of it and its surrounding area bears a scary resemblance to a Xibalba round? Right down to the way it lays with the river?"

"No. But that has a lot to do with the fact that I don't know who or what Xibalba is."

"Mayan underworld," Kody explained. "The word itself means 'place of fear.' And all over the world, there are doorways from this world to others. Doorways we can use to access alternate places."

Nick glanced up at the sinister statue. "Well, that explains Mr. Creepy Clown being here, doesn't it?"

A slow smile curled one side of Caleb's mouth as he let out a low, evil laugh. "This is going to be some twisted fun."

"Malphas!" Kody snapped. "Don't you dare!"

Walking backwards, Caleb spread his arms wide and laughed. "I've got to. I can't resist. It's pulling me, Kody . . . I can't stop." Caleb feigned great physical pain.

Kody growled at Caleb before she took Nick's hand and pulled him after Caleb. Nick wanted to drag his feet, but he couldn't do that if this really would get him to his mother.

Caleb began running, then launched himself straight

up to the very narrow pedestal the clown stood on. Nick gaped at what had to be a twenty-foot jump. Not to mention, Caleb had to balance on something about the size of a narrow two-by-four.

"Forget quarterback. You ought to play running back."

Ignoring him, Caleb reached to the smaller jester head on a stick that Nick had named Mr. Little Creepy.

Nick curled his lip. "Don't touch that thing. You're gonna get rabies or scabies or parvo or something."

With another evil laugh, Caleb touched the head.

"Get your finger out of my nose, daeve!"

Cursing, Nick jumped three feet back as the statue came to life. "I knew it! Damn it all! I knew that thing was a minion of hell!"

The jester went slack-jawed as he turned his head toward Caleb. "Please tell me he isn't one of us."

"Hate to disappoint you, Sal."

The jester made a face of absolute agony. "How far demons have fallen that he can be counted among our family. Sad, sad day." Sighing heavily, he shook his head. Then he glanced back to Caleb. "I suppose you want in?"

"Yes, we do."

The jester held the small head out toward Caleb. "You know the cost of admission."

Caleb bit his finger, then allowed nine drops of blood to fall onto the smaller clown head.

The jester tapped his heart with the little head, then waved it high above. As he moved it, the Riverwalk sign on the right flickered so fast that for a moment, Nick thought he was imagining things.

"Thanks, Sal." Caleb jumped down to land near Nick. "You ready?"

"For nightmares? Sure. Will now have plenty of them, Cay, *merci beaucoup*."

Caleb snorted. "You're such a baby."

Yeah, right. "I'm not the only person who doesn't like clowns, you know?"

Kody patted his shoulder in sympathy. Caleb ignored him.

As they passed the giant Lafayette horse statue beside the Trade Center, Lafayette lifted his tricorn hat to them as his horse reared up on its pedestal. The statue rider jerked its reins and it settled down. "Malphas," he said in greeting.

Caleb inclined his head to him. "Gilbert. Good to see you."

"Et toi, mon ami. Bon soir."

"À bientôt."

His jaw dropping, Nick blinked at Caleb. "I think I now know what it is you do when you're not with me. How much time do you spend here?" Apparently, a lot.

Caleb passed him an innocent stare. "I don't know what you're talking about."

Sure he didn't. . . .

Without another word, Caleb led them under the Riverwalk sign arch that Nick had gone through hundreds of times in his life. Normally, it led to the Spanish Plaza where the humongous, ornate fountain would be on the right and an oyster bar straight back.

Tonight, the air seemed to shiver around them. And as they passed underneath the arch, a flash of light blinded Nick for the merest second. When he could see again, the Plaza had a dome over it. Instead of being dark from night, an eerie green glow made it as bright as day. And the water in the fountain appeared to be blood.

"What is this place?" he whispered to Kody.

"Think of it like an amusement park and holding station. It's where demons who want to enter the human world can stay until they find a way in. Or demons from our world can come and intermingle with nonhumans in a relatively safe environment." She gestured to what appeared to be a row of stores and a building that had strange music coming from it. "There's even a demon brothel and bar."

Great . . .

"It's also where the Hellchasers hold their prisoners until they can hand them off to the right party." Caleb slowed his pace as they neared a man with short brown hair and greenish brown eyes. He wore brown armguards with gold embroidery that started glowing at Caleb's approach.

"Speak of the pain," Caleb mumbled to Nick and Kody. Then louder, he spoke to the man in front of them. "Tristan."

Tristan narrowed his eyes dangerously at Nick and Kody. "Who are your friends, Malphas?"

"Not your targets."

"Yeah," Nick added. "We're not the droids you're looking for."

Kody was aghast. "Don't taunt the Hellchaser, Nick. Most lack a sense of humor."

Without warning, Caleb banked left and headed through a set of glass doors that led to a long, narrow hallway. "All right, Nick. You're up. Sniff out your parents."

"Excuse me?"

"This is the Hall of Holding. If you saw them in a holding cell, it would most likely be one of these."

Nick slowed his pace. "What is this? Like demon death row?"

"No. More like intake."

That didn't make sense. "Why would my parents be in here?"

Caleb held his hands up and shrugged. "You're the one who led us here."

True. He still had no idea who had taken his parents, never mind the why.

With a deep breath for courage, Nick summoned his powers and used them to probe the ether for a sign or signal. His ears grew warm as he finally located them. They really were here.

Thank you, God.

He grinned at his friends. "Got it."

Kody took his hand as Caleb touched his shoulder. Nick teleported them into the room . . . right in front of his father. The instant they appeared, the demons in the walls froze in shock, as did Nick's parents.

Caleb clenched his shoulder so hard, he bruised it. "Uh . . . Nick." He enunciated each word slowly and with great irritation. "You forgot to tell us one itty-bitty important detail." His grip tightened even more as he snarled quickly. "Like the fact your parents are surrounded by thin walls holding back things that want to eat us!"

As if they heard every word, the demons went on an attacking frenzy.

"Baby?" His mother ran to him and grabbed him into a fierce hug. "Are you all right?"

"Fine. You?"

She slid her gaze to his father before she nodded.

Nick turned slowly to face Adarian. This was the first time he'd stood beside his father since he'd been a child. Back then, his father had looked like a giant and had scared the bejesus out of him.

Tonight, they stood eye to eye. And while his father still had him on body weight and muscle mass, he no longer intimidated Nick at all.

And Adarian knew it.

But the one thing that did disturb Nick was how much he favored his father in looks. The only thing different was their eye color. How his mother could ever look at him and not curse and beat him, he had no idea. He was a walking reminder, every single day of her life, of what his father had done to her when she'd been younger than he was now, and not once in sixteen years of his life had she ever let Nick know it.

In that one single heartbeat, the full capacity of her heart and love hit him so hard, he could barely breathe.

And one day, he, who had ruined her entire life by being born to her, would be the cause of her death.

No wonder Ambrose went Malachai. Nick finally got it.

"You are an idiot of the first magnitude," his father

growled. "I should have devoured you when you were born."

His mom turned to defend him, but Nick wouldn't let her. "It's all right, Mom." He stepped around to block her from his father. "I'm not a kid anymore and I'm not afraid of him."

His mother touched his shoulder. "I don't understand what's going on here, Nicky . . . where are we? Why can't I leave?"

Kody put her arms around his mother's shoulders and pulled her back. "Everything's fine, Mrs. Gautier. It's just a bad dream. That's all."

Nick inclined his head to Kody, grateful for her support and strength. When he turned back to his father, he caught his father's unguarded expression as Adarian made sure Kody wasn't hurting his mother.

The worthless bastard really did love his mother. . . .

But the love in his gaze turned to brutal hatred when he met Nick's eyes.

Yeah, they were still at war with one another. No mistaking that look.

"Have you any idea what you've done?" Adarian snarled at him. "They now have us both, and there's no way out of here."

"That's not entirely true."

Both Nick and his father looked at Kody.

"I don't have demon blood. I can open the door. But the problem we're going to have is that your mom is human. She's the Godiva chocolate to all the creatures hanging around here. When we get out, they will all be after her."

"And Kody," Caleb interjected, "doesn't have the passcode for this room. So when she opens the door, an alarm will sound and there's nothing we can do to stop it. The dampeners will come on and we won't be able to teleport. Our powers will be weakened. The only way back to the human realm is to get to the arch and run through it."

His father shoved at him. "You are so stupid."

Nick started for him, then stopped himself for once. This wasn't the time and place for losing his temper. Not while his mother and Kody were in danger.

He glared at his sperm donor. "We are going to fight. One day, one of us will kill the other. That's a given. But today, we have something more important to fight for." He passed a meaningful glance to his mother before turning back to Adarian. "Now, you can be the dick I know you are. Or you can finally be the man my mother needs you to be."

"You don't know who or what you're dealing with, boy." His father went to poke a finger into Nick's shoulder.

Nick grabbed it and shoved his father back. "I'm dealing with a really old and pathetic, dying Malachai, and every second I'm here with you, you're getting weaker and sicker. Unfortunately, while I may have all the power, you have all the control of it. We need each other to get her out of here. So are we going to fight each other, and let everyone die, or are you going to learn how to play on a team for once?"

The expression on his father's face said that they were about to deathmatch.

Nick braced himself for the fight.

His father sucked his breath in so hard that it sounded like a vicious roar. And as he did so, he grew in height until he was twenty feet tall. His skin changed from its normal tawny shade to a mixture of gold and black that swirled in a beautiful pattern. His eyes bright gold, Adarian opened his mouth, showing his fangs.

Completely unimpressed, Nick gave him a cold, dry stare. "Are you trying to scare me? Doesn't work."

Caleb laughed. "Yeah, but put on a clown suit and he'll scream like a girl."

Bristling at his words, Kody cleared her throat.

"You're not a girl, Kody."

She rolled her eyes. "Oh, stop while you're behind, Malphas."

Adarian took a step toward Nick's mother, then

stopped. He glanced to Kody. "Open the door, girl. But once we're back in the human world . . ." His eyes glowed red as he pinned Nick with a murderous sneer. "I *will* kill you."

"Bonne chance." Nick covered his mother while Kody manifested a short recurve bow.

Nocking an arrow, she aimed it for the wall. "Straight and true. One shot and we're through." She winked at Nick, then turned around and placed her back to the wall. The moment her skin touched it, it swung open.

She readied her bow while she held the door. "Go."

They ran for it. But as Caleb predicted, they didn't get far. Demons descended on them like park ants on sliced watermelon.

Kody fired her bow while Caleb manifested his armor to fight. Nick used his fire bombs to attack them.

His father tore the thronging demons apart with his bare hands.

Nick paused as he watched his father fighting. It would be impressive if it wasn't so terrifying.

Step by slow, excruciating step, they made their way down the hall toward the entrance. Nick kept his mother between him and Kody. And just when he thought they might make it, his father slipped and fell to his knees.

Adarian tried to stand, then fell again.

What was wrong with the elder demon?

His father looked straight at him. Nick sucked his breath in hard at the sight of his face. His features were hollow and pale. Gaunt. A thick blanket of sweat covered him.

Nick was weakening his father a lot faster than he'd have thought possible. Guilt stabbed him hard. Without thinking, he reached to help his father up.

Adarian bit at him and hissed. "Don't touch me!"

"You'll weaken him even faster," Kody warned.

Nick put more distance between them. As they reached the front room of the hall, a shadow shot out of the wall. Before anyone could identify it, it grabbed his mother.

He lunged to stop it and missed. Adarian didn't. He grabbed the demon by the throat and brought it down.

Nick grabbed his mother and moved even faster for the door. Just as he reached it, his mother was torn from his arms.

"Mom!" But it was too late. The demon had taken flight with her. Nick shot out his wings and launched himself toward them.

Then slammed into the wall. He cursed at the pain that tore through his entire body. He so did not have the hang of this.

But man, his father did. He watched as Adarian put his head down and streamlined his drag coefficient so that he moved like a bullet. He and the demon rolled and fought in the air.

Taking advantage of their inattention, Nick placed his mother's hand in the crook of his elbow and kicked open the door.

Not much farther.

Yet as they descended down the steps, he came face-to-face with the wolf who'd freed him from Helheim. Blocking their escape, the wolf growled and snapped.

"What are you doing?" Nick asked it.

"I cannot let you pass this time. Not after I freed you. The human is my charge and I *must* keep her here."

Nick shook his head. "Let us pass."

"I cannot."

"You can and you will."

The wolf launched at his throat. Nick ducked and twisted away while Kody moved in to protect his mother for him. Walking backwards to put more distance between him and the women, Nick prepared himself for another attack.

"Zavid!" the masculine shout rang out.

The wolf hesitated. Then he lunged at Nick only to have an arrow land right in front of him.

"Zavid, surrender yourself or you *will* be executed."

The wolf turned and snarled, finally giving Nick a look at who was after him.

It was Caleb's friend Tristan. He nocked another arrow and aimed it for the wolf.

Nick started forward to keep Tristan from killing Zavid, but Caleb grabbed his elbow and held him in place.

"Let it go. The fight's between them."

"I owe the wolf."

Caleb glanced sideways to where the women were waiting, yet still in danger. "Think of your mother."

Nick nodded. Caleb was right. His mother was much more important than the debt he owed Zavid.

Shielding his mother, he made sure none of the demons came close to her. When they finally reached the arch, he let out a relieved breath. A few more feet . . .

Caleb went out first. Kody. And Nick was by his mother's side. He'd just put one foot under the arch when his mother cried out.

A demon had her by the hair.

Cursing, Nick grabbed the demon and twisted its hand until it let go of his mother. The demon fell back.

"Malachai!"

Nick jerked around at the same time his father did. The demon who'd shouted shot a lightning blast at his mother. Acting on pure instinct, Nick threw himself in front of her and wrapped his body around hers so that the blast would strike him instead.

SHERRILYN KENYON

It didn't.

Confused, he waited several heartbeats for that impact. Then he looked up. The demon who'd shot at her was pinned to a wall high above the floor. Nick glanced to Caleb, expecting it to have been his kill. But Caleb stood completely slack-jawed.

As did Kody.

Even more baffled, Nick had a bad feeling settle deep in his stomach. He turned ever so slowly to see his father on the ground with a huge, smoking hole in his side.

No . . .

It couldn't be.

With sharp, jerking breaths, his father reached for him. "Here, boy!" he snarled.

"I'm not a dog." But Nick obeyed anyway. "Why?"

Adarian curled his lip. "I weep at your conception." Then his gaze went past Nick to his mother and softened instantly. "What I give to you, I give for *her* protection. You hear me? Embrace your destiny and let no harm touch your mother." He grabbed Nick's head and jerked him close.

Nick felt something hot and piercing slash through him. It burned and twisted as if it were alive. Agony exploded in his skull. Unable to see, hear, or smell, he fell forward and still the pain worsened.

Crying out, he wanted it to stop. But it wouldn't. It didn't even lessen.

Out of nowhere, a pair of arms wrapped around his waist and held him. From the awful buzzing, he heard Kody's voice lulling him. "Drink this," she whispered, holding something to his lips. "It'll help, I promise."

Nick gulped at it, but still the pain persisted.

With one last roar, his father released him. Nick fell back into Kody's arms.

Dizzy and nauseated, he couldn't breathe. It hurt so much. . . .

Nick met Caleb's frown. By the expression on his friend's face, he knew he must be fugly. His gaze went to his father, who was now nothing more than a dark stain on the floor. There was no blood. No dust. Nothing to say the elder Malachai had ever lived.

A tremor of fear went through Nick. Would that be his fate one day?

"Nick!"

He jerked toward his mother to see a demon trying to carry her off. With a hiss, he launched himself at the beast and caught it about the middle. The demon fell back.

Nick went for its throat and would have ripped it out had Caleb not stopped him.

"Your mother."

Nick nodded. Picking her up, he unfurled his wings and flew her to the arch, then through it.

Only when he was back on neutral ground did he stop to look back for the others. Caleb and Kody were right behind him.

Doubling over to catch his breath, Caleb coughed and coughed. Kody let go of her bow as it vanished into thin air.

His heart pounding, Nick glanced down to see his mother sleeping in his arms. He tucked his wings in and frowned. "Why is she asleep?"

"She's human." Caleb wiped at the sweat on his brow. "She won't remember any part of being on the other side. Humans can't."

That made him feel better.

Caleb shook his head incredulously. "I can't believe your father died for you. That he sacrificed himself for your mother. . . ."

"You're free now," Kody said to Caleb.

Caleb snorted in derision. "I wish. Nick inherited me."

"Can't I release you?" Nick asked.

"Only if you kill me, and for now, I'd rather you not."

Hissing, Nick grimaced as a sudden pain sliced through his arm.

"You're wounded." Caleb took Nick's mother from him. "You need to tend that."

He nodded as he finally saw what appeared to be a violent gash in his bicep. "Thank you. Both. I couldn't have done this without you."

Kody smiled. "Anytime, sweetie."

Caleb inclined his head to Nick's slumbering mother. "Let's get you two home."

They crossed the empty, silent street. At three A.M., there was almost no one out as they trudged toward home.

"Hey, guys?" Kody asked. "Why are we walking? You know we can flash ourselves home, right?"

Nick started laughing as the ludicrousness of his life hit him. "I'm still not used to all this."

Caleb snorted. "In my defense, I'm too tired to think straight."

Intending to flash out, they paused in front of the parking deck at Canal Place. Before Nick could move, the sound of an animal in pain cut through the silence. A bad feeling went through him.

He started forward.

"Leave it!" Caleb snapped.

He couldn't. Not when he heard the ferocity of the fight. Bending his head down, he ran to help.

Nick skidded to a halt just past the gate where

SHERRILYN KENYON

Tristan had Zavid cornered against the wall and an arrow trained on him.

"Put it on!" Tristan snapped.

Nick had no idea what Tristan wanted Zavid to do, but he wasn't about to let him suffer any more. Not after the wolf had been through so much.

Tristan let fly his arrow.

Nick threw his hand out and used his powers to deflect it. To his immediate shock, it actually worked.

That was a first.

Tristan turned on him with a snarl. "What have you done?"

"I can't let you murder him."

By the man's expression, it was obvious Tristan wanted to plant that bow somewhere special on Nick's body.

"Am I too late?" Caleb asked as he joined them. "Did he do something stupid?"

"Yeah. On both counts." With angry strides, Tristan stalked past Nick.

"What is wrong with you two?" Nick went to Zavid, who leaned against the wall. His breathing labored, he wasn't moving at all.

Caleb sucked his breath in harshly between his teeth. "You didn't save his life. Please say you didn't."

"No. I just kept Tristan from shooting him."

Caleb let fly a curse so foul that Nick recoiled from it.

432

Nick scowled. "What is your problem?"

Caleb glared at him with a fury he couldn't begin to fathom. "You wanted to know how your father enslaved me? He saved my life, Nick. That's how it works. When a Malachai spares the life of any demon, he becomes their master until the day he dies. It's another reason we all hate your kind."

Nick couldn't breathe as that news floored him. "Why didn't you tell me that?"

"Because I never thought you'd be *this* stupid."

"Well, you ought to know me better than that, shouldn't you?" Nick's gaze went past Caleb to Kody, who appeared as sick as he felt.

"Stop fighting, you two," she said. "There's nothing more to be done. We survived tonight. We should all be grateful. Now you can do what you want, but I'm getting Cherise home, and then I'm going to soak in a nice, hot bath until dawn." She vanished.

Caleb closed the distance between them. "I'm going, but before I do, I want to leave you with this thought. Your father's dead and is no longer a threat to you. But you still don't have all of his powers. That drink Kody gave you was a binding potion, and it'll help shield you from those who will now be gunning for you. But it isn't permanent, and it can be broken. Intentionally or by accident. But the most important thing for you to digest is that we don't know who kidnapped you or your parents. If your father knew, he took it with him to the great beyond, and your mother will never remember."

Which meant there was a truly scary enemy out there who knew he was the Malachai.

An enemy who knew who his mother was . . .

Crap.

Caleb turned and walked away, leaving Nick alone with Zavid, who had transformed into his human body.

Zavid glared at him. "You should have let him kill me, Malachai."

"You don't mean that. . . . C'mon, let me take you home and get you cleaned up."

"I'm not a pet," Zavid growled ferociously.

"And I'm not a master. I just wanted to help."

Zavid scowled as if he didn't understand the language Nick was speaking. "Is that all you wanted?"

"Honestly? I would give any and everything to have a normal, average life." Sighing in disgust, Nick helped Zavid up and then he flashed them to his condo, where Kody had already put his mother to bed.

Nick showed Zavid how to work the shower, then left him to it.

Exhausted and concerned about the things Caleb had named, he joined Kody in the living room and pulled her into his arms. He pressed his forehead against hers. "Are we good or are we enemies?" he asked her, needing to know where they stood.

"We will only be enemies if you make it so."

Friends could kill as fast as enemies. She didn't say those words, but he was learning to catch those underlying loopholes.

Wanting to trust her, but afraid of what might happen if he did, he kissed her. "I'll see you tomorrow."

"Are you sure?"

He nodded. "We'll try to sort some of this out when I'm not so tired I'm dizzy."

Kody kissed his cheek. "All right. Sleep tight. Don't let the Hel Hound bite."

"You are *not* funny."

She wrinkled her nose at him, then touched his lips with her fingers. "Tomorrow, my Cajun. It'll be a whole new day." And with that, she stepped back and left him.

Feeling older than Acheron, Nick stumbled into his bedroom and threw himself onto his bed. He wanted to stay awake and help Zavid acclimate to this world. But the moment his head touched the softness of his pillow, he was out.

Yet as he closed his eyes, there was a bright flash, followed by a light whisper.

Be careful what you wish for. . . .
You just might get it.

EPILOGUE

"Nick? Honey? You're not really asleep, are you?"

Nick blinked his eyes open as some loud song he didn't know made his ears ring. In fact, he was surrounded by all kinds of noise. Like a party.

What the . . . ?

He lifted his head up from his folded arms to find himself not in the bed he'd fallen into, but at a . . .

Prom?

Scowling, he scanned the darkened room where his classmates were partying hard. His jaw went slack. But what floored him most were the people sitting at the table with him. Caleb was to his right, but instead of the pretty boy jock he was supposed to be, Caleb was a bit heavyset and wore a retainer.

Retainer? Was it a costume party of some kind?

And Simi, who was wearing an understated pink

frilly dress down to her ankles with a sweater buttoned up to her chin, held Caleb's hand. Demon . . . Simi . . .

Casey was beside him, wearing a pair of thick glasses and an outdated dress that looked like something from the 1980s. *Is this a dream?*

It was too real for that, and yet . . .

"Nick, are you okay? You're looking a bit under the weather."

No. He was definitely *not* okay. He felt like someone had just sucker-punched him as his gaze locked on a short, stubby . . . geek whose eyes and hair were all too familiar.

No . . . it couldn't be.

Could it?

"Stone?"

He beamed. "Yeah, buddy. Should I call your dad to come get you? You don't look like you should be driving."

"I can take him home."

Nick went cold at a voice he didn't want to recognize. No, no, no. There was no way *he* was here. His stomach tight, Nick was terrified of where his nightmare would take him this time. *Don't look. Don't.*

But it was like a train wreck. He couldn't help himself. He had to know.

Stop!

The moment he turned, he knew he'd died and gone to the real hell. That was the only plausible explanation that he could wrap his head around. The only explanation that made sense.

Because this . . .

This was the freakfest of all time.

It was Ash—five feet tall with short brown hair and blue eyes. And in a pink tux . . .

Nick laughed at something that was a lot scarier than it was funny. But he didn't know what else to do . . . except scream, and that might get him put in a straitjacket. *Maybe I've already lost my mind.*

Yeah, that was a little more acceptable than this current nightmare.

He swallowed hard, then returned his attention to Stone. "Can I ask a weird question?"

"If you must."

Raking his hand through his hair, Nick tried to figure out why he was having this screwed-up dream. What had he eaten?

But for now, he had no choice except to ride this . . . horror out.

"What's my dad's name?"

They all laughed.

Yeah, so not funny. He forced himself not to insult

them for their ridicule. "C'mon, guys. Just play along and answer the question."

Ash snorted, then answered in a nasal tone. "You know your dad, Nick. Michael Burdette. He's an accountant who works with Caleb's father."

Caleb had a dad, too. . . .

Sure. Why now? And fat, flying fairies made Nick's clothes every night and left them for him in the bathroom.

Nick arched a brow at Caleb. "And your father would be . . . ?"

"What is your problem, Nick? You know my dad is your dad's best friend and has been since forever. Caleb Fingerman? Hello? Mark's my dad."

Nick started laughing and laughing. He couldn't stop. Yeah, this was all insane. "Okay, joke's over, everyone. Ha. Ha. You got me."

"What joke?" Ash, Caleb, and Stone asked while the women looked at him as if he was the one who was nuts.

Unable to deal with it anymore, Nick rose to his feet and curled his lip. "You know, for a joke to work it actually needs to be funny . . . and this is not even a little." Angry at them, he stormed off to the bathroom to splash water on his face and wake up.

Something had to get him out of this hell and back home.

But the moment Nick looked into the bathroom mirror, he froze in absolute horror. Not only was he in an ugly blue tuxedo that he'd *never* wear, his hair was blond, and his eyes were an average gray color.

I'm short?

His heart pounding, he checked his legs to make sure they were intact.

They were.

And yet he was only five foot eight.

No . . .

More than that? His powers were all gone. Every last one of them. He had nothing.

Nick gaped at the face he saw in the mirror that wasn't his. He pinched himself and shook his head. It was him. Somehow he'd morphed into a short, blond dude.

Unable to accept it, he tried everything he could to wake up.

It's not a dream.

Somehow this was real.

Madaug walked in and sneered at him. No longer skinny and nerdy, he was six foot four and ripped. "What you looking at, Burdette?"

"Burdette?" Nick repeated, looking around for Bubba.

Madaug shoved him. "Nick Burdette? Can't you even recognize your own name?" He rolled his eyes. "Damn, boy, how dumb are you?" He went over to a urinal.

Stunned, confused, and horrified, Nick stumbled out to the prom that was filled with people he knew but didn't recognize. Reaching for something, anything to prove this wasn't happening, he pulled his wallet out and checked his license.

It was the "new" blond him in the photo, but what hit him like a kick in the crotch was the name. . . .

Nicholas Michael Burdette.

"What the hell has happened?"

And more important . . . how could he undo it when he no longer had any power and his allies were now woefully normal?